Louisa Young was born in London and read history at Trinity College, Cambridge. She lives in London with her daughter, with whom she co-wrote the bestselling *Lionboy trilogy*, and is the author of twelve previous books including the bestselling novel *My Dear, I Wanted to Tell You*, which was shortlisted for the Costa Novel Award and was a Richard and Judy Book Club choice, and its acclaimed sequel, *The Heroes' Welcome*.

Praise for *Devotion*:

'Young has conjured up another rich historical novel and I longed to know the fate of this tragic cast of friends. These characters demand devotion – they'll get it, too'   *The Times*

'Young expertly weaves politics, race and loyalty into the family's narrative'   *Observer*

'A stirring story of war and its consequences ... tender and convincing. Well-drawn female characters complete an engaging saga'   *Mail on Sunday*

'Elegantly written and compulsively readable, *Devotion* manages to be both thrilling and heartfelt – a real treasure of a book'
                    JAMI ATTENBERG

'A sumptuous portrayal of love and war in fascist Rome'
                    Observer

'Anybody who hasn't read her WW1 and postwar trilogy ... should get buying. An absolutely magnificent trilogy ... three volumes is not enough. I NEED to know more ... and sparking such a n̶... .... MOONEY

'This moving and vivid historical novel … cleverly interleaves the personal and the political, portraying the conflicts of loyalty produced by troubled times with great subtlety … written with real knowledge and affection'   *Tablet*

Praise for *The Heroes' Welcome* and *My Dear I Wanted to Tell You*:

'Young possesses in abundance emotional conviction, pace and imaginative energy, and these qualities will draw readers with her through time and space, as she unfolds the story of the Lockes and Purefoys on their journey through the 20th century'

HELEN DUNMORE, *Guardian*

'Powerful, sometimes shocking, boldly conceived, it fixes on war's lingering trauma to show how people adapt – or not – and is irradiated by anger and pity'   *Sunday Times*

Also by Louisa Young

FICTION
The Heroes' Welcome
My Dear I Wanted to Tell You
Desiring Cairo
Baby Love
Tree of Pearls

NON-FICTION
A Great Task of Happiness: The Life of Kathleen Scott
The Book of the Heart

LOUISA YOUNG

Devotion

THE BOROUGH PRESS

Find out more about HarperCollins and the environment at
www.harpercollins.co.uk/green

The Borough Press
An imprint of HarperCollins*Publishers*
1 London Bridge Street
London
SE1 9GF

www.harpercollins.co.uk

This paperback edition 2017

1

First published in Great Britain by The Borough Press 2016

'Begin the Beguine' words and music by Cole Porter © 1935 (renewed)
WB Music Corp. (ascap) all rights administered by Warner/Chappell North America Ltd.

A catalogue record for this book
is available from the British Library

ISBN: 978-0-00-753290-2

This novel is entirely a work of fiction.
Some characters (or names) and incidents portrayed in it,
while based on real historical figures, are the work of the author's imagination.

Set in Minion by Palimpsest Book Production Limited, Falkirk, Stirlingshire

Printed and bound in Great Britain by Clays Ltd, St Ives plc

To Derek Johns: Agent Emeritus, consigliere, and friend

Part One

1928

Chapter One

An English school, July 1928

Tom Locke, twelve, tall for his age, goose-pimpled and shivering, practically naked in his knitted bathers, was hopping about under the trees at the end of the lake. They were about to be put through swimming, and Tom felt there was a genuine opportunity to disappear up one of the larches and avoid this frankly absurd dunking, the last of term. Yesterday the Beaks had carpeted him because he'd been swimming – well, yes, without permission – and after dark, but so what, he'd wanted to observe the nocturnal bird life and lake-life, he'd explained it perfectly clearly – or would have, if they'd given him a chance – and now they were forcing him in when it was cold and he didn't feel like it. This morning the lake looked like a lake which might give a chap pneumonia.

Soft needles cushioned his feet; grey-black water gleamed in front of him. The other boys, squawking, slapped their hard faded towels at each other. A bit of dank sun slid through the branches above.

Tom had goggles and a phenomenal lung capacity for such a skinny boy. He would go under gracefully and glide through the greenest murk, slipping between spirals of slime, hardly disturbing whoever lurked down there. It was like flying through water. Surfacing, he would go eye to gelatinous eye with half-submerged toads, breathe a little, and sink again. Underwater was lovely to him. But today he didn't feel like it. He flung two quick arms up, grabbed, pulled and slithered, and was up, on a scratchy branch, in the shadows of the shaggy heart of the larch, where cobwebs and grey ghosts of old growth hung in the remnants of winter.

It was bloody cold up there too. *Must be some kind of meteorological front*, he thought, and glanced around for birds' nests, insects, lichens.

As it was the third time this term, in the third school of the past four years, that Tom had decided to do what he wanted instead of following instructions, and as the usual measures had had no effect, his father was called upon to appear. Tom knew perfectly well that his father would not appear. His father had only recently started appearing out of his study, where he had been lurking ever since he came home from the war ten years ago. Why would he suddenly appear in front of the Head? He never had been what one could reliably call reliable, why would he start now? Riley Purefoy would as usual take his place.

This delighted Tom. Discipline rolled off his back, but a visit from Riley was a jewel beyond measure.

Tom was standing outside the Head's study when Riley appeared, and grinned like a loon at the sight of him. Riley grinned back, his constricted harlequin smile. Just then, two

4

seniors lounged past, which distracted Tom for a moment. One of them, Slater, had on a previous occasion suggested that Tom's mother was negligent, as she never appeared at sporting events. 'Oh no,' Tom had said, 'I have no ma' – with a flick of his big blue eyes – very like his mother's, in fact – which had led Slater to think that perhaps Locke's mater was a runaway. 'Has she bolted then?' Slater had asked, scenting prey. 'You could put it that way,' Tom had said, with the slightly amused-looking expression he used for covering what he point-blank refused to talk about. His mother – Julia. Julia. *Joooolia* – had been dead for ten years, died having Kitty, the kid sister – *bad bargain probably*. Of course he didn't talk about her. A chap wouldn't even talk about a living mater, let alone a dead one. And anyway Nadine was a perfectly good substitute.

And anyway if he started talking about mothers he'd have to start thinking about them, and fathers too. Nadine had said, during Tom's last exeat, 'Peter is so much better than he has been, isn't he, Tom, since he went to France with Riley? I'm so glad he's writing his book now.'

The book was about Homer and the Great War. Tom had shrugged. Perhaps when Peter came out of his study he wasn't as odd and unpleasant as he used to be, and he smelt a bit better, but Tom still had nothing to say to him.

Not that any of that was any of Slater's beeswax. So Slater had been confused, and, not being very intelligent, had marked Locke as an enemy and potential victim.

Now, as they ambled by, Slater and his companion caught sight of Riley's face, or to be precise its unlikely shape, and the scars which held it together. They stalled, walked on, giggled, then turned back and behind Riley's head started a little dance of mockery, fingers pulling at the flesh of their own young faces, eyes rolling, at Tom.

Tom flared.

'What is it?' said Riley, turning. The T was lost in the ghost of the cockney accent of his childhood; the entire phrase just caught in his rebuilt mouth.

'Wo' issit?' leered Slater.

So Tom lurched forward, punched him, kicked the other in the balls, and to his shame let the words escape him, 'Don't you bloody laugh at him, you bloody snobs!'

~

Riley, though he felt as strongly as ever the instinctive, instant urge to pull the lad out, restrained himself. His reason was impeccable: if his patched-up face were to suffer a blow he could lose the remains of his jaw, and be a half-head once again, and God knows what would become of him. He had promised Nadine, after the contretemps during the strikes in Wigan in 1919, to be careful. In fact, he'd promised her again last week, when he'd told her about dropping the splint while cleaning it, and needing to see Mr Gillies about a new one. Of course he had learnt that he had to behave.

So he stood back, just barked 'Tom!' and the Head came out. An unpleasant scene ensued. Slater was made to apologise, Riley was made to listen to it, and Tom was expelled.

~

They thought they might as well go home to London immediately, as soon as Matron had Tom's trunk packed up.

Tom, a black eye rising mauve and cloudy on his white face, was simultaneously delighted with his fearsome defence of Riley's honour, and deeply embarrassed by the fact that Riley knew what it had been over.

'Don't do it again,' Riley said. 'It's understandable but not useful.'

'Never?' said Tom. Though many didn't, Tom understood Riley's constricted speech clearly. He wanted to, which helped.

'Never,' said Riley.

'So, you're saying, violence is never to be used?' said Tom.

'It's very rarely a useful response,' said Riley. 'Don't put words in my mouth' – with a little smile. He looked tired.

'Shall we see if we can get a cup of tea?' Tom said. 'Evans will probably make one for us.'

So they slipped off to the sickbay, where Evans the under-under-matron, sixteen and as pretty as a Renoir, laughed and glanced and provided not just tea but digestive biscuits, with a fair amount of 'Oh, I shouldn't,' and 'If Mrs Dale catches us!' and 'He's got us all eating out of his hand, Mr Locke, sir.'

Riley was accustomed to being Mr Locke on such occasions, and let it pass. Evans may well have been wondering why Tom Locke, pale and blond and tall for his age, looked nothing like his broad-shouldered, black-curled dad, but then Tom said: 'I'm off, Evans – been chucked out again . . .' Her face actually fell, and her 'oh!' was small and soft.

Riley noticed that Tom did not notice.

~

7

Walking out to the car, Riley said, 'By the way—' but by the time he said it, Tom had already seen. A long tall figure was leaning against a narrow tree, smoking. Tom found that his face had gone a little hard and he was looking at the ground. He'd have to go in the back of the car now. And – *Peter! Out of doors!*

'Hello, Tom,' Peter said. He dropped his cigarette on the hard muddy path and came forward.

There'll be hell to pay for someone, Tom thought. *Cigarette ends in the grounds.* 'Hello,' he said, with just enough courtesy not to annoy Riley.

'Didn't want to swim, eh?' said Peter. 'Thought you liked swimming.'

Since when did you ever know anything about me? Tom thought.

'Not always, sir,' he said, and glanced up, and saw that Peter didn't seem saddened by this response, and that Riley looked almost approving. *It's so hard to tell with grown-ups if they ever actually feel bad about anything at all. They're just oblivious or happy or angry. Perhaps sadness is only for children.*

It was not the first time he'd thought this. But when you are born into sadness, and normality is based on it, it is difficult to winnow out what sadness actually is. Happiness now – happiness was a recognised stranger, to be welcomed with a big embrace and clung to like a departing parent. Tom always had his eye out for happiness, and grabbed it where he could. For example: Tom had very much looked forward to being with Riley, and talking as they drove back up to London. He thought it definitely worth being expelled for.

But with Peter there, it could not be. As well as Peter being the gooseberry, it was much harder to follow Riley's speech over the engine noise when you were sitting in the back. You couldn't see his face.

Riley said, 'We need to find you another school. Assuming there's any left that will have you.'

Tom's eyes flickered over the dull green fields outside; heavy wet English summer. He appreciated Riley's attempts to interest him in ordinary education and proper work. He terribly wanted to indulge him, but he couldn't care less about education – and how could he say anything important with Peter there?

A while after they reached the main road, Peter fell into a doze.

'There's really no point,' Tom hissed, leaning forward to Riley's ear. 'Books send me to sleep. Anyway it's the hols now.' Without noticing, he repositioned himself so he could see Riley's face in the rearview mirror.

Riley eyed him, and attempted to put to one side how very much he would have loved to have had this boy's educational opportunities.

'Work bores me to sobs,' Tom said.

Riley's mouth twisted a little.

'It's a waste of money,' Tom tried.

'Peter doesn't have very much else to spend his money on,' murmured Riley.

At the mention of his father, Tom glanced at him, his worn and pale face, his thin hair, and grew a little mulish. 'He could buy me a decent pair of goggles,' he said. 'Or a motorbike. I could learn to dive. Or fly! Something useful.

9

There are spear fishers in Italy who live in the sea. I could go and live with them.'

'You must go back to school,' said Riley.

'Why?'

'To make Nadine happy,' said Riley, at which Tom gave him a mock-evil look and said, 'That's below the belt, old man. Totally below the belt.'

'Like that blow you gave that poor senior,' Riley pointed out.

'Different!' cried Tom.

'Why?' asked Riley.

'That was self-defence!' Realising he was on slippery ground, he amended it to, 'I was defending my family honour.'

Riley blinked at him fondly, in the rearview mirror. Tom started laughing.

Riley said, 'What if – all right – you crash your bi-plane on to a Greek island, while on a diving trip to discover Atlantis. A ferocious peasant with a huge moustache and an ancient blunderbuss approaches you. Would you rather know some Greek, or not?'

'I wouldn't crash,' Tom said. 'But say I have allowed some second-rate chap to pilot me, and we go belly up, how ancient is the ferocious peasant? Because we only do ancient Greek.'

'If you speak to him in the tongue of his ancestors, of the wine-dark sea and rosy-fingered dawn, is he more or less likely to shoot you?'

'More!' said Tom.

'Then you reduce me to emotional blackmail,' Riley said.

'I would have liked the education you are having. I need you to continue, so that you can come home and teach me all that I don't know.'

'Totally unfair,' said Tom. 'I'll work as hard as you like but school is wasted on me.'

'Ordinary bribery then,' said Riley. 'Goggles?'

'Motorbike!' said Tom.

'So you're open to negotiation. Good. We can ask Nadine to find the only school left in the country which hasn't yet chucked you out. I dare say she's still got the list.'

'BSA!' said Tom.

'Possible motorbike, when you go to university, if your father agrees.'

'University!' the boy yelped, in new despondency.

'Would you not rather design your own aeroplane?'

'I don't want to be an engineer!'

'Do you want to spend your life at a disadvantage to other men?'

'Well you haven't!' Tom cried. 'And you didn't go to university!'

Riley smiled his crooked smile. 'Thank you, Tom,' he said, and only then did Tom realise what he had said. But the car went over a pot-hole, and Peter woke, and didn't even say, 'Did I miss anything?', just started staring out of the window, his mouth slightly pursed. Tom fell silent. After a while he enquired what was for dinner. Riley didn't know.

Home was not Peter's house, the elegant and pastoral Locke Hill, near Sidcup, where Tom had spent some months before his mother's death. Nor was it the grand cottage of his grandmother, Julia's mother Jane Orris, to which Tom had been snatched during the war. (Mrs Orris was the kind of relative with whom you would have tea if you had to, and whose voice on the telephone filled you with gloom.) No, home now, was in London: Nadine's father's comfortable and fadedly glamorous Georgian house on Bayswater Road, which had somehow become, over the years, Nadine and Riley's comfortable and fadedly glamorous Georgian house on Bayswater Road, in which Nadine's father lived with them.

Kitty was there in the hall, her arms folded across her smock. 'Welcome home I don't think,' she said. 'What are you doing here? It's not holidays for boys yet.'

'It's holidays for me!' Tom said, in his most annoying voice. 'Now go away.' He checked the foreign stamps Nadine had put to one side for him in the hall – *several Italian ones, excellent* – and in passing greeted Kitty with a casual clout about the head. Last time they had seen each other, as he had left for school, he had by a mere slip of the tongue called Riley 'Daddy', whereupon Kitty had kicked him and bared her teeth, making hissing noises. Not that it mattered in the slightest to him what she thought. But order had to be maintained.

Nadine was coming down the stairs, ink-stained, messy-haired and surprised from her studio in the attic, *though she can't be that surprised*, Tom thought. She'd be cross, but Tom knew she wouldn't be for long. She was concerned, but Tom didn't concern himself with that; that was what women were for.

Kitty started scampering around Nadine's skirts, saying 'Tom's been sacked again, he's such a bad boy—'

'Be quiet, darling,' Nadine said, and Tom, while vaguely sheepish, could read on her oh-so-readable face that no, this was not the day on which Nadine would cease to find him irresistible.

'Sorry Mums,' he said, and tried to say 'It was a duel of honour—' but Nadine had interrupted him, saying 'You will be, when no school will have you and you pass no exams and find no employment and you'll be bored stiff all your life and your children will starve.'

He could see Kitty behind her, a '*My* children won't starve' smirk on her face.

'I said sorry,' he grumbled, at which point Dr Aunt Rose, a female relative of the better sort – not a moping romantic, nor a massively tweed-bosomed bossyboots, but a drily amused person who if you asked civilly would show you the contents of her leather medical bag (scalpel, opium, syringes) – appeared from the drawing room and gave him a not unsympathetic look. Suddenly his face felt treacherously insecure, so he barged past them all, heading for the stairs.

In the hall behind him Rose embraced Peter, clapping him on the back as if particularly glad to see him. Grandpa came out to see what the fuss was, patted Tom vaguely as he passed, and mooched off again. And there was Riley, lugging Tom's bag, and calling him to come back out and help with the trunk.

❧

As soon as he could, Tom raced up to his room. He glanced over at Kensington Gardens across the road. The park keeper was trudging by. The heavy leaves of high summer draped almost to the grass, but between them Tom could just make out glimpses of the Round Pond, a horizontal gleam in the distance.

He wondered if the Household Cavalry had been by yet, exercising their stupendously well-kept horses, in two matched, jingling, shining lines, heading round back to Knightsbridge. He thought about going down to the kitchen, where Mrs Kenton might be persuaded to give him some cake. He considered, too, going back down to interfere in the discussions they were no doubt having about his future. He decided against. Whatever they decided made little difference to him. Wherever they sent him, he would, after all, continue to do what he wanted, bear the punishments when they came, and apologise when he had to. And in due course he would be grown up, and free.

The following morning Nadine, her long curls tidied up, her dark yellow eyes calm, benevolently neglectful over breakfast, patently glad to see everyone in the right place – i.e., around a table and within her view – announced that the Italian cousins had invited them to stay during the summer holiday.

Joy engulfed Tom over his toast and milk. A foreign country! Foreign! And it would mean less time at Locke Hill with Peter.

Nobody had ever met any of these cousins. For years

their existence had passed London by, until someone called Aldo Elia Fiore – Tom saw Kitty trying out the name, stretching her mouth round the unfamiliar shapes – son of Nadine's mother's sister and her Italian husband, had written to his lost cousin Nadine. And now she, Tom and Kitty were going to visit his family in Rome.

But Riley was not coming. Nobody was happy about this, but everybody accepted it. He had to go to work, of course. Men usually had to go to work, one way or another. This was the main way of telling that Peter was getting better: he was working now. Writing this Homer book for Riley to publish! There was a manuscript to prove it. Peter had shown it to Tom, with an expression on his face similar to the one Tom wore, on the few occasions when he'd liked a teacher enough to want to impress him. Peter had said, 'Well. There it is. First draft,' and Tom had looked at it and thumbed it, and said, 'That's a lot of words', and that had seemed to do. Anyway, as Riley said now, 'Books don't publish themselves', so he had to work, and not come on holiday, so the joy was clouded. If Tom had paid more attention he might have picked up that strong, tough, humorous, hardworking Riley, who could cope with anything (and had), simply did not want to take a train across Europe to meet new people, to have to talk to them, to stay in a house as a guest with them when he didn't know them, and they would not understand his mangled voice (in English or his remnants of Italian), or know that he could not eat most solid food, or that he had to be able to sleep when he needed to, to stop talking sometimes even in the middle of a conversation, to leave the moment leaving became necessary.

Tom thought he knew all about Riley. Plenty of fathers and uncles had lost arms and legs in the war; Riley had lost part of his face. Plenty of men had wooden legs and prosthetic arms (Mr Tanley at school had one with attachments: he had a spork, a gripper for pens, and all kinds of woodworking tools he could just screw in, and he'd let you play with them). Riley had had his face repaired using his own skin from the top of his head. His black hair was thick and curly; he would comb it back with his fingers over the broad strip of scar when he had to take off his hat. He looked jolly good considering. Tom had always known this, and didn't remember being told. Though he did remember being told about Peter – Dr Aunt Rose saying to him, in the drawing room at Locke Hill, 'Tom, some men are wounded in their bodies and some are wounded in the heart of themselves, in their soul, and your poor dad is wounded in his soul . . .' He had been on the sofa with Max the red setter, and he had thought she was going to tell him off for letting the dog be on the furniture, and she had looked sad, so sad, that he had never wanted to bring it up again.

For a brief period he had thought she meant 'sole'. If Riley could cope with a wounded face, and be kind, then surely only a nothing-kind-of-man would be bothered by a wounded sole? One afternoon, while his father was asleep in his study, Tom had seen his large white feet flopping over the arm of the leather chaise. There was nothing wrong with them.

When Tom realised what it really was – wounded in his soul – the phrase, if anything, made him more scared of his volatile, sharp-tongued, reclusive father.

'You all go,' said Riley, 'and have a wonderful time.'

'But you and Nadine went on honeymoon to Rome!' Tom said. 'Don't you want to go back?'

'I would love to,' Riley said, and Nadine looked over to him, a grown-up look, tender. 'And I will, one day. But at the moment I can't.'

'It's not fair,' Tom said. 'You went to the battlefields with Peter.'

Riley pulled a face at him.

'But they live on an island! In the Tiber!'

'That is a great temptation,' Riley said. 'I will come, another time.'

Tom fell silent. Because of the jawbone Riley had left in France, his refusal had to be honoured.

Chapter Two

Towards Rome, Summer 1928

Crossing France, Tom stared intently from the train window, looking for remnants of the war: tanks, or crashed planes like his one at Locke Hill. No luck, so then he just watched north turn to south before his eyes, cabbage patches to vineyards, apple orchards to olive groves, green to gold. The train stopped for an hour somewhere in the Alps and he leapt off, sniffing the air, letting his eyes rest on crystalline distances. Kitty, who was only eight, and Nadine clambered down after him; they wandered along a lane and found wild strawberries in a field, with snow-capped mountains beyond and a cold stream for their feet. Overhead a slow and tiny scrap of black curve circled: *an eagle*, he decided. *How high? Higher than a plane?* He wished Riley were there.

Kitty saw it, and cried out that Peter would like the eagle.

'Don't be stupid,' said Tom automatically. 'Peter doesn't like anything.'

Kitty squeaked as she dipped her toes in the stream, so Tom was obliged to mock her again. Nadine said, 'Be nice, darling,' as she always did, and flicked the icy water at him so that he squeaked too. The cry of the train guard echoed down, and they grabbed their shoes and rushed back up to the station, breathless and cheery.

The moment they crossed the border into Piemonte he announced 'Something's different here,' even though the goats and the mountains looked much the same and lay under the same blue sky. 'It's different,' he insisted.

The mountains faded from underneath them. At Milan they changed trains, and rattled, rattled, rattled on, itchy, metallic, grubby, south and west: the coastal flats, the sea beyond parades of pine trees, pale cattle with wide amazing horns. It took all day.

They arrived in the sunlit evening. Nadine twisted in her seat, pointing out churches and aqueducts, ruins and piazzas, places she recognised from her honeymoon, nine years before. Tom stared with an immediate and complete jealousy, wanting the adventure she and Riley had had, and the knowledge they had acquired. And then suddenly, right outside the train window, like a massive hot-air balloon crash-landing in front of them, the dome of St Peter's appeared, and was gone again, leaving the vista beyond of roofs and bridges and the ancient world. And the heat! He was sweating in his English tweed. He was enchanted.

A cab took them from the station along the river, past broken arches and massive columns and tall stone doorways leading to dappled courtyards, past donkeys and peasants and priests and endless bold-eyed dark people. Tom took it all in. He wound down the window: the smell was of hot dusty donkeys, of broth boiling, garlic frying in olive oil though he didn't know that's what it was. The light lay golden on white stone. Voices were calling, shouting, chatting, the rhythms unfamiliar and enticing: *Aoh!* he heard, *Aoh!* By the time they arrived, a great and dusty expedition in the small piazza, he was like a big dog in the back of the taxi, desperate to get out and be in this city.

Each of the visitors was to fall like plums in a heatwave for the charms of Rome, but Tom fell hardest.

They were in a piazza, on an island, in the river, in the middle of this city which was more like a painting come to life than any actual place that Tom had ever seen. He was practically quivering.

As they drew up, a man lounging on the far side against the river wall caught Tom's eye through the glass of the window. He would catch any eye. There was something naturally flamboyant about him, an unspoken expectation of attention hanging around his big shoulders and barrel chest. His hair and his coat were long, his waistcoat was striped blue, and he was smoking, with an air both idle and attractive. The bottoms of his trousers, Tom noticed, were soaking wet.

The driver was fumbling with the brakes; Nadine was saying, 'Oh, darlings, look!' and as she opened the car door to get out the man strode up, arm outstretched, black curls going back like a ram's horns from a strong brow, wild eyebrows curling off in all directions. In a fluid movement he opened the door, pulled Nadine up from her seat, and embraced her. Then he pushed her away to look at her, clasped her head with his hands in her hair, and cried out, 'My sister!'

Nadine was startled, yes – but delighted. Tom found himself smiling. *You would think he was in his own house, in this piazza*, he thought. *Welcoming guests*. He launched himself out of the car and stumbled upright. The man turned to him, big brown eyes, a big nose diamond-cut on the bridge and cavernous at the nostril, smiling. Tom felt a flush of infidelity to Riley. He wanted this man to like him. He wished that he wasn't so very blond. *A man should be dark. Like this man.*

Some children had appeared. Two skinny boys, smaller than him. Good. A girl, a little younger than him, quite tough-looking, big eyes, a lot of hair which reminded him of ropes. He wondered quickly if she would choose Kitty or him. He thought he was prepared not to mind if the girls went off together, so long as it didn't mean he had to be with the small boys, but – actually – he knew at first glance that he wanted this girl to want him, and that it was his responsibility to make that happen. First impressions, and all that.

So: 'When in Rome!' he cried, and embraced the girl in a huge, ungainly, long-armed hug. He took hold of her head, kissed her cheeks and cried, just as Aldo had, 'My sister!'

It went down extremely well.

Kitty, pink and fair, saw the tall curly-haired man – the new cousin? – hugging Nadine madly. Kitty was aware that a mother could disappear just like that, and leave one apparently somehow different to other people, so she watched in slight alarm as the only mother she had ever known was engulfed by the stranger. When she had wriggled out of the car, she stared up at him, hoping that he would notice her, and that he wouldn't. He did. He bent from his great height – and picked her up – something she hated from strangers – and actually – ! – threw her in the air, as if she were two years old. He caught her, very securely, in strong arms.

He said, '*Signorina*, sorry. You are sweet like a doll. I apologise for loss of dignity.' He set her down, and crouched a little, and held out his hand, and she had to take it or be rude, even though she was breathless, and his look was so frank and nice that she smiled, and then he kissed her hand and she just laughed, and looked to Nadine, and Nadine was laughing too – so following Tom's example she boldly took the man's hand, and kissed it right back. At which there came a stream of Italian like a waterfall down a hillside. It sounded beautiful. Her eyes widened.

The house was very simple, plain and bare-seeming, the furniture dark against white walls. It was the heat of the day – ferocious heat! – and Kitty had never seen shutters before. The dimness surprised her and she blinked. Her English habit was to welcome any available sun, at all times, under any circumstances. Her entire life adults had been calling to her 'the sun's out children, do go into the garden and run about'. *How strange to block it out!*

The English tried to carry their bags, and Aldo made his small boys help even though they were only about six and the bags were far too big. Kitty kept an eye out for Tom: after helping carry and being introduced, he spun off the side of the group, and went back out to look at the river.

Kitty and the girl, Fernanda, eyed each other. Aldo said something in Italian and the girl beckoned to Kitty to follow her up the narrow white age-smoothened marble staircase.

In a little room at the back, vaulted and whitewashed, the girl said, unsmiling and careful, 'Do you like to reading books?' And Kitty said only, 'Yes,' because despite the preparatory Italian lessons they had all taken, she was so utterly excited that she had forgotten the word '*sì*'. Nenna fetched one: in Italian, but with pictures. Kitty in turn brought one of hers from her little suitcase: *The Legends and History of Rome*, retold for children, which Nadine had got for her from the library. Nenna studied it carefully, smiling at the pictures, looking at the English words and working her way through them. Kitty watched her, admiring her face which was not like English faces: bonier, more golden. It was like Nadine's face though, with the wide eyes. As Kitty watched, a great smile spread across it, and Nenna looked up and thrust the book towards her, pointing at one word: Tarquin.

So Kitty obediently settled in to read about how he had lived and died and how his body was thrown into the Tiber and how – *oh* – *an island* – *this island?* – grew up over his skeleton. Kitty thrilled. *Could it be this island?*

She looked up at Nenna. Was she being unkind? Was she trying to frighten her? But Nenna's face was eager. She grabbed the book again, riffled through it, stopped with a look of delight and passed it back, pointing this time to Aes – Aescu – Kitty could not read it.

'*Esculapio*,' Nenna said, watching. Kitty read anyway. She was accustomed to names she could not pronounce. Aescuthingy did perfectly well. This story told of a medicine god arriving on a boat from Greece to save the Romans from a plague, his staff wreathed with a snake because snakes know the secrets of magic herbs, from crawling on their bellies, and the boat turned into an island in the river – *this island. Well, it has to be. There only is one island. Nadine showed us on the map.*

Nenna sat patiently while Kitty read, and when she had finished took her by the hand, out of the house, across the piazza, and across the road. Kitty was still wondering about how two children could just leave the house, alone, when Nenna nudged her, pointing upwards: above a doorway, a staff, wreathed in a snake. 'Ospedale,' said the sign, and Kitty could read that. Her skin tingled a little. Skeleton, tyrant, hero, god, snake, boat, hospital.

Nenna stood in front of her, tall, languid, expectant. Kitty narrowed her eyes, blinked, and said *sì*, three times. Then she said '*ospedale*', knowing from her lessons to say the e on the end. Osspeddarlay.

Nenna pointed at the snake. '*Serpente*,' she said. Serpentay.

'Serpent,' said Kitty calmly.

Nenna pointed at the ground and said, '*Scheletro*.' Skeletro. There was a naughty look in her eye.

Kitty grinned. 'Skeleton!' she said.

Nenna reached over and pinched Kitty's cheek gently between the knuckles of her two first fingers.

'*Carina*,' she said, and Kitty felt both approved and patronised, and that felt absolutely right to her.

~

Later, Nenna wondered what she would offer the little pink cousin next. Not the river – she was too small for that. That Nenna would save for the boy. Also it was a bit late to go out. So, inside the house . . . the stairs!

So she showed Kitty how to slide on a cushion down the shining marble staircase. When Kitty cried out in joy that it was like a boat going over the rapids, Nenna recognised the word boat, smiled and sealed her loyalty, because that was what she had always thought about this game, that she was a boat tumbling down weirs and waterfalls, and nobody else, not even Papà, had ever noticed. Nenna and Kitty said to each other, '*Barca* – boat. Boat – *barca*.'

It was at this moment that Tom returned: soaking wet, mucky, wildly happy, dripping over the tiled floor in the doorway.

Nenna fell silent, retreated, and watched.

Her mother Susanna, coming into the hall from the kitchen with Nadine beside her, had two hands up in the air, expressing disbelief. She began to shake her head and tut. Her small boys peered out from behind her, interested. Tom gazed at them all with his wide blue eyes.

'Stop that, Tom,' Nadine said.

'What!' cried Tom, defensive.

'Charming her!' she said. 'Kitty, throw him a towel. Tom – dry off, and either keep out of the river or dry off down there. No dripping on Susanna's floor.'

Tom towelled his head, hair sticking up. 'I didn't know if I was meant to strip off or what,' he said. 'So I didn't. I thought that would be best. I'll take them off now—'

Nadine took him by the ear and said 'You're a little monster,' then 'Get upstairs,' she said, pushing him, and she gave him a kiss as he passed.

～

Lying that night in bed Nenna listened to the water outside the window, tumbling over the rocks, and felt its familiar chill in the white and patchy plaster on the walls. Kitty, lying beside her, was restless. 'Nenna,' she said quietly. She pointed to the high wooden head and tail of the bed, said 'Barca!' and smiled. Then she pointed up at the vaulted ceiling of the room, made movements with her hands denoting upside-down, and said 'Barca!' again, pleased and wanting to please. Nenna understood, smiled at her, and said 'Buona notte, carina. Sogni d'oro.' Aldo stuck his head round the door to kiss them goodnight, and Kitty fell asleep with the look of a child who had just discovered that the world was a very strange and potentially glorious place.

~

Sometimes, at night, Nenna imagined the island shaking itself free of the travertine stonework that moored it in place between Trastevere and Sant'Angelo. It would pull its roots out of Tarquin's great skeleton, deep in the Tiber mud, its bonds would fall away, and slow and stately it would begin to move back down the river towards the sea, trailing froth behind it . . . where it was heading she didn't know. She wasn't sure that Kitty would turn out to be someone with whom she could discuss these things.

She lay and thought about Tom, who had been into the river all alone, before she even had the chance to offer it to him.

~

That first night Nadine wrote to Riley.

Isola Tiberina
Rome
17 July 1928

Riley my darling – it sounds like an Irish song that way round, doesn't it? I want to tell you absolutely everything about everything – the journey (easy); the house – yes, they live on the actual island, right in the middle of the Tiber! Do you remember? With the hospital and the bridge with the head with four faces, that you said was a good symbol of the fallibility of the human race: all looking in different directions, not realising they were one creature? The back of the house slides right into the rocks and the river as if it were Venice or something. You look out the window and there it is. SO romantic. Rushing river noise all the time. And of course rather damp. And inside the house we have Aldo, who is terribly handsome and charismatic – I think you'd like him but perhaps not as he does take up a lot of room. He talks all the time – in English and Italian mixed so we are all learning and picking the language up (some (the children) faster than others (me)). He's an engineer of some kind and plays the guitar. The little boys clamber all over him while he's playing and he doesn't mind at all. Lots of hair, big wise eyes like brown honey. He said tonight: 'How do you like me? My enemies say is Aldo more Roman or more Jewish? I look like both, of course' – and he does! You could just picture him in a toga, or in the robes of one of Bernini's marble prophets. They don't seem to be religious at all, thank god – can one thank god for that? It seems rather absurd – anyway, of course he doesn't wear robes, he wears slightly flashy city garb: black suit, a white shirt, a pale blue waistcoat buttoned high at the neck. His English is eccentric but frankly I have no right to complain with my (lack of) Italian. I am reminded constantly of that line of Milton's about educating children, about how 'they may have easily learnt at any odd hour the Italian Tongue'. Susanna, his wife, is quite quiet but smiley. I haven't got hold of her yet but I will though she has next to no English—

Here Nadine was about to write about the delicious dinner that Susanna and Aldo had produced on their first night. Even now, after all this time – perhaps because she was far from home and its everyday habits – it was easy to forget for a moment how unkind it would be to mention such things to her husband whose ease with food had been shot away with his jaw at Passchendaele.

The children are Fernanda, known as Nenna, who has lots of hair and a pale wide face like a *Piero della Francesca*, inscrutable, and the children terribly want her to like them, and two younger boys who I can't tell apart – black-haired, naughty-eyed, tumbling and playful: Vittorio and Stefano, a pair of wriggly black-haired shrimps, who seem to be about six. Perhaps one of them is bigger than the other. Nenna is perhaps ten – a bit older than Kitty and a bit younger than Tom, so that's all right, though I'm not sure what Tom is going to do all day as they – the girls – have already sneaked off upstairs and can be heard singing. The

28

marvellous thing is that the piazza is more or less like the park for us, so they can just go out and lark about and be perfectly safe. I dare say they'll all be bilingual by the end of the week. People pinch Kitty's cheeks between their knuckles and call her a beautiful blessed blonde angel: '*Bella bambina biondina, un angelo, bellissima bionda beata.*'

She stopped a moment as she wrote this, and then in a rush she wrote—

Darling – I'm sorry but it's on my mind again, perhaps because of being here, where we were when we were so young & silly, and when we first so truly came together – tell me, again, please, that you don't hate me for not being able to give you a child of your own? I don't mean tell me, or hate me, I mean – I suppose, thank you, again, for not adding your disappointment to my own. Perhaps I might go and get myself blessed by some saint of fertility – I'm sure there is one – several probably – or perhaps I will just remain grateful that Tom and Kitty needed us – oh, that's come out wrong too. That we were there when they needed us.

She stopped again and considered crossing out the whole passage – which would mean starting the letter from scratch.

No. He could know her thought processes, flawed as they were. One day perhaps her cycle would settle into actually being a cycle; and she'd put on some weight, and her 'system would calm down', as the last doctor had put it.

She continued:

I'll send this now and write in more detail tomorrow. If you see Rose – and please do see Rose, make her come to dinner. She works so hard and you can talk politics and social policy without the children pulling your sleeves and complaining – tell her I will write to her. And make sure she doesn't go to Locke Hill too often. I still fear she's going to decide Peter needs her again. How is he? Lord, see how the habits stick! I am not worrying about Peter, or about darling Rose, or even about my dear dad or you. How is my dear dad? How is my dear you? I love you I miss you and I will do my very best to get thrown out of the Sistine Chapel in your honour and in memory of 1919—

Nadine

It was family legend how during their honeymoon in Rome, in 1919, Riley had lain on the floor, the better to gaze at the astounding ceiling, and been thrown out, and gone back, and been thrown out, five times. Long ago, he had wanted to be a painter, but the war had swallowed that notion. Nadine, it turned out, was the artist.

She really wished he were with them. But so be it. His inability to be there with them was exactly the kind of thing that they, nine years into their marriage, could smile about and accept. She could accept all kinds of things now. She had accepted Julia's death – *because there's nothing to be done about it*. And Riley's wounds – *because look how he is overcoming them* – though she'd hesitate to use the word 'accept' to describe how he was about it. But his practicality, his everyday perseverance . . . yes, there were times when she didn't think about it, and, she thought, nor did he.

And she accepted not being a great artist – *because I am an artist, and to be an artist at all, of any kind, and to be paid for it, is a joy and an adventure. And being mother only to other people's children – ditto.*

But all that said, Rome stirred her up.

~

Tom woke early and tried to head off out without being seen, but Susanna spotted him, sat him down and fed him hard cinnamon buns and milky coffee, by which time the girls and Nadine had appeared, so after a frustrating delay – *Down to Gehenna or up to the throne, he travels the fastest who travels alone*, Tom muttered to himself – they were all sent out to acquire onions. Tom and Kitty saw, for the first time, places that would become so familiar later: the butter-coloured synagogue, the small local market and the big astonishing one at Campo dei Fiori, the piazzas and alleys and temples along the way, the giant pines the shape of umbrellas, the scraps of road and ancient wall for larking on. Sheep asleep in the shade of gigantic arches. A cart piled high with baskets of chickens. Nadine walked like a dreamer, smiling and pointing things out. Tom felt her love like a hand on the back of his collar.

They stopped at a café for cool bittersweet *spremuta di limone*, made from huge lumpy Sicilian lemons with leaves on their woody stalks. Kitty's feet, swollen in her little brown sandals and speckled with mosquito bites, were hurting, so Tom and Nenna were allowed to go on alone.

He walked beside her, suddenly silent. She wasn't chatty as he had seen her be with Kitty. He didn't know much

31

about girls. Some chaps had sisters, some of whom giggled. She didn't seem to be like that.

'*Vuoi vedere le statue parlanti?*' she said, suddenly.

He looked blankly at her.

'*Sì,*' he said, and thought quickly about it in Latin: *parlanti – from parlare, to talk, sounds like a – not a past participle, what's it called – anyway, the -ing one. Talking. And did she say vedere? To see?*

'*Vedere parlanti?*' he said.

'*Statue parlanti,*' she said. '*Vuoi vederle?*'

Statue. Statu-ay. Statue?

She was leading him: up streets, down alleys, round carts, through crowds, through a great marketplace, where onions were forgotten. They came out into a long piazza like a racetrack, with three fountains down the centre; mighty stone figures and dolphins vivid among the water and green streaks of weed. All around, Latin was written across rearing buildings. Tom recognised it from a print Riley had at home, in which it was flooded and filled with boats: Piazza Navona.

See statues talking?

He smiled and imagined how a statue might lean down to you, stone lips moving like flesh, voice creaky and dry, talking Latin. He spun round, his hands in his pockets, to look at everything.

In a small piazza beyond, Nenna stopped, and said, '*Ecco. Pasquino.*'

It was a statue: battered and ancient, with no arms and not much in the way of legs, twisted on a sort of staircase of a plinth which was pasted all over, like the wall behind him, with printed leaflets and notices. A lot of people were bustling about, with bicycles and shopping baskets, and some men in vests and blue trousers were digging a hole in the road.

'*La statua parlante*,' she said.

Tom thought, *It must be an oracle, like Delphi or something. There's probably a procedure—*

'Do you ask it questions?' he said.

She raised her eyebrows at him, and looked brave. '*Va be*,' she said, and straightened her shoulders. Then, with a consciously respectful demeanour and a glance back at Tom, she went up to the statue, pushed herself up on tiptoe and called out, softly, towards Pasquino's distant and lichened ear.

He did not answer.

'Is that it?' Tom said, and Nenna grinned and said 'Yes!'

'*Statua non parla*,' Tom said, having been working on the Latin phrase since seven streets ago.

'*Può darsi una risposta*,' she said, seemingly perfectly satisfied, and Tom realised that he wasn't that concerned about the statue, or the tradition, or the superstition, or even the answer. He wanted to know what she had asked.

'*Quale est domandum tuum?*' he asked, and she squinted at him.

'*Domando tuo?*' he said. '*Domanda tua?*' He knew Italian had vowels where Latin used *us* or *um*. Couldn't remember the gender of the word for question though.

Nenna slid her eyes sideways, and said: '*Segreto*.' Secret.

He wondered whether to tease her to get it out of her. Teasing, in this Latin/Italian mixture? He didn't think he was up to it. But he wanted to know. He couldn't let a girl keep a secret from him. It would be undignified.

They walked in silence for a while, through the hot bright streets, turning into the black shadows beneath high yellow *palazzi*.

Other than physical force and language, what other tools did he have? He was thinking furiously. Nenna glanced at him.

Perhaps she wants to tell me. Why else would she have taken me there?

So I must just give her another opportunity.

As they rejoined the river, he turned to her and said: '*Io credo che tuo secretus dire a me volunta. Se non volunta, perche me ad statuam parlante portare?*' Which he hoped meant. 'I believe you want to tell me your secret. If not, why take me to the talking statue?'

She laughed, of course. And then she stopped laughing, and she stopped and thought for a bit, and then she took him by the hand, which was slightly alarming, and pulled him across the road and into a church: cool, dim, empty. Glancing around, she spotted what she was after, and led him over there.

'*La mia domanda,*' she said, and looked at him fiercely. He nodded.

She pointed at a painting of the Madonna and child, folded her arms in the universal sign of holding a baby, and made the universal rocking-the-baby motion. '*Bambino Gesù,*' she said.

He got it. 'Baby Jesus.'

She pointed to herself. '*Io,*' she said.

'You,' he said.

She drew her finger sharply across her throat. The universal sign of murder.

And that puzzled him.

And she made the universal hands-out palms-up shrug gesture of not knowing. And stared, waiting for his answer.

'*La Mia domanda*,' she said very clearly, '*era se io ho ammazzato il bambino Gesù.*'

From a language point of view he understood perfectly. Her question had been, did she kill baby Jesus?

It was from every other point of view that he was confused – so much so that he thought he must have got it wrong. But the only alternative was did Baby Jesus kill her, which seemed even more unlikely. But then many things are unlikely.

They left the church, slipping out into the day which had grown brighter and hotter even during the few minutes they had been inside the church.

'Why?' he asked. 'Your question. *Tua domanda*. Why?'

Nenna scuffed her shoes on the road, and did a little dance step. She wasn't looking at him.

'*L'ha detto un ragazzo a scuola*,' she murmured, and would say no more.

He held on to the phrase.

~

Dear Heart

Oggi ti scrivo in Italiano! I don't know what the Italian form of Riley would be. Rilino? Reelee? No, not really – today I write to you in English as usual. But I did go

35

shopping with Susanna in what used to be the ghetto, and I said *buongiorno* a lot, to all kinds of people who mostly seemed to be cousins on Aldo's father's side, I think. Susanna introduced me to everybody as *cucina* which I thought meant kitchen but apparently not. Or perhaps as well. It is all VERY Jewish – you know how in England people are only Christian when they're in a church, but here it is a part of everything – food, music, traditional lines of work, all kinds of rules and habits, as well as synagogue. Aldo and Susanna seem to have masses of the culture but none of the religion. Interesting – and nobody seems to hold it against them at all. Aldo has a little gang of chaps he plays cards with – Signor Seta next door is his best chum I think – he has quite a saucy wife who wears her floral housecoat very tight – the men all wear hats and have bright eyes and call for each other like small boys wanting each other to come and play—

This is a short and sweet one – like you! I will be home before you know it. *Ti adoro!* You probably recall what that means.

She had that day taken a long walk with Aldo. Striding beside him she felt like Kitty scurrying after Tom – after all, she'd never had a brother. She smiled. He glanced back, and slowed down for her.

'You know we came here for our honeymoon?' she said. 'I keep catching glimpses of my younger self, loitering in that doorway, say' – she pointed at the vast, shadowy entrance to an invisible courtyard beyond. 'Or eyeing up a statue, or considering the light on the river.'

'Perhaps we passed in the street,' he said.

'1919!' she said.

'Those strange days . . .' he murmured.

'I'd been a nurse,' she said.

'I was a soldier,' he replied, and they looked at each other, and they both knew that they did not want to look back at those times when their countries had just been at war, and at their selves in the shock of survival.

'Ah,' he said, 'life is long, if you're lucky, and who knows – who knows what is coming?' With which she very much agreed.

'Look,' he said. 'The *Arco di Tito*. Come. I give you a tiny history lesson. So. First Jewish people came to Rome two thousand years ago to ask protection against King of the Syrians, and they stayed. Then later, after destruction of Jerusalem and burning of the temple, Emperor Tito brought Jews back for slaves. Look—'

They were coming up to the great arch, looming against the blue above them.

'It looks just like the Arc de Triomphe in Paris,' she said.

'This is the original,' he said, with a little swagger. 'See, look inside.'

The vault of the arch was like a slice through a great church or temple: the ornamental ceiling squares and flowers looking almost Tudor, and the carved stone panels at the sides.

'Look,' he said. 'You see the menorah? Trumpets?'

She looked. 'Oh,' she said.

'And the prisoners carrying them – those are the Jewish prisoners. Jews paid their ransom, and took them into their community – where we still live. Our great great great great etc., etc., grandparents. Good, yes?'

She didn't know whether to smile or cry.

'And Tito had a Jewish *fidanzata*, Queen Berenice. A long long time we have been here.' They gazed for a while and Nadine thought how little she had ever thought about being Jewish.

As they walked on, he said, 'Most of Roman Jews won't walk under that arch. Pride and loyalty. But me, I'm more modern. Not so religious. You?'

'Not so religious,' she said.

He took her arm and tucked it into his. 'Come, my little sister. I buy you an ice cream.'

This full relaxation with this new man in her family made her feel safe, in new territory. A good feeling.

~

Aldo came in to the kitchen with his trousers wet to the knees again. 'Forgive my trousers!' he said. 'I was fishing in boats—' and he set down a bucket on the floor. Tom looked into it: thick coils of shining silver, sliding around over and under each other. 'I make a *marinata*. Susanna, *mi dai l'aceto*! Vinegar, for the marinade. Tommaso, you like to cook?' He was pulling a sprig of leaves from his pocket. 'Oh – are you kosher?'

Tom didn't know what kosher was, but he was pretty sure he wasn't.

'Bravo!' Aldo said. 'It's no problem because anyway eels have scales – the rabbi says not, but they do – but I like no religion. Your mother is not religious.'

38

'Not in the least,' said Tom, wondering whether Aldo knew that Nadine was not their actual mother, and staring as Aldo, a cloth round his hand, pulled a yard of big gleaming eel by the tail from the bucket.

'*Brava*!' cried Aldo. 'Religion is no good – stand back!' and he swung the beast through the air, a great silver arc, and thwacked its head with a loud crack on the marble table-top. And again.

'It's still alive,' said Tom, aghast and delighted.

'No. That is nervous system.' Now he was tying string round its tail, and hanging it from a hook on the wall.

'But it's writhing—'

Aldo was cutting round its neck. 'Now we skin,' he said. 'You take pincer.'

'But it's alive—'

'No,' and then with a look, Aldo took the eel off the hook again, laid it on Susanna's wooden chopping board, and with two blows cut its head off.

'You want to see something?'

Tom wasn't sure.

Aldo dropped the eel back in the bucket.

Tom peered in.

The eel was swimming around, coiling on itself like before, headless.

Tom stared. He could say nothing.

'Not magic. Not a miracle,' Aldo said, with a grin. 'Science. Nervous system continues. Don't tell the girls, eh?' He grabbed the creature again, hitched it back on to its hook and started to rub salt on his hands. 'It moves again with salt: look—' and he put his hands to the skin which twitched

39

and wrinkled even as he started to get a purchase on it. 'Pincer!' he cried, and Susanna handed him a pair of pliers. Gripping, he began to pull the skin off, a thick tight leathery sleeve. Then 'Stand back!' he yelled again, grinning at Tom as he gutted it, strong slashes down the silver abdomen. A little slither of red and blue fell out on to the floor.

Tom blinked.

~

At supper, Aldo asked what they had done all morning, and Tom, taken off guard, said they had been to see Pasquino the Talking Statue.

'And did he talk Nenna?' Aldo asked, and Tom was worried, he wasn't sure why, that he had betrayed her in some way. But she just laughed and went and stood behind her father, her elbows on his shoulders and her head resting against his, her greeny-gold corkscrews resting on his smoothed-down black ones, while he explained that Pasquino and the other talking statues were all nonsense and super-stition, people used to ask them questions, now they stick up leaflets and notices around them. That was all.

'But there are notices stuck up all over Rome,' Tom said, thinking of the ones he'd seen, mostly from the government, against communists, who were dangerous and would prevent jobs and wages and food, or from communists and anarchists, against the government. Plus all the ancient ones in Latin, carved into stone.

'Respectable people sign their notices,' Aldo explained. 'People who put things at Pasquino don't. People say what they want and they aren't punished.'

Tom was surprised that adults weren't allowed to say what they wanted, without being punished. He had only come across that before at school.

'I read some of the notices,' he said. 'They weren't very interesting.'

~

Upstairs, during the siesta, Tom took his little Italian/English dictionary, and worked out Nenna's phrase. *L'ha detto un ragazzo a scuola.* 'A boy at school said it.'

He put the dictionary in his pocket. He would need it, he thought, during these linguistically challenging days.

~

Tom and Nenna were not often alone, and the opportunity did not arise for him to pursue the question of the boy at school and the death of Jesus. Out with Kitty, Nadine or the small boys, Nenna introduced them to every stone animal in the neighbourhood, and many others. Later, in the Piazza della Repubblica, she showed them the fountain full of naiads. Each naiad had a creature of her own: a swan, a horse, a monster, a dragon. Which animal, Nenna enquired, do you want? Kitty walked them all the way back practically home, to the turtle-fountain in Piazza Mattei, because she did not know the word for turtle, and Nenna could not get it from her impersonation, waddling round on all fours, poking her head in and out, much to everyone's amusement. Tom considered telling them that it was a foolish game, but as the idea formed he realised – with a sense of wonder – that he didn't have to. He wasn't at school. He wasn't even at home. He was just with girls, in a foreign country, and he could do whatever he wanted.

'Centaur,' he said.

Whenever they went across into Sant'Angelo, to the ghetto, or Piazza, as Susanna called it, as if it were the only piazza in Rome, which it most certainly was not, they had to touch and greet the four worn and weathered faces on the bridgestone as they passed. It was called the Bridge of the Four Heads, but there was only one head, with four faces. Nenna knew her city so well she could just swagger through it, which filled Tom with a fierce jealousy, because he wanted Rome, he wanted to belong to it, and he – so fair, so pale-eyed – so very clearly didn't. She had names for the skinny wild cats at the Portico d'Ottavia, and for the fat, ferocious lion and the slender greyhound carved into the front wall of the buildings down the road. The madman on the corner who sang opera greeted her: '*Nenna La Bella, bella Nenna!*', and sometimes they sang scraps of Puccini and Verdi to each other, joining together in duets and choruses.

One day early on, sitting on the river wall, Nenna sang: folk songs, Roman songs, Venetian songs, Neapolitan songs, boatmen's songs, songs in dialects, songs in Italian. Songs she knew from her father.

Tom hummed along quietly, picking up words, asking for translations. *Michelemmà* = *Michele mio* = My Michael. *Roma divina!* The warm air, the wind on his neck, the magnificent smells . . . Kitty in turn sang 'London's Burning'. They sang it as a round, and giggled, and tried to think of a more sophisticated song about London, so Tom sang 'Ratcliffe Highway', which Riley's father John Purefoy had

42

taught him, with its haunting tune and tale of the man who kept running away from the recruiting party, and ended up hanged. Nenna stared at him in sorrow all the way through, and sang a Neapolitan song about four *moccatoras*, which they could tell was equally sad, whatever a *moccatora* might be. Nenna taught them a melancholy lullaby: *Lucciola, lucciola, vien' da me, io ti darò il pan del re, il pan del re e della regina, lucciola, lucciola, vien' vicina.* So Tom and Kitty, who did not know that a *lucciola* was a firefly, and did not know what a firefly was anyway, but understood the insect connection from Nenna's buzzing flying gestures, and the *pan del re* from a quick run to the bakery across the way and some gestures into the window, sang 'Old MacDonald Had a Farm', with the animal noises – but then feared that they were trying too hard, and felt foolish, until Nenna smiled and started singing '*Nella vecchia fattoria . . .*' to the same tune.

They were quiet for a while after that, till Nenna said carefully: 'How is it London?' and Tom said: '*È bella. Tu vien vicina. Io ti darò il pan del re.*' It's beautiful. You come near. I will give you the bread of the king.

They sat for hours on the various stone and mud beaches of the island comparing things, playing games, as the river ebbed and flowed. They laid out their opinions and thoughts and preferences for comparison, proceeding with increasing alacrity as each test was passed and each admission approved. Kitty tried to express her regret that they hadn't met earlier. Nenna was able to make it clear that she had always wanted a sister. Tom relaxed in the company of females. It was very satisfactory.

Later, family legends developed about these first meetings: that this was the first time Tom ever embraced a girl and he never got over it; that Kitty, who thought herself plump and dull, saw a Mediterranean nymph with skin like honey and hair the colour of olive oil, and that Nenna, who thought herself plain, saw a princess, a rosebud, a pink and golden creature out of a fairy tale, and a silver-haired prince like King Arthur. Everyone recognised it as some kind of love at first sight, and when it was time to go home, sadness prevailed.

Chapter Three

London, 1928

In a way, Riley liked it when the family was absent. He liked the peace in the house: he and his father-in-law ignoring each other in a manly, companionable way. There was just Mrs Kenton and the char, who lived out anyway and took the opportunity to keep to themselves. (After nine years Riley still wasn't used to servants – he still felt it pure freak that he wasn't one himself.)

He liked the way habits settled in: that Robert would play the piano in the drawing room, while Riley sat with the paper or a book, reading a new manuscript if he felt like it, after a day at the office or the printers. Riley remained a hands-on publisher – literally. No matter how well he scrubbed his hands with petrol, the ink was ingrained in them now and his fingers were grey for life. Sometimes the thought crossed his mind: *if I had lost my eyes, or my hands . . . and if I had, would I be thinking, dear God if I had lost my jaw, my clarity of speech, my ease with food?* And then it floated past, a skein of cobweb on a breeze, sticky only if you touch it.

His was no exquisite press, like Leonard and Virginia

Woolf's Hogarth Press, or the Fanfrolico, or Robert Graves and Laura Riding's Seizin Press. He admired the beautiful books those publishers produced, and did, very mildly, envy the capacity of their producers to ignore the commands of commercialism in favour of aesthetics, both in the content and the look. But it was all very well to have an heiress wife and be the first to publish Ernest Hemingway, or to set up a lovely little enterprise in Paris or Florence. God knows he would have loved to have been in a position to publish something like *The Waste Land* (which had recently become another object of obsession for Peter). Nancy Cunard could wax lyrical on the joys of the dirty hand, and he respected that – sort of – but this was not him. He was not weighing the beauty of the paper and writing odes to the texture and smell of the ink. His hands had been dirty for years.

No, he was building up a business which would keep his family – his ma and pa, and his sisters, as well as Nadine and, depending on what happened with Peter, Kitty and Tom too, and perhaps Rose. And his books were not for admiring. They were for reading in cheap cafés, for learning from on the bus, for carrying round in the pocket of your one greasy jacket while you go after jobs. The how-to books for autodidacts continued to sell solidly; Riley had hired a young man to update the topical ones annually and they were issuing new ones each year (1928's included *A Mother's Guide to Preparing your Children for School*; and *Basic Happy Health at Home*, which Rose wrote). An accountant had been hired too, and an editor with connections among journalists. The detective stories were going so well that Riley insisted his partner Hinchcliffe, who wrote them, give up the publishing side and write them full-time on a contract. Hinchcliffe had turned out to be really imaginative, and to have a great line in American wickedness. He got the lingo, he said, from reading gangster stories, and pinched his plots from the Bible and the Greeks. Riley was proud of having volunteered him to write them.

The family being absent gave Riley an opportunity to visit Peter without the continuing low chill from Tom being an issue, and to go striding about with him on the Downs. It was not even a year since Riley had forced Peter across the Channel to Flanders, at some kind of emotional gunpoint, almost bodily dragging him out of his ten-year post-war stupor, the snug of whiskey, agoraphobia and 1916 which had held him for the previous decade. This last rescue, with its declarations that he, Riley, needed Peter to wake up and come back into the world, because he, Riley, was lonely and damaged too and wanted his friend and couldn't any longer bear to watch him dying by instalments of booze and shame, had been as dramatic in its way as the rescues Riley had inflicted on Peter on the battlefield, and from the sinks of Soho. It really had been ten years – not just since their own wars had ended, but since the War as a whole had ended. It had been Peter's symbolic ten years, the ten years Odysseus had taken to get home from Troy. Both Riley and Peter were more than familiar with the notion that going over the top together, and fighting alongside each other, put a bond between men that nothing will ever break and no one else can ever break into. They thought it grandiose and not worth mentioning, but at the same time they knew it to be true. And then again the last thing they wanted, now, ten years on, was to have to think of themselves as soldiers. They really weren't soldiers any more. Ex-soldiers, yes. That, they acknowledged, they would be forever. Ex-soldiers, friends.

And they had created a new thing out of it all. Riley was Peter's publisher; Peter was Riley's author. Riley had forced the promise to write the first book from his friend, almost in tears. He had thought it would be at worst occupational therapy, at best perhaps some kind of catharsis – either way, therapeutic for Peter. But Peter's book, once unleashed, had raced out of him, and turned out to be fascinating, readable, intelligent and – a surprise to all – funny. Peter was not the only person to discover that he could say in writing what he would never say out loud. *Flanders Iliad and English Odyssey* would be published in November, an item of intellectualism in a sea of war memoirs largely anecdotal, miserable, marinated in hindsight or so far from reality that the sanity of all concerned had to be questioned. For a while now, the main body of Riley and Peter's conversations had been largely professional, about the ways in which experience of the war were being interpreted. But Peter's was not a memoir. It was a work, Peter thought, of literary criticism, looking at Homer through the lens of the war they had all been through. Riley let him think this, but believed it in fact looked at the war they had all been through through the lens of Homer. No matter. It was about soldiering, and getting home. And it was done. They were home.

Riley was proud of making Peter write. *Odd how a hunch can work out,* he thought. *If I'd have thought of it on purpose, if I'd planned it, I'd be very proud. But I didn't. It just popped out.*

Riley's mind wandered about in a different way when his darlings weren't with him. Ideas had time to develop, and silence into which to emerge. He was thinking now about English crime stories, but grubby ones: in the American style, but set in Soho and Clerkenwell, Paddington and the West End. And he was wondering about Corporal Burgess, aka Johnno the Thief, last seen working as a porter at St Mary's Hospital. Johnno and Hinchcliffe had met. Perhaps they should meet again . . .

He liked – God, he liked – not having to talk. He could go and walk about in the park, or not. Wear his ancient trousers in peace. Nobody wanted anything from him.

And then he would go up to bed and look at the smooth sheets, the pillows all in the right place, the absence of a frock and stockings hanging over the chairs, and feel a pang of loneliness as strong as any he had ever had for her, his lovely wife, an echoey emptiness in his chest and his arms . . . And then he would open the window and the curtains, how he liked it, not how she liked it, and climb into bed and lie comfortably on his back all night snoring without her rolling him over.

He did very much like her letters.

Isola Tiberina
23 July 1928

Dear Heart—

It all seems to be settling down really nicely here. Kitty and Nenna have completely taken to each other, and I really had no reason to worry about Tom. He's very self-contained as usual. He's enjoying asserting his age – he's taken to wandering off and coming back with the most extraordinary vegetables, mysterious tales, and slang words that make Aldo hoot with laughter – I hate to think what they mean. Terrible misunderstandings arise. Both the children have a terror of being sent out to buy figs, because of some nameless horror which would descend if they got the gender wrong; Tom caused deep confusion by believing that someone called *la commare secca* – the dry godmother – who had made off with some kittens which had been nesting under the bridge was, actually, someone's actual dry godmother, and trying to find her, to get the kittens back. Turns out she is actually yet another name for death . . . *Come-si-dice-in-italiano*, all one word, uttered constantly, isn't quite a language course, but they're picking an awful lot up, running around.

I've spent some time with Susanna now, she's quite placid and intense. Aldo told me that even though she's Jewish, to the Roman Jews she is practically a foreigner – because she's from Mantua!

Aldo has told us the complete story of the Jews of Rome: did you know they were here before Julius Caesar? I know, it's extraordinary to think. Before Vesuvius, before Jesus even, therefore before Popes? I had no idea. I asked if they were Sephardic or Ashkenazi? – I'm pretty sure Jacqueline's – my – family were Sephardic – and he said, with considerable pride, not either, because they left Jerusalem before the division. And Aldo's father is from that community, and they all lived in Sant'Angelo, just across the river from the island. It was a ghetto, only for a couple of hundred years. Aldo said that sort of apologetically, as if it were nothing much. In 1870, after Italian unification, the Rome ghetto was opened and, as he put it, 'all the young men exploded like seeds from a pod, and land all over Europe, to make fortunes'. His father, Daniele, landed in Paris and came back to Rome after ten years 'with pockets full of gold dust and a young wife of Paris' – and that was Mariana, my mother's sister. As she was foreign that too counted as marrying out, but his father was not religious and couldn't wait to get free of Judaism and religion and the ghetto and everything. So he – the grandfather – bought this house for his mother, so she could be near the old ghetto and the new Synagogue (do you remember it? Vast and modern and yellow, right on the river, with the square-based dome?) and bought himself a little flat north of the Villa Borghese, as far away as possible. I have to say Aldo is most passionate about it all and rather extreme – he calls the orthodox Jews 'those zionist fools down by the fishmarket with their curls and their Hebrew'! I still have to get him round to telling me properly about his mother, but I have a feeling she may never have got a word in edgeways even when he was a child. He is marvellous, but it is quite a relief when he goes to work. He is extremely handsome though and very funny with the children – he has a game of pretending he can't see them, which drives them quite wild with delight and fury – 'I'm HERE PAPÀ! I'M HERE!!!!!' – 'Where? What's that voice? I can't see anyone here!' – Or rather they say 'SONO QUI!!!!' or even 'SONO IO!' which is 'I am me' which comes out rather Freudian, doesn't it? – the ego insisting on its existence to the father . . .

Are you well, my love? Are you lonely? Any news from

Rose? Or Peter? How is the dear dad? I think of you having your peaceful dinners without us, reading your papers undisturbed . . .

all my love to you both . . .

your Nadine

～

The children not being there was lovely and peaceful. The possibility of a pint with Hinchcliffe or a quiet dinner out with Peter, without the nagging feeling that Kitty would not be getting her goodnight kiss.

It had bothered him, when Nadine had brought up the matter of their 'own' baby again. He didn't – he wasn't – he didn't know how to answer, beyond plain reassurances. He loved Tom and Kitty. Any doubts he'd had about taking them on had melted away in the strength of their need. And they were enough for him. If Nadine miraculously got pregnant – and the doctors seemed to think it would be miraculous – and yes, he could admit he did not want to have anything more than he had to with doctors – but if she did become pregnant, how would he feel about it?

God knows.

Terrified, probably. Haunted by that grotesque scene of Julia, dead in her nightdress, laid out on the icy lawn, Peter beside her, smoking, out of his mind with compounded grief. Remembering too being downstairs at home while his mother gave birth to his sisters, and to a stillborn brother, a few feet above him, just beyond the floorboards. No, he did not want Nadine to have to face any part of that danger, that fraught and terrific uncertainty, the ferocious play of hope and fear, let alone the drugs, the blood, the timescale, the effort – he didn't want any of that anywhere near his tender, thin, waxen wife. Her soul had always seemed too big for her skeleton. How could she carry and build another whole body and soul inside her?

To be honest, he would have carried on using johnnies, or her rubber cap, to save them both from all that. But she was in charge of her cap, and when she threw it away he was in her hands. And when the doctor said that pregnancy was extremely unlikely, he was relieved. As was she. Or so she said.

≈

After a couple of weeks he was going crazy with loneliness.

≈

There was, though, one thing that he had to do while they were away. He'd put it off long enough.

In the smart, pale surgery in Harley Street (tall mirrors, white hydrangeas, magazines, a music-box full of sweets for the children), Harold Gillies was a different kind of surgeon to what he had been in 1917, when they were Captain Purefoy and Major Gillies at the Queen's Hospital in Sidcup. The old wounded soldiers were not neglected, but Gillies had other kinds of patients now. He made new faces for civilians: the burnt industrial worker, the bus driver who had had the terrible crash, the cancerous, the ageing film stars with too many chins. As Riley went in, a small girl with a bandaged eye was coming out.

'That's Margaret,' Gillies said. 'Lovely girl. Just fixed her drooping eyelid with a bit of kangaroo tendon. She's doing well.'

Riley sat down, across from him, over the leather-topped desk. He leaned forward a little and placed on it, carefully and respectfully, a small, shiny, greying pink object, arch-shaped and set with creamy teeth. Without this in place in his lower jaw, Riley could not really talk. The spluttery mess which came out of his collapsed mouth when he tried rendered him incoherent, and therefore silent by choice, under the circumstances. It all rather took him back, and as when a thirty-five-year-old sleeps in his old childhood bedroom and feels fourteen again, Riley found, sitting here jawless, that he reverted somewhat to what he had been, back then. *Helpless*, he thought. *Bitter and scared.*

'Well,' said Gillies, his tone changing. 'Old chap.'

Riley heard the words and the change of tone, and decided that everything was for the worst. He knew it; had known it for a while. The pain. It had never hurt before, not like this, with no provocation. *So, what, cancer?* Something coming back to get him; some germ from the mud, some bacteria or mutation that had been lying in wait? He knew what it meant, and he had a mad, vivid thought: *I shall have to kill myself.*

Then, *come on old man. Hold on a minute.*

'It's lasted you very well,' Gillies was saying.

Riley faded out.

'Purefoy!' – Gillies' voice again, as hard and strict as it had ever been at Sidcup. *The voice of authority and knowledge, the voice of the man who saved me, who hauled me back over the cliff-edge I'd already fallen off. The voice which wouldn't let me go. Snap back, Riley*

don't want to. Not fucking going through any of that again
Snap back man
no
Riley!
Fuck off
He snapped back. God, he must have almost fainted.
Fainted! How very manly.
'Would you like a glass of water?' Gillies asked. Gillies knew. *He has seen so many of us, he knows about us . . .*

Riley would like a glass of water. He took out the etched brass straw that went everywhere with him, and twirled it, and when the girl in white appeared with the glass he put the straw into it and sucked, slowly, carefully. He wasn't going to lose dignity in front of Gillies. Anyway, he was perfectly good at this by now.

'As we know,' Gillies was saying, 'the type of splint you've been using doesn't last forever.'

Do we know that? Riley thought. *I must have missed that part. I don't think I did know that.*

'To be straight, you've been pretty lucky to get away with it for so long . . .'

Have I?

'. . . But you've looked after it well, in general . . .'

But?

He just looked at Gillies.

'However, you've managed to crack it – look.'

Gillies picked the splint up. 'See that?' An almost invisible fracture ran across the bottom. Riley squinted at it. 'That's what's been causing the pain,' Gillies went on. 'The edge has been rubbing and I'm afraid there's some ulceration . . .'

Riley nodded wisely, peering.

'If you'd come in earlier . . .'

Riley glanced up. *I came, didn't I?*

Gillies grinned at him. 'The splint is old and broken, there's ulceration and a liability to infection. This old splint's not going back in, that's for sure. Your jaw has changed shape somewhat since you were twenty-two. Riley, this is the perfect opportunity for the osteochondral graft I should have given you in 1919.'

I'm not going back into any of that. Nope.

'I know it's not what you want to hear.' He gazed at Riley kindly.

But I'm already back. Sitting with Major Gillies, being told about things to be done to me, with no choice about it.

Hang on – no, that's nonsense.

This is my life. I don't belong to the army like I did then. I am not that boy, so very out of his depth, traumatised as the head doctors say, shellshocked – was I? God, I don't know – anyway, I'm not him, and I'm not there, and I'm not then. I'm a grown man, thirty years old. With a wife. And children. And ageing parents, and two sisters (one unmarried, the other married to a spiv – secure? I shouldn't think so), and a father-in-law who's beginning, to be frank, to go a bit gaga. And with a company to run, and employees.

Yes, you're really going to kill yourself, aren't you Riley?

'Riley?'

I can't go through all that again. I could hardly do it when I was out of my mind on war; how can I do it now that I am sane and happy and normal?

'We're much better at it now. It will be much simpler.

We can take the piece of rib, your own rib, give you an Esser inlay, which would allow a solid rank of dentures . . . Riley?'

Riley looked up.

'Hear me out,' said Gillies. There was no trace of New Zealand left in his accent at all, Riley noticed. He was balder, as well, though hair was never his strong point. *Things change. How has my jaw changed? Regressed, disintegrated, deteriorated, fallen apart, rotted?* He thought about Jarvis, with the little horsehair stitch at the bridge of his new nose, to keep it narrow. *Well Christ, of course horsehair would deteriorate over fifteen years . . . But that's all right, you don't need stitches once things are healed up. I've been healed up for years! Me and my* – he stared at the pink thing on the desk, his companion, his *sine qua non*, part of him but not. *Vulcanite? It's a kind of rubber . . .* He thought about bicycle tyres and the soles of shoes, ten years old. He wanted to move his jaw gently, very gently, side to side, but without the splint in the flesh it just hung there, empty. Nobody saw him without it. He was not a vain man. Quite the opposite. He didn't like attention.

'The skin is good,' Gillies was saying. 'It can take another bout of surgery. There'd be no flap this time, no pedicles. Our techniques are vastly better than they were. Pain relief, anaesthesia, antisepsis, all transformed. You won't be my guinea pig . . .'

There was a pause.

I wouldn't have had any life at all, were it not for this man.

Riley remembered the boy – what was his name? – who had injected his leg with paraffin wax, to get those ulcers, to get sent home, and ended up with some carcinoma. *You seek to save, and in the seeking it turns out you destroy.*

Riley leaned forward, picked up the splint, opened his mouth and started the procedure: let your jaw hang, relaxed. Left side in first, then crook your finger into the right-hand corner of your mouth to pull it wide to let the right side in, don't choke, mind the ulcerated bit, find the peg on the stub of the left ramus, position, and on the right ditto, position, pulling the mouth opening from side to side as required to make room. Then both forefingers in at once, to the back, to knock it down into place. Bite down. Find some saliva, to ease the discomfort. Not so much you dribble.

'No,' he said, now his mouth was back to normal, and could speak.

'Riley—'

'By all means treat the ulcer,' Riley said. 'And I would appreciate a new splint. But no. No. No.' He smiled politely. 'No,' he said. 'No thank you.'

～

As he left, heading down to Oxford Street to get the bus, Riley had in his mind a phrase that he had spotted once in somebody else's notes at Sidcup: 'Refusal not considered reasonable.' He knew Gillies hated that he wouldn't let him finish the job. *But it's my head. It's not unreasonable to not want your head dismantled again.*

He was not going to tell Nadine about this. Certainly they told each other everything, but that didn't mean telling each other every stage of everything, when it might make the other unhappy, unnecessarily.

So you're worrying about upsetting her and thinking about killing yourself, simultaneously? He laughed at that. Good old self-mockery.

It felt very strange. Such similar emotions to those of ten years ago. But so different now.

He settled into a corner seat, and gazed out at the limp, thick green leaves in Hyde Park, great pompoms of trees with the parkland beneath them wide and golden like a savannah.

~

'So that was all a grand success?' Riley asked, when they came home, sunburnt, lugging bags of polenta.

'Did you miss us?' cried Kitty, embracing his middle.

'Hello darling,' said Nadine, shining at him, removing Kitty, and hugging him, her arms inside his jacket, as if they were still nineteen. Tom grinned at him from across the room.

'Rose is coming to dinner,' Riley said. 'I knew you wouldn't mind.'

Within days, it was as if they had never been away. Only of course it wasn't.

Chapter Four

South of Rome, 1928

Aldo, on a train rattling south the day after the English left, considered the cousins from London, and their visit. Inviting them had been an experiment, of course. He half expected individuals from perfidious Albion to be as perfidious as their rulers, those arrogant old men who had denied Italy justice at Versailles, keeping from her territories which had been promised and for which he, Aldo, had shed his blood and got slight frostbite of the toes. But he was a modern man. He knew well enough that you do not judge somebody by where they come from. That kind of *campanilismo*, that loyalty to your own town's belltower, is what keeps the world in the dark ages. *My bell rings wide and clear across the world*, he thought with a little smile, and the thought pleased him. In fact he was pleased overall. The warmth and beauty of the English cousins pleased him; their willingness to come was itself an honour and a declaration of their faith in him and in Italy, but more than that – he liked them, and they liked him and his family.

Did Nadine look at all like his mother? No. To be honest, no.

The hair, of course . . . He smiled. English family! *Her husband must be very fair indeed, though. Those children are not in the least like her. They're as blond as the ones St Agostino saw when he first went to England and declared them non Anglii, sed angeli; not Anglos, but angels.*

He had been thinking, since his darling mother had died, about something she said to him once. He had expressed, years ago, an interest in synagogue and shul; other children went, other families, why not them? And she had explained: 'To your grandmother, and her generation, religion holds you together; to your father, religion holds you back.'

Well, Aldo wasn't interested in religion, but he was interested in holding together. And in religion as a cultural thing. He was now in a position, as a free and prospering Italian in the twentieth century, to reconsider on his own terms some aspects of it that his father had had to throw off in the interests of leaving the ghetto. For example, he could invite his relatives from another country. He had beds for them to sleep in, food to feed them. He had the freedom to treat them properly, as a man should, a cousin and a host. *They don't know so many things,* he thought. He had watched their ignorance with some fascination. Food, for example. They were so surprised to see Aldo cooking, and knew nothing of ordinary food.

'We don't have nice food at home,' Kitty had said, but when Nenna had asked why not it elicited a look from the boy to the little girl meaning 'Stop'. The little girl had stopped. She looked as if she always did.

'English food is less of a fuss than Italian,' Tom had said, and so Aldo had put it down to English pride, and watched

61

amused as they encountered pasta and fried artichokes and tiny fried fish and creamy melting mozzarella. Tom liked to stand by Aldo, Susanna, and Ilaria, the family's servant, learning. He was, he said, going to make lasagne and cannelloni and polenta, for his father. Nenna told Aldo that the boy planned to fill his suitcase with pecorino romano and mozzarella and tomato seeds to grow at home in a greenhouse. Susanna offered to write down for him the recipe for the little fried cakes they called ears, crunchy and sweet and delicious. *Well, all children like them,* Aldo thought, and instructed Ilaria to make them every day during the visit. The boy didn't seem to think his father would want them though, and declined the recipe.

And then, today, on their last day, there had been a bit of a fuss. It turned out the boy had bought mozzarella to take home, and when Nadine had said that it wouldn't travel, Tom had gone off to Campo dei Fiori and found a man who would sell him a buffalo calf. He was halfway to making a deal for it when Aldo caught up with him and was able, laughing and teasing, to talk him out of it.

How sweet, youngsters, with their unexpected wisdom and then their complete ignorance! Though to be honest how could a child be expected to know that you can't take a calf on a train in England?

Sweet cousins, sweet extension of family, the coming together.

It was not that Aldo had forgotten his father's stories, and his grandparents'. Far from it. The past dwelt constantly in the low foothills of his consciousness, and occasionally wandered into active consideration. Even sixty years after it had come about, he was delighted, every day, by the unification of the various states of the peninsula into one Italy. He had a trunkful of suffering and chaos, like any man. He remembered perfectly well what the ghetto had been like before the handsome yellow apartment blocks and the noble new synagogue were built on the site; and those memories were why he was now an engineer and not just a musician, as what he thought of as the Lesser Aldo would have preferred. The new Italy did not need guitar players. It needed roads and irrigation systems, railways and sturdy housing. He remembered perfectly families in rags eight to a room, when babies died regularly and mothers died at forty-five. The smell of people trying to live decently with practically nothing. The sound made by a grown man who has fought over a fishbone and failed to win it. The ghetto's gates had been opened before he was born, but by no means all its inhabitants had found their way out through them. Many never would. His father's flight meant Aldo had been born to freedom. Others of his father's generation and of his own were still stuck. To them freedom meant danger, and only the ghetto was safe. He pitied them. And he despised them, a little, for not taking hold of the opportunity they'd been offered, for not stepping out into the sunlight.

Blessings on you all, he thought. *My parents, my grandparents, all of you, for what you have suffered and what you have feared. Thank you, Garibaldi and all the great souls of the* Risorgimento, *for uniting Italy as a country, and for opening the ghetto just in time for me to be born free.*

It wasn't so long ago, only twelve years, that he, aged

twenty-one, had been walking up a frozen river, struggling and cold in a struggling and cold troop, heading to the pass, he didn't know which pass. 1916. It was a pass many had used before them, the previous winter, but this winter was harder. His lingering memory was of staring down as he trudged and scrambled, his gloves worn and his boots not originally his, the underfoot so irregular he could not look ahead. Thinking about food and his mother. Unlikely to see much of either in the near future. And noticing, gradually, disbelievingly, under his trudging feet, under the dishevelled ice at which he stared, something familiar in the shapes and colours within the twist and darknesses. And then a man somewhere ahead slipped, and there was a moment of pause and breathcatching, and Aldo saw, quite clearly, what it was. Beneath his feet, deep in the ice, a man lay sleeping. His position was uncomfortable, Aldo could see that, but he could see too that he hadn't moved for a while. He knew, of course, that he was dead; he must be dead, he wasn't under the ice, he was inside it. He thought: *Oh! he is ancient: a tattooed mountain wanderer, a caveman, an iron-age vagabond tricked by the severity of a three-thousand-year-old winter* – But iron-age men did not wear military tunics, and between the clear and milky streaks of the ice the tunic was present – an arm within a sleeve, a shoulder out of kilter. The feet were naked; socks and boots reclaimed by those who could use them. His own feet, which he could scarcely feel in any case, shrivelled a little. But he couldn't take his young eyes from the face. The dead man was in profile. He could – well he *could* – have been sleeping, but that he was pressed, distorted, only a little but enough, God yes, to haunt Aldo's dreams that night and for several years: the man from the severity of last winter, or the winter before. And then, once Aldo had recognised the pattern and shape of the frozen human body, so it began to reappear, as the order came to trudge on, other shoulders. Other feet. Other faces within the clear and shining ice. Suspended, in some kind of eternity.

After a while, trudging over these frozen brothers, he no longer saw them. They were like the multi-coloured pebbles on the seabed, greys and ivories and whites, shapes. If they threatened to become again what they really were, he blinked and crossed his eyes a little, recasting his focus. He prayed for their souls as he went. Though he was not religious he *was* religious; this didn't confuse him. Emotionally he was religious; politically not. If walking up this ladder of dead men demonstrated his commitment to a better future, so be it. If it helped the redemption of the Trentino, the Alto Adige, Trieste, he would do it. If Italy needed him to see men die; to run screaming at strangers, to sleep in barns, to walk forever, to gaze helplessly at the Isonzo week after week, and lurch himself at it over and over like a chained dog at a window, then he would do it. To end the war you had to fight the war. Only then could you rebuild. Those mountains, though. Those ravines and cliffs and zigzag paths – he'd be happy if he never saw a mountain again.

Confusion was his strongest memory; a confusion which leached between what had happened and how he felt about it still. He had not been able to make sense of what he had actually done. At Caporetto in October 1917, he had not run away – though 400,000 other people had. And 300,000 had been taken prisoner. Of each division which had deserted, afterwards, one in five men had been shot in punishment, platoon by platoon, and some of them shot their officers, and anyone without a rifle was shot, because *why didn't you have your rifle? You threw it away to run away faster didn't you?*

No Sir—

DIDN'T YOU?

NO SIR

and nobody knew if they'd be lined up and shot or lined up and made to shoot the others. That was the end of the war.

It was not a time for clarity. It was hard to know, in fact, if you had deserted or not. He thought, as best he could put it together in his mind, that having done his honest best he had found himself in the firestorm alongside someone who was trying to organise an orderly retreat, and he went with that flow. He was driven back among his fellows, and found himself way back in the Veneto, shamed and furious, and all around him men spoke of Russia, Russia – where the Bolsheviks were taking unspeakable liberties with authority.

And deserters – men he knew had deserted, properly deserted, deserted their companions who depended on them – were walking around, smoking cigarettes and drinking coffee and talking about the future—

Everything he had thought he was protecting was broken. The Pope said the war was a scandal, a useless slaughter – the Pope should be taken off and hung. And the government – talkers! Neutrals! Old men! They knew nothing. They had never really been behind the army.

Aldo coming home, in uniform, 1919, was mocked in the street. In Bologna a gang of youngsters, working men, thin desperate men, jostled him, shouted at him that he was a lackey and should be ashamed. He stopped, unafraid, to remonstrate with them. '*Ragazzi*,' he said, 'I've been in the war, what's the matter with you? I've been fighting to win back Italian lands that were stolen from us – this is no shame, this is honour.'

And the least uncivil of them suggested he had been fighting for the rich and powerful, that the working man would see no benefit till the communists set Italy free – and the most uncivil of them spat at Aldo's worn-out boots. 'The war starts now, brother,' they said, 'here, in Italy, now' – and Aldo stared at them with such total incomprehension that instead of passing on by they laughed and cried, 'Come with us!' and he could not get away.

So Aldo, aged twenty-three, trying to get back to Rome, thinking of his mother's soup and a better world, in that order, found himself in the tight middle of a crowd of howling demonstrators and strikers all hurling stones and chanting. *Occupying a factory? Rioting?* He hardly knew, it disgusted him so. These children with their lock-outs and their strikes – and men old enough to know better. Communists, anarchists, Marxists: the shame of Italy, uncontrolled by the weakness of parliamentarians and liberals. The rot. What future would this build? No wonder the greybeards at Versailles were disrespecting Italy even now.

Aldo, the young man, was full of love, full of desire. He was in love with his saviour, Italy; his homeland, Rome.

He saw it suffering: no food, harvests lost, families shredded, everything torn up by the war. He had read Dante; Mazzini; Crispi: he saw a bigger picture. As when the poet Gabriele d'Annunzio, for whose inspired and glory-filled passages he had always had the greatest respect – *now there is a man of the future! There is an Italian!* – headed for Fiume with his band of freedom fighters and reclaimed the disputed city and just took it! *And ruled it with such a manly, fiery sweep of inspiration! D'Annunzio! There was a man who was prepared to actually bloody DO SOMETHING.* But Aldo had been away from home for too long. This chaos across the country frightened him, and his very bones ached for his own city. There were so many voices caterwauling round this precarious Tower of Babel: not just the communists and the anarchists but all kinds of rebels and crazy people, nebulists, idealists, cliques and recidivists, all blaming each other and leaping headlong to conclusions. *Italy has not existed for very long. How can she hold when her children are in such a state?*

Aldo had such a very different idea of how his world should be. He longed to mend, to heal, and to get on and build. He nurtured an idea of great glory: the Third Rome. After the ancient Empire when Rome ruled the known world, and the glories of the Renaissance when the wealth and creativity of Rome was without comparison, should Rome not rise again a third time? The Risorgimento had not, after all, been completed . . . *Think what we could do with this magnificent country, if we could only harness our abilities and our strengths, if we could organise ourselves – Imagine if we could drain our malaria-infested marshes to make good farmland. Imagine if we could help the* contadini *to farm more easily, more fruitfully; if we could build up the industries of the north, mine our minerals and educate our children. Imagine the roads, the bridges and tunnels, the aqueducts and the plumbing, clean fountains at every corner, electricity. Imagine if we could bring water to Sicily . . .*

It was quite a thought, when you were slogging home, in someone else's boots.

So, he had studied, qualified himself in engineering, with a sideline in surveying and hydraulics, married his wife and started fathering his children. He started straight in, working, building, helping.

In particular, Aldo was grateful that after all the weakness and chaos of the birthing pains immediately after the War, Italy had moved into such a magnificent period, where the struggle was clear, the direction was forward and the leader was strong. It was a wonderful time to be Italian. In fact if there was anything wrong for him it was that he was always slightly distracted by the possibility that his gratitude for being released from the ghetto and left unbothered might not have been adequately expressed to the authorities concerned. But then his optimism would burst through – *left unbothered? Ha! No, you are part of it . . . You are part of it!*

He was looking forward to next year, 1929. The Duce had taken to Parliament the proposal to drain the great swamps south of Rome, the Agro Pontino, and Parliament had accepted it. Next year they would start the clearing and levelling. Left unbothered! Far from it – he would be joining in!

The train scooted on. He could smell some late stubble

burning, over the metal smell of train. *They should be ploughing by now*, he thought, looking out over the framed land. *We'll make so much more farmable land. The ditches and canals we'll dig, the roads we'll lay, the lovely fields and homesteads and little towns . . .* He knew the stories about the Agro Pontino, of course – the snakes as long as a man, the quicksands, the bandits, the treacherous tangled forest and scrub. Stagnant pools and backwaters, seasonal riverlets with nowhere to drain, ghosts and wicked spirits, streams drying out, nothing but frogs and eels and mosquitoes can live there, malaria, malaria, malaria . . . And it wasn't consistent: from one dip to another it would shift and trick you – and it changed with the seasons, and the weather: lush with green weed one week, underwater the next, mud the month after that. Putrid clay-clad pools that never dried out. Islets and strips of land that might look secure, but only a fool or a drowned man would dare to step on them . . .

This swampy chaos was to be mapped and divided and controlled. To the north-east were the Lepini Mountains. To the south-west lay the Tyrrhenian sea. Between them lay two long parallel sections of disparate marsh, separated by the ghost of the coastline of hundreds of thousands of years ago: a long long dune, more or less parallel with the coast and the mountains between which it reclines, known as the Quaternary Dune. This dune made a barrier just high enough to keep inside it all the water from the mountains and rivers around: it all ended up there with no way over the dune to the sea, trickling about aimlessly on the flat, flooding the whole plain each autumn, leaving all the silt and mud it brought down with it, vaguely making its way forty kilometres south-east to Terracina, solidifying a little as it dried out in the summer, before welcoming a new season's rain and silt. This was the plain of Piscinara. Outside it, between the dune and the new coast, lay the second sweep of marshes. Nero had dug a canal through the Quaternary Dune to drain Piscinara; it had silted up. Napoleon and Garibaldi and Leonardo and countless Popes and Prussians and speculators and aristocrats had tried and tried to drain these places. And failed.

Aldo was smiling as the train drew in. He'd stared down at the marshes from Sezze and Cisterna. The surveyors were ready, maps and designs on their way.

We're going to dig a bloody great canal from the top of the plain to the sea, and all the water will drain into it, the mountain streams and the rivers, the Fosso di Cisterna, the Teppia, the Fosso Moscarello . . . all the rain, all the snowmelt, all the sludge. We're going to bring electricity from Cisterna in giant cables, blow up any rocks that get in our way, dig and dig and dig.

Next year, Aldo thought, with a little shiver of pride. He had been having ideas as well for the other end of the project: how about mosquito netting; lovely little netted-in verandahs on the front of each house, so people could still sit outside but have an extra layer of protection? *Just until we've wiped the cursed insects out . . .*

What a job! What a wonderful job!

Next year, he thought, *I'll invite the English down to see how we're doing.*

~

Susanna Norsa had spent her early life praying, sewing, and listening politely to her aunts and their friends as they prayed and sewed. She fully expected to spend her entire life in variations of this scene: moving up in role from niece to aunt, from aunt to great-aunt, perhaps; to mother and grandmother, if her father arranged things so. She hadn't thought much beyond it. There was no reason to. Nobody had ever suggested it. And she loved to embroider. And outside was quite dirty.

One of the aunts, a tiresome dissatisfied Aunt Rebecca, given to sighing and wishing for things, told her one afternoon behind the white linen curtains, in the shaded hush of siesta, that there was a painting, in a church, of their ancestors. Susanna could hardly believe her. Church was nothing to do with them. Why would Christians have a painting of Jews in their church?

'Our ancestor Daniele did something very wicked,' Aunt Rebecca whispered, toxic and gleeful. 'He and his son Isaac. I don't know what so don't pester me asking about it. You will never know. It is forbidden. It is the church on via Monteverdi. Santa Maria della Vittoria.'

Susanna asked her father. She was not afraid of him.

He – bearded, arch-browed, a man unchanged for generations – said: 'It's the way of things that we are tolerated, not welcomed. It's always been thus. If we are quiet, all is well.' She did not press. She had never felt the need for her own wisdom, and she liked quiet.

The year Susanna turned fourteen, a quick and vicious surge of something incomprehensible rose in her, and she found her customary logic and her habits of obedience quite unsatisfactory. For absolutely no reason, coming home from school one afternoon, she turned away from the route, removed her headscarf, tucked in her white collar, and strode off, guilty feet striking the street, to via Monteverdi. There was a church: white, stucco, its portico the gay shape of a woman curtseying in a long skirt, holding up the cloth. It was not that one. It was naked brick, tucked into the corner, small and imperturbable. Her pause at the door was brief. It had to be, or she would never dare enter. She entered. She did not burn up like a dead leaf in a fire. There was a painting, and another . . . she found her ancestors. Two men and two women, in a row, on a panel alone at the bottom of a painting of someone else's glory. The younger man would be Isaac.

Susanna's rebellious surge did not last long, but she retained this one small act of independence: going without permission, in clothing as un-Jewish-looking as she could muster, to the church where the painting hung, to look at Isaac's handsome face, full of *ritegno*, a holding back, a dignity. She developed and bore, on his behalf, a rich prideful resentment which gave purpose and value to the dappled shadow of shame that her name, in that town, had carried for hundreds of years. When she learnt the complex story, of how Daniele had whitewashed over a fresco of the Virgin Mary on the wall of his house, and paid a dozen punishments for it, it simply made her prouder of Isaac. He had stood by his father, suffered alongside him. She felt the blessing of not being alive at that time, four hundred years ago, when a Jew could be fined and tormented over and over for doing something he'd been given permission to do. When she visited Isaac, she talked to him. Soon enough she came to love him. She prayed for him when they prayed for the dead.

When she met Aldo, the handsome engineering student, he looked to her like Isaac Norsa – only with the ineffable advantage of being alive. Aldo knew and loved the past but his talk was all of the future. To him Trent was not ancient anti-Semitic scandals about who had accused who of making matzohs with the blood of a small boy in 1475, but Italian land redeemed, finally, from foreigners by the blood of Italian soldiers, including a little of his own. He had served on the Isonzo, he had been one of the straws whirled on the vast chaotic floodtides of Caporetto.

When Aldo spoke of the new Italy; of the sacrifices made, of the need for discipline and cleanliness and order and common sense, Susanna's rather weary young heart lit up. Hers was not a fancy family; not wealthy, not ambitious. All that was required was respectable survival at a level which permitted charitable donations and decent marriage prospects. Had Susanna's infatuation with the portrait been known, it would not have been comprehended in the slightest. Her infatuation with Aldo produced much the same response, among the embroidered linen tablecloths and the carefully polished glasses.

But to Susanna, here was a man with passion enough for two. Yes, he lectured. But so he should! He knew so much, and he shared it. He knew about Daniele and Isaac – and he knew about the future too. She listened carefully, head down, ears wide open. 'The regiments who let us down at Caporetto – do you know who they were? They were full of the munitions workers from Turin – the ones who had been rioting. Yes! Sent to the middle of our campaign as a punishment. Not the most intelligent bit of planning. And everyone knew they were going to give themselves up. Why would people like that have any loyalty to their country?' Susanna could not answer. She knew nothing. But that was all right, because no answer was required. 'They made no secret of it. Their officers locked themselves in at night, in fear of their own men. They didn't even consider themselves to be in the army! Some of them refused their tobacco and charity socks – they said they didn't qualify to receive them – tell me, Susanna, how can good Italians be brought to this treachery? To plan in advance to surrender, and for nobody to notice that?'

She shook her head sadly in agreement, and glanced up at him. 'For our generals,' he would continue, 'to put these revolutionaries, these communists, right in the middle of this most important battle – ah, my dear, don't you think we can do better? Aren't we the oldest civilisation in the world? Can't we save these misguided men from the tempting garbage they hear from the communists? And give them back their pride?'

Her adoration transferred as easily as a leaf falls. Leaving Mantua with Aldo, she chose to leave behind there her respectable relatives alongside the ancestral *innamorato* and all that he entailed, and devote herself instead to the future, to faith and trust and the glorious light of the sun, and to the beautiful Italian children she would have with this ador-able, important man.

Of course it had not been quite like that. But he worked

hard, he kept the family well. And he was so sweet. When he was playing the guitar and Nenna crept up on him and stole his hat, and put his box of cigarillos and matches in it, and sneaked it back on his head and in the joy of playing he didn't notice, until ten minutes later he would take the hat off and everything would fall out – oh, he made them laugh.

And what had he seen in her? A beautiful girl, who didn't say much, who adored him. As for so many men, that was enough.

~

Both Aldo and Susanna considered themselves to be very lucky Jews. They'd met a foreign Jew once who didn't even believe they were Jewish, because they were so Italian. That amused Aldo very much. He said, in all his travels he'd found that most Italians hardly knew what a Jew was. It made Susanna a little nervous though. To laugh about being taken for a gentile! Things change so fast.

Chapter Five

Rome, 1929

Kitty, Tom and Nadine went to Rome again the following year, and the one after, and the one after that. All the previous pleasures awaited them, freighted with the added delight of now being familiar. A person could think, *this is what I do*, because they had done it before and would quite possibly do it again. They could perhaps think, *this is where I stay, when I am in Rome. This is the fruit stall I go to. The signora greets me.*

Kitty announced that she was Italian. Challenged by Tom, she said, 'Well, I have eaten lots of Italian food, and breathed lots of Italian air, and drunk lots of Italian water, and I have had lots of Italian lessons to help me talk Italian, so I am made of Italian things, so I am Italian. Partly.' It made perfect sense to her, and she was annoyed when everyone laughed.

Aldo was working south of Rome, 'where new cities are rising from the swamps', Nenna said. Kitty thought of a city like a dinosaur, dripping weeds, lurching up, until Nenna explained. 'Everybody dies who spends a night in the swamps,' she said. 'Papà is draining them, so the poor people

77

can live. Drain the swamps, kill the mosquitoes, build the cities. He has to take a pill every day so the *anofele* don't give him malaria.'

One morning, going over to the bakery in Via del Portico d'Ottavia, Kitty observed as if for the first time the great number of churches in this Jewish area. Nenna said: 'At every gate of the ghetto there was a church, to be easy for Jews to convert.'

Tom asked why they would have to convert.

'Christians want us to,' Nenna said. 'It's what they most want from us. So they can all go to heaven, I think.'

'And why does a ghetto have gates?' asked Kitty.

'A ghetto is walls,' said Tom, with one of those looks that made her feel stupid.

'Oh,' she said. 'I thought it was a place.'

'All the Jews had to live inside,' Nenna said. 'Didn't you know?' And she walked Kitty and Tom along where the walls had been. She showed them two buildings abutting: one had been inside the ghetto, one outside. They were the same height, conjoined, part of one long wall of buildings along the side of an alley. But the one outside had tall stone-mullioned windows, yellow stucco, and three storeys; the one inside had unframed windows, bare brickwork, and six storeys. 'The wall was across here,' Nenna said. 'Big houses and nice tall rooms out there on Piazza Mattei, low ceilings and people packed in, inside.'

Kitty gazed at it, imagining the wall opening up like her doll's house, revealing the different levels of floor, the cramped ceilings, the poor families on the left hunched over, ragged and numerous; the rich families on the right swanning on pale carpets beneath chandeliers way above their coiffured heads. Just a wall between the two lives. On one side paintings hang on smooth stucco. Cracks split the other side.

'It's not fair,' said Kitty.

'Yes.'

'I'm sorry,' said Kitty, not quite sure why.

'Why? You didn't do it. And you are Jewish too. Your mother is Jewish.'

Kitty got the little dizzy feeling which happened when that topic came up. It was nice to say nothing about the parent situation, and never think about it, just laugh blankly if the matter of hair colour was mentioned, or resemblance (lack thereof). Nobody really expected a child to say or think much anyway.

She looked to Tom. These were their shared secrets, family mysteries which a girl could not address unilaterally. They were not hers to give away.

'Nadine's not our mother,' Tom said. 'We don't talk about it much.'

Kitty thought: *Nenna might not want to be my cousin any more now.*

Nenna said: 'I won't tell anyone,' and waited.

'Our actual mother ran away and got ill and died, and our father is still a bit sick from the war.' Tom said it bluntly, amazing his sister. He glanced at her – a flash. 'We can tell you,' he said, 'because you're like family, and we trust you.' At this Kitty nodded. 'Also you're a foreigner and you probably won't tell anyone we know at home. At home,' he said, rather fiercely, 'it seems that only our family has anything

79

wrong with it. Everyone else seems to be terribly all right. Though of course they may all be covering up too.'

Nenna smiled. 'People think the English are very cold and calm,' she said.

'I wish we were Jewish,' Tom said. 'And Italian. More fun than being boring old polite old cold old English . . .'

'Let's be,' said Kitty, shy to propose a pretend to Tom, who was getting so old now, but then it was his idea – so perhaps—

'Good idea,' he said. 'Nenna, you show us how.'

'How to be Jewish? You don't eat salami. You marry other Jews.' She stopped to think. 'Do you want to be like us? Or like the proper Jews?'

'No salami!' cried Kitty, who had only just discovered it, and felt this was too unfair.

'Like us then. *Bene* – it's easier.' Nenna pointed to a yellowish church beyond the bakery, and said, 'I continue your history lesson. That's where the Jews were forced to go, to listen to Christian sermons.'

'Sermons are bad enough if you're Christian,' said Tom, and they got on to a discussion of hymns, and Nenna sang them a favourite bit of Kiddush, as sung by the Romans, and said yes, she went to temple sometimes, for the special days, Hanukkah and Passover and New Year, because she loved the music, and everybody went, and the cloths were so beautiful, all the gold and silver, brocade and beautiful needlework—

'But the people aren't rich,' Kitty said, and Nenna told her how the Jewish women were the best seamstresses, and the ladies of Rome would give them their old dresses, and the Jewish women would remake them to dress the Torah.

'Does Susanna do that?' Kitty asked.

'No,' said Nenna, rather vaguely. 'I said. We're not really very Jewish now.'

'Do the other Jews mind?' Kitty asked, but Nenna didn't hear; she was leading them to the synagogue. Perhaps Kitty was scared to go inside, to tread on the toes of a different religion that would think she was dirty; some religions she knew didn't seem to like girls, or foreigners, which was what she was, here – but Nenna took her hand and led her inside. She gazed up: a high ceiling spattered with stars; candelabra covered in pomegranates and bells.

'Bells to jangle like the hem of the Chief Rabbi's garment in Jerusalem, so the unclean have the chance to get out of his way,' Nenna said.

'And why pomegranates?' Tom asked, and she laughed and said, 'Because a pomegranate has 613 seeds.'

'Why 613?' he pressed.

'Because that's how many different types of Jew there are, and yet we are still one fruit.'

'You like being Jewish more than your father does,' Kitty said.

'Oh, he doesn't mind,' Nenna said. 'And I like the cakes.' She was still laughing.

~

Occasionally, through her childhood, Kitty had wanted to know about her mother. But as youngest children always are, she was born into a family already formed before her arrival. Even in a family as unorthodox as hers, there was an existent mood to which Kitty had not had the opportunity to contribute. The fact of her, of course, did – but it was beyond her influence. Julia and her death were not secret or denied, but nor were they much spoken of. As a result, Kitty's first emotion was insecurity. These parents were not her real parents. They were not really hers. So she would have to work harder to make sure she was loved. She was a warm little girl; it came easily to her. But she never relaxed.

Occasionally, she had asked. She asked Riley first, when she was seven or eight. (She hadn't wanted to rock the boat by asking Nadine – of course Nadine knew she wasn't Kitty's actual mother, but mentioning it out loud seemed rude almost.) It was bedtime, and he had come up to kiss her goodnight. Kitty had dithered between asking what had happened to Julia, and what Julia was like, and decided on the latter. When she produced her enquiry, cautiously, Riley had fallen silent, rubbed at his chin, stroked her head, and finally said: 'She was very pretty, and she loved your father very much, and she loved you.' (Looking back on that as an adult, Kitty thought it sounded like the letters people had saying how their fathers had died in the war: bravely, and without suffering. Every one of them.)

A year or so later she asked Mrs Joyce, the cook housekeeper at Locke Hill, what had happened. Mrs Joyce asked her what she wanted bringing that up again, it had been very sad but what's done was done, now get out from under my feet there's a good girl. So Kitty had plucked up an immense courage and asked Peter, one day when he was quiet in his little house in the woods. She remembered it clearly: he had been on his big old chair where he always was, and she had run in and said, 'Tell me about Mummy.' He had turned his head a little towards her, and without hesitation said, 'She was too good for me.' Kitty had pressed: 'Tell me a story about her.' And he had shaken his head, sucked his cheeks in, and fumbled for a cigarette. 'No,' he had said. 'Oh no.'

For a while that was all she had. Her mother was beautiful, she loved Peter, she was too good for him. It was sad, and nobody would talk about it. So after a decent interval she picked up her courage again and took this information to Tom, the beloved, the older, the all-knowing, the unreliable. He had smiled at the question, realising his power, and then sat her down with great seriousness, and sworn her to secrecy. He was always doing that. It added to the importance.

'Kitty,' he said, 'I am sorry to have to tell you this. Our mother was no good. I remember her clearly. She was very beautiful with golden hair, but she was no good. She upset Father by never leaving him alone. She let her mother steal me when I was a baby. She ran away from home without telling anybody. She was always crying and being selfish. And then she did a very terrible thing which you must never mention.' Kitty squirmed, and promised. 'She did something terrible to her face,' Tom said. 'She sort of burned it off with chemicals, and after that she looked like a terrible frightening clown.'

Kitty had trembled, she'd bitten her lips closed, she'd wept and denied, and then she had to run away. For years

83

afterwards she had dreamt of the bad mother with a glaring white clownface, carrying a suitcase, running down a railway platform, waving from an airplane, coming into her bedroom at night. She never spoke of it to anybody.

~

Later, upstairs, Tom was surprised to hear Kitty ask, 'If the Jews had just converted, would they have been let out of the ghetto? And so, why didn't they?'

Nenna shrugged. 'God would be angry I suppose,' she said.

'It's the same God, though,' said Tom, who didn't believe in God. 'Isn't it? It is. Jesus was Jewish, after all. So why would God mind either way?'

He didn't know. He couldn't imagine. It was like Shakespeare, or the Bible. People always doing ridiculous things for God, when you never even knew if he was real or not. How could they really believe in hell? He had read the whole of Shakespeare the year before and had been quite concerned about *Measure for Measure*. Would a girl really let her brother die rather than lie with a man? Not that he was sure what lying with someone entailed, and not that his English teacher had had much to say on the subject – but really – let your brother die? He wouldn't let Kitty die. Or Nenna. Not if he could save them by doing something perhaps just a bit bad. The lesser evil being justified if it prevents a greater evil, and all that. If God did exist, if he was any good, he'd understand anyway.

Tom was annoyed by Kitty's questions. He felt that he should know about these Jewish things. Nadine had been his mother first – she *was* his mother. So that made him Jewish.

At dinner that night, Aldo being away, they asked Susanna, cautiously, the question about conversion. Tom asked. He had told himself to be bold in Italian, or get nowhere, but so many delicate matters crumble under a badly chosen word. 'I mean to say,' he said, 'you're not religious. Nor is Aldo. So why didn't people just, you know, stop being religious before? If it would help them?'

Susanna stood to start clearing the plates, which for a moment the children took as a sign that they were not going to get an answer. But Susanna was thinking.

'The modern world is very different,' she said, after a moment or two, clattering a little. 'Our ancestors, in the old Italy, had nothing other than religion. Nobody would have let them escape their religion. Nowadays, we have united Italy to believe in. Not everybody makes the same choice, but now we have a choice.'

That didn't seem to make any sense either. If the Christians were so keen for Jews to convert, how could they not let them escape their religion? Surely they wanted them to escape their religion?

'Riley says it's the same God anyway,' said Tom. 'Jew or Christian. Or Muslim! It's all offshoots from the Jewish god, and people have given him different names.'

That night they decided that the best way for Tom and Kitty to become Italian and Jewish was if they all became blood brothers, which had the added advantage that it would make Nenna English as well. It was particularly important because they saw so little of each other. After bedtime, a

85

small knife was procured from the kitchen, jabs were made in fingertips, and fingertips were pressed together in a rather bloody mess, for probably longer than necessary. The squeaks of excitement at this mass martyrdom alerted Vittorio and Stefano, who bounced in and, once they realised what was going on, insisted that they too should be blooded. Vittorio made a huge fuss about it, and then let Kitty swaddle his finger in a grubby handkerchief.

Kitty fell asleep clutching her sore finger, tightly. She was happy.

~

This was the first year they went to the lake. After Rome, the lake was a vision of a different paradise, like something just beyond a wall, glimpsed through an arch in a Renaissance painting, tiny in the distance through the just-discovered law of perspective. It was a place one could become thirsty for, Tom felt, as he approached it for the first time: the hills behind him, black with forest; the green irrigated meadow beneath his feet, rolling down to the shores; and the great blue limpid eye of the lake itself, dozing in the sun, relaxing in the arms of its tree-robed promontories. Look at it! Flat, cool, reflective, a surface like blue slate. Over to one side, a handful of chestnut horses stood in the water, long-legged sentinels of the little harbour. They raised their heads at his appearance, up to their ankles in their own perfect reflections. A very strange effect.

Everyone walked down together.

'Show us the other beach, and the stream,' Nadine was saying to Aldo, but Tom had already pulled off his shirt and kicked off his shoes and was running out through the shallow sweet water to dive into the perfect surface, and revel. About twenty feet out, the sloping muddy-sandy lake-bed dropped off beneath him, suddenly, into deeper, colder water. *Tectonic plates!* he thought. *Marine cliff-faces. Here be monsters.* The drop-off was marked by a swathe of tall narrow tubular reeds, growing like an inner halo all around the lake. (Later he knew them well. You could break them off and use the pointed ends to pick your teeth. They'd draw blood on your gums if you weren't careful. If you broke them open the inside was a strange almost-solid white foam.) Then just beyond the reed-bed was a bed of weeds: to go out into the lake proper, to dive and frolic in deep water beyond this little safe shallow harbour, you had to swim through those weeds. Their long subaqueous strands bore leaves like the glass leaves on Venetian necklaces, and jewel-coloured dragonflies were alighting on their tiny tufts, which just pierced the surface, as if for that very purpose. Below, the misty slime-clad stalks gradually became invisible, disappearing down into the cold depths. They trailed against Tom's legs like something which might grab his ankle and pull him down. Tom swam through fast, front crawl, legs kicking mightily. The water was superb; an unspeakable joy.

He came out shaking parabolas of iridescent water drops off into the sunlight, and lay himself down. *Can't I be a lizard, and lie in the heat, on the black sand, immobile? I shall soak in all the sun till the sun is all used up; I shall radiate, I shall never ever move.* Above him, twinkling poplar leaves, tiny blades against the bluest sky. Around him, a very low buzz, the quietest hottest most silent sound: one insect, perhaps, dozing off. Beneath him, a thin worn towel and the heat of the black sand coming through it. To one side: the lividly green field, riven with swampy irrigation channels, and spangled in the mornings with bright blue chicory flowers which, he would learn, at the stroke of noon folded their stringy petals in and disappeared till the next day. And just there, inches from his pale toes, the round and lovely lake. No wind yet – that, he would learn, came later, after the chicory had retired. No movement, no ripple. A slight smell of what Nenna called *mentuccia* – mentoooooooo-cha. How she mocked his accent. How he mocked hers. Late morning. Summer. Bliss. Swallows and swifts dipping and softly cheeping, way overhead. When he asked the name of anything, he got a shrug and a word meaning something like 'fat face' or 'Chatterbox', or else 'you can't translate it'. He looked things up in the Latin dictionary, in case there was a connection, like *lacerta* and *lucertola*: lizard. *Rondine, rondone, rondicchio*: swallow, swift, martin. He kept sketchbooks, and wrote everything down: sizes and colours, where he'd seen it, what time of day, what it was doing. His little drawings were not only accurate, they were charming.

Nadine and Kitty came wandering back. They had seen a massive tree stump, semi-submerged, which looked like a horse's head. You could see the castle of Bracciano from just round there, and there was a rock you could sit on, out in the water. Kitty and Nenna had swum out to it; they looked such mermaids with their hair.

And now they could hear Susanna calling them to lunch; her voice faint down two fields and across the little road. Tom's greed woke his hunger, and he rolled over. He could see Nenna, out in the water. She had made a coronet out of the emerald weeds and was putting it on her father's head: he emerged from the water like a Triton, hairy chested and dripping, Nenna a naiad beside him, laughing. They shook themselves, water flying off their thick curly hair, and pulled on their sandals to set off up the field. Tom dragged himself off the towel and followed them, muttering under his breath the names of all the delicious pastas which Susanna might have made: *in bianco, con ragù, carbonara, all'amatriciana, all'arrabbiata, l'aglio e olio, alla puttanesca* . . .

They walked on up.

'Come on, perfidious Albion!' Aldo called back to him. Tom took off at a run, and overtook them at the gate, vaulting it: hands to rung two on the near side and rung one on the far, body horizontal, fly over – yes! He landed skidding on chamomile. The dusty scent of it erupted at his feet, and Nenna smiled. He walked up the hot white-dust road to the shade under the umbrella pines and the pale gigantic eucalyptus.

∼

Nadine wrote to Riley.

Bracciano
August 1929

Dearest,

The children are just in heaven, I think. This is an entirely new heaven. Nenna told us that Romans don't like lakes, traditionally – because the Etruscans live there, so it's all left over from Lars Porsena of Clusium swearing by the nine gods and so forth . . . but Aldo finds the seaside too busy, and has enough of it trying to drain it at work. This place is a kind of agricultural ruin, part of a farm belonging to some Roman princes who never come here. One of them, Don Alessio (?) is a bigwig on the Board of Drainage, and an admirer of Aldo's work at the Agro Pontino, so when Aldo wanted to rent it Don Alessio said yes. It used to be a stable, and still has great stone troughs and iron mangers inside, but from outside it looks more like a tiny castle, with a tower full of pigeons, floors more or less of brick, and the roofs held up with wooden beams. The walls are speckled with lichen, greens and gold, and somewhere on top of the tower, rooks and bright blue sky. It's a bit of a camp – water from the well, milk from the cows. Farther up the path live a bunch of lovely men in vests – Renzo, Roberto, Armando, Angelo – and their families, in small farmhouses. The men look after the cows and the women make vast vats of tomato sauce in a tiny stone house specially for the purpose. Barns and fields and vineyards recline in the golden sun on all sides; there's a stream down the side where a Frog Orchestra quack and trill all night long.

High up in the vaulted kitchen (so-called, there's no stove and no sink; just a stone basin and a big fireplace) ceiling there's an iron bar for hanging hams off so the rats can't get them. The very first night, there was a bat hanging from it! Like a trapeze artist, or an acrobatic mouse. Tom made Nenna really laugh when he tried to explain to her why acro-bat was funny, in this context. She got the joke and he was so proud and happy.

Sorry! Forgot to finish. It's two days later. The lake itself is round in its volcanic crater like an egg in a mountain of flour (this is how you make pasta – I'll explain when we try it at home) surrounded by boggy emerald meadows and Etruscan legends. A soldier made of solid gold lies asleep on the lake's bed, silent in the deep water with nothing but eels for company. Last night little bats were flying in and out of the children's bedroom window; livid green crickets cackle all night. I don't know if it's the same grasshoppers with scarlet underwings that fly across the meadows all day. Tom is looking it up. Kitty sits for hours damming the stream by moving stones and rocks, daydreaming and talking to herself, tying her wrists with strands of tiny pink and white striped bindweed, and not noticing when dragonflies land on her . . . Aldo loves this of course, and told her he does exactly the same at work. Sometimes he sits and joins in with her, pointing out the pitch of the land, and how water always takes the shortest course downhill. She got awfully bitten by mosquitoes, and one of the women here said '*Sei tutta rovinata!*' – 'You're all ruined!' She does look rather dreadful but they all say these aren't the malaria kind and it's the wrong time of year – So—

'The dragonfly hangs like a blue thread loosened from the sky' – What song is that from? That lovely one – Vaughan Williams? Tom swims, all day if you let him. The rubber mask and snorkel for staring at fish is very popular. I think he might be beginning to entertain ideas of being a naturalist. There's a little wooden dinghy; Aldo is teaching them to sail. Tom and Nenna are old enough to go out alone together; Kitty, much to her sorrow, just can't swim well enough yet. Yes we're taking our quinine!

I will post this – I haven't been to town yet so I haven't had the chance. Day five or six now.

Angelo and Renzo have taught them how to milk a cow! On a three-legged stool, with their cheeks resting against the great beast's smelly side. The milk comes out warm and scary, and it tastes quite different to English milk. The rough-tongued calves with little nubs of horns on their curled brows come up and lick our hands; they sucked appallingly on Kitty's fingers as if they were udders, and she thought they were going to pull them off. Even so she wants to be a dairymaid, or a cowgirl. There's a gang of ugly lumpy-faced ducks who line up on a stone water trough by the cowshed which I'm certain must be an Etruscan sarcophagus (Kitty then decided perhaps an archaeologist would be more interesting). They do their homework, play cowboys in the barn, pick peaches as if they were apples, and take jugs up the dusty lane to where huge wooden doors open into the hillside, and Angelo's wife fills the jugs with wine from a tap on a barrel twice as tall as a cow.

All my love to you my dearest—

Nadine

~

And so Italy became regular. 1928, 1929, and then the 1930s, so modern and new. Each summer's visit became a part of a whole, studding the overall experience with its individual jewels. The year Kitty could swim. The year Tom fell out of the tree. Memories grew on memories. And it was all lovely. And each passing year the children were different in themselves as they grew.

Kitty progressed from cute-like-a-doll to rather stout and serious and, in her eyes, unwanted – unlike Nenna, who, in Kitty's eyes, was wanted by everybody, especially by Kitty herself. This led to an uneven combination of envy and desire, a watchful attitude, and a sense of dumpy plainness which was not entirely justified, and – had Kitty only known it – more the result of the stultifying school she attended in London, with its obsession with sport and manners over intellect or joy, than of any actual plainness in herself.

Nenna became aware that she didn't entirely want to be a girl. Not that she wanted to be a boy, but she wanted to stay free, an unregulated sort of companion-at-arms to boys, one who could take them or leave them. She was not amused by the responsibilities of girlhood: cleanliness, white socks, helping in the house, being told when to be back. Being worried about. There was a march where the boys of the Balilla swung by with *novantuno* rifles, and the girls with baby dolls. She didn't mind real babies, and God knows there were enough of them about, but why would one want a toy one? And also she felt rather put on the spot. Understanding instinctively that nobody would want to hear about this, she said nothing. In fact she developed something of a habit of silence, and grew charismatic, attracting attention by not wanting it.

And Tom? He wanted everything. To swim, to fly, to run away from school, to fight, to swear eternal loyalty, to mind. He wanted to be older. He wanted to get into trouble.

∼

It was in the summer of 1932 that Nadine found herself confused by something which should have been very simple – writing a letter to Riley. They were staying a little longer than usual that year and perhaps that extra exposure made it all that bit stronger.

Darling,

It is lovely to be here again. The beauty! I know it's so dull to go on about it and I promised myself not to be one of those English people who wafts about Italy saying 'Isn't it lovely isn't it beautiful' all the time, as if nobody else had ever noticed, and it was in any way an interesting thing to say – but it's awfully hard. Because it is so beautiful! I allow myself to do it only on the first day, and after that I just say it to myself. Aldo has been teaching us to fish, off the little boat. The lake fish are called *coregoni* – they don't even have a name in English. Did I tell you about Ferragosto? The night of celebration of the Virgin Mary's ascension into heaven? We all walked round the lake in the evening to Trevignano, a loopy road, and when we got near (Aldo had to drag Kitty some of the way I'm afraid) we could see the little fishing boats all lit up with coloured torches, and fireworks were launched from the decks of *Il Batello*, the lake's ferryboat: they reflected off the dark water and it made the strangest effect, as if all barriers collapsed between two sides of anything – between water and sky, above and below, then and now . . . life and death, hope and fear . . . I wanted so much to have you there to lean back on and share the beauty with. It was almost spiritual for a moment – even though all to the sound of fairground music and the taste of warm nut brittle. Usually, apparently, the ruined castle up the hill behind the town catches fire from the flares marking the path up through the dry dry grass. One year, Aldo was telling us, it didn't, and everyone was disappointed, so the young men grabbed up the flares and ran about setting the fire on purpose. Then all the older men had to set up a run of buckets to the lake to put it out.

Where was I? Sorry, Susanna called us for dinner and I have been quite bad about helping out – well, we're swimming every day, obviously; eating far too much and getting as fat as little olives. The bats are driving Kitty quite bonkers. She read somewhere that they get tangled up in your hair . . . also she's reading *The Castle of Otranto* which would keep anyone awake at night. She said yesterday that she's writing a story about bats, so I hope that will get it out of her system. Tom is quite superb, diving and sailing and swimming, drawing a lot – not in his mask and snorkel obviously. I love to see them all together – each year I am worried that age and distance might mean they don't get on so well together, but they do, every time.

all my love,

Yours not in flames,

Nadine

Oh dear I didn't post this and now it's two days later! Who would have thought being so lazy would take up so much time? I am drawing a lot though – close-ups of leaves and any little creature I can get to stay still long enough. Beautiful scorpions and spiders with sections, if you see what I mean. I am terribly lazy about going into town –

No desire whatsoever! Even though I could stroll about in the market looking for fresh *burrata* and ice cream to bribe the children with. I am sorry. How's Papa? How are you darling? But don't write back, the post is awful – I don't even know if you have written, we haven't received anything. But now we'll be leaving the day after tomorrow so we'll be home before you get this. I am beginning to miss you rather a lot now. I'm trying to soften Aldo up to bring them all to London next year, but I don't know if it's going to work. He seems to think there's too many of them, but I shall hold out. —He has decided that Shakespeare was Italian! – or at least stole all his best stories from Italians: *Romeo and Giulietta*, from Verona, *Two Gentlemen*, also from Verona, *Giulio Cesare*, from Rome, also *Antonio* (from Rome) *and Cleopatra*, *Tito Andronico*—! They've been translating that bit of *Antony and Cleopatra* for him, because Nenna has decided that Cleopatra's barge, as Enobarbus described it, sounded like their island:

The barge she sat in, like a burnished throne
Burned on the water. The poop was beaten gold;
Purple the sails, and so perfumed that
The winds were love-sick with them. The oars were silver,
Which to the tune of flutes kept stroke, and made
The water which they beat to follow faster,
As amorous of their strokes.

I'm writing it out for you in full because it does sound beautiful in Italian. Not sure of its grammatical accuracy but here it is:

La galea dove sedeva lei, come trono brunito
splendeva sulle acque. La poppa d'oro;
Viola le vele e profumate tanto che
i venti vi languivano d'amore. D'argento i remi,
in cadenza al tono dei flauti, e l'acqua
battuta di loro li seguiva rapida,
quasi amorosi di quei loro colpi.

And Aldo's response? 'Shakespeare stole the story from Plutarch, and he was a Roman . . .'. To which Nenna says, surely he was Greek, and Aldo says 'Roman citizen' – you'd think every half-way talented person in the world was Roman to listen to him. So Nenna says, all innocent, 'And Shakespeare, was he Roman?' 'Crollalanza,' says Aldo, with his devilish little smile. 'Sicilian name.'

Anyway my love we'll see you soonest soonest. I will have to post this now, or be utterly embarrassed by having brought it back to London in my suitcase.

Your Nadine

She looked at the letter as she folded it. It really was quite long – five sides! Full and chatty, lots of news, how he liked it. A good letter.

And yet. And yet.

It was not entire chance that she hadn't got round to posting it. It was so easy out here to neglect things. So relaxing. But that wasn't it.

Something in me didn't want to post it. She could acknowledge that. Because it was not an entirely honest letter. There were several things she hadn't mentioned.

97

On Saturdays, when the other Jewish children were at synagogue, Nenna and the boys, in smart little uniforms and clean white socks, went off to Little Italians and Children of the Wolf.

There was a song, 'Giovinezza', that she really didn't like. It was too military, and the children would march around to it, and sing, and once or twice she had snapped at them to stop.

Earlier that week, at Trevignano, a bunch of young men in black shirts had walked into the main café in the piazza as if they owned it. They laughed too loud, and ordered beer, and they didn't seem to pay for it. They were *braggadocio* in action and she found herself moving the children outside sooner than she would have.

And there was the Day Camp to which Nenna and the little boys had gone, to which she had not wanted Tom and Kitty to go – not that they could have, as they weren't members of the club that organised it. Aldo had said he was sure they could go as guests, and she had said no, they had some reading to do for school, which wasn't really true. The excuse was the worst thing. *If either of the children mention it to Riley, I will have to explain . . .*

And before they came up to the lake this summer, she had visited Aldo in his office. He laid out drawings before her, in the tall cool room, large and precise. He showed designs for the giant pumps whereby salt water was being sucked out of marshes and beautiful farmland was being revealed. 'Julius Caesar planned to do this,' he said. 'He wanted to bring the Tiber down through the marshes all the way to Terracina, and drain off the water all the way. Leonardo da Vinci too – but it was not done. But we are succeeding.'

She looked at them politely: they were beautiful, vast and powerful. But she was distracted: a photograph of the Duce, framed, perched on the wall right above Aldo's broad and tidy drawing desk.

'Would you like to come down there?' Aldo said, beaming and keen, like a small boy offering a turn on his best toy. 'I could show you,' he said. 'I'd like to so much.'

'Next time, perhaps,' she said, but she looked at him and smiled, so it wasn't rude.

'We are digging more than fifteen thousand kilometres of canals and trenches,' he said, and she kept the smile. *Fifteen thousand kilometres!*

'Quite something!' she said. *But Riley despises Mussolini. He's publishing a pamphlet about him this autumn and it is not a fan letter.*

'It's such an important job,' Aldo said. 'For the people. There's so many men down from the north already, rebuilding their lives. We see the results of our work, every time we raise our eyes. Nadina, it's such a joy!'

He looked so happy. *Dear Aldo!*

But but but.

The photograph bothered her. Up there in his hat and his Sam Browne, looking like he thought he knew everything. *Odd how people think he's handsome. He looks like a lump. And there's too many pictures of him everywhere.*

She hated leaving things unsaid. It held a horrid cargo of potential upset.

So, a long letter, emptier than one would think.

Part Two

1932

Chapter Six

Kent, June 1932

Peter and Riley were striding about on the Downs. Part of the idea of walking, though this too was unspoken, was that striding along, eyes not meeting, mild distractions constantly to hand – 'Isn't that a kestrel—?' 'Ah, look, St John's wort' – was a convenient forum for the exchange of confidences, should either of them be inclined. One could not escape, but neither could one be forced. But today – a drowsy, bee-heavy day, where even the river ran a little slowly and the sweet-bitter smell of clover blossoms languished across the thick meadows – this was not working. They had left the house a little too late; it was too warm for any actual effort. Their muscles were soon limp and their clothes itchy.

The lure of the river and the removal of shoes was too strong. They rolled their trousers up, sat on the banks among watercress, slow worms and kingcups, and kicked crystalline spray up into the sunlight to make rainbows.

After a while Riley said, 'Oh, well, for God's sake,' and took his shirt and trousers off, and folded them (which made Peter smile) and plunged in like a shaggy dog, submerging among weed and minnows and rising again, gasping and shaking his head.

'Beware, beware, his flashing eyes, his floating hair!' called Peter, humorously, and Riley made a face.

Peter had a secret.

Sitting there, the sleeves of his shirt rolled up above the elbows – *God I am so white* – and his collar open, he wanted to tell it to Riley. But he wasn't going to. Things were not calm enough. It is always hard to be rescued – to maintain one's dignity, and accept that one must be grateful – and Riley had rescued him three times now. Looking back on these rescues, Peter saw how it worked: Riley could drag him out of chaos, yes, but that was as far as it went. Riley couldn't deliver Peter into a safe and happy haven. He could only leave Peter on the outskirts of what used to be his life, and let him work out his own way back – which is what Peter tried to do. Of course there was nothing to be done about Julia. He could continue to rage, or he could accept the cruel joke that just as they had begun to regain each other, she had to die – and of the most ordinary, everyday domestic tragedy: childbirth. The woman's equivalent of war, he had realised, after talking to Rose about it, about how many women die that way. In every thousand births, fifty women will die. One in twenty. *One in twenty*! *Can that be right*? Rose, who worked with Dr Janet Campbell on her project for a national system of antenatal clinics, had told him about Pasteur and Semmelweis and Alexander Gordon, one of the first to realise that doctors themselves might be passing the infection that caused puerperal fever among the women they were caring for, who for his reward was chased back into the Navy by a horrified medical establishment who did not want to believe what he was saying. Rose had taken Julia's death hard. She felt she should have been able to help. *Poor Rose,* Peter thought. *Always so helpful, and then, when it was really needed, she simply hadn't been there. Poor Rose.* She had told him something else: before the war, one in four babies born in poverty died. *Only one in ten fighting men died in the war! Only – of course only is not the word – But one in four babies!* It wasn't that he didn't feel so sad for the babies. *But those mothers! What women suffer – and people go on about men's sufferings in the war – trauma and shock – and all the time, which I never noticed, women were suffering under our noses.* He couldn't stop thinking about this. *It's a form of mourning, no doubt –* he thought. *Mourning for Julia.*

But I'm not dead.

His book had been respectably received, had an excellent review in *The Times* and two reprints. This having transformed him in his own eyes into a man of perhaps some value after all, he was preparing a second. It was about this battle, the woman's battle. Starting with Sparta, the leaving of children on the hillsides and so on, and those Incas in Peru. Rose was to help him, and an obstetrician colleague of hers was going to steer him right medically. It would be dedicated to Julia, about whom nothing could be done. And yes, he hoped that it might be somehow good for his own children.

He had hopes of the children. With them, he thought, he had time. But though Kitty was willing, Tom held out still, and for all Riley's optimistic declarations, would not love his father. There had been a moment, though, a curious moment, slipping between the leaves of timing and possibility, which had revealed to Peter that he and his son could come together, one day. They had all – Riley, Robert, Nadine, Kitty – gone to a concert of Schumann. After one passage of surpassing beauty, Peter had glanced up and seen his son, two along from him on the velvet seats, looking at him, facing him, from a rank of profiles. For a second Peter was embarrassed to think what entranced expression might have been hanging on his own face, but he quickly realised that Tom's expression was not of mockery or derision but of recognition. And then, a little later, Peter had forgone the pleasure of being carried away by another intoxicating section in order to observe Tom, and he saw on his son's face the ecstatic removed look of a human immersed in musical joy, just as he had worn moments before, and he saw it followed by a swift shadow of embarrassment as Tom realised he was observed, and then he saw Tom realise that the look on Peter's face was, in turn, not mockery or derision but recognition. And their eyes met, and each gave a rueful little smile.

The moment glowed in Peter's heart like a rising sun. *Time*, he thought, and the great victory was that he believed now that he had time, and that he was capable of the patience and dedication he would use it for, to win back his son.

His new secret, however, was unlikely to be conducive to a reunion with Tom. Peter could see that.

And telling a secret, Peter thought, *is usually a request for help.*

Am I thinking Riley could help me with this, as with so much else?

He wasn't sure. He wanted, really, to share joy.

Peter leaned forward, the sun warming his shoulders, his feet like pale tenuous fish in the water.

'Riley!' he called. But Riley was underwater. Hooting and sploshing and gasping, 'Riley!' Peter yelled, and caught his attention as he surfaced again. 'Come here. I have something to tell you.'

~

When Mabel Zachary met Peter Locke for the third time – well of course, it wasn't the third time. It felt like the third time, because it was the third episode. Even as she saw him walk into the shop that dingy November morning, she knew that this was what it was going to be.

He came in, confused slightly by some interchange between his gloves and the door handle, taking off the gloves (soft leather, black, gentlemanly), and looking up. And looking up he saw her, and seeing her, he gave her a mild, surprised, enchanting smile.

And immediately she thought: *Do I want this? Am I ready?* And then it was already happening.

She saw the ghost of the charm he had had in 1918, when they had first met at the Turquoisine, when everyone was crazy and drunk, and he no crazier nor drunker than the rest of the crowd, just more elegant and more polite and more understanding of the deep sorrow at the root of it all. She saw too the hunger he had had in 1919, when they had run into each other on Chelsea Embankment, and he

107

had been so drunk for so long that after a few weeks she had had to extricate herself from his chaotic ways, and retreat, and leave him to it.

And now, because it was 10 a.m. and twelve years later and he was clean, sober, shaven, upright, looking younger than she had ever seen him look, and smiling, she knew that the involvement of drink was no longer the entangling imperative it had been before, and she smiled back.

'Hello,' he said. His blue eyes were clear: no misery, no bovine defiance, no shame glittering in their depths.

'Hello,' she said. And then she was almost embarrassed, because something in her really quite guarded heart was simply melting, melting away, at the sight of him looking well, and being here, smiling at her, and saying hello to her, in his voice.

'Do you take a lunch break?' he said, just like that.

'A half hour,' she said, 'at twelve thirty.'

'Perhaps you could leave your job,' he said, and he may have been serious, but she started laughing and said 'No', in a gentle and affectionate way.

'I'll have to wait, then,' he said. 'Would it get you into trouble if we were to chat?'

'It's quiet,' she said. 'Of course if a customer comes, or if Mr Moores comes in—'

'Oh but I am a customer!' Peter said. 'Show me all your latest American imports. Tell me what is good. What are you listening to? And who are you singing with? What news of Mr Sidney Bechet? Florence Mills? And why are you working here? You *are* still singing, tell me you're still singing . . .'

108

She told him she was still singing. She'd just finished a run in *Porgy and Bess* at the Theatre Royal, chorus, but on stage with Paul Robeson! She told him she had recorded, with some of the guys from the show's orchestra, and they had a band now. Of course he wanted that record. She brought it to him: there she was on the cover, smiling her huge high-cheekboned smile, big eyes gleaming, wearing a feathered little thing on her head. She looked cool and hot at the same time. On the back she was described as 'New York's Newest Singing Sensation', which was quite funny, as she had been in London since she was fourteen. They laughed about that. She told him she worked three days a week at the shop, and that it was great to get to hear all the new records early. (She didn't tell him that before *Porgy and Bess*, or *Porgy and Bless*, as she secretly referred to it, she had been working at the shop six days, working bars and singing in the evenings, or that before Mr Moores had offered her the job in the shop she'd been cleaning houses too.)

He admired the picture. 'I have never had a photograph of you,' he said, and she said, 'Well,' and he said, 'What, *why would I*? You know why I would. Don't you?' And she was about to say 'I'm just a girl' when she realised she mustn't because he would say something and she would say something and suddenly they would be in a place neither of them were prepared for.

She turned back to the shelves behind her and said: 'New Orleans? Chicago?'

'Chicago, I think,' he said.

'Jazz or blues? I have Bessie Smith's "Black Mountain

Blues" here,' she said. 'You heard that? Or, the Famous Hokum Boys? "Saturday Night Rub" is the new one . . .' She gave them to him. 'Have you heard the new stuff coming out of New York? Here—' She passed him another disc: Bix Beiderbecke, 'At the Jazz Band Ball'. 'Cornet player,' she said. 'With Adrian Rollini on bass sax. He's something else. You know even Louis Armstrong has moved to New York now?'

'I haven't heard anything for a long time,' he said. She wondered if he'd been avoiding jazz as a way of avoiding drink, and looked at him with that thought in her eyes.

He blinked at her and said, 'But you'd have seen me, if I'd been going to any clubs.'

There was a record player behind the counter; he handed back 'At the Jazz Band Ball', and she put it on. The music started straight in, gay and ghostly, something mournful in the rhythms and the chords . . . As she turned back he was looking at her as if he were going to ask her to dance.

Oh my Lord, dear Lord, she thought. Peter was the only white man she had ever been to bed with. Her mother didn't hold with white men.

He did, he held his arms up in a 'dance with me?' position, and raised his eyebrows.

She shook her head and smiled. 'Need to stay this side of the counter,' she said. Her heart was going pitter-pat.

We've leapt up some ladders and down some snakes in the past twelve years and you don't even know, she thought. But the music made her shrug her shoulders and swing her hips a little. She couldn't not. And she was very pleased to see him.

They played records and talked about jazz and blues for

two hours: Duke Ellington, Fletcher Henderson, Coleman Hawkins, Lead Belly, Big Bill Broonzy. Sidney Bechet was in Berlin, she'd heard – he'd been deported! No, twice! From London in, what, '22? And then from Paris, there'd been a shooting at Bricktop's in Montmartre – well, yes, actually she had been there – not performing that night, no, but Henry Crowder had been in on his way back from Venice, with – well, anyway, Sidney was in Berlin, was the word. But there were no new recordings. Had Peter heard the 1923 tracks, with Louis Armstrong? 'Texas Moaner Blues'? Ooh, she'd get those out for him . . . She broke off from time to time to serve customers, and then he watched her, and a smile lingered, at her square shoulders, her gentleness, her courtesy and quiet enthusiasms.

'Your voice hasn't changed at all,' he said. 'It's no more English. Does it still get more American when you've relaxed?'

'Uh huh,' she said. 'Or excited.'

'Or on stage?'

She smiled.

Then he bought all the records she had shown him, and took her to the Gay Hussar for the fastest goulash ever known. She told him not to come back with her, but he was waiting outside at five thirty, and only by agreeing to his coming along that evening could she get rid of him for a couple of hours before she started work.

~

Mabel was living in two rooms at the top of a narrow rickety Georgian house in Lexington Street, Soho. All afternoon she had been thinking, and she was thinking now, heading over there, and indeed she had been thinking for twelve years. But now a great big snake had been slid down, and she had to make her decisions. She had a half-formed song in her mind, and as was her habit she was working through it as she walked, because Lord knows when she'd be able to sit down at a piano and finish it. The melody was bluesy but pure, E minor, and the lyric was a Bible verse: *Take ye heed, watch and pray, for ye know not when the hour is . . .* She'd assumed it was about death, and maybe it was, but yeah, it could be about anything. *Ye know not when the hour is.*

The tall black door was open onto the pavement and Reginald, the Jamaican trombone player who lived below her, greeted her as she slid past him into the shaded hall. She smiled, and gave thanks that she was no longer provoked into hunger and envy by the frying smells dripping down the stairs from his room. The goulash had been huge – and they had been sitting in a dark corner, so when Peter had left the table she had shamelessly taken the larger pieces of meat from her bowl, wrapped them in her smooth white napkin, and stuffed the package, fraught with the potential to leak gravy, into her bag. She didn't really need to do that sort of thing any more, but she couldn't abide waste. She was sorry if the loss of the napkin would cause trouble for any of the staff. She would bring it back. The meat she knew did not count as theft, as it was Peter's gift. He would, she thought – *would he?* – be glad to give it, if he knew where it was going.

But that's the big question, isn't it? Will he be glad?

She was steeped in sin, she knew it. It all led from the

one recurrent sin: that she would not always fight men off. Well, and well. It wasn't her coveting her neighbour's wife, it was her neighbours coveting her. She had been through that with God on many occasions. It was unfair of God to have made men so attractive, and to have made her so attractive to them. And to put her in this white world where so many men were unable to approach their own women (women their own colour and class) unless with a view to marriage, yet thought a woman like her (different colour, and kind of unclassifiable) only too approachable. Approachable, that is, for buying a drink from, or buying a drink for. For service – in a bar, or domestic, or sexual. Housework, church, marriage, prostitution of some kind. And that, as a set of limitations, she had never liked. But a negro woman had a particular responsibility towards men. Knowing the hardships the black man suffers, she above all must not give him more. She learnt this from her mother, and all around her. A woman must be kind and service him and not knock him down, and by her womanhood she must let him be a man in a world which so often denied him his manhood. She must marry him and bear his children and look after them and cook for him and not hassle him for money and understand when he has to walk out on her. She must not shame him. And for sure she must not take his work.

To sing was all right. A girl singer was always a girl singer, that was fine. But instruments? No. Jazz is a male language, females can't do it. When she played piano, they didn't like it. She didn't even bother to tell them – her friends, her band – that she wrote songs. She sang them and played them just for the guys to learn them, for the real pianist to take over – and when someone said, 'Whose song is that?' she said, 'It's one of my daddy's.' *My daddy's pretty up-to-date and productive for a dead guy.*

So of course when a man appeared with something other than that in his eyes or his talk, it was a rainbow on a grey day. The first was Thornton Williams from Charleston Carolina, so pure a musician that he only saw her talent, and wanted to teach her. From him she had learnt to read and write music and frame a song and play Bach and Scott Joplin. Thornton was a composer and taught at the Royal College of Music; he'd helped her so much with how music actually works, how you can dismantle a song and put it back together. She'd always done it on a wing and a prayer before. When he introduced her to musical literacy, to tell the truth he had dismantled her and put her back together also. And he'd recognised Iris's baby skills on the piano, and said, get her lessons. Every black musician doesn't have to be self-taught. Every black musician doesn't have to play jazz. Every black musician doesn't have to play in church and clubs – he said it with a laugh because Lord knows they'd both done enough of both.

And most of all – every black musician doesn't have to be a man. It wasn't that a girl couldn't be fully musical, it was just that other people didn't want her to be. Mabel had been so pleased to clarify this that as a result, ironically, she would have cooked for him happily, gone back to the States with him even, if he'd wanted . . . but things didn't go that way, and the man died in '25. Thornton's copy of the Goldberg Variations was still in Iris's music bag. He'd taught her himself: big hands curved over small hands on the keyboard: 'Imagine you're holdin' a little mouse in there. You don't want to squash him, but you don't want him runnin' away . . .'

And Peter was the second: a man who talked to her, and listened. She'd told him, back in the day, about her childhood in her mother's troupe, flinging her limbs around dancing while Mama – Betty Zachary – sang 'Why You Make Dem Goo Goo Eyes at Me'. The little dancers, known as Betty's Pickaninnies – they were meant to be boys, but Mabel had been a skinny kid, and kept her hair short, and that was a way for Mama to keep her with her on the road and to keep her safe. Mama took her up and down the US, Florida to Chicago, LA to Harlem. Her bed was often enough a train seat, or a fur coat thrown into a tuba case. And thence to the other side of the world, St Petersburg, Paris, and London; Salford, Birmingham and Skegness. Mabel's aunties were dancers and singers; her fathers sax players and piano men. It was romantic and uncomfortable and funny and bitter and tough, and hers, and she threw it over when she had her child.

None of this was what she wanted for Iris. Iris was to have piano lessons, and one home. She, Mabel, was providing it. You could depend on nobody in this world.

She didn't want to have to fit into this system of men and women, black and white. She hoped for something easier and better, with more room for her to do what she wanted. Sometimes it seemed to her that the easiest thing might be just to accept how things were and shut up about it. Marry someone and cow down. But only sometimes.

'Hey, ladies,' Mabel called softly, as she pushed open her own door. Mama was in the chair, dozing, a gleam of light resting on her wide cheekbones and the gold crucifix on her breast, her mouth like carved stone. Mabel bent to kiss her cheek – a swift breath of rose hair-oil and talc.

Iris, doing her homework at the scrubbed table, glanced up and said, 'Hey Mumma.' She stood for her embrace, tall and fair-skinned, and looking, Mabel realised, really very like her father.

~

Night after night Peter came to hear Mabel sing, to take her to supper, to walk her home. He kissed her in squares and telephone boxes and backstreets and doorways. She felt she needed great ribbons strapped round her ankles and tied to a lamp post or a tree to stop her from flying off. The suddenness and the implausibility and the familiarity made it irresistible. She took to laughing out loud in the street.

Peter would not take her to a cheap hotel, and she would not take him home. So as it was impossible for them not to be together, they became, briefly, that winter, familiar with the Savoy. Even Peter was not so naive as to imagine they could go up together. The first time, he booked and paid in advance, but when she went there, ahead of him, the smart expressionless young man in charge would not give her the room key. The next time Peter went first, and she was prevented from following. He came down, claimed her, outstared and out-embarrassed everyone present. Upstairs, finally, he watched her sit on the vast smooth

116

cream-coloured satin jacquard bedspread with an implacable look of combined resentment and acceptance on her face.

He said 'Well, we shall just have to get a flat. Where is nice?'

By nice, he meant, though he hardly knew it, 'possible'. If he had thought, he would have thought he meant 'possible for a negro woman'. If he had thought a little longer, he would perhaps have got round to thinking 'possible for two different-coloured people'. He would never have thought that she would be thinking, 'An area where no one who knows my mother will see us.'

'I really am surprised at the Savoy,' he said. 'I thought they had more class.' He smiled at her, held out his hand. 'Belgravia,' he said. 'You can walk in to Soho, and give up where you're living now.'

Her smile was quizzical, and he felt he ought to make things clear.

'I won't let you down,' he said. It felt extremely important that she knew that. He had had no interest in any woman for years. He had, since Julia's death, spent several years wrapped in a deep and shattering grief for the cutting off of the reunion they had only just begun. Before that, whores and hallucinations and violence and filth, and the two terrible occasions, riddled with drink and lust and misunderstanding, on which he had fathered his two children, so dear to him, so far from him. The distant memory of the early nights with Julia, under the chandelier in Venice – no, don't look back that far. No. Mabel was the only woman in whose arms he had ever found anything like peace, let alone desire, and joy – and here they all were, still. All the tiny possibilities of love which you suddenly realise are love, if you only have the eyes to see it.

'I won't let you down,' he said.

~

Every time his talk wandered into these territories, she silenced him – and indeed herself. She could not look at it too closely because it would melt away under any examination. It was too extraordinary! At her age! And with him! This joy they were feeling was not possible in this wicked world. So she would keep it separate.

The flat was beautiful: the first floor of a tall house some aristocratic family could no longer afford to run, white stucco like a wedding cake, windows almost the height of the tall ceilings, low February sunshine lying on the black branches of the plane trees outside beyond the balcony. In the evening the damp smell of the garden square rose and crept over into the room like the promise of a continent beyond. Imminent spring. *The leaves will dance in the summer, out there,* she thought, and then thought it best not to think ahead.

Four rooms and a parquet floor. And a kitchen.

At the flower stall in Sloane Square he had offered her a big spray of something expensive and hothouse – orchids? Some glamorous lily? – and then caught sight of her face, and bought the violets instead. She said, once they were alone, 'Thank you. The others were kinda—' and she had been going to say 'mistressy', but she didn't even want to think that word, Lord forgive her. He took her arm, and she thought, as a passer-by glanced, *I don't suppose that in public we will ever really be alone.*

He was saying, 'That's not how I think of you. As something expensive and exotic, to show off. That's not – that's not it.'

If Iris didn't exist, she thought, *what a wild joy I would make of this, spitting in the eye of everything, just loving him and going places and fighting everyone who criticised or looked sideways at us, and breaking rules and having such fun – I'd go to his places and he'd come to mine, and none of it would matter because our love is pure no matter what anybody thinks.*

But I must tell him soon. I must work this out.

She was scared. She wasn't used to fear. She had not been brought up that way.

Well what's the worst can happen? He'll just quit me and that's it, like nothing ever happened. So I'd better do it soon. But the idea of him quitting her – *no. I've earned this,* she thought. *I've lost him twice already. I don't want to quit. I want to keep him. I want him.* That part of it was – terribly simple.

'You'll need a maid,' he said, unlocking the door, smiling sideways at her, and she smiled at his idea of necessity. She thought of Reginald's eldest daughter, Rebecca – but then how could she bring any other girl here where Iris could not come? She thought, briefly, madly – *I'll bring Iris, pretend she is my maid, then she can live here in this sunlight—*

Then, *Oh Mabel,* she thought.

'I'll see about it,' she said, but she kept the rooms herself. She preferred it that way: such calm in solitude. Anyway, bringing anyone else would be too much like reality.

After he left, she surveyed her empire. There was hardly any furniture. *We could have a room each*, she thought. *Mama in that cosy one, Iris in the sunny one, she could have a little desk in there and hang her clothes up properly – me in this one –* 'This one' was small but on the corner, with windows south and west, a fireplace framed with twisted carved leaves and columns, a mirror the same. All so clean.

She put a tiny table in front of a window, and on it the violets in a little vase, and she lay on the bed, and she wept.

~

'I knew it!' crowed Riley.

They were sitting on the bank, smoking cigarettes and letting their white shoulders glow like ivory, grass tickling their knees. A damselfly kept settling on Riley's toe as he lifted it in and out of the water, reminding him of Nadine, and that song about the thread of blue.

'No you didn't,' Peter said. 'How could you know it? What do you mean?'

'Knew it in 1918,' Riley said. 'She was so – lovely. Fabulous eyes.' She had been serving at the Turquoisine; he had asked her to tell Peter that he was there to take him home, and there had been a look in her eyes – he could picture it now, a sort of veiling that passed across, a look of loss, expected and accepted loss, deserved loss, even, as if she knew she would never be allowed the thing she wanted. What had she said, about Peter, or to Peter? He couldn't remember the words. Something implying an intimacy. He remembered what she'd said to him, though, back when his scars were fresh and his voice just healing. As he had dropped his scarf to speak – to croak – this beautiful girl had looked him in the eye and said, 'You still cute.' A chap doesn't forget that.

'Oh rubbish,' said Peter, but he glowed a little at that description of her.

'Not rubbish,' Riley said. He smiled. 'Then you told me later. 1919, was it, you were with her again?'

'A few months, after . . . after Julia left,' Peter said. 'I let her down, then. The old drink. I know you might think a girl like that might expect to be let down but—'

'She's not a girl like that,' Riley said.

'No she's not,' Peter said. 'Exactly.'

A silence sat between them, companionable and open.

'So, I'm beginning to think,' Peter said.

Riley grunted.

'It's not like normal!' Peter cried. 'It's not tennis and dances, we're not twenty-two, I don't know her people, I don't even know if she has people. We're practically living together, Riley! Except she won't let me. Two nights a week, it's as if we're married. Otherwise, I'm packed back off to Locke Hill. Too much work! she says – days in the shop, nights singing. If it were any other kind of work I'd have her stop, of course, but it's music, it's her heart – I'd go and listen to her every night of the week but she won't let me. She says people have noticed me, and there's been talk. I haven't even been to where she – where she really lives.'

Riley glanced round at him.

'Husband?' he said. 'Boyfriend?' He had a sudden image of Peter being beaten up by a vast and jealous jazz musician.

Dear Peter, so innocent despite everything. 'Someone keeping her?'

'No,' Peter said. 'Pretty sure not. She's – honest, you know. And proud. She doesn't have a bean, really. Rather hard to get her to accept the slightest thing, too.'

Riley knew nothing about these things. He had gone straight from war into Nadine's arms, had only ever had Nadine to understand or be understood by, and Christ what a woman she was for understanding . . . For a moment he thought to tell Peter to speak to Nadine about it – but then no. There was something delicate about this. But if Nadine did know, what would she say? She'd say, when you don't know what to do, get more information. Which means, going up a notch.

Peter was leaning back on his elbow now, one knee bent, his arm with cigarette dangling, languid. For a moment, seeing him thus against the livid green, Riley recalled the morning of Julia's death, the mad tableau of Peter sitting just so by Julia's dead body at the end of the frozen lawn, the collar of his greatcoat up, cigarette dangling just the same way.

Riley bit his reconstructed lip, and let go a huge sigh. *I never saw a man who more deserved happiness,* he thought.

'Have you told anybody?' he asked. 'Rose? The children?'

'Good Lord no,' said Peter.

'Probably best leave it where it is then,' Riley said. 'See what happens.'

'But,' said Peter, and Riley glanced at him.

'But?'

'I want more,' Peter said simply.

'Then you need to go up a notch,' Riley said, but the word notch was difficult, so he said, 'Up a level' to make it clear.

'How?' asked Peter.

'More information,' said Riley. 'Keep talking.'

'What, ask her?' said Peter, looking slightly aghast.

'Well I don't think you should get a detective,' Riley said, and shot him a look, and slipped back into the water.

Chapter Seven

London, July 1932

A few weeks later, Nadine and the family were at supper in the garden at Bayswater Road, evening sun limpid, and London just beyond the soot-blackened wall. It was Tom's first day back from school. Rose had joined them, looking stern and cheerful, and smelling slightly of carbolic soap, and Kitty was staying up for dinner with the adults. They were having shepherd's pie: too heavy for the weather, but Riley's favourite. Tom was complaining about his trunks. Matron had written to Nadine during term saying the elastic – or the trunks themselves – needed replacing. But nothing had been done about it and now it was July; the old ones were hanging by a string, and Tom wanted to know, was he going to have to go to Italy with no decent trunks to wear? Talking of which, when were they leaving? Because he had plans . . .

And Nadine said, girding her loins a little and not looking up from the dish, 'We're not going to Italy this year.'

'Aren't you?' said Riley, looking up. 'Why not?'

'But why?' Tom said. He looked aghast.

'It'll be nice to have a holiday in England for a change,'

said Nadine, as if it were nothing much. 'With Riley.' She did hope Tom wasn't going to kick up too much fuss.

'What about my polenta supply?' Riley said, cheerfully. Nadine looked across at him and said, 'Wouldn't you rather have a proper family holiday than polenta? I thought we might stay at Locke Hill for a change.'

Tom was quiet, and Nadine saw the stew that this proposition opened up for him, and was sorry. She thought, looking at his face, *he still does not love Peter at all* – and that made her sad, all over again. She recalled Riley saying to Tom once: 'I wish you'd known your father before the war made him what he is,' and Tom snapping back: 'Well I don't' – but that was a long time ago. *Hadn't things changed?*

If they had, it hadn't been enough. The resentful set of Tom's mouth said it all: he still wasn't interested in his father. Of course, she thought, a boy that age isn't expected to talk about loving his father, but he's meant to feel it. She wondered if Tom might be somehow aware of that, and a bit inchoately ashamed of it, without perhaps really knowing it. Certainly she could see it all adding up to 'Who on earth would want to go to Locke Hill, where we have to go at Christmas and Easter anyway, when we could be in Rome, and on the lake?'

'Riley could come to Italy,' Tom said, flashing his blue eyes upwards. 'They'd love him to come.'

'You know he doesn't travel, darling,' Nadine said, and a look crossed Riley's face, a little sad frown, and Tom glanced at him. For a moment restraint sat at the table with them. Rose noticed, of course.

'I hope I will come, one day,' Riley said, almost apologetically, and Nadine felt suddenly tearful.

Kitty said, 'It will be nice to be with Daddy. Locke Hill is lovely anyway, and we can ride.'

'I'll have your trunks ready in time, darling,' Nadine said after a moment. 'The river's quite full this year. And you know, it is your home.'

'I'm coming too,' said Rose. 'I'm taking some proper time off. My poor patients have all agreed to do without me for two entire weeks. I've made them all promise not to die or have any sick babies.'

'I love Dr Aunt Rose,' said Kitty dreamily, and Rose eyed her sideways and grinned.

'I don't understand,' Tom said, at this series of betrayals. 'Why should we suddenly not go? We've always gone before—'

'Four times,' said Nadine. 'It's not a lifelong tradition.'

'Well it should be,' Tom said. 'They're our—' and with that, of course, he realised that actually they weren't what he had been going to say, 'our cousins'. He frowned.

'Of course they are,' Nadine said. 'We're just not going this year. That's all.'

'Then I'll go on my own,' Tom said. 'If nobody else wants to come. I am old enough – I've been old enough to go away to school for years, so I'm old enough to go to Italy.'

Riley gave him a look.

Tom sank back into thought, furious.

Riley had some work to catch up with so it was Nadine and Rose who sat out among the gleaming white roses in the dusk, drinking a little wine and talking.

'So what was that about?' Rose asked conversationally.

Nadine glanced at her. No hiding anything from Rose. Knowing she would have to explain, she wondered how she would phrase it.

'Don't you like them any more?' Rose was saying, with kind curiosity.

'Gosh no,' Nadine blurted. 'I just wanted them to come here for once, and they couldn't, and now it's rather late, and of course we should spend our holidays together, as a family, with Riley. It's been selfish of us to go gadding off without him . . .' She ran dry, having over-explained, and thus revealed that she had not given the real reason. Because of course there was the other reason, beyond friendliness and natural hospitality, why Nadine had tried to get the Fiore family to come to London. And Aldo's refusal – for the perfectly good reason that there were too many of them – and insistence that she and the children should go to Rome 'as usual' had meant she had to take this other tack.

That photograph of the Duce was the reason. Nadine was not a political woman – she drew, she painted, she was engaged with the children and with Riley. If she was polit-ical at all it was social policy which engaged her, with Rose at her surgery, helping with her campaigns for public health and education and women, discussing ideas at length. They'd set up a weekly children's art class at the surgery, which Nadine ran, and they hoped to expand it to other surgeries in deprived areas. That was Nadine's politics . . . But she could see that the Duce, for all his social policies, was not their kind of politician. She knew that Riley, with his Fabian ways and his clear-eyed, humorous idealisms, and Aldo would lurch naturally into political discussions, and would disagree. With Aldo in London, she felt, it would be less of an issue.

'And I don't think Aldo and Riley would get on,' she said.

Rose raised an eyebrow.

'Politically,' Nadine said.

'But Riley wouldn't be going,' Rose said. 'So why not go anyway, as usual, with the children?'

Because I am on the verge of lying to Riley about Aldo, Nadine thought. *I am withholding the truth, already. Am I? I think I may be. I am not open with him.*

'It's a little more subtle than that,' she said. 'I suppose.' She didn't want to say it to Rose either. *All the more reason why you should then. Go on! Spit it out!*

She took a breath and blurted. 'Aldo's keen on Mussolini,' she said. 'I don't say this to Riley, because he wouldn't like it.'

'Ah,' said Rose. She thought for a moment. 'Ah yes. Do you fear that Riley would say that you can't be friends with him, and the children must not be under that kind of influence?'

'I just—' Nadine said, and stopped.

After what she and Riley had been through already as a result of not being open with each other, during the war when he had lied about his face, wanting to protect her by breaking with her, and almost breaking both their hearts by it, it was inconceivable to her not to be open with him. So, clearly – well, fairly clearly – the thing to do was to retreat from the cousins. She could write to Aldo still; they could be fond relatives at a distance. She didn't have to upset anybody; not the children, Nenna, Susanna, nor the men. They'd only visited for four summers! It wasn't as if she were breaking a lifelong joy for the children. She was being responsible.

I don't have to make a big thing of it, she told herself. *The Duce probably is rather awful but people out there do seem to really love him and one doesn't want to be judgemental.*

'No,' she said. 'It feels like a kind of lying, to Riley, and I don't want to go on with it.'

Well, Rose understood that all right. She had been right at the heart of their first great misunderstanding, when she had been Riley's nurse. She had had to read Nadine's letters, and some of his.

'Is it not dishonest not to tell him why?' Rose asked.

'I don't want to upset anyone . . .' Nadine said. 'And I'm not exactly telling Tom the real reason why either!'

'Well, that's different,' Rose said. 'One shouldn't tell children everything. They're not equipped.'

Nadine was annoyed. She liked the cousins so much! But of course she could do without Aldo for Riley's sake. It would be for the best. *Let it fade, and then you will never have to lie to Riley.*

Lie to Riley! She laughed. Never never never again.

Riley was in bed, reading something by George Orwell. She was glad to have talked with Rose, because she would have felt somehow naked, having these thoughts in mind, in front of him – he who could almost read her mind. He looked up as she came in.

'Rose all right?' he said.

'Mm,' she said.

'You all right?'

'Love you,' she said, taking off her robe, and sitting. Sometimes she adopted, without noticing it, the brevity of speech patterns that he had developed, thanks to his damaged mouth.

'What, still?' he said, in pretended amazement.

'Still,' she said.

～

The next afternoon Tom announced to Nadine that he had written to Nenna and invited her to come and stay. He was very bland about it.

'She can come to Locke Hill with us,' he said. 'And she'll love London. We can carry on practising our languages. It would be a shame to let them slide.'

Where on earth did he come up with a phrase like that? Nadine thought. Probably heard a teacher use it, and imagined it would go down well. She stared at him for a full twenty seconds.

His eyes were wide and frank as he said, 'I've posted the letter. It would be awfully rude to try to cancel an invitation.'

She tapped her finger on her desk. 'You are a very cheeky little blighter.'

She could see him wondering which way it was going to go.

'It's a good idea,' she said. 'But you should have asked.'

'You're not going to say no, are you?'

'Well,' she said. 'Are you planning to carry on being manipulative and presumptuous?'

'I wasn't!' he cried. 'I was being generous and welcoming!'

'To her, yes. But not otherwise. To me, you were – those other things.' She didn't want to say them again. They were such strong words.

'Well I didn't mean to be,' he said.

'If you'd been acting in good faith, you would have asked. There's no need to be manipulative in this family.'

He was a little crestfallen. She went up to him, and took his face in her hands, and raised it up. He was just her height – five foot six, and so skinny. Any minute now he would overtake her. Blue blue eyes – Julia's eyes, Peter's build. She had to support the strength in him that neither of his parents had been able to maintain. Heaven forbid that he will ever have to go through what they went through – heaven protect him, even under the best of circumstances, from his father's weaknesses and his mother's vanities.

'I'm going to think about it,' she said, 'and I'm going to talk to Riley about it, and to Peter – we can't just foist guests on them. And while I'm doing that you are going to draft a letter rescinding the invitation, in case it is needed.'

Lord! How tough I am being. Is it the right thing?

Yes. Though part of her wished she'd just said, 'Oh you monkey, of course she can come', and ruffled his white-blond hair.

'You wouldn't,' he said, aghast. 'You couldn't.'

'I'm going to take everything into consideration,' she said. She gave him a look as she left which she hoped conveyed to him the clear message that this is what he should have done in the first place.

Though actually, *what a good idea!* she was thinking. A wonderful let-out. And it might rather cheer Kitty up too.

Nadine was pregnant. She hadn't told anybody, not even Riley, not even Rose. It had come out of the blue, and she only just dared to believe it. She held it close.

~

Kitty's school was killing her, but nobody noticed. Within weeks of arrival all that she had valued in herself – her cheerfulness, her wit, her affection and intelligence – had been mocked and distorted by big girls with hockey skirts, lacquered hair and private languages. Very quickly it became apparent that in this world, where she was now to live, she was nothing. She accepted this judgement with a weak compliance which made her feel it was her own fault. On her way home each afternoon she bought apple pastries and ate them in the park, standing under wide-spreading plane trees, the sugar a comfort on her lips. She longed for the tender life she had had at her little prep school with only eight other girls in her class and dear Miss Jenkinson, whose favourite she was, a life of *Stories from Dickens* and museum visits and shared jokes, tea and cinnamon toast in the little sitting room, and everything happening at the pace they worked out between them, which was not very fast. School, now, was hard and quick, from the shiny floors to the talk to the expectations. Though plump, Kitty was bendy: she could do the splits and a back bend, but the gym teacher didn't notice. She had no puff. She once caught the ball during lacrosse, and was so delighted that she forgot to pass it. 'Cradle, girl, cradle!' yelled Miss Calthorpe, and Kitty wanted to die. Not for her the coloured canvas girdles of sporting success and social acceptance. Not for her the kudos granted to a slim waist and an easy manner. She was relegated to brainbox, in a world where that was an insult. She was short, and so was her neck. Sidney Carton, Jane Eyre and pastry were her friends. She no longer liked the outside world. The holidays were going to be a magnificent period of respite, and the news that Nenna was coming was a shaft of sun in a dark sky.

When they all went to meet her, Kitty said to her the sort of thing the girls at school said: 'You've arrived on the warmest day of the year, isn't that wonderful!' But she knew it was still wrong.

And anyway Nenna was wearing a jumper. 'My special jumper,' she said to Tom, rolling her eyes and shivering. '*Estate!* Your most hot day! *Dio mio . . .*'

Tom said, po-faced, 'Don't worry, I arranged with Pluvius the rain god to give you a truly English experience,' at which Nenna pulled the jumper's collar closed round her neck and made a face and said, 'Please bring me one big English umbrella for my formal attentions to Pluvio.'

Kitty looked on, and didn't know what they were talking about. And that was just the start of it.

It was Tom who took Nenna out and about. Kitty was too young. *They'll put it on my gravestone*, she thought, *even if I'm a hundred when I die I'll still be younger than Tom and I'll still be a girl.*

'Did you have fun today?' Nadine asked over supper at home, and Tom and Nenna would giggle – giggle!

'Today,' Nenna said, 'I have identified all of London landmarks with Roman landmarks: St Paul's is St Peter's. Trafalgar Square is Piazza Navona. Your Thames is my Tiber of course, but you have no island, it's sad. Marble Arch is the Arco di Tito, Buckingham Palace is the Vittoriano . . .'

'The Typewriter,' said Tom with a droll look, and Nenna gave him the look of the person who likes the naughtiness while pretending to disapprove.

'Tower of London is Castel Sant'Angelo, only the angel is flown away to Piccadilly Circus . . .'

Kitty was starting to hate them. It was a clever funny way to understand a new city. But she was sure they were having more fun than that. She hungered for what she thought they had.

And it was Tom who introduced Nenna to Riley. Kitty had thought that perhaps as that was something which didn't involve going out perhaps she might be allowed to – but no. She couldn't push herself forward for things. She knew the answer already – No, you're too young you're a girl you're too fat – so rather than risk hearing the words or seeing the look in anybody's eye she answered the questions for herself before even asking them, and made that process part of herself, and fell behind.

When the much-anticipated meeting finally happened, anyway, it was a let-down. Riley had been away for a few days, for work, and the timing was off: he came in tired, and Tom sort of pushed Nenna at him, and then suddenly it turned out to be rather formal. Riley said 'How do you do?' and Nenna couldn't remember what you were meant to say to that – only that you shouldn't say, 'I am well, thank you.' She seemed shy of him, and startled by his face, even though she had been forewarned. Kitty, observing from a distance, was surprised. She had begun to think of Nenna as super-capable.

And then there was an embarrassment as Riley, though courteous and attentive for a moment, needed to get by with his bag, and Nenna was in the wrong place. As Riley went upstairs Tom was already saying to Nenna, 'What do you think of him? What do you think of him?' but of course Nenna could have no answer.

'I don't know,' she said. 'I hardly met him.'

Kitty could see Tom was frustrated, that he needed them to love each other. Or admire each other. Or admire him, for being favoured by the other. Kitty wanted it too, in so far as she could admit to wanting anything. Why could it not be immediate, like electricity? Turn it on and up it lights? She wanted Tom to have what he wanted.

Tom took Nenna to meet Rose, and she thought it strange and frightening that a woman could be a doctor, but somehow marvellous as well. She came away quiet from that encounter, very thoughtful. It was Tom who took her to the park, showed her the statue of Peter Pan ('He doesn't talk') and the ducks on the Round Pond, which were more various and smart than the farmyard ducks at the lake. And *he* showed her the Italian paintings in the National Gallery, reporting back that she had said, 'Well, we conquered you, so perhaps is fair.'

Kitty, while all these outings were going on, was doing extra French and maths, to make sure she didn't have to stay down a year.

Nadine went to Soho for special Italian food that Nenna would like. In the evenings they sat together. Kitty watched them, and thought: *Nenna looks like Nadine.* She studied them: Nadine was more slender and pointy, Nenna stronger-looking and fairer. But their wide cheekbones matched, and the yellow-brown of their eyes, and their sallow skin. She realised with a little jolt that their eyebrows were the same. A few days later, in the park, a woman – a friend or something – spoke to Nadine, and she said, 'Oh is this your daughter?' Kitty looked up, happy, because that was her favourite thing – but the woman was looking at Nenna, and they were all smiling and laughing. Kitty looked again at Nenna and Nadine together, and a thin film of ice moved across her heart. *I do not look like them. I have stupid pink cheeks. I look like a stupid bowl of milk with red bits. I look like a cream bun. They look like cypress trees and olives and skinny cats.*

When they went down to Locke Hill, it was easier for Kitty to hang around with them, and she couldn't bring herself not to, although her position was humiliating. Even so, it was Tom who introduced Nenna to Daddy, *even though he doesn't even like Daddy!* Peter was charming to Nenna, and Kitty could see from Nenna's surprised little glance to Tom that they had talked about Peter before, and Tom had complained about him, and Nenna was going to say to Tom now, 'but he's charming, your Peter', and then the two of them would talk quietly and confidentially about her father, and she would be told to go away.

And then Tom showed Nenna his aeroplane, the German ghost from the War, whose metal bones still lay there silently falling apart in the woods. They clambered into the rusting holes, and he said Nenna made a most satisfactory rear gunner, and he let her sit in the pilot's seat. At that, Kitty went running back through the woods, her humiliation compounded by the understanding that running away through the woods was a stupid immature reaction.

Later that afternoon Nenna, being kind, took Kitty into conversation, drew her to the sofa, and asked about school, and friends. She said many sweet things, but she also said, 'Being fat makes you go about less, I think, also maybe in your head.' Kitty knew that she didn't mean it to sound harsh. She knew Nenna would not say something so unkind on purpose; that it was a trick of the language, a misjudged translation. But – who would pay attention to a girl who reads all the time, and runs off like a baby, and is dull? *But even if I was amusing nobody would notice* . . . And when nobody is interested in a girl what can she do except read? What Nenna said felt true, and that was the harshest thing.

Nenna was not fat. She went about, in her body and in her mind. She beat Tom at tennis and ran faster than him. She was quite Amazonian, with her strong hair and long legs in shorts. She looked like those flat female figures Nadine liked, sculpted by Eric Gill. Heroic and maidenly, on equal terms in the world. They swam in the river and Nenna's hair was like weed underwater. She and Riley got over their first hiccup, and she made him laugh. She was beautiful and clever and in every way preferable to Kitty. Of course they would rather have her as a daughter, a sister.

~

Kitty was in her den under the piano at Locke Hill, with an Agatha Christie and a pocketful of nuts and raisins stolen from the kitchen cupboard, though probably Mrs Joyce would have given them to her if she'd asked. She didn't want to ask.

Nadine had not got out of bed that day. Not like her, Kitty thought. She could hear Riley striding about; he came in to the drawing room every now and again to say something to Peter. Apparently the doctor was coming. She glanced up from her hidey-hole: his expression was tight and unfamiliar. She slowed her breathing. She didn't mean to be sneaky.

'Do you still think about her?' Riley said, suddenly, in the swing of a turn round the room. The French windows were open onto the mild morning, but he did not seem to want to leave the house, or even to step over the threshold into the garden.

Peter, from the sofa, was staring at the corner where the walls met the ceiling.

'Julia?' he said, and Kitty froze. She had never to her knowledge heard her mother's name on her father's lips.

'Yes,' said Riley.

'No,' Peter said, after a pause. 'Or – very seldom. It's all gone to sleep. They're all dead, that's all there is. They are in another land, and I must leave them be.'

'Good,' said Riley. 'And this doesn't—' He sort of waved his hand, as if hoping it would express something.

'No,' said Peter mildly. 'It turns out that it doesn't.'

Kitty closed her eyes tight. She didn't know what they were talking about. Julia, in her father's voice.

'And – how's Mabel?'

'She's well,' said Peter, but Kitty wasn't listening. *It's all gone to sleep. They're all dead, and that's all there is.* She repeated the words, to remember them. *They're all dead, and that's all there is. Julia. Very seldom.*

I'm not dead, she thought.

She peeked up, and saw Riley clasp Peter by the hand. Two daddies. Two daddies. She had never really minded before. It was just normal. It was what she had. She wondered for a moment what Vera and Jennifer at school would have to say about two daddies – then blocked the thought. She had agreed with herself not to think about school during the holidays. *But you sort of don't have any daddy, if you have two daddies . . . And you can't block all your thoughts. And whichever way you look at it it's not much good, is it? Two daddies that don't add up to a proper one, a dead mother and another who'd rather have Nenna than me . . .*

Kitty took an almond from her pocket and nibbled it, pointed end first, to and fro, tiny little squirrel movements with her clean little teeth. *Perhaps Peter will want me more. Perhaps he might notice that I need somebody.* It didn't sound very likely.

Riley had gone out into the garden. Leaning forward, she saw him through the window, falling to his knees on the lawn, as if in fear, or prayer. *But he doesn't believe in God*, she thought. *He doesn't go to church.* Even as she thought it, he laughed suddenly, as if at himself. *Suddenly you want God's help*, Kitty thought. She wondered if God would help her. She didn't think so. God wasn't really her father either.

She crawled out from under the piano, and stood by the window, looking out at Riley. Glancing up, he saw her, and waved distractedly. She waved back, a little movement, and withdrew behind the curtain. *They don't notice me at all. And it's hardly going to improve, is it?*

But then that was what parents did, after all. One way or another, sooner or later, they lost interest and went away.

Nadine was in bed for several days, and they were not to visit her, because she was tired. This terrified Kitty. Was Nadine going to die? Would anybody even tell her? And because she was scared she became angry. When Nadine did emerge she was very pale and everybody fussed over her, but Kitty was still angry with her. Let Nenna be nice to her, she thought – and Nenna was nice to her. When Riley had to go back to work, Nadine and Nenna sat together on the chintz sofa reading, with their matching cheekbones and their womanliness, and so Kitty went back under the piano, and felt unloved.

~

At supper on one of those slightly awkward evenings when Nadine was upstairs, and Riley and Peter were doing their best, Kitty jumped up from the table, declaring that she could see a firefly outside the window. Before anyone could say anything she rushed out of the room and out through the French windows in the sitting room, back round, searching, and losing it as it flashed and disappeared.

The night was warm and not very dark; the sky a rich blue and a small moon riding high. She scanned the garden – had she imagined it?

The others were behind her – Tom and Nenna together, and behind them the men, moving more slowly, indulgently. 'We had fireflies here when I was a boy,' Peter was saying.

'I haven't seen any for years.' Kitty could smell his cigarette smoke.

'Look!' called Nenna. Kitty saw the dark form of her arm rising to point down towards the river – and yes, there it was – in fact more than one—

She raced down there. *They're my fireflies*, she thought. *Nenna has her own fireflies in Italy. I found these they're mine.* She wanted to get there first.

They were enchanting. So hard to track! They glowed in one place, then in another – you couldn't really see how many there were. Ten? Twenty? They were moving about in the darkness, a magical sight. *Fairies*, she thought. *Tiny spaceships.* She imagined that they let out a low hum, that they were swimming like fish in the air. She didn't know what they really looked like, and wondered.

'Do you remember the song?' Nenna called. '*Lucciola lucciola vien da me, io to daro il pan del re—*'

'*Pan del re e della regina, lucciola lucciola vien vicina . . .*' Kitty murmured it, remembering.

'This one's not moving!' Nenna cried. 'Let's look—' It was in a bush, in shadow, flashing. While Tom ran back to the house for his torch they peered at the little light: on, off. On, off. Kitty could feel everyone smiling, and snuggled in between Riley and Peter as they bent over to see. Then Tom was back, out of breath, triumphant, and the torch beam shone down. The light of the firefly was drowned in it, faded in the greater light, but still flickering, on, off, on, off. But that was not what caught the eye. What caught the eye was a spider, busy with captor's web and mandibles, carefully eating the firefly.

'Oh Christ,' Peter said, and Kitty couldn't really make it out, and for a short, long, timeless moment they stared, before Tom flicked the torchlight away.

'What!' Kitty cried. 'What's it doing?'

'Nothing,' said Nenna. 'Nothing' – but the word came out stiff with disgust and the edge of tears, and the sweetness of the search and the magic had dissolved.

'Look, there's some more!' said Riley, pointing back down towards the riverbank. 'Shall we look?' But nobody was falling for that.

'Come on Kitty,' Nenna said, and took her hand. 'Come on' – and that warm kindness took Kitty back to the house and away from the confusion, and there was still pudding to be had, Summer Pudding full of currants and raspberries, everyone's favourite, which Nenna had never had before.

It wasn't until much, much later that Kitty realised what she had seen, and even then she got it wrong. After she found out about sex, she decided the creatures had been mating, and everybody had just been terribly embarrassed.

The day Nenna left, Tom was already asking for reassurances about going to Italy the following summer. Riley snapped at him. 'Nadine has been very ill, and this is not the time to bother her with plans for your social life in a year's time,' he said. Kitty listened, and heard this: Nadine is going to die. She took to turning down Nadine's bed at night, putting her slippers out to warm, and going downstairs to ask Mrs Joyce to make Nadine's preferred cake, the one with boiled oranges and ground almonds.

~

'Well, I don't think we can go this year, Tom,' Nadine said, when Easter came.

'Riley says we can go,' said Tom heartlessly. 'He says we can afford it. He says that amazingly enough the company is doing all right. He said so.'

Nadine smiled, and said, 'No.'

~

After Easter, Tom said: 'Well, as you've clearly given up on going again, I'll arrange to go on my own. If I'm to do modern languages, I might as well do a course in Rome or Florence or somewhere.'

Nadine said, 'Well, you must talk to your father about that—' and even as Tom was saying 'Which one? Riley or Peter?' Kitty said, suddenly, and loudly, 'And so will I.'

'No, Kitty,' said Nadine. 'You can't go alone. Or with Tom.'

'Why?' said Kitty. 'Because he's a boy, I suppose.'

'Because he is older,' said Nadine.

'He's always older,' she said. 'It's because he's a boy, isn't it?' her mouth running away with her now. 'He can do what he wants because he's a boy. Miss McDonald says women's lives were transformed by the war and there's no reason a girl shouldn't do anything a boy can, now.'

She knew Nadine was in favour of Miss McDonald, who wore green tweed suits and scarlet lipstick, and had sleek black hair and a Boston accent.

'It's because Tom is nearly sixteen,' Nadine said, 'and you are twelve. It's because he wants to study Italian some more before university. It's not because he's a boy.'

Kitty set her mouth firm. 'He's fifteen and I'm nearly

thirteen,' she said. 'It's because you love him more than me.'

This made Nadine cry. Kitty felt a pig. But she had nobody. If she wasn't allowed to go to Italy, her nobodiness was compounded.

Chapter Eight

London, 1932–3

Mabel sometimes looked up from what she was doing – writing a song, wiping a table – and felt side-swiped by a mad wave. Her arrangements had been imperfect but under control. Now she was all at sea.

Why?

Peter.

Why Peter? She asked herself that too, and answered it. Because he was so damned kind. He was honourable. He was faithful. He was everything the dashing heroes in novels weren't – those who in real life any sane woman should rush from. The kind of heroes beloved of young women who haven't yet learned that life will throw them enough pain and danger without them having to look for it in a man.

Every time Peter did something kind or honourable, her heart lit up slightly, and slightly more, and slightly more, and its burdens, bit by bit, slipped away. And why did this leave her all at sea? Because she had for years been in charge of her own safety, and letting somebody else contribute to it threatened it. Ironic, she knew that. And she knew she was right. Her answer was to go very very slowly.

They only wanted to be alone. They spent their hours together in peace, laughter and love-making, and left each other's lives alone. There was an electric loveliness for them, lying in twisted sheets in the beautiful flat, talking of nothing in particular. Their conversation was abstract; their shared quotidian life made up of: 'What shall we eat?' 'What shall we listen to?' 'How was your day?' 'Come here.' The restfulness! They slept well in each other's company, which neither of them did alone. And they both knew, though they chose not to touch on it, that the rest of the world might prove to be, or to have, a problem with them as a couple. They managed to keep that up for more than a year before the little fishes of outside attention gathered to nibble at them.

~

They touched once or twice on his sobriety. She wondered how it had come about, after the last time she'd seen him in 1919.

'Do you remember what I said to you?' she asked.

'You paraphrased Homer,' he said. 'You said I needed to eat a little more and take a little less wine. And that I should change myself, not the company I was keeping.'

'And you said you weren't fit for company.'

'I wasn't,' he said, and a little shiver went over him, because he remembered all too well.

'So what happened?' she asked.

'I – after a while – some years – I started to feel that I didn't deserve to be drunk. Not that I deserved better. That

I didn't deserve the relief it brought me. Drink was a prize or a solace for good men who had suffered. I felt I didn't deserve the solace of it. So I banned myself from it. I know not everybody can do that. But it worked for me. I talked to myself as if I were someone else. Looked at myself from outside, and – I suppose – once I wasn't drunk all the time I realised I wasn't such a dreadful character. I had to acknowledge, I suppose, that I had done my best, and that thinking everything was my fault was another kind of vanity, of self-obsession. Claiming all the power, as it were. As if I could have had the power to stop history!'

'Oh!' she said. 'And?'

'Best thing I ever did. The biggest prize. In the long run. I see chaps now . . .'

'Mmm,' she said, for she too had seen chaps.

'But you are a good man,' she said.

'Hmm,' he said.

'You are,' she said. Then, 'We most of us live in the fear of the fact of ourselves.'

'What do you mean?'

'I'm not sure. I read it in a novel called *Home to Harlem*. It was about being negro—'

She stopped, and he looked at her.

'But I was thinking, whatever we are, people expect us to be what they think that thing is . . .'

He smiled a little. 'As in, a drunk is a drunk and a failure; an English gentleman is an English gentleman, a negro is a negro . . .'

'Whereas a gentleman can be a drunk.'

'And a negro can be a gentleman,' he said.

She kind of smiled, and looked away from him, and said perhaps it was time they got up.

'No,' he said, and drew her back into his arms with a gaze, and they each thought, in their own way, how extraordinary this is, better not look at it too closely, this blessing we have tumbled into . . .

~

Iris Zachary, twelve and clever and skinny, her hair in plaits and her eyes an unexpected blue, grew impatient. Why did Mumma stay out all night twice a week?

Mabel said, 'Work goes on too late for me to get home, so I stay with a friend.'

Iris said, 'Which friend?' Her mother's friends were funny and interesting, with chocolate and saxophones and stories.

Mabel said, 'You're all right here with Grandma, aintcha honey?'

Iris shrugged. She liked her Grandma. Who wouldn't? But she still didn't look very happy about it, so Mabel said, 'Sweetpea, I'm sorry, it won't go on forever.'

And that was all very well, but when Mabel said it, she sensed that Iris sensed that something was not all right: a little whiff of sorrow passing over. Iris put her head to one side. And Mabel thought, *Well, yes, in a way I do want it to go on forever. Because change is dangerous. Is Iris sensing that?*

Lord, of course not. You're thinking too much, baby.

Mabel had decided, about the situation. Peter would be her secret pleasure, her private life, and private. Not just for the obvious reason, but for personal ones too. It was not that she did not trust him. She did, for herself. But for Iris? No.

A man can love a woman, that she knew, but a man loving a child is a different thing. She knew that Peter had children, and she knew that they didn't live with him. He hadn't invited her into his past life, his family life, but he had been open in all kinds of ways about it, trying to get her to be open too. She knew he lived in a place in the country out by Sidcup, and had a mother in Scotland. He had told her, cautiously, about his wife Julia: her leaving, her returning, her death. With a little thought Mabel could see where her own past encounters with Peter fitted into the interstices of that story, and felt, for a moment, so second-best she wanted to scream. Why the outsider? Why, even here, with a man who loves her, Iris's father, why even now the outsider, the Johnny-come-lately – *why must whatever joy I'm allowed have to be secret and at the expense of the real wife's life?* She bowed her head under the weight of her anger, and waited for it to pass. It passes, it always passes, it has to pass. It passed.

He had told her how useless he had been, after the war, how he had thought he would never get himself back. He had told how much Riley had helped him, and how he never wanted to be useless again. He had told her that he had not been a good father, and that as a result his children weren't very interested in him, though perhaps things were getting better. He had told her they lived with Riley and Nadine, and her fury roared back on a sudden hideous wave of injustice: *another woman is bringing up Peter's motherless children, when I am the one who loves him, who has his child—*

149

What, you want to bring up his other children? When you won't even tell him you have his child too?

Yes I do. I do—

She stopped it. That kind of fury did not keep a life together, didn't keep a child fed and an old woman warm. She used to indulge her furies when she was younger, and her mother had been looking after her – but no grown woman with responsibilities can afford a temper like that. *Bite the bullet, darling. This all proves the same point. That is his life, and Iris is mine. Iris is not for risking. Better to have no daddy than a late-coming unknown-quantity of a daddy . . .*

So, she didn't tell him anything. Not about Iris, about Betty, about Pixy, about Thornton . . .

Why not?

Fear.

If I tell him about Iris he might leave me. If I tell him my stories he'll become part of them and part of me and I'll never be able to extricate myself, and when he leaves me I'll be left gutted and gaping, pulled to shreds by the ties that bind—

≈

Mabel didn't know who half the fathers in her family were. She didn't know who Betty's father was. She didn't know when, where or how often the white blood that gave her her fair complexion or the Chinese blood that gave her her high cheekbones had come into the family. She knew about her Grandma Pixy, and she knew that her father was called George, back in Georgia. George from Georgia. She knew she had older brothers, in Chicago, San Francisco and

Montgomery, Alabama. The name Zachary was Betty's through Pixy – so, through Pixy's owners.

This is what Pixy did; the story that Pixy told Betty and Betty told Mabel. Pixy cosied up to her owner Mr Zachary. (Mabel was not certain what exactly that meant.) She cosied up to him and she played him. (Does that mean she let him sleep with her and then blackmailed him? Mabel didn't know.) She talked him into giving her time off each week. (*How?* Mabel wondered. Perhaps she told him she had to go to church to pray for her soul and his after the wicked adultery they had performed. Perhaps she told him he would go to hell and she wanted to save him.) She used that time to work – *What work? It had to be secret, or he'd have known she wasn't in church* – and worked so hard, and saved every cent – *but how much could she have made, a black girl, there, at that time, with those limited hours?* – and using that money – *How long must it have taken her!* – and arguments from the Bible, she bought herself from Mr Zachary. Yes she did, she bought herself back. *Stop a minute to think about that.*

He was glad to see the back of her in the end because she talked so much and was so pretty. And then she went north, taking that long and difficult road, alone, where she started out again, working so hard, again, and saving every cent, again, and she went back down there and she bought her own father from Mr Zachary. She was fifty years old by then and her father seventy. And she would have done it again, and bought her mother, if her mother hadn't been dead.

Pixy had Navajo blood, and was small and tough, and her hair was long. In her free life, she earnt a living playing violin day and night in a bawdy house in Chicago: any time a man made a go for her thinking she was on the menu she'd whip him across the face with the bow. She was famous for it. Some men came specially to be whipped across the face by Pixy. The proprietor was half in love with her and she made him pay for a new bow each time it got broke: this was to guarantee her some protection from the lowlifes. A fiddle bow gives a good slap around the face and leaves a welt sometimes. She was popular. The way she sang and played, all the white men came down, and the whores were busy all night. This was the story. Mabel wondered if maybe Pixy was really a whore, and then she felt ashamed even for thinking it. But if she didn't think it, she felt she was being naive. Anyway, by now, what did it matter? *Pixy did what she had to do. She turned our family around. Pixy set us free and lifted our curse and sent her daughter into the world with a way of living that was neither whorehouse nor plantation. Pixy blessed us and freed us with the sweat of her body and the quickness of her brain and the fullness of her heart. By her pride.*

I provide for Iris. I'll give her no false dreams. We just live, little human creatures on the surface of the planet. We own ourselves, and that's all. And it's a mighty blessing. Even though it shouldn't be.

$\approx$

Mabel knew Betty's thoughts on taking up with white men. 'Mabel, don't go giving yourself to one of them for free.'

$\approx$

Iris was not a girl to show her cards. She had always known when to keep quiet and when to speak out, how to be loyal by being sneaky. You learned that kind of thing pretty quickly in the alleyways where she played, or when she was out with Mumma and trying not to be sent home. It's not that people are mean, but when there's not always enough to go around you learn to be protective. If Mumma was unhappy, Iris would find out why.

~

Grandma couldn't keep her in and didn't try to. Iris did her schoolwork and had nice manners. The vicar even trusted her with the key to the church room when she went to practise the piano. She could get away with things. She had a habit of picking her mother up from the shop at 5.30, and walking home with her, picking stuff up from the market on Brewer Street as it closed up, having tea with Grandma when they got in. Mumma would sing snatches of new songs, ones she was writing or ones she was performing or ones she'd heard. She'd warm up for her evening show, and Iris would do the exercises along with her, and Grandma would make comments. These were their habits, calm and nice. Then Iris would get ready for bed as Mumma got dressed to go out to whichever club it was. Iris did not like it that on Tuesdays and Wednesdays Mumma didn't come home.

So one sunny afternoon she followed her. She stood on the corner of Great Marlborough Street across from the shop, hiding behind a lamp post and a man with a big dog. She saw her mother come out, and head off towards Regent

Street instead of south down Poland Street towards home. Across into Mayfair – Mayfair! – and further west, the heels of her little shoes clickclicking, skirting the park at Hyde Park Corner, moving on into the fairyland beyond, where buildings as clean and white as wedding cakes rose around green lush squares, and kids like Iris did not go.

Iris went, stomping and determined.

Her mother stopped outside one of the buildings, and was looking in her purse as if for a key, and as she did so a tall white man came up, and with a quick glance around – which did not catch Iris, standing against iron railings in the fall of a rich-blossomed lilac – slipped his arm around her waist, and kissed her hair.

Iris raised her chin. She thought he was – *what? What is he doing?*

They went in together.

Iris sat on the kerb and stared up at the building, the tall white columns holding up its porch, the smooth broad steps, the black and white tiles, the rising layers of large clean windows and fancy plasterwork, up and up to a bluer sky than the sky she saw between Soho's huddled buildings. She didn't actually know the way home from here. This, she supposed, would be where Mumma stayed. She stared at it with hatred.

After a while, the white man came out again, alone. She stood up to stare at him – and he looked round at her. He gave her, suddenly, a most radiant smile. 'Good afternoon,' he said, and his voice was gentle.

'Good afternoon,' she said.

He nodded and moved on.

Mabel came down soon after. She crossed the road straight to Iris, and said: 'What did he say to you?'

'He said "Good Afternoon", Iris said. 'Am I in trouble?'

'Uh uh,' said Mabel. She put her arm round Iris's shoulder. 'Come on, let's go home.'

''Cos you're in trouble,' Iris said.

'Not for you to tell me I'm in trouble,' Mabel said. 'I'm the mother here.'

'I want to go in there,' Iris said.

'No, honey.'

'Why not?'

'Later, sweetheart.'

'Who is he?' Iris asked.

'Later,' Mabel said, speeding up, blinking.

Back in Lexington Street, Iris said coldly, over tea: 'Is it later yet?'

Looking across at her, Mabel saw a firmness in her daughter's eyes. Glancing across to her mother, drinking her tea in her chair, wearing her pink satin gown and a cap, because she had not actually got up today, Mabel saw a questioning, and shift of position – tiny – suggesting: what's this?

'You promised her something for later, child?' Betty said, the smile spreading across her glossy cheeks.

They were like pincers, the pair of them, coming at her from each side. Very gentle loving pincers.

'Something you goin' tell her, maybe?'

'No,' she said. *If I tell them it will all go wrong. Things will change – heaven forfend things should change! When things change they change for the worse.*

'She went into a big white house miles away,' said Iris.

155

'With a white man. And he came out and he said "Good Afternoon" to me.'

Betty turned her face slowly round to Mabel.

'He's her boyfriend,' said Iris. 'He looks like Leslie Howard. The one Marion Davies should've married in *Five and Ten*.'

'Go to bed, Iris,' said Betty.

'It's not even—' said Iris, but she went, mouth tight, giving Mabel a look – support? apology? rebellion? – as she went.

'Close the door after ya,' called Betty.

Iris closed it.

Betty hadn't stirred: she just sat in her chair, and looked. She took a cigarette, examined it, tapped it on the side table, lit it, took a small, delicate puff. Looked up.

'It's her father,' Mabel said.

Betty blinked, and looked at the back of her hand, and took another puff.

'What are you hopin' for, my child?' she said.

'For nothing to be ruined.'

'Does he know about her?'

Mabel was silent.

'You still ain't told him. You're hangin' by a string, honey,' Betty said. 'You're gonna fall. You know that.'

'Not yet,' Mabel replied, with a tiny smile.

'Hangin' by a string,' her mother said again. 'How long's it been?'

'Bit over a year,' she said.

'Tellin' lies . . .'

'Keepin' privacy,' Mabel retorted.

'Tellin' lies,' her mother snapped back. 'To him, to me and to Iris.'

156

That, Mabel thought, *is not the problem. The problem is that I want to keep them both – such a demand! to have your man and your child! – and if I reveal each to the other, either of them – or Lord help me both – might . . . they might . . .*

'I'm not bothered by the lies so much, Mama, forgive me, but by the potential for loss. I love the man.'

Betty gazed. 'Love!' she said, and she hauled herself up a little in her seat. 'I think it's time for you to lighten up a little, Mabel. Get yourself a new man. Reginald likes ya. You're young enough, they all still like ya. Get one with a steady job. One you don't care about.'

'Mama,' she said.

'Have another baby, if that'll cleave you to him. But this white father – no.'

'Things have changed, Mama,' she said.

'No they ain't. He won't want a negro child. Leave her be. A negro child. Don't go making her think she can be white. Don't cast that unhappiness on her.'

'Things have changed, Mama,' Mabel said again, though the repetition sounded empty.

'So why you lyin'?'

Mama, you hit the button.

I want everything, Mabel thought. *I don't believe it's wrong to want everything. But nor do I believe it's possible to have everything. But I want everything.*

Her mother was looking at her. 'Mabel,' she said softly. 'You don't have to do everything yourself.'

'I do!' she cried.

'Why?'

157

'Because you did. You and Pixy both.'

'Didn't you just say times have changed?'

He has this kindness, Mabel thought. *Don't cut me in half – he's the one I want. The only one.*

~

She wondered if she would ever tell Peter about her family. Could he possibly understand what she came from? Well of course not. She couldn't even understand. She knew, yes, and it was part of her, blood and bone – but understand? No. Here she was, sixty-five years after emancipation in America, living in England, with her English-born, English-fathered child, yet what had been abolished thirty years before her own birth was still ruling how she could lead her life. Only thirty years before. And then after that it was just her and Betty, moving, moving, moving, carrying no family, the brothers wherever they might be, Lord only knows, their blood lost – nothing of Pixy but the memory, for she was dead by then, wore out, Betty said, by all that working and saving, and thus she was reduced to the handful of tales and a look in Mama's eye.

Mabel just wanted her own life. *To own my life . . .* To write her songs, be a good mother, be a good daughter, make a bit of money, not have to think about . . . everything that had happened to her forebears, and was happening still.

It's not that I don't want to be coloured. Being coloured never proved so difficult for me. But I ain't everybody. And whatever I want for myself, I am attached to everybody. A great river of blood flows through all of us, bearing the sufferings. White people don't have that to fret them. Except maybe Jewish people. Irish people maybe. Foreigners in new terrains. But we are so damn visible! A Jewish man can cut his hair and lose the cap. An Irish man can learn to talk different. But being coloured ain't just unchangeable, it's so damned significant.

She wondered: *in Africa, in the countries where everybody is coloured, do they think of themselves as coloured? Do they even have to think about it at all, until some white person walks in and tells them they're coloured?*

From time to time when she was younger she used to go along to meetings and social occasions beyond Church and Jazz. There was a bunch of folks known as the Coterie of Friends, which was black people from all over getting together to share what they learned and earned. Africans, West Indians, students and academics, musicians, all types. There was one medical student from St Mary's Hospital in Paddington, Harry Leekham – she'd liked him. Not just the Trini accent – he was a good man. And of course Thornton . . . The Coterie of Friends had been, to be honest, a Coterie of Men Friends, men who had time to talk about improvements and rights and responsibilities and law and opportunities and the advancement of coloured people. She admired all of that, she truly did, and dear Lord if she had only had the time . . . But she didn't have the time. And after Thornton died it wasn't the same.

Thornton had told her a great joke though:

'What do you want to be when you grow up, son?'

'A musician!'

'Well make your mind up, you can't do both.'

159

Ah, Lord, it's all just adjectives. A female, musical, coloured person.

~

Peter decided, on that beautiful evening, to walk to the station for his train to Sidcup. It had been a beautiful unexpected treat to have that hour with Mabel, outside their usual timetable.

Timetable! They were getting very set in their ways. He'd said to Riley that it was as if they were married, two days a week. Now, he was thinking about home, about Locke Hill, and this woman.

If my mother hadn't sold Chester Square, he thought, *I would have invited Mabel to live there.*

He was trying the thought on for size, really. *Would I have?* he thought. *Would I really?*

Steps along the pavement, blossom hanging in the trees above. For a moment he was reminded of Riley and Nadine's wedding.

I hope I would have. I have after all got her this flat – which is empty half the time. Like me. He barked with laughter at that image. *But it's true. It's all very well, this. It's marvellous – but it's partial.*

Could he take her to Locke Hill?

For goodness sake, old chap, you're an English gentleman, you of all people can do exactly what you like. I could take her to Locke Hill, as my girlfriend, my mistress or my wife, I could épater les bourgeois like Baudelaire or Oscar Wilde . . . not that it would be very nice for her – would it? To be a full-time outrager of the bourgeois? No. And anyway she needs to sing . . . She needs London – she doesn't need to work at Moores' though – she needs to be looked after . . .

He wanted to look after her.

He didn't know what she wanted. He still didn't even know where she lived. It had been revealed that she lived with her mother, and thought he wouldn't like her mother, or accept her – or *vice versa! Perhaps she thinks her mother won't like me! Or perhaps she lives in a place which is completely negro, and I wouldn't fit in . . . perhaps I'm an embarrassment.*

But we're not children. It's not 1830.

He wanted to be with her. To wake with her and go to sleep with her, put his head on her shoulder or hers on his, find her arm round his waist, or his arm round hers, slip his cold feet under her legs in bed, every night, not just two in seven. That was it. That was all. His body wanted her, his mind wanted her, his heart wanted her.

That Scottish woman had married the Sultan of Johore, after all. And another Scotswoman had married a Pathan prince and was living on the north-west frontier. Which might be easier than for a London negro woman to live outside Sidcup . . . She was writing a book about it: *My Khyber Marriage.*

For goodness sake, Peter, have you less courage than a Scotswoman?

Again he found he was laughing at himself.

Laughing!

He bought his ticket, found his train, and settled in. His delivery of books from the London Library should have arrived. He had work to catch up on.

The clubs where she sang were full of mixed couples. *Not married couples though.*

Paris? In Paris you see mixed couples.

He thought about that. But he was not at all comfortable thinking about it. He didn't see why it needed thinking about – he resented it.

Would people really make a fuss, if he just drew her in?

~

He had talked to Riley about it. Riley had been sanguine. 'Some people,' he said, 'will be quietly polite and deeply shocked, and will never get over it, out of embarrassment. Some will be prurient and over-interested. The ones who matter will be happy for you.'

The more real problems people have to deal with, Peter thought, *the less likely they are to provoke a problem out of something which really isn't a problem.*

'But yes, some people will be unpleasant about it,' Riley said. 'You may face cruelty, or scorn.'

'What the staff at hotels say,' Peter said, 'is "No you can't have a room – it's not us, of course – but we host so many Americans, and we must respect their wishes and expectations . . ." So you get that, plus the unspoken assumption that she's some kind of prostitute—'

'Whereas she is a perfectly respectable mistress . . .' Riley said, and Peter snapped: 'Riley, I'm in love with her. She's the one.'

Riley was sorry.

'Hinchcliffe,' he said, 'reads all the scandal mags. They

162

are agog about Nancy Cunard, apparently. An heiress, and a publisher. Do you know who she is?'

Peter did know.

'She keeps getting into fights in nightclubs over her negro boyfriend, Hinchcliffe tells me. Doing it to annoy her mother, while living, apparently, on her mother's money. Of course it's different, and who knows, and I'm sorry even to mention it.'

'Yes, it's perfectly likely to be unfair,' Peter said. 'But it's not necessarily different. Aren't most things about money and sex and love, and trying to defend people? What do any of us know about the secrets of Nancy Cunard's soul?'

'Yes, it's gossip,' Riley agreed.

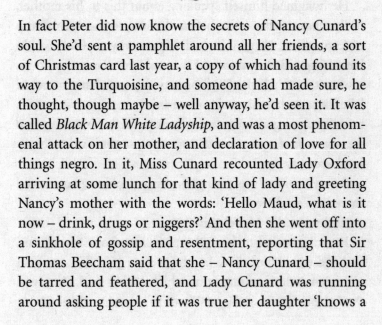

In fact Peter did now know the secrets of Nancy Cunard's soul. She'd sent a pamphlet around all her friends, a sort of Christmas card last year, a copy of which had found its way to the Turquoisine, and someone had made sure, he thought, though maybe – well anyway, he'd seen it. It was called *Black Man White Ladyship*, and was a most phenomenal attack on her mother, and declaration of love for all things negro. In it, Miss Cunard recounted Lady Oxford arriving at some lunch for that kind of lady and greeting Nancy's mother with the words: 'Hello Maud, what is it now – drink, drugs or niggers?' And then she went off into a sinkhole of gossip and resentment, reporting that Sir Thomas Beecham said that she – Nancy Cunard – should be tarred and feathered, and Lady Cunard was running around asking people if it was true her daughter 'knows a negro' . . . And the second half was an account of the history of the negroes of Africa. *Well written*, Peter thought, *and strong stuff*. And an account of a legal case going on in America, the Scottsboro case, where nine young black men had been sentenced to death, a great injustice. And thirty negroes lynched in the first six months of 1931. *Lynched! Repellent.* There'd been a leaflet for contributing to the cause. Peter had sent five pounds.

And what people think is unthinkable, is that a white person and a negro might be lovers. I don't think it's unthinkable. It's just people being who they are, with who they want to be with. I think it is good. I think . . .

It was all so distasteful. And why did it have to have anything to do with him and Mabel?

He imagined himself speaking about this to his mother, to the chaps at the office before the war, to the Archbishop of Canterbury. He genuinely didn't see why anybody would have any good reason to find it a problem. Slavery was over, it wasn't as if half the US economy depended any more on labelling a certain kind of human as inhuman. Was it embarrassment and guilt? *We treated you so badly for so long that we cannot find a way now to stop being so utterly, immorally unpleasant to you?*

Surely, if there was no reason for a problem, how could there be a problem?

And what did Mabel think?

Peter had tried to keep the pamphlet from Mabel, and had succeeded, but there had been a very similar article in *Crisis*, an American magazine which Mabel read. Peter was then the embarrassed one. He didn't want to think about them in those terms. He didn't want to think that other people might think about them in those terms. *If even I, an English gentleman, am getting annoyed at being thought of in particular terms, how does it feel for her? For negro people in general? It must be absolutely horrid; insult to injury, on top of all the practicalities like not getting a room, or a job. Anywhere you go, people don't think, oh there's Mabel or there's Henry, they think there's a negro. Even if you're Paul Robeson. Except presumably in their own world . . .*

She has another world, he thought, *which is not mine. What do I think about that?*

Though what I think about it is not, probably, the point.

Partly to put Riley at ease about all this, and because Riley was the only person who knew and Peter needed him strong by his side, Peter invited him along to hear Mabel sing. Riley did not want to come. Clubs, going out – no. It was all an oppression to him. He didn't like the noise, the being looked at, the having to decide how to conceal himself, the being spoken to and not being able to speak back easily, the not being understood, the staying up late, the having to drink more than you wanted to in order to make it all bearable.

But he went, because it was Peter, and it was important. Peter arranged for them a small table, at the back, sheltered; he pre-ordered the wine, he sat between Riley and the crowds. It was crowded. Smoky, clattery, laughter and scent, chiffon and cocktails. It was like another world to Riley. He smiled quietly, sat himself down, took out his brass straw, and twirled it. It stopped him smoking too much. Smoking was making him cough, and coughing was difficult.

Mabel came out on stage in a gold dress, dripping with sequins and glass beads, fringed with bugling. Her hair was slicked back and gleaming, her smile wide and red. She waved to them across the room: fluttering fingers with scarlet long nails. She cracked a few jokes, sang a few funny numbers, and then said, 'Droppin' a gear now, boys and girls. This one is for a friend o' mine out the back there, don't look at him now, he's shy. I ain't seen him in a while, and I hope he don't mind this song and this dedication. Our mutual friend quoted me this. It's for them.'

She came up close to her microphone and began, a slow blues, a smoky voice, a slinky melody:

> *Courage . . . Courage . . . Oh courage . . .*
> *for the big . . . Problems . . . in life . . .*
> *Courage –* (and the notes rose, crescendo)
> *Oh Lord courage, give it to me.*
>
> *Courage,* (a righteous shout)
> *for the big,*
> *problems,*
> *in life . . .*
>
> *Oh Lord courage, give it to me.*

Riley sat transfixed as she continued, quiet again, smooth and intimate, a beseeching prayer, right up with the microphone:

166

Oh Lord and Patience,
oh Patience, for the small . . .
Patience, sweet Lord patience, for the small . . .

By the time she got to *Be of good cheer, God is awake*, tears rolled down his face. If he had heard this ten years earlier he would have felt their ghosts all around him, clamouring; now he heard them turn in their graves as if in their sleep, a little shift, a sigh. Ferdinand, Dowland, Dowland's brother, Burdock, Knightley, Atkins, Jones, Bloom, Bruce, Lovall, Hall, Green, Wester, Johnson, Taylor, Moles, Twyford. Merritt. Captain Harper. Captain Jessop. Baker. And above all Jack Ainsworth, whose prayer this was, whose scrap of paper was still, worn and creased, these words on it almost illegible, in Riley's wallet.

~

She came to join them at their table afterwards, her silky coat slipping from her shoulders, her make-up a little worn. Riley was about to be polite, formally refer to their previous encounter all those years ago, roll his eyes at the passage of time, but she just slipped into the booth beside him and said: 'Was that all right? To use your friend's words for the song? If you don't like it I won't sing it again.' Her hand was resting gently on Peter's shoulder; relaxed, quietly protective, affectionate. Giving strength.

'The only problem is how to get Sybil Ainsworth down to London so that you can reduce her to tears too,' Riley said, and Mabel smiled, and said: 'I'll go to wherever she is, and I'll sing it for her wherever she wants.' And she meant it, and Riley saw that the offer was as honest as her word-less concern for Peter, the big heart she offered up when she sang.

'Did you know about this, Peter?' Riley asked, leaning forward – but Peter hadn't known. Didn't even remember quoting the prayer to her. 'When was it, darling?' he said – such a settled-couple thing to say, Riley thought. Peter was drinking soda water, and smoking. They looked beautiful together. They seem right, Riley thought.

Mabel caught his eye as he said to Peter, 'D'you want another of those?' – the eye catch that says, I am noticing. Each of them noticed the other's affection for Peter and concern for his well-being, and each was glad to see it. Peter, of course, did not notice this noticing.

In the end, that first time they went to hear Mabel sing, Riley had said – at least Peter thought this was what he'd said, but it had been dark and quite noisy – 'Actually, you should do yourself a favour, Peter, and just marry her.' Of course he might not have said that at all.

By the time Peter got off the train at Sidcup he had decided to talk to Rose about it. Rose, cool-headed fount of understanding, would help.

By the time he reached home, he had decided not to after all. If he told Rose, he would need to tell Tom and Kitty, and would they not hate him for it?

Part Three

1933–4

Chapter Nine

Rome and Bracciano, 1933–4

The following two summers, 1933 and 1934, Tom went to Italy without his immediate family. Being there liberated him, and he was entranced by the magnificence of the liberation. He and Nenna played tennis, and went about on bicycles. *I am a young student,* he thought. *I am studying in Rome.* It gave him great pleasure to think it and know it was true. He was rather full of himself, wrapped and seduced in the glamour. Then, as he became used to it and relaxed, it became true.

Later, he asked himself: *but when did that happen? What was the progress? How did the little things add up to become big? When should I have noticed? Why didn't I notice – was it just because I was otherwise engaged? Not so much with the irregular verbs as with –* and he had to acknowledge for a moment his youthful obsessions, and admit his folly, his natural folly – *Nenna, and the beauty, and the strangeness, which remained strange?*

1933 – what happened in 1933? My summer between school and Cambridge.

He'd had his interview that spring: Natural Sciences. It seemed to have gone all right, or perhaps it went terribly, he couldn't tell. So he went to the pub, the Blue Boar, feeling rather adult and swaggery, and tiny underneath, at the sight of these grown undergraduates: the biggest boy in school acknowledging that he would be the smallest boy at university.

There were some other interviewees in the pub and they chatted, and – how did it happen? – the subject of Oswald Mosley came up, and a languid toff said to him, with a repellently suave little smile, something along the lines of 'I don't know why you're fretting, whoever you are. People like us will always be all right . . .'

People like us! Tom could have explained to him that though they were both blond, human, male, and applying for Cambridge, the similarity ended there. He could have explained that he didn't define what kind of a person he was by his accent, his blue eyes or his pale skin or the name he used for God, but by his thoughts and his actions, his beliefs and his heart and his guts and his morals. He might have taken the twit home and shown him Nadine (Jewish blood); Riley (common, disfigured); John Purefoy (a railwayman! Good Lord!). He might have pointed out, mildly, that actually he wasn't that interested in being 'all right' himself, if everyone else was suffering – that didn't really seem to him to be what 'all right' meant. The clue, perhaps, being in the word 'all'. He should have said, perhaps, that if you're going to divide humanity up into types, and generalise about them, then perhaps rather than dividing them into races and religions you might divide them into open-hearted honest kind people who believe in justice and have a sense of humour, and self-serving bastards who build their power and their personality on greed and fear and violence and an incomprehensible notion of their superiority.

But what he wanted to do was hit him. He really wanted to – right there in the pub just down the road from the college he wanted to take him in, his instincts were telling him it was worth it, to shut this smarmball up – this idea, that because one was all right one didn't have to be concerned about anyone else—

But he had absorbed Riley's lesson, from that day he'd blacked Slater's eye. Violence is very rarely a useful response. He did agree with that.

The smarmball was raising his eyebrows at him.

Tom blinked and thought about Riley. The moment passed.

Look what I nearly threw away, he thought, and he said, mildly: 'That rather depends on how you define "people like us".'

A very Cambridge answer, he thought, as he walked up to the station, resolving always to do his best to keep his temper and define his terms.

And how were Nenna and I then?

She used to laugh at me a lot, and I didn't mind.

He laughed at her too. They had a foundation of trust which neither of them ever thought about. They really were like brother and sister, except that the affection between them had to be made the most of, because his visits were limited. This made them uncritical of each other, which made them like each other more. The natural superiority he had by dint of being older – he would never have knocked around with a fourteen-year-old girl at home – was compensated for by her being in her home city, talking her native tongue. They were equalised.

That was the year that one day hundreds of pamphlets came tumbling down over the city, from a plane. They stared up into the bright sky, the tiny shining plane seemed close enough to climb up to, and the pamphlets fell, flicking and turning on the wind like doves as older people cried *Anvedi oh che roba!* and the younger ran around to find them: writing falling from the sky! Tom took one home for Aldo, who said some people were never satisfied. Some people were very ungrateful and didn't know when they were lucky.

Nenna and Tom spent most of the time at the lake, that year. They were immersed in the nature – the black volcanic beach, fields prickly dry or lush with irrigation, ruins, looking up from books to admire the hills and the rocks, shining blue and green rollers and bee-eaters which had flown north from Africa, crimson cyclamen on the dusty roadside, fat black and yellow spiders, little amber-coloured scorpions, ruffled millipedes. They drew a lot, and had picnics.

It was while lounging among the rubble of the ruins of the little Roman villa in the neighbouring vineyard, after a picnic lunch of hard bread and salami, that Tom found himself noticing the golden hairs on Nenna's shins glinting in the sunlight. In the same moment, because she was sitting with her knees up in her tennis skirt, her back against a bit of low tumbled wall, he saw the golden hairs on her thighs, and just as quickly he realised that he shouldn't be looking at her thighs – so he raised his eyes, thinking to observe how lush and big the fig tree craning from a crack in the wall had grown, or to stare up in wonder at the great umbrella pine in whose fragrant shade they lay. But it seemed that his eyes did not want to look at the fig tree, or the umbrella pine. They wanted to look at the golden hairs on her thighs.

He glanced back at her. *Avoid the thighs.* His eyes caught, helpless, on her T-shirt, and the curve within it, which had not been there last year.

So he closed his eyes instead. Inside the pink glow of his eyelids, he cast them down. They re-opened on white dust, dry grass, and the long pale brown tweezer-shapes of last year's fallen pine needles. He picked one up, and poked the back of his hand with it.

He knew about sex. Horses did it, and stags, in season, and he'd seen a dog doing something quite peculiar once with what must have been its own penis, which had made some older boys laugh in quite a disturbing way. He knew that the wet dreams and embarrassingly gloopy sheets which had got him into trouble at school were something to do with it. But he didn't know why he had this sudden exceptionally strong urge, now, to hug his cousin, and push his face into her neck.

'Look,' he said, poking at his hand, pricking the skin with the sharp pine needle. 'If you did this long enough and hard enough it would look like a rash, and you could get off school.'

Nenna gave him a most bemused look. 'What are you talking about?' she said, and for that he had no answer.

'Let's go for a swim!' he said, to cover the moment, and then realised that swimming, far from solving this issue, would exacerbate it. He put out his hand to help pull her up – a gentlemanly gesture he had been making automatically for years: she landed inches from his face, smiling and sun-warm. His body, for a moment, thrilled.

In the turn of a moment, his life had become a chaos. Fraught.

'Come on!' he cried, over-perky—

—and from then on his days were spent in a web of perils: a shoulder too close when they sat reading together; a breath on his ear if she leant in; the swing of her walk, half boyish, half – something else. Her utter relaxation with him. The way when he glanced at her and she glanced back she would say, 'What?' and he could say nothing. *She's a child. She's fourteen!* But she wasn't exactly a child. But she was fourteen.

He was at the fishmongers with Aldo one morning in Anguillara – eeltown! – where the fishmonger indeed sold giant lake eels from lake-water tanks carved out of the rock beneath the shop on the quay. If he leant and peered, he could see them, four or five feet long and as thick as a child's forearm, coiling and gleaming in the dark water. Aldo would buy by the metre, and later split them and grill them with bay leaves on hot orange embers. His caveman side, which sat amusingly with his vanity.

'Aldo, what shall I be when I grow up?' Tom asked.

Aldo snorted. 'You are grown up. How old are you, seventeen? Do things now!'

'Do what now?' Tom asked, horrified – *are my thoughts about Nenna visible?* It wouldn't be surprising. He was, he'd begun to think, obsessed, and he didn't like it. *It's not right*, he thought. *It's not decent.*

But no. Aldo said: 'Come shooting. Learn something like a man.' And Tom smiled, because Riley didn't like guns and Tom had never used one. And because a manly business like this would keep him safe from this growing obsession.

Up in the dark wooded hills, alongside Aldo and a small crew of local blokes, Tom, with old coat and borrowed gun, learnt the difference between a rifle and a shotgun, between birdshot and buckshot, a quail and a blackbird, an ancient Carcano *novantuno* and a not-that-old Winchester, the comparative merits of Franchi and Beretta, 20-gauge or 28-, or even, maybe, 12-, *sovrapposti* and *paralleli* and the tale of the Sicilian who once appeared in the neighbourhood trying to sell a sawn-off shotgun that he called a Lupara. He learnt terms in dialect that he would never know in English. He learned when to talk about these things, and when to be silent in anticipation; the joy of the wind coming up just before dawn, and with it the sound of wings. He turned out to have an eye and an ear: the sight, the creak, the dog pointing, the glimpse, the decision and the shot! And the triumph or failure, the laugh, the next one, the moving on . . . He caught eyes with the other men over each triumph, collecting a prize, feathered and still warm. He learnt the swift movements required for gutting and plucking; making a fire, sharpening a knife, stripping green twigs for a spit, roasting your catch then and there in the woods. A bit of bread, cut sideways with a hunting knife against a wool-clad chest, a sprinkle of salt. Swigging home-made red wine or grappa from the other man's flask. Sitting back against a tree trunk, listening to them sing. Aldo bought him a hunting knife at the market in Bracciano, identical to everyone else's, sharp in its own brown leather sheath, to hang from his belt.

Occasionally the talk turned to things beyond the wind, the birds, the guns and the lunch: light mockery of Aldo for being a decent man despite being a Roman and a *forestiero*; heavier mockery of Tom for thinking a *forestiero* was someone from the forest, rather than someone from Fuori – outside. 'So I am a *forestiero*?' he asked, to howls of laughter and the response – 'People from Trevignano or Tolfa are *forestieri*! You are a little green man from space!'

Aldo explained on their way home, heads aching slightly from the woodland siesta after wine, about this thing, 'This *campanilismo* – the spirit of the *campanile*, the belltower – this universal belief, this self-fulfilling prophesy, that the people from just over there' – he waved his arm, generally – 'are idiotic foreigners who hate you. It's left over, of course, from all the tiny states and small towns. You've seen the Palio in Siena? You must go. Pure *campanilismo*, from one building to the next. You know what they say in Milan? *Dal Po' in giù l'Italia non c'é più* – South of the Po, Italy no more. In Lucca? *Meglio avere un morto in casa che un pisano alla porta.* Better a corpse in the house than a Pisan at the door. Pisa is no distance from Lucca! Half an hour in a motor car. Which is the point – those closest to you are the ones who can make the most trouble!' Here he gave Tom a little glance, rueful, humorous. 'It takes no time to reach you when they want to steal your cow, insult your wife, burn your barn. Down at the marshes, the original inhabitants from the mountains call the new northerners who've moved down Vikings. And the Vikings call the southerners Wogs. Which is why Italy loves the Duce. He reminds us we are Italian in the modern world, not terrified *contadini* in the sixteenth century.'

'I read the other day,' Tom said, 'that he said Fascism was not something for export.'

'Yes,' Aldo said. 'It is designed for us, for our history and our needs.'

'So England doesn't need it?'

Aldo side-eyed him. 'What do you think?'

'I think not,' Tom said, after a moment.

'You're right. England, Great Britain, you are a much older country, you are united, you have your great Empire; you have proved your discipline. You are a different kind of people.'

Well that was true. Tom laughed. *Good old Brits, so cool and disciplined* . . . and that thought brought an image of Nenna, and the recognition he was not, naturally, entirely, cool and disciplined.

'I don't think Fascism would ever take, in Britain,' Tom said. 'We have Fascists, of course, and plenty of people really admire the Duce, and Herr Hitler too—'

'Oh, it's all different things!' Aldo cried. 'We are not German, you are not Italian. Your Mosley is idiotic. We are all free humans within our countries, living in the real world . . .'

179

They walked on. Tom was considering this opportunity. Usually, if Tom didn't bring something up, Aldo didn't mention politics. Ideals, yes. History, yes. Current politics, beyond admiration of the Duce, no. And on ideals, they agreed: peace and justice and respect and family and prosperity . . . *Well, even Herr Hitler would probably agree on all that,* Tom thought. *Except the justice and respect and family and prosperity is only for Nazis. Not for the people he's annexing . . .* Campanilismo *writ large? That's the rub with that type – it's all for them, and nothing for anyone who is different, or foreign.* Tom had seen that close up; blue-eyed, blond-haired Tom, about whom people sometimes made assumptions. *That ass in Cambridge . . .*

'But, Zio Aldo,' said Tom. 'What about the violence? The *squadristi*? And the Duce had Matteotti killed, didn't he?'

Aldo turned to him, stopped him, put his hands on his shoulders. For a moment Tom was alarmed – had he gone too far?

'Aoh,' Aldo said. 'My boy. Listen. Here is something: One: do not slander the powerful. How old were you then? Six years old? You do not know what happened. Here is another thing. The Duce acted like a man. He took responsibility for what had been done by men of his party, full responsibility, because he is the leader of the party. He did what was honourable. And then, though he had many enemies, and the law is strong, he was not prosecuted. Would he not have been prosecuted, by those enemies, if there had been evidence? There is no proof or evidence that he gave the order. But here is another thing. A more important thing. If he did, so be it. The English did not build England or your Empire without shedding blood. Power is dirty. Now, your government can run the country all by the rule of please and thank you and oh excuse me; you don't need the Tower of London and the cutting off heads. Good for you. But one must be realistic! A wise leader knows what his nation can afford. Matteotti was undermining the Duce's efforts to build Italy, with his whining about this and that, about necessary discipline and rigour and, yes, violence. As if he thinks you can win without fighting!'

Aldo took his hands away and gave a little sigh. 'Matteotti was an enemy,' he said, 'not of the Duce, but of Italian advancement. That is the truth. Sometimes violence is a tool of development. Also' – and he turned again to Tom, with a knowing this-is-not-our-fault, this-is-how-things-are look – 'It's a man's nature. Isn't it?'

Tom thought of the little toff, and laughed, and rolled his eyes. Yes, it was a man's nature.

For a moment, he thought of Riley. *Well, it's different for Riley. Riley had enough violence, and it did more to him than to most people. Of course he feels differently about it.*

They walked on, and after a while scuffing through the dust Tom, enlivened to confidences by the wine and his quasi-uncle's gentleness in the face of a difficult question, asked him another: 'What was your father like?'

It wasn't that Riley wasn't a good substitute. It was that a boy who ever needed a substitute will always have some kind of vacancy available.

Later, the term 'it's man's nature' returned to him.

Man's nature, eh. Sex and violence.

His mantra that year: *she's fourteen.*

~

Kitty missed Tom unspeakably when he went off to university. All right, he was an oaf, and didn't seem to care about her at all, and was being a grown-up now, with patches on his jacket elbows, and all those tall friends who didn't know she existed, and just talked about bumps and chaps and philosophers and yards of ale. She'd managed to worm her way into his room to join them one time over Easter, during his first year, and one of them pointed at her and said 'Locke, there's some kind of tiny munchkin lurking in that corner. What can it want?'

It is not right, it is not right. Why such humiliation just because I am a girl?

Their cricket games were now grown-up affairs: six-footers in whites, with girls watching, and mothers, and cucumber sandwiches. No more bunches of children all with muddy grassy knees. They wouldn't even let her play chess with them. They wouldn't let her sit with them. And anyway, they weren't there: they were out, in places to which she would never go. She was defenceless.

She wished she had a sister. Or a bicycle she was allowed out in the streets on. Or a crow that would sit on her shoulder, and fly off, and come back, and talk to her and only her. She lay on her bed and rolled her eyes so far back in her head they saw universes, and hurt. She resolved to read the Bible all the way through, and even made it through an entire chapter of Enochs and Mahalaleels begetting each other, but the first mention of a girl being begot was when the sons of God saw the daughters of men that they were fair, and they took them wives of all which they chose, and then she cried, because no son of God would choose her because she was fat and fluffy, and anyway she didn't want to be chosen, or to get married, she wanted—

She wanted—

I want—

Well at least I can agree that I want, she thought, and went outside to water the sweet peas. It was that spring, watching the emerging leaves each day, the astounding strength of the power of tiny shoots against black London earth, little drops gathering and running down the sharp-folded leaves, the plant throwing up its hairy stalks and wild cycling tendrils, that she thought – *I bet no man will ever write a book about why there aren't any exciting women in the Bible – all you get is to have a baby, even if it is the son of God, or weep among alien corn, or cut some man's head off and get thrown to the dogs . . .*

I don't have to be like Mummy. I don't have to have babies and get thrown to the dogs. I could be like Daddy, and write books. It's either that or I must run away from home. She was not brave enough to run away from home. She didn't want to.

Sometimes she would listen at Nadine's studio door, and hear her humming happily to herself as she worked. She knew she could go in, and Nadine would be kind, and give her some paper and charcoal. But she didn't want to disturb Nadine's strange joyous world of concentration, which though she could sense it she could not yet achieve for herself. It seemed to her to be a precious thing.

She cleared the surface of the little desk in her bedroom, and thought: *this is not my bedroom any more. This is my room.*

She started her first novel the afternoon she watered the sweet peas, in a shiny blue notebook: '*The True Story of Etheldreda Emmerham,* by Katharine Locke', and spent most of the next three hours thinking up new noms de plume for herself.

~

Summer of 1934 then, Tom was thinking. *What happened in 1934? First long vac from Cambridge – I took the language and Italian culture course, and met Carmichael for the first time, and spent a fair amount of time with him.*

Nenna was running around with one of the Seta boys, Daniele, a nephew of the Setas who lived next door. That's what happened. She had turned idiotic. She was rolling her sleeves up in some special way, and giggling a lot, and he had turned his back, rather, because she was a silly fifteen-year-old and he was eighteen now and at university and frankly, he had more important things on his mind, as a young man would. Dante, for example. He and Carmichael – Johnny – walked the streets, bought their own coffee, took up smoking. They carried their Boccaccio and their Dante and read them where they liked, in the Forum, on the Capitoline, with their backs against white marble and their feet in the river. Carmichael rather specialised in street slang and Romanaccio, and getting it a bit wrong: '*anvedi oh!*', he'd cry, at anything unusual, and '*namo a magnà?*' when inviting Tom to eat. Together they learnt the names of the many marbles on the floor of St Peter's, and teased the children in the piazza, playing football with them and joking.

Tom really wasn't bothered by Nenna and the Seta boy. Though her parents were, rather, and would suggest Tom as a third – a gooseberry! – when Nenna wanted to go somewhere with Daniele.

Nenna, Tom felt, was rather fast. Out with Carmichael, or back in Cambridge, he didn't mind girls being fast at all. Rather older girls, more interesting and with more to offer. But he didn't want Nenna to be.

Other than that, he read a lot, and went back fairly soon to London. University actually required quite a lot of work, it turned out.

Chapter Ten

Rome, 1935

When he saw Nenna again, in the summer of 1935, suddenly it was all different again. He practically threw up his hands in submission. Jesus, the beauty. What is a man to do. Jesus.

And now, apparently, she was old enough to be taken on trips. Out for the day, by bicycle or train: 'Just keep her out of trouble,' Susanna said. But more often, it was out for a few hours with the baby.

The baby! There it was, fully formed, a calm, fluff-headed infant with saintly ways, a knowing look, hands like starfish and a dirty laugh which made everybody about her laugh too. Her name was Marinella, and even Tom acknowledged her qualities: he played the drums on her tummy which reduced her to fits of giggles of such charm that he stuck his finger in the honeypot and let her suck it, gurgling and smiling her curly smiles.

'It's so unfair,' Nenna murmured, taking her sticky little sister in her arms and blowing raspberries on her. 'I can never have one of my own without having some husband, some boy, to be its father—'

'You could have your choice of boys,' Tom said. 'They all love you. When you're not shouting at them to behave.' Signorino Seta had disappeared. His aunt, the chirpy saucepot next door, seemed rather disappointed. *Ha!*

When they took Marinella out with them, strangers thought she was theirs. There was a particular approving look that came with all the cheek-pinching and cries of '*ma che bella*' and all that. They were stopped thirty-three times on one day alone in Campo dei Fiori by people needing to admire the baby.

'*In Campo dei Fiori, son già trentatré!*' sang Nenna, to the tune of '*Ma in Spagna son già mile e tre*', Leporello's song about how many women Don Giovanni slept with in Spain.

It was as if they both retired a little from the previous times, and for a while a strange apologeticness was on them, as if they could almost acknowledge what had disrupted them the summer before. And then that dispersed like morning mist, and they looked at each other anew. Anew, but all the ballast of the past. Everything to play for. Nineteen and sixteen. Sixteen, actually, was not too young.

But if that was true, another territory opened up for Tom, the gist of which was: did he mean it? This wasn't something he could do anything about. He couldn't tell her, or kiss her, or anything like that. This wasn't some bold-eyed Girton twenty-one-year-old with her own fags and plans for a flat in London next year. This was family. Marinella, smiling up at them, demonstrated exactly where all this stuff led.

But it had lurched back. He glanced at her and she looked away. She glanced at him but he was thinking about something else. He thought, *She is not even on the same page as me. She is too young. I should not be thinking these things. Feeling these things.*

Damn.

They sat out in their old spots on the low walls of the island, the river rumbling away beneath; they retreated into the house, to Susanna's cool and respectable rooms where they had to sit upright in respectable chairs. And then they wanted to go *out out out.* Being out was the real involvement. Being in the house was a limitation; being out was really being in – being in the world, in what really mattered. In the great human reality of it all.

When the family left Rome for the lake, Tom and Nenna broadened their expeditions: to Tarquinia to see the towers and Etruscan tomb paintings; up to dusty Tolfa for the Donkey Palio. Two lakes north, at Bolsena, they ate their lunch in a miniature Palladian temple on an island of miniature Palladian temples and dived off a small boat to a sunken sarcophagus. Back on shore they sneaked into the church of an ancient nunnery, where Nenna sang arias and showtunes – Puccini and Verdi and 'Stormy Weather', and 'Indian Love Call' – and Tom was surprised at how strong and real her voice had become, echoing in the dome. They ate ice cream, read each other's diaries, and plotted itineraries for when they could go to Florence and Venice, when Tom had his motorbike, when they could go anywhere. They swam in new lakes, Bolsena and Vico, and the bewitching indecency of her swimsuit contradicted him very effectively when he tried saying to himself, still, she's too young.

Their eyes caught, from time to time. He wanted to kiss

her, all the time. All the bloody time. Well, most of the time. He had not the slightest idea what she wanted.

~

Nenna, of course, recognised Tom's perturbation immediately. She had been wondering when, rather than whether, Tom would start behaving like every other moo-faced idiot male she met, whose inability to ignore her *bella alta bionda* body in favour of her interesting mind and sarcasm and capacity for shenanigans she was starting to find quite . . . cramping. After Daniele Seta – which was nothing, really, nothing! – Aldo and Susanna had forbidden her from going round with boys at all. Not even the dull cousins from the ghetto were allowed, so Tom's arrival was a blessing dropped straight from heaven – but if her parents were to notice that Tom was also starting to moo, then no doubt he too would be banned – but thank God, he was English and so repressed that no one had spotted it. Apart from her.

She responded as she did to them all. *Let's see what you mean by it. Is this just you being male? Or is it about me, in particular, me? Let's wait and see.* Meanwhile the admiration soaked in, and was transformed by that alchemy of adolescence into a self-confidence which in turn radiated out again, shone like the sun in her hair and her walk and her look – and drew more admiration in.

And then, when they were back in Rome, a ludicrous upsetting thing happened.

They were heading out to meet Carmichael and go to the cinema. *La Moglie di Frankenstein!* They hadn't told Susanna that was what they were going to see. Strolling through Piazza, *passeggiata* time, a girl Nenna knew from about the place appeared on the other side of the road: Stella, pale, broad-browed, black-haired, with her eyebrows plucked like a movie-star's and her pouty, droopy cupid mouth.

'Stella!' Nenna called out, and she looked up, like an animal hearing its name and looking around, a little sleepily, for the caller.

'Stella! Over here!' Nenna cried, and as Stella identified her, her unfocused face lit up with a slow smile, a little twist to the plump lip. Nenna had reached her by now, and was saying, '*Ciao, amore*, what are you up to?' Stella's smile spread to her creamy cheeks. 'Walk with us?' At this Stella beamed; silently she tucked her hand behind Nenna's upper arm, and hugged it a little. She turned to glance at Tom, and gave him a coy flash of her big eyes.

'*Salve, Stella*,' he said. '*Sono Tommaso.*'

Stella didn't reply. She just glanced up again, like a celluloid doll: painted irises, up/down eyelids, and a brush of thick lashes.

'Stella doesn't talk much,' Nenna said. 'Do you, darling?' Stella kept her smile, her eyes down.

They walked like this as far as via del Portico D'Ottavia, where it seemed to be time for a little ritual.

'So d'you want a bun, Stellina?' Nenna asked. And Stellina did – they smiled complicitly – so they went to the bakery on the corner to get one of the really hard ones that Tom practically broke his fine English teeth on, but that everybody else loved.

Stella grabbed it and laughed, making a sideways head-wobble denoting joy, gratitude and affection. Nenna felt the satisfied glow of a person who has done a simple kind thing on a sunny morning, when Stella, after a moment of hesitation, suddenly reached up and, putting the bun-holding hand round the back of Nenna's neck, kissed her, on the mouth.

It was sweet, gentle – a little open, a touch of breath. Nenna jumped in her skin, recognising it instinctively for what it was: sexual. She was electrified. Stella retreated a little, smiled demurely, and batted her great lashes, as if waiting.

Nenna was rigid, with shock, outrage and an undercurrent of thrill running all over her. She pulled herself together with a little shakedown and said: 'Stella, no. You mustn't do that. That's wrong.' She looked as if she wanted to laugh. Or something. She wiped her mouth.

'No, Stella,' she said firmly.

At the word 'No', at the insulting wipe of the mouth, Stella's face clouded. Eyebrows and mouth drooped, the chin went back and under. Hurt gathered. Then she pouted her lower lip and gave an actual little hiss at Nenna, like a cat. For a moment Nenna thought Stella was going to thrust the bun back at her, but instead she clutched it closer to the front of her dress, and turned, and stalked off.

'Oh dear,' said Nenna, shaken. Tom, having no idea what to do with a girl who has just been kissed and then hissed at by another girl, went to put his hand on her shoulder, then didn't.

Nenna turned to him, a little breathless, and said: 'My first kiss! Dio mio – but she really mustn't – oh dear . . .'

'She's presumably not all there,' said Tom, looking worried, as if concerned for Stella's moral vulnerability, which he was, and so was Nenna, but Nenna said 'Don't change the subject! That was my first kiss. That! So much for young love!'

And she did start laughing, shaking her head, and then she had to sit down.

Around them the street was neither crowded nor empty, but nobody seemed to have seen the moment, for which she was grateful. 'It's lucky nobody noticed or I would have to marry her!' she said, and her laughter turned into the choking, teary kind, so Tom was able to pat her back helpfully, and her arm, until she said 'Do stop that, Masino.'

'She is going to get into trouble, though,' he said.

'She'd always do anything for a bun,' Nenna said. 'It didn't really matter when she was a little kid.'

'She is a little kid,' said Tom.

'She's about fourteen.'

'A child,' said Tom.

Nenna rubbed her mouth again. It felt as though she was rubbing the kiss in, not off.

Tom thought: *I could kiss her now.*

It might help.

God no of course I couldn't.

But he looked at her and thought: *there will be a first kiss for us though. It will happen. I will do it.*

Aldo took Tom with him to see the new towns. They stopped outside Cisterna, at the edge of the hills, and looked down over the plain, wide and smooth, divided in quadrants by roads and canals, flat as a tablecloth carefully laid. Graceful eucalyptus trees, small and floaty in the distance, lined the banks and ditches. Beyond lay the blue sea, no flatter than the land. Tom smiled.

'Before we made our *bonifica*, our reclamation work, it was dinosaur country,' Aldo said. 'Weeds and reeds and pools and swamps to the end of the eye. You imagine diplodocus and brontosaurus walking about. We found a mammoth skeleton . . . But now it is just frogs – do you eat frog?'

'No,' Tom said.

'You should try it. It's delicious. We'll go and see Olivieri, and buy a few. He's been trapping them here for years. Eels too . . .'

Aldo pointed out the towns. From this height they were star-shapes and circles, geometrical urban paradises set in the chequerboard of green fields and brown. Littoria, opened in 1932; Sabaudia, 1934, and Pontinia, which was still in progress. 'It won't take long,' Aldo said. 'We built Sabaudia in two hundred and fifty-three days. Littoria – look at it now, how beautiful it is – was a mess hours before the opening. There was a terrible storm, mud and flooding everywhere.'

'I thought the *bonifica* had stopped all the flooding,' Tom said.

'Mostly. That night, not. The men worked all night, and they have a tale that the ground underneath the piazza opened up and swallowed a tractor whole. Every man working on the town,' he said, making the expression that means indulgent disbelief in the face of peasant cunning, 'was holding on to the rope, and saw it fall. They tried to save it but it was too heavy, and they had to let go.'

'Is that true?'

Aldo shrugged, made a moue with his mouth. '*Beh*,' he said. 'Everything was nice by morning when the Duce came to make his speech and plant some trees. They do say the driver had a kitten, and it couldn't be saved, and you hear it mewing on stormy nights . . .'

'So is the tractor still under there?'

'So they say. Or maybe someone sold it. It was just a tractor – not one of the huge Tosis with all the buckets – oh, you haven't see the Tosis – come, let's go and find one.'

Aldo grinned and gleamed as he drove Tom down on to the great tablecloth, taking him on a brand new road along a brand new built-up bank to where a great dinosaur of steel and electricity leant its long neck over into a wide vale of water and mud. It was festooned with a row of vast buckets, which constantly moved along like beads on a gigantic necklace, shunting each other into the mud and water below, and in turn scooping, scooping, scooping, and then dumping, dumping, dumping. Farther away, in a canal bed of thicker mud, sinewy brown-faced men in shirtsleeves and caps dug, and dumped, and dug, and dumped, and dug, and dumped. In the distance, hovering almost above the plain, Tom saw three more diplodoci, leaning their long necks, buckets scooping, dumping, scooping, dumping, and crowds more men, digging, and dumping, and digging, and dumping. The smell was revolting and the noise tremendous. The dance lurched on, both primeval and industrial. Tom was entranced.

Aldo was saying something about explosions, having to blow up rocky outcrops. Tom pictured volcanos of mud bursting into the sky.

'The workmen are from the north,' Aldo was saying, his face misty with pleasure at the rightness of it all. 'Ex-soldiers. They will have a house and land of their own; quinine every day against the malaria. They are building Italy, and Italy is building them.'

Turning back, leaving the raw landscape where the men and machines were still slogging to win land from water, they came to the salvaged land, flat and perfect with tiny fruit trees, fields that had yet to see their first harvest, new houses, blue with red tiles, pretty and neat, dotted about regularly on the empty land. Aldo waved at people as they passed: women working in the fields, children. They waved back. 'Every house has mosquito nets built in,' Aldo said, and for a moment he looked as if he was going to cry.

'Come,' Aldo said. 'I'll show you the pumps. They're down at Mazzocchio; six of them as big as aeroplanes, and as noisy. They pull nine and a half thousand gallons of water a second, and send it through the canals down to the sea.'

'What would happen if they broke down?' Tom asked.

Aldo gazed about. 'All under water again,' he said. 'One week maybe.'

'It all looks so perfect,' Tom said. 'Like a toytown.'

Aldo smiled.

'Did anybody live here before?'

'Not really,' Aldo said. 'Maybe a few.'

'What happened to them?'

Aldo didn't know.

Heading back up the via Appia to Rome, Tom asked, 'Have you met the Duce?'

Aldo glanced at him in surprise. 'Of course!' he said. 'All the time! He comes down to admire the works – and to help. Shirt off, digging, helping get the harvest in. Also' – and he gave Tom a look – 'he has a girlfriend down this way. He comes on his Moto Guzzi to visit. Then we pretend not to know it's him.'

'Have you talked to him?'

'Of course!' Aldo said. 'Everybody talks to him. He listens to everybody. And what's more he gives you a straight answer, and he keeps his word.'

When boys yelled at foreign girls in the street, '*Eh, bionda!*' and so forth, in not at all the same way that their grand-mothers used to coo the same words to Kitty, Nenna yelled back with a mouthful as dry and salty as anchovies. They did not yell at her twice. Word got round.

It's a great big hokey cokey, Tom thought. *Yes and no, to and fro.*

'It's because they get a cheque for seven hundred lire when they get married,' he teased. 'They want you for the money.'

Tom did not shout at girls in the street. He was, like it or not, an English gentleman. He wasn't sure, now, that he did like it. He could tease her, and make her make that face, the one she was doing now, narrowed eyes, pouty mouth, the 'Yes, yes, I know what you're up to' look, but he could not – *cannot what?* he thought. *If I were not an English gentleman,* he thought – but the thought stopped there. He was an English gentleman, and there was nothing he could do about it.

But English gentlemen touch women. They father children. They hold girls too close at dances. They go out on to the verandah with them, they kiss them in cars, and stay for hours in the car park outside the tennis club. They cuddle up with barmaids and town girls and – he'd heard about this – they give money to girls they meet in stations and pubs, to do the kind of thing some of the chaps at school did for each other . . .

None of this was anything to do with Nenna. Nenna was – well, she was nothing to do with any of that.

'They want those blondies for their lovely Aryan genes,' Nenna said. 'And men with plenty of children get better jobs, so they have to start young. I suppose I'd better marry one now, and get a good start.'

'You're far too young,' Tom said, bringing out his mocking tone, which would make all his dirty thoughts go away. 'A mere child.'

'Younger than I are happy mothers made,' she said, with a little laugh. 'But don't worry Tommaso, I'll wait for you. We can marry when we're old enough to know no one else will have us. When we're twenty-five.'

'But if we leave it so late how will we fit in our seven sons?' Tom asked, grinning gaily as his mind filled up suddenly with fantastic images, shocking images, of him and Nenna creating sons, images of golden thighs and coiling hair and breasts and mouths . . . 'Five thousand lire apiece, don't forget!' he cried. *Dear God, I am becoming a lunatic.* 'But what if we have seven daughters too?'

'Life insurance!' said Nenna. This was another kindness from the Duce to his people: if anything happened to the patriotic mother there would be an insurance payment for the upkeep of her seven fine Italians sons. 'You know the signora with twenty-four children? She's pregnant!'

'Imagine!' cried Tom. 'Twenty-five children dressed like Vittorio and Stefano in their little shorts and their hats like acorns, marching across a desert to invade Abyssinia, singing' – and he sang – '"*Ti saluto, vado in Abissinia, cara Virginia, ma tornerò*." If they'd invaded somewhere else, of course, they'd have put in some other girl's name . . . I'm going to America, dear Angelica; to Albania, dear Grainne – it's an Irish name, Nenna.'

This is better. Sort of. At least it's changing the subject.

'Bulgaria, Maria,' Nenna said.

'Haiti, Katie,' said Tom. 'Uganda Amanda.'

'Bolivia Olivia,' said Nenna.

'Tanganyika Veronica!' cried Tom.

'Nigeria Valeria!' from Nenna.

'To Guinea, dear Minnie,' said Tom, 'and Chile, dear Millie' – at which they fell about laughing.

By the end Tom was physically sitting on his hands, red-faced, and Marinella was watching them with huge eyes and an expression of vast wisdom.

∽

Was it because I was so engrossed in her? Was I just blinded?

∽

Tom wrote to Nadine and Riley.

Dear Old Folks. Everyone's well. The baby is very sweet, though everywhere is festooned in urinous cloths as a result, which is not really my cup of tea, talking of which I'm longing for one. The autarchia thing is getting really quite extreme. Nenna has a particularly nasty coat which is apparently made of milk. It's called Lanital. Sounds like a medicine or something to clean the bathroom with. Aldo is very keen on it all and quite believes that coffee is not good for us and chicory is not revolting – also leather shoes are not necessary, we must wear cork or rubber. I feel quite privileged to be allowed my English brogues which are of course not unpatriotic because they are English and so am I. I managed an entire week at the lake before term began and have elongated my capacity for staying underwater, unfortunately as I have not invented a way of reading a stopwatch underwater or of persuading Nenna that timing me is an interesting project I still don't know how long exactly I can stay there. I was about to start training up Stefano as my assistant in this experiment but alas he had homework and now everyone has to go back to school, so my ignorance remains intact. Having had a look at Tiber water under a microscope last summer – positively oodling with life forms hitherto unknown to man, or at least to me – I don't think I'll be continuing my research when we get back to the island. Been to a couple of rallies and so forth, all jolly stirring but somebody said the tanks were made of wood, so—

Anyway, Aldo etc send their regards – it is now dinner

time, so *accubituri te salutant* – those who are about to lie
down and scoff salute you. I won't say I'll write again because
I probably won't— Yr lvg Tom

A conductor had left the country because he wouldn't play
'Giovinezza' before his concerts.

'Idiotic,' said Nenna. 'Why not play it? It's his job and it's
a lovely song.'

Tom said he had read in the paper that a senator had
slapped the conductor's face once for not playing it.

'Well, he felt strongly about it,' said Nenna. 'Songs can
be very strong. You remember how we used to march up
and down . . .' They remembered: Nenna and Kitty singing
Giovinezza, giovinezza, primavera di bellezza . . . Youth,
youth, springtime of beauty . . . You couldn't sing it without
marching up and down.

Nenna was back at school. One weekend her gymnastics
troupe took part in a display: Tom went along with Susanna
and Aldo and the boys, to watch. Johnny Carmichael, also
on the new course, came along.

The Duce was up there somewhere, thumbs tucked into
his belt no doubt, swaying his stout chest around, being
adored. They peered and craned but they didn't get a
glimpse. So many ranks of people passed by! Young men
with charms dangling from their hats; boys from the Balilla
walking with their bent arms swinging alternately right
across their bodies so their elbows pointed at their shoes.
Everyone so very much in time. So much saluting. Aldo
and the boys cheered and stamped their feet, and as
Nenna's troupe came cartwheeling by, bouncing and spin-

ning along like great white flowers, Tom's spirits rose – with the general enthusiasm, of course. And, yes, with the sight of her legs flying, long and strong. Her hair was tied up tight around her head. He realised, seeing it tied so tight, how glad he was that she didn't cut it short and hold it in place with clips, like the other girls – and her face was bright with exertion and pride as it flashed by, upside down, spinning. Her arms, flexible and brown, were curved with muscle, her belly stretched and smooth under the white shirt.

'There she is! There she is!' shouted Stefano and Vittorio, and Susanna, beside Tom, put her hand on his arm and turned to smile at him with a maternal pride which made him flush with shame. On his other side, Carmichael whispered, 'What do you think of all this? Rather ridiculous, don't you think? But impressive.'

'Mussolini is a great statesman for Italy!' Tom said. 'Every Italian knows they need discipline and a strong leader. They're not like us English, naturally hardworking, and reasonable.'

'Stop that,' said Carmichael, giggling.

'Stop what?' Tom said.

'You're joking, aren't you?'

'You sound like Papà,' said Stefano.

Carmichael fell silent.

~

Tom was bemused about what was going on in Abyssinia. There was some disagreement, and Mussolini had sent soldiers, and the League of Nations had got involved.

201

Tom wasn't convinced about invading other countries. How was it fair?

Aldo, just back from another rally, bluff and cheerful, laughed and laughed at that. 'From a son of perfidious Albion!' he said. 'The country which – have you heard of the British Empire? Dear boy, allow me to quote.' He turned to the bookshelf, and took a paper from the pile. It took him a moment to find the right thing.

'Here,' he said, and read: '"As soon as the British have sated themselves with colonial conquests, they impudently draw a line across the middle of the page in the Recording Angel's book, and then proclaim: 'What was right for us up till yesterday is wrong for you today.'"'

Tom thought for a second, and supposed he had a point.

'But Anthony Eden is brokering for peace,' Tom said. 'Peace is better, surely?'

'Arms embargo!' said Aldo, and snorted. 'You lot are trying to tell us what to do. Listen. The Duce wants to take back what is naturally ours, that you lot – Albion! – messed about with at Versailles. And it is the duty of a powerful country to spread civilisation. Don't we all have empires? France? Russia? Germany? And if we invade, the darkies will benefit from Roman standards! They will be delighted.'

Tom thought for another moment, and supposed that he was proud of the Empire, and supposed, in a way, that of course Italy would want one.

'There is slavery in Abyssinia!' Nenna said. 'It's terrible! These things have to be challenged.' Her eyes were wide and shocked. 'Don't the English newspapers tell you these things?'

He hardly heard the words, her eyes were so beautiful.

'You lot watch out,' Aldo said. '*Inglese italianato, diavolo incarnato.*' The Englishman Italianate is the devil incarnate.

~

Tom really tried to settle to work. For several weeks he persuaded himself that he was revelling in the deeper involvement: working hard, seeing more of the chaps from the college. He'd be back in England for university early in October, but wanted to stay as long here as he could. He read the papers – English or American ones if he could get hold of them: Joe Louis the Brown Bomber beat Max Baer, the former champion (Aldo wouldn't like that: in June Joe Louis had beaten Mussolini's boy, Primo Carnera the Ambling Alp, despite being 9 inches shorter and 65 pounds lighter). Howard Hughes had flown the plane he himself designed, at 352.46 mph. Hitler had put through the Nuremberg Laws depriving German Jews of citizenship; aviator Hubert Fauntleroy Julian, the Black Eagle of Harlem, had volunteered for the Ethiopian air force, and was on his way to meet Haile Selassie – that gave Tom a pang. He had loved Hubert Fauntleroy Julian ever since reading about his flights and parachute jumps in New York, years ago, where he wore a red suit and played the saxophone as he descended, crowds rushing up and down the streets of New York as the wind blew him this way and that. One time he had landed on the police station in Harlem. Or something.

Aldo was a little moody. The latest phase of the *bonifica* at the Agro Pontino was finished, and everybody had been laid off – thousands of men. 'It's good,' he said. 'They were getting restless with the sacrifices that have to be made. As if you can achieve anything without suffering.'

Tom asked, 'What have the men been suffering?'

'Oh, the usual complaints. The camps are too crowded, the wages are too low, the food is bad, things are dirty, there's not enough doctors—'

'And is it true?'

'Of course it's true! It's not the *Dopolavoro*! They can't expect to sit about playing *briscola* all day! But anyway, now they're all sacked, so they've nothing more to complain about. For the next phase, they'll employ men with more enthusiasm. Me for example!'

~

One evening early in October Tom was reading when Nenna came and grabbed him, saying, 'There's a big speech at Palazzo Venezia, come on.' He let her drag him. Vittorio and Stefano, smelling excitement, followed in tow.

It wasn't far, just through Piazza and up via dei Delfini. The crowds were out en masse, pushing and scurrying in expectation of good news. All Rome, it seemed, was filling the streets, up the steps of the Vittoriale/Vittoriano/Typewriter/Wedding Cake/Vittorio Emmanuele monument – the vast white building with the parades of columns, and flying chariots on the roof, Tom never knew what to call it – and beyond. Everyone was moving in the same direction, moths to the same flame: soldiers and *contadini*, sailors and matrons, children and old men, girls and youths, Fascist badges, ribbons and medals, soup-stained ties and worn-out shoes, black shirts and breeches, skirts and nylons, soft hats and suits, three-legged dogs and squalling babies. Tom grabbed the boys by the hand so as not to lose them as they craned and wriggled to see. Above by the famous balcony on the first floor of the red palazzo, the loudspeakers swung with echo and delay as the Duce appeared, trim and strutting, and raised his voice above the chants of *DU-CE! DU-CE! DU-CE!* Nenna glanced across at Tom, her eyes aglow, eyebrows raised in complicity, then turned her bright face towards the palazzo and the man.

'*Dux, mea Lux!*' wailed a woman beside them, holding out her arms in something between the Fascist salute and a yearning reach for a lover. Leader, my light. '*DUX, MEA LUX!*'

'Steady on, old girl,' Tom murmured. But everybody was lit up. A kind of pride and clarity illuminated them, all looking the same way, bound together in certainty, all calling the same phrases, the bass line of *DU-CE! DU-CE! DU-CE!*, the ecstatic free-flying cries above of *DUX MEA LUX!*

They all fell quiet as he started to speak.

'Blackshirts of the revolution!' the Duce cried out. His manner was as usual brusque, friendly and strong – relaxed, like a school teacher who knows he is loved. 'Men and women of all Italy! Listen' – and listen they did, as if their dad had called them together to tell them something important. 'Listen. A solemn hour is about to strike in the history of the fatherland. Twenty million Italians are at this moment occupying piazzas in every corner of Italy – twenty million people, one single heart.' Cheers erupted. 'One will.' Cheers. 'One decision. It is not just an army which is moving towards its objectives, but an entire people of forty-four million souls.' Cheers! 'A people against whom attempts have been made to commit the blackest injustice: that of depriving us of a little place in the sun – we have been patient for thirteen years, during which the noose of selfishness that has stifled our natural energy has been drawn ever tighter! With Ethiopia we have been patient for forty years! – Enough!'

The ripples ran over and through the crowd; the deliciousness of being one heart, one will, under one leader. Tom glanced around at the faces. They weren't hysterical. They just loved him. *It must be rather nice*, he thought. *You wouldn't get the English all out in the streets like this for the King . . .*

'It's all your fault, you know!' Stefano cried naughtily, when the speech was done. 'Britain is so selfish! So rich and greedy, and won't let Italy have what it needs in Abyssinia.'

'You know why?' said Vittorio. 'Because England is afraid! Because England is old and weak, and Italy is so young and strong! The Duce is Julius Caesar and we conquered you before!'

'Shut up, you little beasts,' cried Tom, putting on his evil face and tickling them exactly as they liked him to do. They were still just small enough for him to keep both of them in place, if Nenna helped.

'We're going to show you!' the boys yelled. 'We're going to show everybody!' as Tom swung Stefano on to his back in a fireman's lift, and galumphed him down the street, scattering and annoying the dispersing crowds, leaving Vittorio and Nenna laughing like fools.

~

The young boys went on home, cutting across to the island, like feral creatures with their own pathways through the city, their own adventures to have. Nenna didn't want to return immediately.

She said, 'Come on.' She wanted to walk along the river. 'You're leaving so soon,' she said. 'I haven't seen you properly for ages. All this work – I've been thinking perhaps you were avoiding me.' Her eyes were sparkly and the evening was drawing in, a little damp and misty, a sense of chill off the water, and the scent of dying leaves.

She looked, to Tom, as if she knew everything, understood everything, and forgave everything.

A terrible thought came over him: I'm going to kiss her. *I'm going to kiss her. This is terrible, I'm going to kiss her.*

Resisting that became his only responsibility. He could move his feet, in this ostensibly innocent stroll, and he could resist this thought.

He didn't kiss her. After only a few yards of strolling, she, overcome by how much she was going to miss him, flung her arms girlishly around his neck and kissed him, on the cheek, and rested her head against him, hugging him tight as she would Marinella, or a beloved dog, and saying, 'Give me a proper hug, you've been so offish with me.' And he, poor Tom, overwhelmed by the innocence of her gesture, indeed the innocence of her entire person, was simultaneously overwhelmed with the most unavoidable, the most inconvenient, the purest, hardest flood of male desire. His body could not but thrill to it, while his mind said, *You sneaky shit*; his body revelling, coiling in response, and his mind shouting, *You are required to ignore this!* He tried desperately both to glory in and not to notice the soft, irresistible impression of her breasts against his chest; her thighs, *God help him*, against his, her breath on his neck. Meanwhile his hands spread wide and stark as starfish inches from her flesh, trying not to land on her back or her – *oh God* – and his voice strangled, trying not to gasp her name.

It was not possible—

This was the situation when Aldo walked up, tapped Tom on the shoulder, turned him round, and punched him in the face.

Tom reeled. It was a good punch.

Nenna shrieked: 'Papà! Papà what are you doing!'

Aldo, without looking at her, advancing again on Tom, bovine, his arms swinging, said, 'No, what are *you* doing, *puttana*? Go home and tell your mother.'

Nenna yelled. Her outrage was magnificent. From the still centre of his spinning head, Tom heard and admired. But something was said that he missed, and when he was able to look up and see, she was not there. Clutching a handful of blood, from his nose? His mouth? – Tom coughed and tried to say, that's not it, Aldo, it's not what you think – but something in him knew that Aldo had recognised what Nenna had not, and that Aldo was right, and Tom stank of lust and was guilty, and therefore could not hit him back.

'It's not her fault,' Tom said, to which Aldo replied, 'Of course it's not, you goat, you tramp,' before hitting him again.

Tom found himself on the road, suddenly, a horse going by clip clop clip clop very loud, the bones of his arse jarred, his eye shut, his head ringing. Looking up he saw Aldo swaying about – two Aldos, and some other people – men? They dissolved back into individuals under the streetlight. Aldo, and two men, one of whom was swinging a cudgel.

'Don't want to go messing with Fascist girls,' said the cudgel man, in a wheedly voice, and fear bit into Tom deeply – but Aldo, his eyes on Tom, had his hand out towards the man, low, in a gesture of 'we won't be needing that'. He put his other hand out to Tom: an offer of assistance.

Tom eyed it, and got up on his own, his fingers delicate on the cobblestones. He took his handkerchief from his pocket and Riley came into his mind: *dignity, pride,* he thought. He put the handkerchief to his nose, breathed gently – through his mouth – and said, carefully: 'This was not what you think, Uncle. However. I won't mention it to my mother. And Nenna has done nothing wrong. I'll go for my bag now, if you don't mind.' Then one of his teeth fell out.

They all looked at it. Tom carefully folded himself down to pick it up: a gob of bloody pearl on the slate-black cobble.

'Hm,' he said, and put it in his pocket, and unfolded himself upwards, carefully.

He pushed past Aldo, tempted to bash him with a disrespectful shoulder as he passed, but resisting. His head hurt to buggery.

Just go back to the house. No more damage here. Hardmen with a cudgel! Jesus.

∽

Back at the house, Susanna insisted on cleaning up Tom's face, and he let her. He was still so surprised! Aldo coming at him – *but we're family!*

While washing out his mouth with salty water at Susanna's instruction, he had a slow and important thought: he retrieved the tooth from his pocket, rinsed it in the glass of water, and carefully put it back into the gap it had left. Somebody – Nadine? – once said this was the thing to do. It was an upper tooth; gravity was not on its side. He clenched his jaws to hold it, grinned and said to Susanna, unclearly but very politely, 'Thank you for everything, I must leave now.' He collected his things, and said, through his teeth, to anyone who came near him, 'Nenna is not at fault. Aldo has misunderstood. Nenna is not at fault. Nothing improper has occurred.'

Nenna was standing like a ghost at the door when he stood. He said to her: 'I believe I may be in love with you. I'm awfully sorry. And really it is a terribly bad idea for Italy to invade Abyssinia. They only have thirteen planes, you know, and four pilots. And one of them is Hubert Fauntleroy Julian.'

There was a night train going north; he just got on it, and off it rattled, and his head, his teeth, his thoughts, his feelings. *I'm being churned,* he thought. *A lovely mozzarella of clarity will emerge from this milky mush. Fetid thought will drain away leaving islands of good solid intelligence . . .*

He had thought it was good strong nationalism, with a touch of the buffoon. But it was not.

What would she be thinking now?

Thirteen planes! Not even a rugby team. And four pilots.

'Don't want to go messing with Fascist girls.'

Dux Mea Lux.

A folksy, charismatic, dangerous brute.

Building Italy – into a stinking mess of corruption, violence and wrongness. Power is dirty – but that dirty? It wasn't as if he had never heard of the *squadristi* and their violent ways with people who didn't play their game.

Matteotti, Matteotti, Matteotti . . .

He did know that Mussolini loathed democracy (two foxes and a chicken discussing what was for dinner, Riley calls it – and himself a complete democrat, a Fabian even). It wasn't that he hadn't seen the faces of Blackshirts before.

Aldo! So unnecessary—

Yes it's all very manly, national strength is good, patriotism is a natural urge. Those little blue houses are very clean, those fields very big—

Look at it. Actually look at it.

There were swamps in his mind from which he could salvage nothing. Uncomfortable, he fell asleep, head jolting against the seatback, images of Riley, Nenna, Aldo, and the Duce bobbing through his dreams.

He woke with a start, God knows where, to the mighty shunts and jerks of train and carriages coupling or uncoupling. He was thirsty.

Jesus! I told Nenna I love her!

Also—

The compartment had filled with young men; their strong legs, their canvas bags, their five-o'clock shadows, their stertorous sleepy breathing building up a fug. Some pools of light from outside illuminated their faces.

211

They're my age, he thought. *Born into it. It's normal for them; they know nothing else. It's different for me. I should know better . . .*

Being young is no excuse. This has been self-deception.

In London, it had seemed obvious to him that the English didn't understand the Italians. In Rome, he usually only saw Fascist newspapers, anyway, because there was nothing else.

There has been a thick layer of scales over your eyes—

When are you meant to realise?

—and each person's scales are stuck on with different glue, and each glue is soluble in a different moment of truth. And time passes and things add up and sooner or later you look up, you grow up, and you realise. You see how tidelines have shifted and boundaries flexed; the lighting has changed, the angles tilted. What was is no longer. A turning was made which you didn't notice, and in the trick of the eye strength became tyranny, determination became bullying, patriotism became xenophobia, self-respect became arrogance. Aldo swore obedience to a noble-looking little plant. He could not know the man-eating jungle it would grow into.

Would Aldo swear himself to Mussolini now? If he saw him now for the first time?

But so what. Here we are: Uncle Aldo, Nenna, and the whole lovely family—

Fascist to their teeth, proper Fascist—

And you know, Tom, what Fascism is.

~

Do I love her?

He was so ashamed to have been concealing the obvious from himself. In the low, debilitating way we know things we cannot bear to know, he had always known. Strange the veils which hide the obvious, when you grow up in the middle of them. And how very cold it felt, suddenly, without those veils.

He pulled his jacket round him. He could hear voices shouting outside, but he couldn't remember where the train was going. The spot on his head where he had landed on the cobbles was seething with pain. It felt very late.

The train started to move again, very slow, halting.

Was it the cudgel? Was it just that this man was all ready to dole out punishment with a weapon like that, for no reason, that the violence and the instant judgement was so close under the surface they could be called up, just like that—

No, it's Hubert Fauntleroy Julian.

It's the combination. It's everything.

He did not blame himself for not having recognised earlier what was going on, just as he did not blame Kitty, who was a kid, or Nadine, who was a woman. Or Nenna, who was born into it. Or—

You couldn't expect them to know – could you? But then, what do you do about it?

He couldn't think how to point it out to them.

Or indeed how not to. Should he?

What, when it might very well break their hearts?

But the hypocrisy burned under his skin. Truth once unveiled cannot be dismissed. Even if he wanted to dismiss it. Which he didn't.

I want . . . to have the courage to do something about it, and some inspiration as to what that something might possibly be. And I have neither.

He feared – a terrible fear – that Nadine had understood all along, and didn't care.

Well. There was a further paralysis in that thought.

There's only one question, really, he told himself, though the moment he phrased it that one question sprouted another three and each of those sprouted further ones of their own. He couldn't get comfortable. The side of his cheek was against the cold glass of the window. In the darkness beyond, half his own face looked back at him. He whispered his questions to himself:

Question: *Do I speak to Aldo about the fact that Fascism has gone horribly wrong and Mussolini is a fucking villain?*

Sub questions:

Do I tell Nenna?

Will they care in the slightest what I think?

Why would I say it?

Do I want to convert them from this love of the Duce?

What good would that do them?

Is it my business?

Will Aldo shout at me?

Will Nenna hate me?

Will Nenna hate me?

Will Nenna hate me?

I'm nineteen years old, I'm at university, I should be able to say what I think.

They won't care. They're so . . . soaked in it. It's been Nenna's whole life, her normality. It's their blood and bones. They have nothing else.

This was not how he had wanted to leave Rome. It seemed so far away already. He wondered if he would ever go back.

⁓

When the young men got off at Milan, a magazine was left behind on the seat. Tom stared at it for quite a while. He had never read it.

He sighed, leant over, flinched at the pain in his mouth, picked it up. A drivel of anti-Semitism greeted him. His stomach churned.

But they're Jewish.

How can they—?

He didn't understand.

⁓

He woke up again: the land outside hilly, early morning sun.

It was simple, really. At the beginning Mussolini had looked like Italy's saviour angel, and he had turned out to be something else. Mussolini didn't used to be anti-Semitic, and now, ganging up with Hitler, he was.

The mistake, he thought, *is not to realise that things change.* From which it was only a tiny leap of thought to *I have changed*. Or perhaps even, *I am changing*.

The worst enemies don't come dressed up as monsters, yelling their threats. They come as friends, helping you, and when you are in their debt of course you forgive them. You've given up your sense of proportion.

I've been bamboozled.

Chapter Eleven

London, Autumn 1935

'I got in a fight,' Tom said, before Nadine or Riley could say anything. 'Just a stupid thing.'

They accepted it, not that happily, and for that he was grateful.

It was Nadine who said, quite quietly, while helping him pack for university, 'Aldo mentioned you left in quite a hurry.'

Tom paused for a moment, stared at the small pile of poetry books in his hand, Tennyson and T. S. Eliot, and said nothing.

'That you didn't say goodbye properly before you left. Nenna was upset,' he said.'

Tom cast his eyes up to the ceiling for a second, then broached the matter.

'Did you say goodbye?' he asked. 'Before you left?'

She looked at him steadily, and *thank God*, he thought, did not say, 'What do you mean?' She knew what he meant.

'I didn't know what to say,' she replied, after a pause. 'I pretended I couldn't see it, or that it wasn't real, or that it wasn't important.'

'Then what happened?' he asked.

'I saw it through Riley's eyes,' she said. 'I thought, what if I have to explain it to him? I felt that I was lying to him.'

Tom had been prepared to be angry with her. He had wanted to be – it could be her fault, as an adult, for not warning him, or explaining to him. But she disarmed him with her frankness and the look in her eyes.

'And have you spoken to Riley about it?' he asked.

'No,' she said. 'Oh no.'

'But you should,' he said. Then stopped. He was unaccustomed to moral ambiguity. 'Shouldn't you?'

'I don't think so,' she said. 'I don't see that there's any point. It would upset him, on our behalf.'

'But—' he began – and stopped, because there was nothing to say. It wasn't right, but—

But—

'Sometimes things just aren't right, darling,' she said, and she folded a jumper. *I'd better just look after myself,* he thought, and then wondered where the thought had come from.

He and Nadine had been, in some way, got. And then they had jumped back, almost, each of them separately, like children caught in the act of some naughtiness, and assumed an innocent expression – *who me? Oh, no, I don't know anything about that. Do you, Nadine? No, Tom, I don't.* Perhaps they hadn't believed that Jews could really be Fascists. Or that Fascists were somehow not as bad as some people thought. Or that Italian Fascism was really different to National Socialism in Germany.

Suddenly and strongly, Tom didn't want to go to

university. He wanted to go out, to be elsewhere: running, riding a horse, a motorcycle. Flying. Fighting. He wanted to shoot something. He wanted to be clean and fast and strong.

'I'm going for a swim,' he said. The green waters of the Serpentine would hold him, solid as glass as he powered through.

⁓

That first week in Cambridge, strolling into the Porters' Lodge, trying to feel as if to the manor born, *I'm familiar with the streets of Rome and London, Cambridge holds no fears for me*, he found a letter waiting for him. The sight of her handwriting did give him a thrill of excitement, and he tore it open crossing the green and grey purity of Great Court, a satchel of books over his shoulder.

Caro Masino,

I have been thinking perhaps it would be best to forget the last hours you were here. What Papà did, and what you said. It seems so odd that I am not sure it happened at all. But you are not here. This much is real. I am so sorry for what Papà did. I don't know what he thought – well, I do know what he thought. But I don't know exactly what he thought. I am showing him my anger by not talking to him; he is showing his by not letting me go out. So I have all the time in the world to read a letter from, perhaps, you.

My friend, my brother, whatever you are, sayer of an important thing which perhaps you regret, perhaps you

218

don't feel is true now you are back in England, in the land of the cold—

Papa wrote to Zia Nadina. I don't think he told her what he did.

Perhaps you have written to me, and a nice letter from you is caught on an Alp, fluttering in the wind . . . no letter has arrived here.

It seems a waste of postage not to fill the envelope, but I have nothing else to say until I know what is on your mind.

Write to me!

from Nenna with love

He stopped a moment in the draughty Gothic gateway, holding the flimsy piece of paper with a kind of respect. He liked how delicately yet directly she said what had to be said. He had never met a girl who was at all like her; who was human, and open, like this. But what did that mean – what could it mean? When only two days ago Mussolini's troops – her hero's troops – had attacked Abyssinia. The tune of the song sprang up in his head like a mockery: *Faccetta nera, bell'abissina* . . . Little black face, beautiful Abyssinian.

He had been laughing with her about those songs . . .

He was on his way to a tutorial, so he picked his feet up swiftly again as he strode across Great Court. His lecture schedule was full, and a chap on his staircase had said he was to try out for the boat club, but his first port of call was going to be the University Air Squadron . . . *This is a different world* . . .

He knew what he ought to do. He ought to write her a straight honourable letter saying look, Nenna, I'm not a Fascist, you are, in most cases political differences don't need to make that much difference but in this case, I'm afraid our principles are—

How pompous!

'Seeing your face all lit up at that rally while that big oaf—'

No.

'As long as you share your father's attachment to—'

And then what? It was pretty common knowledge now what was happening to anti-Fascists – *you lose your job, your*—

The problem wasn't Nenna. The problem was Italy.

In which case.

The solution was simple! And what a fool he had been not to have thought of it before!

He ran up the steps and through and out again into Nevile's Court without a glance at the architectural beauty which floored the world, skirted the lawn, slipped under the arcade and into the College Library. At a dim desk among the book stacks he sat down and wrote to her.

Nenna, my love

Listen, I have had the very best idea. Why don't you come to England to study? You liked it here, didn't you? You could stay with the family. Of course I would be here in Cambridge but the terms are very short, or – even better, yes, this is it – you could come up here – there's women's colleges and language schools – though to be honest you could probably teach in one – earn while you learn! – and teacher training and a hospital – and there are lots of marvellous courses in London too, and you could learn anything you like. You could start after Christmas. Nadine and Riley think it's a wonderful idea

(He hadn't told them – he'd only just had the idea – but they would think it a wonderful idea, the moment he gave them a chance to.)

and only a nincompoop would disagree. You, not being a nincompoop, will of course recognise this plan as the best idea anybody ever had, and start putting it into practice. You know what you have to do! I will ask Nadine to send details of colleges, etc.

He raced back out: courts, lawns, Trinity Street, post office, letterbox. Done. He laughed out loud, breathless.

Damn. Late for his tutorial. 'No running in Great Court, sir,' smirked a bowler-hatted porter.

It didn't matter. It was an inspired idea.

Later, he wrote to Riley and Nadine about it. Nadine in particular said Yes! what a wonderful plan, and took on the business of finding out about courses.

A second letter came. It seemed Nenna had not received the first:

221

L'Isola – Ottobre xx

Tommaso caro,

I know Papà can be a *capoccia grossa*. Is it because of him that you don't write to me?

He is busy all the time, working down in his swamps and busy with party activities. The Duce came to open another new city. It is amazing the work they are achieving. But if you are angry with Papà, just remember I am not him! There are boys here making eyes at me; I don't know if I can make eyes back, I don't know if there is someone I like who has made a claim on me – Masino, listen, if you have made a claim on me, please, repeat it, make sure I have heard correctly. Because it's not nothing, such a thing. And if you have not, I need to know. Because if you have—

Well.

Marinella sends her love and waves her little hands at you.

She had cried as she wrote that letter. To be stuck in her little room after school every day, the white ceiling and the white floor and her dark bed and outside all the sun and the cries and the people and the evening and the river.

And Aldo swinging about the place, and Mama just rolling her eyes and telling her to have patience, he'll get bored, he'll forget . . .

So she had nothing to do except schoolwork and thinking about Tom.

≈

This didn't change a thing. He did not regret the first letter at all. It all lay out before him like a beautiful landscape: she would be here, he would look after her, he would respect her and keep other boys off her, he would not try to seduce her, she could learn to fly too! And they would work hard and they would get married and have a beautiful exciting life together.

'I am not him!' He laughed at that. *No, you're not. You can be saved, I can save you.*

Her next letter said:

Tommaso,

You are a genius. No idea has ever been better. I have asked Mama, she is going to talk to Papà. This would be so good! Tell me, please, which schools I can write to. I do want to be a teacher I think, Papà says it is a good work for a woman, so he is more likely to agree. Then I can teach English here and Italian there – does anyone in England want to learn Italian? Or I can teach little children – or be a proper *professoressa*. I am very excited and you are very clever. Thank you!

Your not-nincompoop (I had to look this word up. I like it very much), Nenna

Something about this letter made him so happy that he replied with the extravagance of a telegram:

DEAR *NON-NINCOMPOOP ONLY FAIR TO SAY WHEN IN ENGLAND NO ENGLISH CHAPS ALLOWED TO MAKE EYES LOVE*

When that went winging its way, he felt a great sigh; an expansion and a settling. A decision made. A path ahead, clear and well-lit. He felt happy.

~

Meanwhile, he acquired a motorbike. At first, he tried to talk Riley into talking Peter into paying for it.

'Earn the money or ask your father,' said Riley.

Tom, heartened by his new independence as an undergraduate and inviter of women (women! Women? Was Nenna a woman?) from overseas, asked his father. He made Riley go with him, and Riley smiled all the way through the conversation, because this was the first proper conversation Peter and Tom had had since – well perhaps ever.

They met for lunch, the three of them, at a little restaurant in Kensington. Tom realised he had hardly even seen Peter for months. Walking in, he felt for a moment like the small boy, the cross boy, that he used to be – but then – no – he had an overcoat now, and was as tall as his father.

He held out his hand: 'Hello Father,' he said. And Peter took it: 'Hello Tom.' And each saw what a matching pair they were, how very alike in looks, in manner, in carriage. Tom blinked. He had spent his entire childhood insisting he was not and would never be anything like his father. But his father was sober and clean, his face was in focus, clear.

'How are you, sir?' Tom asked, as the chairs were pulled out and napkins snapped.

'I'm very well,' Peter said, and gave him a little smile and nod, and something unspoken and very British slipped into place between them. Tom was mystified. Was it manhood, in some way? A silent acknowledgement of adulthood? He glanced at Riley, but Riley was looking at the menu.

Mild embarrassment, small talk and mutual observation covered the soup and the main course. Riley compèred, with chat about Nadine, and mention of the Italian girl who they hoped would come over to study. After the steak (shepherd's pie for Riley) seemed to be the moment to bring up the motorcycle. Peter raised his pale eyes to Tom's and said: 'Tell me why you want it,' to which Tom responded thus: 'I will need it for taking Nenna around, and also getting out to Duxford, and I'll need to get out to Duxford because I'm an Officer Cadet now, and I am to learn to fly, and if I can't learn to fly I'm not staying at university. I could easily go to the bad in the London fleshpots, that would be all right for me but I don't suppose any of you would care for that, but I think the best thing for me would be adventure. Travel, and so on. Souks and temples – from above, of course – the sky and the stars. I might volunteer with Miss Earhart, or fly the mail from Florida down to Rio. And then if there is a war I can come back and die heroically for the RAF. What do you think? Would that do?'

His head was just a little bit cocked; he felt defiant and certain, full of his own plans.

Peter blinked at him. 'The RAF won't let you die heroically without a degree,' he said, not in the least bit truthfully. 'I'd stick with the sciences if I were you.'

'And the motorbike?'

Peter looked a little puzzled, and said: 'Well of course.' Then, as if it were an afterthought, 'Just don't crash it.' And he gave his son a sudden, rare and tender smile, which Tom blinked at, before leaning forward across the table, to the peril of the salt and pepper, to shake his father's hand and say, 'Thank you, sir.' Peter's other hand rose, as if to touch his son's arm – but then he stopped and said, without looking at Tom, 'You can come and talk to me any time, you know. You don't have to need something. You don't even have to bring Riley.'

Tom sort of half raised his eyebrows, then dropped them again, as if they had surprised him.

'Thank you, sir,' he said again, and sat down.

We don't seem to be on bad terms, he thought. *Everything seems possible!*

He celebrated the feeling by collecting Kitty from school. She came out on her own among groups of laughing, self-aware girls, and the droopy unmoving angle of her head revealed her loneliness among them, her need to be wanted, and the desire to be left alone that had grown up around that, trying and failing to preserve some dignity. When Tom, elegant with his collar up, hailed her from across the road, every straw-boatered hairclipped head turned. He saw it, and called her 'darling' loudly, bestowing his handsome smile on all around, and resolving to pay a bit of attention to her, she looked terrible. 'Today, my dearest,' he said, loud enough to carry, 'You are going to come and help me choose a motorbike' – and the ripples swelled into waves of wonder and whispering – Kitty! Little fatty Kitty Locke!

Tomorrow I'll bring her into school on the bike before I go back to Cambridge, he thought.

Of course she wasn't really going to help choose. He was getting a BSA Empire Star – the one with the removable

226

electric headlight on a cable so you could check for faults in the dark. 'Though it has no faults,' he said, gesturing, at the motorcycle showroom on the King's Road, 'because it's the Masterpiece of the Industry. Look, it says so here . . .'

He did let her choose the colour of his extra crash helmet. 'But I'll tell you a secret. It's really for Nenna. She's going to come and live in England. She's going to be my girl!'

'Really?' Kitty said. 'That's wonderful.' And though it came out wistful, she seemed to mean it, which stopped him for a moment, and made him look at her.

'You happy about that?' he said. Extraordinary that he should be asking her opinion, really, he thought, but—

'I am!' she said, and she smiled a real big glowing smile, with her blue eyes full of sweetness, and Tom gave her a sort of hug, and found he was ruffling the hair on her head.

'Tom,' she blurted. 'Some girls at school said I was anti-Semite. They took my diary from my locker and read it and I'd written that I was glad Deborah Schwarz couldn't come on the school trip because it was Passover and she's Jewish so she couldn't come, but I wasn't an anti-Semitic, I just don't like her because she was trying to get Eleanor Hardwick off me and Eleanor's pretty much my only friend . . . if you can call her a friend . . . and nobody else likes her very much except for me, and I don't think Deborah would like her for very long either, so I was glad she couldn't come, so I said I can't be anti-Semite, my mother is Jewish and they said well then why don't you go to Jewish Prayers then, instead of ordinary prayers like everyone else, and I didn't know what to say except tell them Nadine's not my real mother but I wasn't going to tell them that; they called

227

Susan Mack Floppy-Doppy Baby and she wasn't even really adopted—'

'Would you like me to kill them?' he said. 'With my bare hands? I could, if it would help?'

She smiled.

'Otherwise, it might be more convenient, you know, if you just – when they start talking like that – imagine them on the lav, you know, having a bit of trouble, straining . . . Then you'll laugh, and that'll spook them and they'll run away.'

She smiled some more, and looked down. Pleased.

He gave her a sort of hug, and said: 'Good oh! Now come on, Titch, put this on,' and he helped to strap her into it, her yellow hair fluffing and her hairclip needing to be removed. He could feel Kitty's joy all the way back to Bayswater, through the leather of his new jacket and the howl of the engine. *How little it takes to make her happy*, he thought. *I shall be nicer to her.*

All of which made Nadine's news all the harder. She had had a letter from Aldo. Absolutely not, he said. Nenna was too young, she was needed at home, it was out of the question, an absurd idea. What father could allow it – a daughter that age, going to another country, living away from home? He was amazed Nadine would even suggest such a thing. No further discussion. Absolutely not.

Nenna's letters were full of fury; her father's injustice, her mother's spinelessness, Vittorio's passivity in his sympathetic agreement that their parents were outrageous; Stefano saying 'well I never wanted you to go anyway'. Tom's were full of Nadine's advice: be patient, this can happen later. Time will pass. This wasn't what he felt though. What he felt was pure incomprehension. It was such a good idea! Why would Aldo forbid it?

Tom didn't write to Aldo to seek to persuade him. He still felt the look in Aldo's eye before the second punch. The look which knew exactly what Tom wanted. Tom suspected – knew, really – that he, Tom, was the reason why Nenna was not permitted to come.

He closed his eyes at the thought, and decided to calm it all down. Cool off. Wait.

Trinity College, November

My dear noncompoop,

So we are not allowed to start our adventure yet. Never mind. Every day we get older and nearer to being able to do exactly what we want. Pacify your old dad, and let's see how it goes. It all seems to have got rather heated so let's keep our heads down . . .

Masino,

The reply came soon. Papà really has gone off you. I mentioned that we'd probably see you in the summer, and he blew his top. Partly I want to blow my top right back at him but why bother? He will always shout louder than me. But today has been a happy day – the *Giornata della Fede*. I went with Mama and Zia Seta to the Temple where she gave up her gold wedding ring, and was given in exchange

229

a band of patriotic steel. Then we went up to the Vittoriale, to the altar of the Unknown Warrior. It was so beautiful! Thousands of women, with choirs, and braziers, and the Archbishop of the Armed Forces leading the ceremony. It was as if everyone was marrying the Duce, all of them – Mama, all the aunties, Christian and Jewish, old widows and young brides marrying the Duce and the army, declaring their faith and giving their wedding rings. And all the husbands looking on and approving. Papà wasn't there though, he was at the inauguration of Pontinia, you remember, the fourth new city of the Agro Pontino. The Duce made a speech: 'We inaugurate Pontinia today on the Day of Faith – the day on which all the fruitful mothers of Italy give, on the Altar of the Fatherland or other monuments to the fallen, their wedding rings – but a day also of the faith of the Italian people in their rights, a day of certain and undefeatable faith in the destiny of the Fatherland.' They were both so happy when they came home, so proud and joyful to be part of something so powerful and productive. We are so lucky to have our Duce.

It's so clever isn't it that it's the same word, fede, for faith and for wedding ring. I wonder who thought of it. Really, Masino, I wish you could have seen it. It was as if everyone is in love with him, and with Italy. It's so personal. I stood with my girlfriends and we all wished we were married, so that we could give our rings too.

This letter made him furious. It made him think: *there is no time. I must get her away from him, from them, from It. Before it poisons her any further.*

There didn't seem to be anyone he could talk to about this. He wasn't going back over this ground with Nadine. Riley, clearly, must never know the levels of Aldo's Fascism. Carmichael? No. Kitty crossed his mind for a moment, as a confidante, and that made him smile. But there was nobody he could think of.

~

Peter decided that everybody was to spend Christmas at Locke Hill. He was thinking about telling them about Mabel. Preparing the ground for telling them. The double life – *it is a double life,* he thought, *like some sordid man in the papers. How did that happen?* – was tiring him. He wanted to invite her for Christmas too, but she wouldn't come. She had to stay with her mother, and he was to go ahead and have Christmas with his children and Riley's family. She was quite insistent. So, he was looking forward to seeing everybody and was sorry when Riley rang to say that Kitty was not well, and they would have to delay their arrival at Locke Hill by a few days. Kitty was the pleasure he was looking forward to – she was so easy to cheer up.

Tom did not get the message, and Peter thus found himself, for three days, alone with his son.

Tom arrived halfway through dinner.

'I don't need anything to eat,' he said, his hair sticking up and his eyes shifting. 'Thank you, but really. I'm jolly tired, actually, so I'm just going to go on upstairs if that's all right.'

He's so formal. He's so—

Peter sat on his own at the table laid for two, and ate his

mutton chop. It seemed ridiculous. Mrs Joyce looked in and Peter didn't care to catch her eye. He picked up the bone to gnaw it, listlessly, then wiped his hands on the napkin and went into the sitting room, where he collapsed on to the sofa. *God, I'm making old man noises when I get up and sit down.* He picked up the telephone receiver.

'Mabel?' She was out, of course – no answer, she'd be working. He read for a bit, knowing she would ring him when she came in, and she did. He spoke to her then at length about how much he wished he could be a better parent to his son, who was now almost grown, and whether it was all too late, and what he could do.

Mabel was quiet. 'You always do your best,' she said. 'You can't do more.'

Peter took those sweet words up to bed with him.

Tom heard his father's footsteps passing. He wondered why Peter was up so late. He'd heard the telephone ringing – after midnight – and the low rumble of voices from the room below. It reminded him of being a child, that sound of adults talking downstairs, having dinner. That must be a very old memory, he thought. *You left this house when you were, what, four?* He wondered if this would be his oldest memory. He wondered who was calling his father at this hour. He wondered if he wanted to know, and why he didn't know, and acknowledged that he simply didn't know his father.

The next day Peter had to go to London, leaving early, back in the evening. But Tom that night went out with a friend in the neighbourhood; a longstanding promise, he said as he left, even his strides looking more and more cheerful as he headed off down the drive. Peter sat down alone to dinner again, and wished he'd stayed in town. He could have stayed the night with her.

It was embarrassing.

He could not bear it.

No, that was not what he wished. He wished his boy would sit down to dinner with him.

Peter had bought a clattery wooden backgammon board in Athens before the War, with a zigzag of dark and pale inlay and four vast dice. Before dinner on the third night he whipped it out, saying: 'Come on, it's about time I taught you something.'

Tom jumped slightly at this.

'It's what fathers do, isn't it?' Peter said, mildly. 'Teach their sons?'

Tom raised his eyebrows and agreed to sit across the low table in the drawing room. The fire was blazing; the sherry dry. Peter had set it all up.

He laid out the board. Tom watched dutifully as the stacks of pieces took their positions.

'Best of three, to start with,' Peter said. 'Throw the dice – ah! Three and five, very good. Classic move – here – five from here, three from here – and you've built a block, do you see?'

He guided his son through the game: 'You go that way round, I go this. Don't leave yourself open or I'll take you. You want little stacks of two or more – ah! Five and a six – the lover's leap – do this. You see?'

Tom smiled. The lover's leap was a neat little move.

The thwack and rattle of the dice and pieces were a soothing sound.

'Is it luck or skill?' Tom asked.

'The perfect balance of two,' Peter said.

Tom won the first two games, with Peter's direction, then lost two, then won two more on his own.

'Extraordinary how various it can be,' Tom said. 'And rather more . . . lively . . . than chess.'

Dinner interrupted them.

After the ham pie, Peter looked up at Tom and said, 'Tell me the most important thing.'

Tom was startled, but Peter said nothing more: just looked at him, clearly. And so, much to his own surprise, Tom answered honestly – thoughtlessly almost, as if bewitched.

He said, 'If you love a girl who has filthy politics, but only because her family and background have filthy politics, do you save her from herself or throw her over?'

Peter felt a weight shift inside him.

'How filthy?' he said. 'The filthier they are, the more you have to save her.'

He saw that Tom had not expected that, and sat quiet for a moment. Perhaps he had jumped in too bumptiously.

'Italian Fascist,' Tom said.

Peter thought a moment.

234

'The cousin,' he said – and Tom threw back his head, and acquiesced.

'Oh dear,' Peter said.

'Do you see?' Tom said.

But Peter was so happy to be confided in that he almost could not hold in his heart at the same time sorrow for Tom's dilemma.

'She wishes she were married so she could give her wedding ring to Mussolini.'

Peter recalled Nenna's long hair and bright eyes.

'Then why do you love her at all?' he said, and Tom acknowledged his injustice, and said, 'Of course she is more than that.'

Of course, Peter thought. *Of course she is more than that* and he saw in that bright moment that his son was in the same situation as he was – he loves someone he shouldn't. He loves where there is a problem.

But it is not the same. There is nothing wrong with being negro. The wrongness is all in how you are treated. Mabel being a coloured woman is immutable. The Fascist girl chooses to be Fascist. It's in Mabel's body; it's in this girl's mind. There's something to think about.

'Love is not to be sniffed at,' he said, buying time.

'No,' said Tom.

Peter wanted, suddenly and very strongly, to tell Tom about Mabel. He didn't. *This is Tom's moment to talk to me. Not mine to as it were trump him.*

'I was in love all the time at your age,' he said. 'Different girl every week.'

'I do like Nenna, as well,' Tom said. 'And she's like family.'

Peter wanted for Tom never ever to be hurt. That was all. There had been enough pain in this family. Admitting that dashing Italian to the inner circles would, he could see, bring more pain. Riley was putting out another bunch of pamphlets, on Abyssinia, on Mussolini's policy in Spain – he would not be welcoming a Fascist girl into the family – but then—

'Does Riley know they're Fascist?' Peter asked suddenly.

'For God's sake don't tell him!' Tom burst out. 'Please. Please.'

Peter was taken aback by the strength of it, and the pieces fell into place.

'Does Nadine know?' and Tom's expression told him the answer.

Good Lord. That is a mess already. That's why she stopped going there. And Tom insisted on continuing – well.

'I see your dilemma,' he said after a moment. 'I know you like them but my feeling is you should have nothing more to do with them. For your family's sake and your own. If they – or she – change their politics, of course, that's a different matter. But people have to change themselves, in my experience.'

Tom was looking at him.

Peter smiled low and gave a dry little laugh and thought – *oh – I'm going to say something now* – and he did. It leapt from him like something released.

'You may remember something of how very hard a lot of very fine people tried to change me,' he said. He looked up. 'Do you remember any of that?'

The air around them, between them, had shifted. There

was heaviness suddenly, as if ghosts, for years concealed in the long velvet curtains, had stepped quietly forward to listen more closely to their conversation. Peter felt underwater.

'I see that you have changed,' Tom said. It came out stilted. 'And that it took a long time.'

'I changed because of other people,' Peter said. 'You, for example. Your mother' – he blinked – 'Rose, and Riley – but other people did not change me, or force me to change. Despite their best efforts. And believe me their efforts were the very best.'

'Me,' said Tom.

'Yes,' said Peter 'And I'm sorry, for all of it.'

Tom looked confused.

It's too much for him, Peter thought.

'Tom,' he said. 'If you are even asking these questions about the girl, thinking in these terms, perhaps this is a love you are thinking about sniffing at. We can talk about this again if you like, but now let's have our rice pudding and then you can thrash me some more at backgammon.'

'Of course,' Tom said, still sort of paralysed. He looked up at Peter in a kind of shock, and saw him for the first time.

~

Tom read the *Giornata delle Fede* letter again, and thought about what Peter had said.

I'm thinking about what my father has said! Quite extraordinary.

Am I getting a father? Something of a father?

237

The idea thrilled him. *He apologised! He said he changed, for me, because of me.*
Am I to forgive him, and get to know him?
Am I forgiving him?

~

After Christmas, back at Cambridge, Tom got this letter:

Epifania, 1936

Masinuccio mio,

I will not be cast down. You may not write to me often enough but I will write to you. Things are the same here. Papa is well and bossy; Mama is well and quiet, the horrible boys are well and getting bigger, the lovely little girl is well and lovely. The Nenna is pretty well, though she misses her friend. You know Faccetta Nera is not to be sung any more? They're worried about the slavery of love bit in the lyrics. And the *quando saremo insieme a te.* They want to change it to *quando saremo vicino a te.* Near you, instead of with you. It's because of miscegenation. They don't want to encourage brown babies. Why? Brown babies are so pretty. *Insieme* is a very personal word! Sounds like *inserire*/insert and insemi-nate/ *inseminare.* And inside, in English. And there's all that being kissed by the sun and wearing the Blackshirts' shirt . . . it sounds like a marvellous romantic escapade. Are you impressed with my English? I am working hard on it and reading Dickens.

(Tom, sitting in the corner of the Eagle with a pint of bitter, thought, *yes. I am impressed with your English.*)

I was thinking, about the night you left, when Papà thought you were kissing me. Before, I thought Papà was wrong – but now I was thinking – you did want to kiss me, didn't you? I recognise it now.

(A worm wriggled in his guts. *Why do you recognise it now? What has happened, that now you know more about kissing?*)

And anyway, here comes 1936, cold and damp so far, a New Year and what will happen? *La Befana* – who despite our being 1) atheists and 2) Jewish always used to bring me something, has this year brought me nothing – because my mother says I am too old. Perhaps she – *la Befana*, not *la mama* – will bring me something else nice, something direct to me, suitable for a more grown-up girl.

Auguri to you, Masino, even though it is hard to speak to you when you don't answer. I am here.

Nenna

He wrote:

Cara Nenna, noncompoopa,
    I mean it. I meant it. I love you. Don't kiss anyone else.

He didn't post it.
Want, not want. Push me pull you.

239

What could he give her? *Aldo is right: she's too young. And I'm too young. And Peter is right: she's a Fascist fool in complete thrall to her daddy who is in complete thrall to Daddy Duce and oh, God. I don't need these people.*

And anyway he was very busy.

~

Come spring, Tom saw on the newsreels the scenes of mad delight in Italy when the Italian army entered Addis Ababa – the Duce stepping out on to his balcony like some high priest being adored in a vast temple. Riley gave him copies of the new pamphlets, which he accepted with a feeling of grubbiness. He read Haile Selassie's denunciation of the Fascists' use of poison gas against the civilian population. He noticed, wearily, that Fascist Italian troops were fighting republican Italian Brigades at the Battle of Guadalajara, in the Spanish Civil War. He read, not long afterwards, how Carlo Rosselli, head of the Matteotti Battalion, and a Jew, had been murdered by a Fascist gang in France. He saw the Duce parading around Berlin with Hitler, the puffed-up pigeon alongside the cat that got the cream. He saw news-reel of Florence draped in swastikas along with the beautiful Florentine lily, and felt sick, physically sick; Cellini's Perseus gazing on with eyes blind to history. *We were going to go there*, he thought, *and be in love.*

No. Push it away. She wants to give her wedding ring to Mussolini. Forget about it.

A person being deluded doesn't mean, does it, that there is nothing good in them? That they're not your friend any more?

Forget about it.

Forget about it?

What, really?

Then, what, write to her and tell her you're forgetting about it?

He wrote less, and shorter.

He bit his lip, and re-read the letter about the *Giornata delle Fede.*

He thought, and considered, and decided one way, and then another. He wrote a long letter to Aldo and Susanna, and didn't send that either.

When it came down to it, it was her choice, between him and Mussolini. And because he knew she would choose Mussolini, he didn't ask.

He missed her. He felt evil, as if he had left a child in the care of a wicked old man, with pinch marks all up her arms.

Part Four

1938

Chapter Twelve

London, Summer 1938

In the spring of 1938, Betty died gently, kissed and blessed, with Mabel at her side. Mabel's sorrow was bitter and dusty: yes of course she knew it was going to happen, but now? Now? Now she was alone, without her mother. When an old lady dies, having lived a life which had improved incredibly, then it is a passage, Lord yes, as history slips away with her deep eyes, but it is . . . normal. Mabel hadn't thought very far ahead, though. Now, through her mother's slipping away, she, Mabel, was a different generation. She held Iris very close, and thought, *Perhaps God is true. Even though I don't think God is probably true for me, please may it be true for Mama?*

Rather to her own surprise, after the initial grief Mabel's response was to grow suddenly bold. Without Betty, there was nothing, it seemed, to hold her back. Nothing to stay polite or careful for. What, not Iris? No. Iris, she felt, could now only benefit from boldness. *She's eighteen years old!*

This, Mabel knew, was a turning point, if she wanted one. And she decided she did. The past has glided on by;

the future is a strange beast: how about tackling it directly? It was as if Betty had taken with her old ancestral notions of shame and behaviour, of keeping your head down and operating within some invisible architecture of properness and fear. Mabel felt fearless now. Now, she was the mother – the only mother. Betty had borne her burden for decades, back in the States and here in Europe, she had been a God-fearing woman, a strong hardworking woman, and she had placed herself just so in everything she had done, because she had to, to survive. Just as Pixy had in her day. Nineteenth-century women. *But I am twentieth century*, Mabel whispered to herself. *I hold the power and the responsibility now. And I'm coming free. My girl grown and my mama gone.*

It was about one thing, really. It was wrong that Peter didn't know, and that Iris didn't know. Times *had* changed, and needed to be changed a little more.

All these years she had been Peter's three-times-a-week girlfriend in the beautiful flat in Belgravia. All these years she had gone back to the dark little flat in Soho where her mother and daughter lived. All these years she had kept quiet to Peter about her other life, and he had accepted it. And for eighteen years she had kept quiet to Iris about her father. *Eighteen years!* She rolled her shoulders back, and felt a cool wind around the back of her neck. Enough hiding.

So one very warm summer afternoon she took Iris to a café and bought her an ice cream sundae: vanilla with strawberry syrup and a cherry on top. She let her take two bites and said, 'Sweetheart, I have to tell you something important and I hope you ain't going to be mad at me.' She'd thought she'd be nervous, but she wasn't.

Iris looked up.

'I have found your father,' Mabel said. Plain and simple. 'I found him a couple of years ago and I've been keeping an eye on him to make sure he's good enough for you, and I think he may be. I want you to know that he doesn't know of your existence. He hasn't been ignoring you. He didn't know about you. I'm going to tell him soon, and then if he's the man I think he is you two will be meeting.'

Iris's spoon hung in mid-air like a cat going over a cliff in a comedy cartoon. Her eyes behind it were vast.

'Today?' asked Iris. 'Is that why the ice cream?'

'Not today. Like I said, I have to speak to him. But I wanted to tell you first.'

Iris's hair was slicked and curled like a grown young woman's; her face was suddenly childish.

'What if he doesn't like me?' she said very quietly.

'Doesn't matter,' said Mabel. 'More fool him. I do think he will, but if he doesn't, well, you know you can do without a father, having never had one up till now.'

Iris blinked.

'I should point out,' Mabel said, 'that I believe you saw him one time. When you came to the big white house beyond the park. There was a tall man who said hello to you.'

Iris remembered him. He had been so unlikely. That whole little outing had been so unlikely.

'That white man?' she said.

'Mm hm,' said Mabel.

'Is that still where you stay when you're not home?' she said. 'Or do you have some other boyfriend now?'

'Iris!'

'Well how would I know, Mumma?' She stared at her mother quite clearly, and Mabel found herself flushing. 'All I know,' Iris said, 'is I was born out of wedlock and you never told me anything. So excuse me, if you suddenly decide to confide in me about my own self, that I might have some questions. You've been keeping an eye on him? What does that mean, Mumma?'

Mabel couldn't speak.

'Does it mean that you've been going to look at him through a window every now and again?' she said. She had put down the spoon. 'While staying out half the nights of my life with some other guy? Or guys? Or, have you had him on approval like a car all these years? Since I met him? My father? To make sure he was good enough for me? And I never got to see him, to meet him, to have an opinion on him? *My* father?'

Mabel closed her eyes and said, 'Yes.'

'Yes what? What are you talking about – is he the friend?'

'Yes,' said Mabel.

'The boyfriend? All this time?'

'Yes.'

'Why didn't you tell me?'

'You were too little. But you're big enough now.'

Iris was looking at her. She was biting the side of her thumb.

'Let me get this right,' Iris said. 'Since I followed you to that house and saw him, all that time and maybe longer, I have had a father, living nearby, and you have been seeing him two or three times a week, living with him almost, and

I have never been allowed to see him, and he doesn't know I exist.'

'I'm going to tell him tonight,' Mabel said, 'and see how that goes.'

'No,' said Iris. 'Oh no. Just wait a moment. What I just said; that's all true. Yes?'

'Yes,' said Mabel.

'And now I'm big enough to know . . .'

'Yes.'

'. . . how you have cheated me.'

'I—'

'It's when a child is little that she needs a father.'

'I—'

'If you weren't the only parent I have, I would—' Iris said.

'Iris—'

Iris was shoving her fingers into the remains of her ice cream, and scooping it up. For a moment she stared at it on her fingers. Then leaning forward, she stuck her hand at her mother's face, and smeared it, to and fro, across and back. 'Ice cream,' she said. 'Ice cream.'

'Iris,' Mabel tried to say, but her mouth was obstructed and she was starting to cry.

Iris took her hand away, and stood up.

'Did Grandma know?' she said, and Mabel, who would often later wish that she had had the quickwittedness to lie, said, 'Yes.'

'Well,' said Iris. 'Both of you. That's—'

'I'll make it right,' Mabel said quickly. 'We'll give you both a little time to get used to it. If he likes the idea maybe

249

we'll go and live in that pretty flat. If he ain't keen on that, then how about we go and live in Paris?'

'Paris?' Iris said. 'Ice cream, and Paris? Can you add turning back time and behaving completely differently? Because if you can't—'

Mabel was wiping her face. 'Iris,' she was saying.

Iris shook her head, her body tensed and she turned away. 'Don't do anything, Mother,' she said. 'Don't talk to him. You're not in charge now,' and she moved away. 'Oh,' she said. 'What's his name?'

'Peter Locke,' Mabel said.

'Peter Locke,' Iris said, thoughtfully. 'White man!' Then, 'Don't go back to that flat,' and she walked off.

~

Iris was angry, but it was not anger that propelled her. It was curiosity and a very pure, immutable pull. It brought her through Soho and Mayfair down to Hyde Park Corner, across the roundabout, and into the white maze of Belgravia, where the houses were taller, the roads were wider, the squares leafier, the people fewer, their shoes shinier. It was a discreet area. The houses had no expression beyond prosperity; if anyone looked out it was a servant, and not the kind who would chat or reveal.

Iris assumed that Peter Locke lived at the flat all the time. It was him she was drawn to.

She didn't know where the flat was, which street, which number. They all looked very similar. She remembered . . . black railings at her back, a junction to her left, a lilac tree in bloom, which wouldn't be blooming now, or would it?

She had no idea. A garden square divided into four by roads? Second house in from the corner? She wandered. She came across something likely: Eaton Square. Quartering it like a harrier, she came to a corner and saw, hanging above her among dusty leaves, the rusty spikes of dead lilac. Sliding between two low and glamorous cars, she leaned against the railings and looked up. The casements above were blind and silent. Any of them could hold him.

She stayed there, thinking: *a father would have a job. Perhaps?* He'd be out, anyway.

He'll be surprised. He might not be pleased. He might be angry.

She remembered him coming across the road to her. He was tall. Even though she had been little he was really tall. He had a nice voice. *Posh, though. I am not posh.*

He won't be disappointed in me, not once he gets to know me. Not if he gives me a chance. He'll like me because I'll be a bit like him. He'll be happy. I think. But he'll be surprised, and—

Probably he's at work.

But he might hate me.

White people often don't like black people.

But if he's my dad I'm half white.

But it doesn't work that way does it? It's not maths. It's not fractions.

~

And Grandma had known too, and not told her, and she had been left out. Iris had always thought of her family as the Three Musketeers, three ladies on their own looking after each other. And now she was only one. Not one of three at all.

But he likes Mumma.

~

After two hours, Iris left. She'd come back in the evening. That's when fathers come home.

Mabel, who had been watching her from around the corner, fifty yards away, followed her, saw that she was going home, and slipped into a telephone box.

~

Peter had been going to come to Mabel's show that night at the Serpentine Room. She said, let's meet earlier, how about the John Snow. He said he'd had no lunch, let's eat before for a change.

Things had looked up for Mabel, professionally. She had fans, and more salubrious dates. She'd been selling her songs and writing for other bands too. She sometimes even admitted that they were her own, and not her daddy's. She only sang four nights a week now. Top of the bill. Tours round the country sometimes, and regular seasons in Paris. Her own band, much of the time. Reginald played trombone. Peter sat night after night; came in after a day either at the firm, or writing. They had their routine. It wasn't that she was bored with it.

So they went to Sheekey's, and ate dover sole. Peter sang the old rude song softly under his breath: 'The sweetest of fish, When placed on a dish, are soles, are soles, are soles!'

She found her heart was beating exceptionally strong. But there was no point looking ahead and fearing. She didn't even stop to think what it was she feared. The truth was the truth and the time was now. Iris's anger only made it more important.

He had just put a forkful of buttery fish into his mouth when she slid a photograph across the white tablecloth. Black and white, semi-posed, Iris, fourteen years old in school uniform, holding her own hands in front of her and squinting a little into the sun in the garden of Soho Square. Plane-tree dappled light. A sweet smile.

'Hello,' said Peter. 'Who's this?'

'My daughter,' said Mabel.

'Daughter!'

'Iris,' she said, and observed him. He looked – surprised. Not shocked or horrified. Surprised.

'Is she dead?' he asked.

'No!' Mabel yelped. *Unsay that! No she ain't dead! No!*

'Sorry,' he said. 'But – where is she then?'

'She's the reason I've been so private these years,' Mabel said.

His eyes were puzzled and frank.

'Protective,' she said.

'From me?' said Peter, bewildered.

Mabel gazed at him and her face broke apart into a scared, hopeful kind of smile.

'Honey,' she said. 'I've been a mother on my own for a long time. I've made some mistakes and I don't think this is one. This is our daughter. Yours and mine. I reckoned you're both ready to know about it. I told her today about you. I'm telling you now about her. I'm happy to introduce you any time.'

He was silent. An absolute silence in the clatter and clink of the restaurant. All she heard was the soft chinks of his thoughts falling into place.

'You never told me,' he said. 'Why on earth have you never mentioned this before?'

'Is that the most important thing?'

'No. But neither is it nothing.'

Silence.

'How old is she?' he said.

'Eighteen.'

'That's almost adult!'

'Yes.'

'Such a long time.'

'Yes.'

'I could have—'

'What?'

'Been a father.'

'No,' she said.

'No, what?'

'You couldn't have been a father.'

He raised his chin. His mouth twitched. 'What on earth—'

She said, softly: 'Do you want me to remind you?' and he blinked. 'About how we were, then?' she went on.

He turned his head.

'About how you were?'

And yes, he knew all about how he had been.

'I was a bloody mess,' he said. 'Unfit for decent company,

or any other, let alone for a woman to depend on. In such a situation.'

'You were,' she said. 'And that is why.'

'But for so long!' he cried, and his raised voice brought a look from a neighbouring table, and she said, 'Yes, it takes a long time, doesn't it? To get over things, to learn a little trust . . .'

'I wish it had been different,' he said, and he was suddenly afraid he might weep.

'It can be,' she said.

They paused, and breathed.

'Was that your only reason?' he said.

'Is that not enough?' she asked – but took pity on him then, and said, with a funny little laugh, 'Scared?'

'You're not a scared kind of woman,' he said.

'But Peter,' she said. 'You're an exception and a miracle. Not all men like their children born out of wedlock.'

He squinted at her, furrow-faced.

'Then we must marry!' he cried, and she said, without thinking, 'Oh, no, that's not what I meant' – but he grew excited. 'Would you? Shall we? It would be – then I can – please. Darling. Please. I really have been terribly remiss in not asking you earlier. I don't know what I was thinking. Please! Marry me!'

His enthusiasm grew a little noisy, and people at neighbouring tables were looking. Some of the younger ones, theatre-looking people, smiled and laughed. An older man flared his nostrils, caught eyes with his wife, and looked away.

Peter quietened. He took her hand across the table. He

255

said, 'Shall I go on my knee? Here and now? I will. Or just say yes. Then I can meet my daughter as her father sworn as well as by blood. Say yes. Please. Marry me.'

'One thing at a time,' she said, a little flustered. The spirit in the room was embarrassing her, though Peter didn't seem to notice it. She knew the piano player.

'I love you and you make me happy,' he said. 'I'll look after you forever. You can carry on with your music of course, if you want to – we'll be being awfully modern anyway, so why stop there? I won't be that kind of husband. My children will love you. And her. Please.'

His innocence seemed almost sacred to her. How could she squash it? He was what the world should be like.

'There are things we would have to face which even now you hardly know exist,' she said.

Marry him! What, and go and live in that house in the English countryside where she'd never been? With English countryside people who've never seen a black face in their English countryside lives?

'My dear girl,' he said. 'Surely we've come far enough that we don't let that sort of thing ruin our lives?'

He's right – it ain't about that. It's about love and freedom. Marry him and prove your point. Iris lives it, is it, in her flesh and blood. What hope is there for her if you can't even put it on paper?

She was gazing at him: fifty years old, those pale blue eyes, what he's seen, what he's done, what he is. What he's been through to get to where he is now. How he loves her. This is his response – real joy.

She leaned forward and whispered to him, 'Shh.' Her eyes

flashed up. 'I will. But secret for now. There's things we need to talk about. I don't want you tied to something you can't handle.' And he looked at her, and said: 'It's not about that. It's about you and me being happy together. And our daughter. What's her name again?'

'Iris,' she said, and she laughed.

'Pretty name,' he said. 'And you'll marry me?'

'Yes,' she said. *Sweet Jesus yes I will.*

And he jumped up and cried out: for joy, for champagne – 'Not for me darling, for you' – for the wedding march on the piano, for congratulation and love and amazement . . .

It being a theatrey kind of crowd in the West End of London, everybody laughed and joined in and were happy for them. Some, undoubtedly, were a little scandalised, though largely delighted to be so. *How modern!* they thought. Champagne was brought. The piano player made a perfectly friendly face at Mabel, and played a few chords. 'Hey Mabel,' he called out. 'You gonna sing for us?'

'You know I can't!' she called back. 'You know I'm contracted to the Serpentine Room tonight!'

'Ain't every night you get engaged to be married,' the piano player called. 'Come on, let's do it.' And that gave Mabel an idea.

Eyes were rolled, laughs shared. The maître d' made an announcement, and Miss Mabel Zachary whispered to the piano player with a smile. The chords started to rattle out. Her voice over the top, laughing and saucy, and every note sung through a beaming, glorious smile, as wide as love. 'Birds do it,' she sang. 'Bees do it. Even educated fleas do it. Let's do it—'

The maître d' sent the busboy out for roses; he pressed them into Mabel's arms. They smelt of honey and happiness.

Two couples, only, stood and ruffled themselves and left. Mabel noticed; Peter didn't.

Never mind them, thought Mabel. *They're the Old Days. Bye bye Old Days.*

∾

After her show, Mabel sent Peter back to the flat alone while she went up to Lexington Street. Iris was in Grandma's chair in the kitchen. Mabel woke her gently.

'He's at the flat if you want to see him now,' she whispered. 'Or you can go in the morning. He's waiting for you. I'll come with you, only if you want.' She sat on the arm of the chair and waited for Iris's head to move towards her, so she could put her arm round her, so they could be together again.

Iris looked up at her. 'It's not that easy,' she said.

'It's a start,' Mabel said.

'I might not want a start,' Iris said.

'Whenever you're ready,' Mabel said, humbly. Then, quickly: 'I gave him a photo of you. He's so excited! He's not angry or upset about any of it. He just wants to see you and to get on with it. He wishes I'd told him years ago.'

Iris tipped her head a tiny bit further.

'Uh-huh?' she said.

'He wants to marry us,' said Mabel. 'If you see what I mean.'

Iris met her mother's eyes. 'He does?'

'Mm.'

'You in love with him Mumma?'

'Always was, sweetie.'

Iris closed her eyes again. 'Waited long enough,' she murmured. 'Can wait till morning.'

~

At the root of everything, a child wants its parents. But then at exactly the same root, a child doesn't want its father suddenly to produce a secret girlfriend. When she thought about Tom and Kitty, Mabel had a very tight little feeling under her breastbone.

~

'You mean you're married?' Riley exclaimed, when Peter rang him.

'No!' Peter said. 'She won't actually marry me until I've told everyone in my family and they're happy about it.'

'Ah,' said Riley.

'Oh don't be like that,' Peter said. 'It's lovely news and everyone will be delighted for us.'

'No they won't.'

'Yes they will!'

'Have you told your mother-in-law?'

'Riley, don't be unpleasant,' Peter said.

~

Mabel was being alarmingly helpful. It was as if she was making up for the years during which she had said nothing. She wanted to be there when Peter and Iris met, to introduce them, to control it, to protect them from each other.

'My dear,' Peter said. 'I know you want to help. And I dare say we will need your help. But for now, I would like to see my daughter alone.' He saw her pupils shrink.

'Our daughter,' he said. 'Sorry.'

She smiled.

～

Peter met Iris in Piccadilly Circus – her choice. He saw her standing there in the middle, underneath the heavy grey Eros. She was upright and motionless in the swirling crowd: a tall calm girl, a little gangly, short hair under a little hat, a flowery dress with buttons down the front, a handbag held in front of her and a holdall at her feet.

Is she nervous?

Am I?

He wondered how he looked to her. Tall, a little gangly, short hair under his hat. He laughed, and walked up to her.

'Hello,' he said. 'I think that's what I said to you last time we met – of course it's what people always say, when they meet, so I suppose there's nothing particularly special – but it is perhaps worth noticing that it's the only thing I've ever said to you . . .'

He ran dry.

Her face was long, like Mabel's but bonier, like his but more beautiful. She had the slight indentations at the temple that his father had had; she had his mother's wide, mothlike eyebrows. She said, 'Well then, hello!'

'I do have a plan,' he said. 'It seemed a good idea to, for such a momentous occasion. Of course we must have some lunch. But I thought we might go to the pictures or – more literally – to the pictures, I mean the National Gallery, if you preferred that, so that we would have something to talk about, if we found ourselves growing shy or overcome, or with nothing to say to each other.'

'Oh don't worry,' she said. Her look was both mildly humorous and dead straight. 'I have plenty to say to you.'

'All right!' he said. She made him feel bold. She was superb. He wanted to – take her arm.

'I thought we might go to Sheekey's,' he said. 'It's a—'

'Oh, I know Sheekey's,' she said. 'I love Sheekey's.'

You're a mystery to me, he thought. A veil of wonder started to wrap itself around him, and infiltrate him. *I adore you.*

'Come on Pappa,' she said. 'No need to stare.' She was starting off up St Martin's Lane. He stared.

She turned back, and took his arm. 'Come on,' she said.

~

Peter was well known at Sheekey's. So, it turned out, was Iris. The maître d' looked from one to the other, and furrowed his brow mildly.

'Piero,' she said. 'This is my daddy.' Piero's eyebrows bounced around.

'And this is my daughter, Iris,' said Peter, courteously.

Piero blinked, and then rose like a zeppelin to the occasion.

'So, a bottle of Krug 1909,' Peter said. 'We've only met once before.'

Piero nodded and snapped his fingers to a minion. 'Congratulations,' he said, and then with a slight edge of

261

boldness, he said, 'And will . . . Madame Zachary be joining you?'

Peter's heart was pounding, soft, excited, healthy.

'Not immediately,' he said. 'But in general, yes.'

They went to their table giggling.

Iris said, confidingly, 'I think we're doing very well so far.'

He could have wept with gratitude.

'I always liked you,' she said, factually. 'Since I saw you in the square and thought you looked like Leslie Howard.'

'Leslie Howard?' he said. 'Do I? Well I suppose I do—'

'And I like him because he always plays the decent man.'

'Yes,' Peter said, and a fist squeezed his heart. 'I'm not sure I have been decent, though.'

'Well, you just haven't been here.'

'I—' he said, but she continued.

'Not your fault,' she said. She had a square forehead, and tiny freckles on her cheekbones. 'That's Mumma's fault.'

'Well please don't be angry with her about it,' he said. 'She did what she thought was right.'

'But you're a nice man,' Iris said calmly. 'And she knew I'd seen you. She should've told me who you were earlier. I am angry.'

'Well if you are, you are,' he said.

'I am,' she said. 'I don't think it's ever going to be the same for me with her. She stole something pretty big from me, keeping us separate.'

'She had reasons,' he said. 'I wasn't always a nice man,' and he stared at her frankly for a moment while a million things passed through his mind, and then he said: 'Am I to treat you as an adult, or as a child?'

'I'm eighteen,' she said.

'But where do we start?'

'We've already started,' she said. 'I started with you a long time ago. In that way, I have the advantage of you. I didn't know who you were, but I always knew you had to exist.'

That hadn't occurred to him. But of course.

'And will you help me?' he asked.

'Sure,' she said.

'But I'm your father. I should be helping you—'

'I'm sure you will. But you're not allowed to boss me around.'

'Jolly good,' he said. He felt he could talk to this girl about anything. Anything! Look at her. What a blessing. She felt somehow like him. He could see his blood in her veins. How magical, that she should appear, fully formed, so unknown, so familiar. So like Mabel, so like him. All this time, they had been joined together by this third creature. So much herself. Sitting across from her at the clean white tablecloth, he felt it like a sacrament. *I will do everything good and right.*

The champagne arrived. The charming ceremonial of popping and aahing and pouring and clinking was achieved.

'Now I don't take this stuff any more,' Peter said. He moved his glass a little away from him. 'It's not good for me. But I want its blessing and significance. So—' he turned his head swiftly for a moment, thinking. Then he quickly dipped his finger into his glass and, leaning across, he gently touched it to her forehead, and to his own. 'There,' he said. 'A sort of christening for us.'

She lifted her glass and said, 'I've never had champagne before.'

He smiled. The tradition proceeded: the first sip, the bubbles up the nose and the giggling.

'And now,' he said, 'speak to me. Tell me, ask me. Continue—'

'I'm coming to live with you,' she said. 'I brought my bag.'

His head fell into his hands.

When he looked up he said, 'Don't celebrate finding me by losing her. Don't do that.'

She was biting her lip, her face hard with unshed tears.

'And anyway,' he continued, 'we're getting married. Sort of all of us. You will have both of us.'

Even as he said it, he was thinking of Tom and Kitty. Three of them. A lot of ground to make up.

Something very unexpected happened. Mrs Orris, mother of Peter's late wife Julia, went to a nightclub.

Julia, in her day, had rather liked nightclubs – or at least the idea of them. In reality, they had always been beyond her reach: not the sort of place a respectable woman could go, not the sort of place Peter, then, would have taken her. Had Julia lived into the 1920s; had Peter's relationship with drink been different, had Julia not become jealous of everything he did that she did not understand, she might have found a way to lead a racier life, and sit listening to jazz late at night with a cigarette in a holder and a string of pearls down her magnolia back. But Mrs Orris? Never would such a woman be seen in a nightclub. Not even at the dangerous ages of twenty-one or thirty-five. And now, she was seventy-eight, as grand as ever, still with her air of a vast ship manoeuvring in three-point turns around the 1890s; still festooned in furs, her hats still unhappy, her voice still unleashed only in instruction, self-satisfaction or complaint.

Mrs Orris had been silenced, at lunch one day with a small friend, Antonia, by the small friend's son. He was of what Mrs Orris considered 'the unfortunate type', which meant that though he came from a decent family, he had turned after the War to the motor business. He wore blazers, smoked in front of women, and his moustache was over-thought-out. Had Mrs Orris known that Percy would be joining them for lunch, she might have made her excuses.

Percy, over the vegetable broth, was keen to tell Mrs Orris the latest. He took the full facial-expression tour through doubtful, concerned and apologetic before throwing 'the latest' out between the three of them: Peter Locke was running round with a negro girl! Yes, Percy had had it on the most reliable authority. Frequently seen in public together. At clubs, of course, but also apparently . . . during the day.

Antonia almost quivered with schadenfreude, and immediately began throwing glances. Mrs Orris listened politely, and blinked.

During the day!

'Well thank you so much,' she let slip, pleasantly, in Percy's general direction. 'So many peculiar things people say, these days.'

'When I say the most reliable authority, Mrs O, I mean, my own two eyes.' He paused, and stared at her. 'A "night-club singer", I gather,' he said, with a knowing and vulgar emphasis on the words. 'Rather well known! I saw her at the Serpentine Rooms.' He leaned forward a little. 'Jazz,' he murmured. 'You know, saxophones, that sort of thing.'

Mrs Orris murmured, 'Indeed!' and threw a look to Antonia, a woman-to-woman look which meant, 'Has he been drinking? Oh my dear, I am so sorry for you.'

Percy leant back triumphantly, and lit a cigarette. Mrs Orris was regularly a cow to his mother.

Mrs Orris gazed at him kindly. 'Dear Percy,' she said. 'So kind of you to be concerned for me. But you know it is a very long time since I cared about anything Peter Locke does.'

Antonia looked a little shocked. 'But your grandchildren, Jane,' she said, quietly.

'They are living very happily with Sir Robert Waveney's daughter, and her husband the war hero,' Mrs Orris said. 'As you know, Antonia.' This version had served her well for a long time. What would she do with children anyway? It had been bad enough having Tommy during the war, but there had been no choice then, one had to do one's bit. Tommy and Katherine were charming children; their annual lunch together was hardly a burden to any of them. Peter, of course, was beyond the pale. So even if this was true, she didn't care.

~

Only she did. Her dead daughter's children! Which is why she and her fox stoles ended up at a small table at the back of the Serpentine Room, sarsaparilla and opera glasses at the ready, next to an orchid in a pink cut-glass vase. She had come alone. There was nobody with whom she could share this quest – *and after all*, she thought boldly, *if one is forced to enter this modern world, one might as well take advantage of its liberties*. Apparently it is all right for a woman to go out on her own. Very well. Mrs Orris would go out on her own.

She received many stares and the odd snigger. They fell away before her progress like the high seas before the prow of the Queen Mary.

She settled herself, took a sip from her glass, raised her head and surveyed the room. The light was not very low, the tables well spread apart. The crowd looked thoroughly disreputable, the women half naked – but even Mrs Orris knew that things could be far worse. These were not common people, not cheap. The jewels were real, and the louche atmosphere was not vulgar. In fact, she recognised that it was rather fashionable.

She saw Peter almost immediately. He was unmissable, so tall and pale, like a heron. He sat down to the right, with – well. Mrs Orris took a deep breath. There he was, indeed, with a negro girl. She looked so young! Mrs Orris's lips tightened, and she thought, for a moment, with what she thought was pity and loving sympathy, *The fool! Can't he see how ridiculous he is making himself?*

Not that Mrs Orris would have known what one looked like, this girl did not look to her like a gold-digging floozie.

A nightclub singer. An adventuress. *Oh, say it: a prostitute. But perhaps not looking like one is part of it.*

They were chatting easily – the girl leaning in and laughing, Peter looking fond, relaxed. Happy.

Oh my poor Julia, Mrs Orris thought (which was more than she had ever thought while her poor Julia had been alive). *How thou art foresworn.* A very strong strange anger was coming over her.

The light changed, the band hotted up. The compère announced the singer—

Mrs Orris was confused. She thought Peter's – Peter's – well, that she was the singer. But the girl stayed with him, looking up keenly at the stage, anticipating.

Someone else appeared on stage. An older woman, a blacker woman, in a gold dress and an unmistakable cloud of glamour. A surge of applause rose around the room. Lazily smiling, the woman fluttered her fingers at Peter's table, and the two there glowed back at her. She clicked her fingers to the band, shrugged her shoulders, and slid off into that world, the audience at her feet, following and adoring.

Mrs Orris lifted her opera glasses, and saw, circled in their lenses, the gleam and glister of sequins and gold fabric tight over flesh; then, higher, the glowing, moving face of the singer: a happy woman, a musician, a professional, an ecstatic. The circles moved across: the dark hands, gesturing and flexing by her sides and up by the microphone; the mouth, the lips, curving and mobile as she sang and smiled.

Well. She'd seen what she came for. Her grandchildren's father with not one but two negro women, waving at one and laughing with the other, as if it were perfectly normal. She found she was giving little nervous tics of her head, shaking it. Leaving the room, shuffling through the shadows towards the exit, Mrs Orris felt a hundred years old. Only later, trying to get those sensual circled images out of her mind, did it come to her that the singer's left hand, making that starfish shape as she turned her head to profile, had been wearing an engagement ring.

~

The tragedy of being an unkind person is you have no friends. Even if you do, they do not like you and you do not trust them. Mrs Orris had nobody to talk to. Not even a pet friend like Antonia, the sole purpose of whom was to agree with Mrs Orris, could do in this situation. There was precisely nobody to whom Mrs Orris could admit vulnerability.

She returned to Berkshire, and was even more unpleasant than usual to her servants. She stared out of the window, and thought perhaps the vicar? But no. Not the vicar. The shame!

She was terribly terribly angry. It couldn't happen. It was unspeakable. Was it legal?

Did the children know? Did anybody know? The people in that unspeakable club? Did they accept it? An engagement ring – for all the world to see? What kind of a world was this becoming?

Well, she wouldn't let it.

She would speak to Peter.

~

Mrs Orris's invitation to meet for a cup of tea was delivered with a tone of insistence, and seemed unavoidable. Peter rolled his eyes, and went along on the appointed afternoon to the Devonshire Street Hotel, the respectable little place where Mrs Orris stayed when she was in town.

The tea was hardly poured before she opened her mouth and started. It was unspeakable. It was outrageous. It was to be put a stop to immediately. Did his mother know about this? Did the children know? Had he lost his mind? To imagine even for one moment that such a thing could be countenanced; of course she was fully aware that society had gone to the dogs and there were no standards anywhere any more, but some things, Peter. Some dregs of respect, if nothing else, surely, for the memory of his dear wife, her poor sweet Julia—

At this he raised his eyes and stared at her.

She continued — would surely give him pause, make him realise what a cruel and foolhardy thing this was, bound only to cause — here she stopped and her lips curdled with distaste and the inability to express quite how – how—

'Do be quiet,' Peter said.

'You've gone too far, Peter,' she said. 'If I hadn't seen for myself—'

'Be quiet,' he said. 'What are you talking about?'

She sat a moment, silent.

'What? What is it?'

'I hear you are getting married,' she said.

'I am. And?'

'To a negro,' she said, and her eyelids began to flutter, very fast. 'A singer. A—'

'To a woman,' said Peter. 'So, as gossip has told you before I had a chance to, there we go. I think that's all, isn't it?' He stood, and looked to a waiter for the bill.

'Peter!' she pronounced, in a tone of doom.

He looked at her, there on the little hotel sofa, all bundled up like something nasty you found in the attic.

'Peter!' – in desperation now. 'A negro!'

He leaned in. He couldn't help himself. 'Shut up, you horrible old woman,' he said. 'I don't give a damn what you think.'

She blanched, jerking back as though stung. He turned. *Oh Lord I've done it now.*

She said to him, 'Sit down, Peter. Peter, if you proceed in this madness, I will make such a scandal. Such a scandal.'

'What scandal?' he asked. 'This isn't 1885. It's not a Henry James novel. I'm an adult widower and Mabel is a free and single adult. There is no scandal.'

'Oh Peter,' she said. 'You are so naive. You will call it off. You can imagine the headlines, surely? Negro Jazz Singer Entraps War Hero?'

His fury was rising.

'I can't imagine what the children would feel about that,' she wailed. 'Can you imagine, Peter? At school? And poor Nadine Waveney . . .'

'Purefoy,' he said. 'They've been married since 1919.'

'After all that family has done for you,' she went on. 'To shame them so. To shame your children and the memory of poor sweet Julia – Peter, you will of course call this off.'

271

He stared at her. Amazed, really. *But perhaps that is foolish of me. Perhaps I should have expected this. Perhaps I have underestimated how much some people enjoy causing trouble for no reason at all.*

'Or I *will* make a scandal,' she was saying. She had on an insufferable 'for your own good' expression.

He flung himself back into his chair and grinned, suddenly. A wolfish grin. 'Waiter?' he called. 'Could you bring me a telephone?'

He stared at her and drummed his long fingers till it arrived, important on a tray, long black cable trailing. He picked up the receiver.

'*The Times*, please,' he said. 'Thank you, operator.' Grinning at her all the while. 'Diary, please. Yes, hello? Is this the Diary? I have a person here who wants to announce a wedding. No, for a sort of gossip piece, I think – excuse me—' he scarcely covered the mouthpiece with his hand and said, loudly: 'Mrs Orris, do you want to put the wedding in as an announcement? Or was it as a bit of gossip? Scandal, wasn't it you said?' He turned back to the telephone. 'Yes, hello. She wants to make a scandal. Can you help with that? No? Oh, wouldn't you speak to her? No? Oh dear.' He sounded genuinely disappointed. 'Well, in that case, may I give you the wording for the official announcement? Here goes: The engagement is announced between Mr Peter Locke of Locke Hall, Sidcup, and Miss Mabel Zachary of New York and London W1. The wedding will take place in October. Will that do? Good-oh. Send the bill to Locke Hall, would you? Thank you so much.'

She was silent before him. Crumpled.

'You're not invited,' he said. 'If your grandchildren ever want to see you again that's up to them. Goodbye.'

He left her quivering, an old blancmange in furs.

~

Peter walked furiously to Eaton Square, bashing the pavement with each step, shoulders taut and eyes blind. *Stupid bloody bigoted old cow. As much as called Mabel a prostitute. Snobbery and bigotry and racial prejudice and hatred and fear and stupidity.*

He let himself in and banged up the stairs. Iris was in the room which her mother had earmarked for her all those years before, reading.

'Oh dear,' she said, jumping up and coming into the sitting room.

'Iris,' he said. 'I'm beginning to see how the world can be nasty. I'm sorry. I – no don't say anything—' and she didn't. 'I refuse to be part of it, I refuse to engage with it. Now you know your mother and I are going to marry. And sort of put you right, for the future.' Here he smiled, and she smiled. 'That past business. We can get over that, I think – forgive each other and so on – you and I, your mother and I. You and your mother – I hope. All of us. But this black and white business, this negro or white business. Listen. We're us. Is that all right?'

She blinked at him. 'Well I hope so,' she said. 'But I can only speak for me.'

'Of course,' he said. 'I just want you to know that if it, um, affects you, if that hurts you, ever, I am here, and we are us.'

273

She blinked at him. 'Pappa,' she said, and he smiled at the word. 'You do know you're a white man?'

'I am aware of that,' he said. 'My point is, if ever requested to take sides, I'm on our side.'

'Well good,' she said.

'Good,' he said in turn. 'Good,' again, and patted her. 'Where's Mabel?'

'In her flat, I suppose,' Iris said, with a little hardness.

He gazed at the floor, his hand still on her shoulder.

'It's all right,' Iris said. 'We haven't been fighting.'

'This can't go on, you know,' he said. 'I shall spend the night with her there, if you're still insisting . . .'

'She can come here,' Iris said, drawing herself up. 'I'll just go where she isn't.'

'It can't go on,' he said again.

Iris picked up her book and headed to the sofa. 'I can't help it,' she said. 'I could lie about it but I'd rather not.'

'The point of our marrying,' he said, 'was to put things right, and now they're wrong again!'

'Sorry,' she said, and her lip went out like a child's, and he frowned. Had it been Kitty he would have hugged her, but this young almost woman was too much of a stranger to hug.

Oh God, Kitty.

'You know I was married before,' he said.

'Mm.'

'And that I have children.'

'Mm.'

'You should meet them,' he said.

She stared at him, her face silhouetted against the window so he couldn't see her expression.

'I should?' she said.

'Yes,' he said.

'Do they know about me?'

'No,' he said. 'Nor about your mother. I'm trying to see how to tell them.'

Oh God the announcement in *The Times*. He must cancel it.

'Would you like me to?' asked Iris drily. She moved her head a little and her smile, as it came into the light, was small and gentle, as if she'd lived for a thousand years.

'Good God, child,' he said. 'In some ways I shouldn't even be talking to you about this.'

'Why not?' she asked, and so he went over and sat on the sofa with her, and found that he could pat her head with his long hand, and say, 'How things change, my dear.' Then, 'Please, please, forgive your mother. Take your time, but please.' His eyes slipped in and out of focus, and he said: 'I shall give you two bits of wisdom, from the temple of Apollo at Delphi. Number one: *Panta rei*, which means, things change. Number two, *Gnothi seauton*, which means, know thyself. I don't suppose you've been taught Greek.'

'No,' she said. 'I know they had gods. Grandma didn't like them.'

'Religious woman, was she?'

'We all are,' Iris said. 'Except maybe Mumma.'

'Quite right,' Peter said. 'Keep ahold of that as long as you can.'

'What do you mean?' she asked.

'If you lose religion, you may well look for something else to fill the gap.'

Again, she asked, 'What do you mean?'

He smiled at her suddenly. 'I like it that you say that,' he said. 'Would you like to learn Greek?'

'Sure,' she said. 'Would you like to hear me play the piano?'

'Do you play the piano?'

'I'm quite good,' she said.

Peter thought about his cello, and the melodies he used to make up when he was young.

'Please,' he said.

~

Mrs Orris took her humiliation and fashioned poison from it, and she filled her pen with the poison and wrote a letter. *The Times* was not the only newspaper.

Dear Editor,

I wonder if you are aware that a negro jazz singer known as Mabel Zachary is attempting to entrap Peter Locke of Locke Hill, the war hero and director of Locke & Locke, the well-known law firm, into marriage? It might make an interesting story for your society pages.

Yours sincerely,

A Well Wisher.

It wasn't enough, though. Peter had made his point perfectly clear, but the children were a different matter. If Peter wasn't prepared to see sense on their behalf, she would speak to them directly. In the meantime, she was going back to Berkshire to rewrite her will.

Part Five

1938–9

Chapter Thirteen

Soho and Rome, July 1938

Kitty was, and it felt most peculiar, happy.

Why? she wondered. *It's worth thinking it through, for the next time I am miserable. But perhaps that's like sticking a pin through the butterfly, binding to myself a joy and thus the wingéd life destroying, when I should be kissing the joy as it flies and living in eternity's sunrise.*

No, I want to know why.

She was happy because she would never again have to go to school. Never again wear a horrible uniform and be told what to do. Tom had come and picked her up on the motorbike on the last day. She hauled her school skirt up around her thighs and straddled the bike like Boudicca on the run – Tom her chauffeur, not she his pillion. *I'll have my own motorcycle,* she thought. *Ride myself wherever I want to go, do whatever I want to do.* Vrooming away through the gates of summer: there was never going to be any more maths or physics or biology or chemistry, and she had won the French Prize and was five foot six and she would never see any of those creeps again, except Susan Westenra of course because she, Kitty, had directed her, Susan, in *Antigone* – in French! – and she had been superb. They both had.

She was happy because she wasn't going to university or anything like that. A typing course, if she had to – then work, money and life.

And she was happy because they were going to Italy again.

It had been very difficult to persuade Nadine. Kitty had tried over breakfast lunch and tea for weeks, and just got No No No. No reason given – or rather, a vast pile of reasons, none of them any good.

'We're not invited,' Nadine said.

'We soon will be, if we invite ourselves,' Kitty replied smartly.

'They may not want us.'

'Of course they will.'

'It's been a long time.'

'All the more reason to go!'

'I don't want to go travelling again without Riley.'

'Riley can come too!'

'No he can't.'

'Why not?'

'You know why not.'

'No I don't.'

Short silence, small frown.

'He doesn't travel.'

Gleam of triumph from Kitty:

'But he's going to the Venice Film Festival! That's travelling. That's Italy even. And if he can go to Venice with Mr Hinchcliffe to see someone possibly get a prize then surely he can come to Rome with the two women who love him best in the world, to meet your family?'

Nadine was quiet, and Kitty delighted. The unlikely development of one of Hinchcliffe's novels having been made into a film which was up for a prize was the star of her armoury.

'We must ask him at least! Perhaps he'd like to! We could all go to Venice . . .'

Kitty could not see why Nadine was being so bullish. But then Kitty never read the papers, and wasn't very good at putting things together.

'I don't want to go,' Nadine said.

'Then I shall go alone!' said Kitty, her final arrow shot. 'Tom did. I'm much older now than he was then.'

~

Nadine stewed with it. Stewed.

She stewed for a while with the various possible results of a reignition of the relationship between the families. Kitty might stir anything up there, if she went on her own. The risk of Riley finding out what Nadine had kept from him. The pash Tom had had on Nenna, for the decline of which Nadine couldn't be more grateful, and which she did not want revived in any way. The affection she, Nadine, had had for them all, and had been so sad to have to quash, when it became apparent which way the wind was blowing. *Poor dear Aldo, my blood relative. Pretty much my only one.*

Thoughts like that made her rush to her darling old father, to sit beside him at the piano and kiss his white head and make sure he had no egg on his tie.

No, no no.

'Well, I'm going,' Kitty said. 'You can't stop me. Why would you? You can't. I'm eighteen. It's just to visit my family. Peter will let me go.' She said this a lot.

And at last Nadine lost her temper, and said: 'Very well! Very well, we'll go. You and I. While Riley is in Venice, and then we will go and meet him there. Venice! How lovely.'

Actually, it wasn't the worst way out. She could at least keep the visit short; she could control a little what was going on, she could protect this dear but explosively naive smartypants from both her own folly and the attentions of the Roman male, and she could – she could be in Venice with Riley! The joy of that idea made her smile.

So that was the plan. ∽

Tom walked up Berwick Street on a hot July morning a month after graduating. He was thinking about what you could control and what you couldn't.

He had a summer job and a shared flat in Meard Street. Through his obsessions with flying and undergraduate journalism, he had achieved a shockingly bad degree, and so had turned from science with a humiliated nose-in-the-air shrug, and acquired a menial post as a junior reporter and, it sometimes seemed, as everyone on the *Daily Chronicle*'s personal researcher and slave. But today was his day off, so he was free to delight in the grubbiness and sophistication of summer city life. It was hot. Hot and grubby. This still only meant one thing to him: Rome. Which was on his mind anyway: for some inexplicable bloody reason that he could not fathom, Nadine, Kitty and Riley – Riley! – were all heading there at this very moment.

First Kitty had insisted she go again. Fair enough. No reason why she shouldn't want to. Hitler's visit in May, the Duce building a bloody railway station specially for him, and meeting him off the train with the King in tow, and laying bloody wreaths at the bloody Vittoriale monument and having bloody banquets at the Quirinale might put some people off, but Kitty's life is her own. That Nadine felt she must go with Kitty was fair enough, under the circumstances. Their Venice plan made sense – and then this morning he received this telegram: 'Riley arriving Rome please come can't do this without you love'.

I have a job!

And, more quietly: *I don't go to Rome.*

It was not that he blamed Nadine or Riley or – well, perhaps – Kitty for the situation. It was not that he didn't have a locked and frozen love for his cousins and for Italy still tucked away in his heart. Far from it. A part of him remained paralysed between the rock of his love for them – for her – and the hard place of his disgust with Fascism. But nothing that had happened in the past three years had made Italy, or them, any more approachable. Quite the opposite. *When that evil clown is gone, or my cousins see the light, then I'll go back.*

At the little specialist newsagent he picked up a handful of foreign newspapers including, for the sake of being well informed, the Fascist rag *Giornale d'Italia.* He strolled on towards Gino's Caffe. Coffee, the papers. A sunny London morning. *Be of good cheer,* he told himself – that sweet old phrase of Riley's. He did not want to think about it all. He wanted coffee. And a nice lunch.

And he was, for a moment, of good cheer. But then after his lunch he picked up the Fascist rag, *Giornale d'Italia*. Page three was headed *Manifesto degli scienziati razzisti*. He made a face, and read it, translating as he went, over his coffee.

'Manifesto of the racist scientists.' He took a sip.

'One: Human races exist. The existence of the human races is no longer an abstraction of our spirit, but corresponds to a reality that is material and perceptible with our senses . . . To say that human races exist does not mean a priori that superior or inferior races exist, but only that different human races exist.'

I wonder where they're going with that, he thought.

'Two:' it continued. 'There exist large races and small races. It is necessary not only to admit that the large classifications which are commonly called races and which are identified only by a few characteristics exist, but it is also necessary to admit that smaller classifications exist (as for example the Nordics, the Mediterraneans, the Dinarics – Serbs, Croats, Montenegrins) – identified by a larger number of common characteristics. From a biological point of view, these groups constitute the true races, the existence of which is an evident truth.'

He really didn't know what that meant, in Italian or English. It certainly wasn't any biology he'd been taught.

'Three: The concept of race is a biological concept. It is therefore based on other considerations than the concepts of a people and of a nation, founded essentially on historic, linguistic, and religious considerations. So, the differences of peoples and of nations are based on differences of race. If the Italians are different from the French, the Germans, the Turks, the Greeks, etc., it is not only because they have a different language and a different history, but because the racial constitution of these peoples is different.'

But Italy's only been a united country for seventy years – what about before? And why are the Milanese generally tall and fair and the Sicilians short and dark? And what about the rearrangements of the northern border after the war? What about the Trentino, and Alsace Lorraine? What about Nadine, half French, half English, and Jewish? This is idiotically simplistic.

'There have been different relationships of different races, which from very ancient times have constituted the diverse peoples. Either one race might have absolute dominance over the others, or all became harmoniously blended, or, finally, one might have persisted unassimilated into the other diverse races.'

'Blah blah blah,' he murmured.

'Four: The majority of the population of contemporary Italy is Aryan in origin and its civilisation is Aryan . . .

'Five: The influx of huge masses of men in historical times is a legend. After the invasion of the Lombards, there were not in Italy any other notable movements of people capable of influencing the racial physiognomy of the nation . . . while for other European nations the racial composition has varied notably even in modern times . . . the forty-four million Italians of today have arisen . . . in the absolute majority from families which have inhabited Italy for almost a millennium.

'Six: There exists by now a pure "Italian race". This premise is not based on the confusion of the biological concept of race as the historical-linguistic concept of a people and of a nation, but on the purist kinship of blood which unites the Italians of today to the generations which have populated Italy for millennia.'

Millennia, or almost a millennium? Make your minds up.

'This ancient purity of blood is the greatest title of nobility of the Italian Nation.'

He thought he must be reading it wrong. Perhaps his Italian was not as good as he had thought. It was all upside down, even if you went along with that kind of thing. He read it over, and made no more sense of it.

'Seven: It is time that the Italians proclaim themselves frankly racist.'

Tom snorted. Well, that's clear enough.

'All the work that the regime in Italy has done until now is founded in racism. Reference to racial concepts has always been very frequent in the speeches of the Leader—'

'That's not even true!' he cried, causing Gino to look over at him across the café.

Tom said: 'Does the Duce ever talk about race? Did he ever?'

Gino gave a little moue, and said, 'Not much. Not like Herr Hitler.'

'Have you seen this?' Tom asked. 'This manifesto?'

Gino glanced at it. 'Why are you surprised?' he said, and turned, and picked up some cups from the next table, and went. The sun was warm through the wide glass window.

Tom continued reading. 'The question of racism in Italy

ought to be treated from a purely biological point of view, without philosophic or religious intentions. The racism in Italy ought to be essentially Italian and its direction Aryan-Nordic.'

'But what is this?' Tom exclaimed. 'Its direction? What does it mean? It's a nonsense—'

Gino looked across at him, and stepped back over. He leaned down, and said gently, his eyes sorrowful: 'Signore, it's a fool looks for sense in the pages of the *Giornale d'Italia.*'

The look Tom gave was almost grateful, and he carried on, out loud, in Italian: 'This does not mean, however, to introduce into Italy the theories of German racism as they are or to claim that the Italians and the Scandinavians are the same. But it intends only to point out to the Italians a physical and especially psychological model of the human race which in its purely European characteristics is completely separated from all of the non-European races. This means to elevate the Italian to an ideal of superior self-consciousness and of greater responsibility.

'Eight: It is necessary to make a clear distinction between the European Western Mediterraneans on one side and the Eastern Mediterraneans and the Africans on the other. For this reason, those theories are to be considered dangerous that support the African origin of some European peoples and that include even the Semitic and Camitic North African populations in a common Mediterranean race, establishing absolutely inadmissible relations and ideological sympathies.'

Make a distinction! Make up a distinction more like. These scientists are really tying themselves in knots.

'Nine: Jews do not belong to the Italian race. Of the Semites who in the course of centuries have landed on the sacred soil of our country nothing in general has remained.'

And here he stopped in his steady, angry, reading.

'Oh,' he said. 'Oh.'

Gino said, '*Cos' è adesso?*' Now what is it?

'*Gli ebrei non appartengono alla razza italiana,*' Tom said.

'So what?' said Gino, going about his business. 'Why should they? So long as they work hard and talk the language, who cares?'

Tom smiled.

'Even the Arab occupation of Sicily . . .' he continued, to himself. The details melted and blended. They didn't matter. '. . . left nothing outside the memory of some names; and for the rest the process of assimilation was always very rapid in Italy. The Jews represent the only population which has never assimilated in Italy . . . blah blah . . . Union is admissible only with European races, in which case one should not talk of a true and proper hybridism, given that these races belong to a common stock . . . The purely European character of the Italians would be altered by breeding with any other non-European race bearing a civilisation different from the millennial civilisation of the Aryans . . .'

So Jews are not Italian, or indeed European, and union – i.e., what, marriage? Family? – is admissible – what a nasty little word – only with European races. So, Nadine is not admissible? And the Fiores are not Italian? After two thousand years?

All this was detail. *Once you've divided the human race up like that, into some arbitrary Us and Them, you are half way to announcing that They aren't actually human anyway.*

For a moment he sat in the glow of sun that fell through Gino's window, the warmth of it on the side of his face and his shoulder, his coffee cooling in front of him. Into his mind floated the image of Piazza Venezia, a little man, thousands of faces all turned up to him as if he were the sun, shining on them, making everything possible for them. A great field of sunflowers diseased with uncritical devotion to this false sun. And that sun with its own diseased devotion to an even bigger false sun.

We are meant to think for ourselves, aren't we? We're not children in some horrible orphanage, to be marched around and hypnotised into dumb obedience. Are we?

Gino let him make a couple of calls, including one to the paper. The girls were travelling by car, and had stopped off for a few days in Paris. If he left tonight, by train, he could easily be in Rome before them. It seemed to him now absolutely necessary that he should be. Only a worm would not be there now. This could, actually, be a wonderful opportunity.

He headed for the Tube station.

~

It was as he passed the corner of Lexington Street that he saw the family: man, woman, girl. They caught his eye because the man's silhouette was like Peter's, and made him think he probably should tell Peter he was going away. Then he saw that it was Peter. Then he saw that it couldn't be, because as they stepped into the sun the two women – the girl was almost a woman – revealed themselves to be negro. Then he saw, definitely, that it was Peter.

They were walking seemingly easily, cheerfully, and a shaft twisted from surprise, disbelief and guilt speared him to the spot. *Why? Who?* And, *you've walked in on something. Walk out.*

He stared, unable to remove his eyes from this unlikely target. Then he ducked suddenly away, into Silver Place. His eyes did not follow him quite quickly enough: the girl looked up, and fixed on him. It was only for a moment, but it was quite clear. *I see you.*

He turned to walk on quickly: up, away. Head down. The pavement was warm and the alley stank. Keep going.

It wasn't that he forgot what he'd seen. He just didn't believe it. There was a lot going on.

≈

Tom did not go to the Fiores' house on the island when he arrived in Rome. Instead he looked up Carmichael, who was working now at the British Consulate.

'Ah, you're back,' Carmichael said, in what seemed to Tom a rather knowing manner. 'Good.'

'What do you mean?' Tom asked.

'Well, are you here to save Italy from herself? Or to save your pretty cousin from her Fascist birthright?'

'Don't rub it in, old man,' Tom said. 'I know why I'm here, I've no clue how to go about it, though.'

They met for supper at a little place by Campo dei Fiori. Carmichael brought a friend, a quiet, well-dressed young man who worked in the Vatican. Very quietly and intently, this man, Michele Bertolini, told Tom about his uncle in Florence. The story was brief and bloody. The uncle was a known anti-Fascist. He had been kidnapped and beaten, and blinded. His friends had rescued him, taken him by carts and byways down to the coast and put him on a boat to Sardinia. Nobody had heard from him since.

Tom blinked. Bertolini kept his dark eyes downcast, his slender fingers resting on the edge of the table.

It's here, Tom thought. *It's real. Look.*

'Was this an official punishment for something?' he asked, tentatively.

And Bertolini raised his heavy eyes and said, 'I'm afraid it's not really like that at the moment. Not if you have the right friends and the right slogans.'

They had other stories too, and Tom listened carefully. Various addresses were mentioned, neighbourhoods where it was best not to go without the party badge on your lapel, things to say or not to say.

'I don't know about your school,' Carmichael said. 'But it's rather like school, with no beaks, just the big nasty boy's gang in charge. And there's no comeback.'

'My uncle,' Tom said, 'described it much the same way. Only he said the Duce was the leader of a gang so powerful it stopped all the other gangs from fighting between themselves, and so it was a good thing. People could just get on with their lives. And that's why everyone loves him.'

'Do you think that?' Carmichael asked.

'No,' said Tom. 'But I see why people do. Otherwise they'd have to admit that the person they put all their faith in, who made everything right for them, is some kind of monster.'

There was a silence across the table as Bertolini and Carmichael looked at him.

'So,' said Carmichael. 'Are you staying at your uncle's again this time?'

'No!' said Tom. 'No. I . . .'

Their gaze was exceptionally straight. It was Carmichael who leaned forward and said, quite gently, 'because you are going to have to decide,' and in that phrase Tom saw, in a flash of clarity, that it was real, it *was* beginning, it *was* more than his fears, more than his family – and bigger than them too – and that it was going to be a long haul. He closed his eyes for a moment. He thought. *It's clear. It's right and wrong. It's simple. But it won't be easy.*

He looked up at them and smiled. 'Here goes then!' he said. 'Johnny, Michele – my family from London are arriving tomorrow – my socialist pacifist war-hero pa, my pretty apolitical ma, and my ridiculous kid sister. My family in Rome are Jewish Fascists, now under threat from the very man to whom they have dedicated their lives. I'm sorry to sound portentous. But which decision am I to make?'

Without hesitation, Bertolini said: 'You cut them off. They are Fascist.'

'They are family,' Tom said. 'You don't understand.'

Bertolini dropped his sad scholarly eyes for a moment, and then said, quietly: 'Yes I do understand.'

Tom looked up at his face: hooded, blank.

'You cut them off,' Bertolini said.

'I can't,' Tom said.

Bertolini's mouth tightened the tiniest bit, like glue drying. 'If I can,' he said – and he left it there, as if he couldn't speak.

'Oh,' said Tom. Helplessness loomed in him. *Really?* he thought. *But*—

'I'm going to their house,' Tom said, 'and I'm going to make them see sense.'

'Good luck with that,' Carmichael said. 'Only twenty years of solid top-class propaganda to unravel.'

After Bertolini left them, Johnny told Tom that two of Bertolini's brothers had been involved in the uncle's disappearance. Tom winced, but said: 'I have to try though, haven't I?'

'Doesn't matter if you have to or not,' Carmichael said. 'You're going to. And you're still going to have to choose a side.'

'I'm on the side of the human, Johnny,' Tom said.

'Well just get a move on.'

~

He stayed that night at Johnny's, sleepless, and went early to the island. Sheepishly, he stood across the piazza watching as they came out and started packing up a little green car: Aldo, Susanna, and two long lanky teenagers with soft black moustaches, *the little boys*, he thought. No sign of Nenna. *All right*, he thought, and was about to stride across, a bold *Buon giorno!* on his lips—

A voice behind him. 'Eh, Masino.'

He couldn't stop the smile.

He spun round, and there she was, a quizzical smile on her face, little Marinella clutching her hand. He only had time for the thought *I didn't really think this through, did I*, before a swift and deathly drama broke out inside him:

his heart ricocheted, helpless, alarmed, and his default English manners swept quickly in to make his face smile, his hand stick out to be shaken and his mouth utter the words, 'How lovely to see you again, Nenna.'

Jesus, the beauty. Not her being beautiful – though she was. The beauty of her being her.

Her mouth fell open. 'How lovely to see you too, Tom,' she said. She put a comical little emphasis on the use of his English name. Tom. Very polite.

I am a fool, he thought. *Nenna. Nenna.*

Later, he would remember this moment, and how he should have kissed her, swept her over the wall into a waiting boat, hauled her down river to the sea, out and home to safety – her and Marinella too.

Everybody was delighted to see him. Time dissolved, past insults had never existed, and all was joy and welcome. And everybody was busy: packing, lugging, closing, locking, forgetting, remembering, arranging, changing arrangements. He caught them just as they were leaving for the lake. The boys would go by bus; there was room for Tom in the car, of course! How not! All the way, Nenna's leg was against his in the back seat, and Aldo talked loudly about wine-making; when they got out into the country the roads were terrible, and then Aldo insisted on stopping to wait and pick up the boys, which meant a great squash in the back, and on giving them turns at driving, which involved much yelping, instructing, and shrieks of horror and delight, so Nenna and Susanna said they would walk, with Marinella, thank you very much, so Tom said, no of course I will walk, and he walked, with Nenna.

The bastard formality which had frozen him in the piazza would not let him go. He threw glances at her: she had grown tall and fine, physically sleeker, though her stripey mane of hair still sought to escape the control into which she had twisted it. Her skin was sallow, her hands rough, her dark yellow eyes were humorous. She was glad to see him. She teased him for staying away so long, accused him of having grown handsome – and yet he could not speak naturally to her. She made him blush.

Am I just to launch in? Challenge this golden morning with news that her government rejects her? The calmer the dark hills and the blue sky around them, the rustling of the bamboo canes by the stream, the jumpier he felt. He even found himself asking her what she was doing now.

'Teacher!' she said. 'Depending how well I do, either little children, or, I was thinking, history.'

'And?' he said.

'I don't have my exam results yet. But – I asked my old teacher at school, and he said, "Women cannot teach history". So I said that I thought I could, and that I would work very hard. And he said, "No, you don't understand, it's against the law."'

'It is against the law for women to teach history?' Tom asked, just to be sure.

'Yes.'

'Why?'

'Because women are hysterical and inaccurate, and allow

emotion to influence them. History must be pure and factual. There is no room for debate and argument.'

'Oh,' said Tom.

'That is what he said. Very calmly! And it made me think of my father's argumentative, hysterical friends, of all the men who shout and argue in the cafés and in the streets. And of my quiet mother.'

'But—'

'I said that too. But. And my teacher said "There is no room for But."'

She glanced over to him.

'This did seem wrong,' she said.

'It *is* wrong,' he said.

'But, never mind,' she said. 'There's always a way. Perhaps I will teach some history to the little children . . .'

'But Nenna, it's not fair, or right' – at which she laughed, and said, 'Oh you are so sweet,' and the phrase *long haul* swept into his head, so he laughed too, and he said: 'I meant it more in a revolutionary way, *fiore*, not in a sweet way.'

'Fiore!' she said. 'Are you calling me by my surname like your public schoolboys? Or are you calling me flower?'

'Both,' he said. 'Expressing my respect for your pure factual masculine intellect, and admiration for your beauty.' And she laughed, so it was a little more like the old days, except, of course, that it wasn't.

~

On arrival at the lake, everybody was busy again, unpacking, cooking, sweeping, making up the small metal beds.

There was no way in, through all this activity. He didn't know if they'd seen the manifesto. They must have! But if they had, how could they be continuing so oblivious? They must, surely, understand the implications. But they were just – continuing. There was an air around the family, a density, which he didn't remember and couldn't break through. It was as if they were all held in orbits and circuits with each other, and space was delineated. The whole universe of it was protected by a membrane, which he was outside. His words and his presence prodded it gently, but no impression was left. Tom could not make the declarations he had been rehearsing. His determination, which had been dissipating since the border, and encouraged by Carmichael and Bertolini, flagged again. *Long haul,* he murmured again.

Lugging buckets of water from the well for the kitchen, he remembered the acro-bat. Little bats, tucked into their cool dark corners; soft-bellied lizards gloating in the hot sun. It was here that he had decided, years before, that he was going to be a naturalist. And perhaps he would yet. He had had an offer to go in September to Palermo, to help a friend of his tutor to list beetles.

Before lunch they walked to the lake, to sweep the dust and sweat of the journey from their bodies, down the dusty track, towels round their shoulders. Marinella skipped about ahead, squelching and squeaking with her feet when they reached the meadow with its grassy irrigation channels. Nostalgia seized him, and he was momentarily helpless. How could he break all this perfection?

Because it's not perfect. It only looks it.

Can't I let it carry on looking it? Until someone else breaks it, or it breaks itself?

❧

Aldo was looking splendid in a wilting crown of lakeweed, smoking a Florentine cigarillo after lunch beneath the vine-covered pergola.

'Only three things good about the Florentines,' he said, reaching for his hat as the sun moved round. 'Their cigars, their hats, and their Italian. Oh, and their steaks.'

'And their painters,' said Nenna.

'And their architects,' murmured Susanna.

'And their TRIPPE!' Aldo yelled suddenly to Nenna, to alarm her, or amuse her – it wasn't clear which. It was their old joke: when she was younger the mere mention of Florentine tripe would make her shriek, because nothing in the world was more horrid, chewy and rubbery and clad in tomato sauce that anywhere else would be delicious but on tripe looked like blood on a dead thing . . .

'Tripe, tripe, tripe . . .' he chanted now, comically, waggling his eyebrows, and Nenna gratified him with a yelp, and went and hung round his neck. Tom recalled her as a small girl, always sitting on her father's knee, hiding in his coat, climbing into his pocket, burrowing in under his beard. Aldo used to pick her up and carry her under one arm like a parcel. She seemed to wish he still could.

'Papà,' Nenna said, helpless. His presence on the holiday was a luxury. She wrapped her arms round his head, and said again, 'Papà'.

Tom was silent, watching.

298

Part of him very much wished that he were a young boy still, and could tell himself that if Aldo thought everything was all right then everything was all right.

But that, he thought, *is not true*.

Looking at Nenna, as in love with her father as her father was with the Duce, he recognised his way ahead. *I will not lie*.

Chapter Fourteen

Bracciano, Summer 1938
It doesn't matter Nenna thought. *It was a long time ago, and one short moment.* Several boys had told her since that they were in love with her – Lord in Rome you only have to walk down the street to be hailed as a miracle. Nenna had thought that from an English boy, a cousin, it might mean something else, and when he turned up, unexpected, older, for a moment yes, a little flicker had . . . flickered . . . It had been something of a shock.

It wasn't that she had forgotten about him. She had put him in a special sentimental part of her heart: *my beautiful big cousin, who I don't see any more, since Papà alarmed him. My delicate blond English cousin, spooked by a bit of big Italian drama which actually passed within a few days. My dear cousin who stopped writing to me, or did I stop writing to him? And well, time passes, and other things happen . . . and so, he is just the first boy who said he was in love with me. It was sweet. We were babies.*

And so suddenly here he is: her cousin who wasn't coming though the others were; and who then totally unexpectedly did. Her cousin who is taller, older, and behaving very oddly. He didn't look at all sweet now. She'd stared at him, down at the lake, when he'd pulled his shirt off over his head.

When the English arrived in their car, before dinner, Tom was there like a policeman, watching as Aldo came out, big and cheerful in his shirtsleeves, to meet his cousin's husband. *Il famoso* Riley, meanwhile, allowed himself to be grinned at and have his hand wrung, and then embraced, and kissed on both cheeks, impassive to Papà's friendliness, only raising his eyebrows, and looking rather charmed.

Why is Tom so nervous? she wondered. *He looks like he's expecting them to have a fight.*

Papà suggested a swim, and stroll around the place as the afternoon cooled off, and Riley said that was an excellent idea.

Nadine looks nervous too.

Kitty was the only one who was happy and relaxed. She greeted Nenna with the biggest hug, and had bought her a book of postcards from Paris. 'It was that or scent,' she said, 'and I couldn't afford scent, and I didn't think you'd like it. It absolutely stank. Now come on, teach me Italian again I've forgotten it all except *scheletro* and mozzarella' – but then she was entranced by Vittorio and Stefano, and they took her off to show her her room, and the stream, and their bicycles.

~

A Russian pianist, married to an American heiress, came up from Rome for dinner, with an absurd little dog which wore a bell and blue ribbons in its hair. They laughed and

301

play-acted about the rather pastoral nature of the hospitality, which involved a long-drop latrine in the mimosa thicket, and they had brought a friend of theirs, an English artist called Mann. Nenna was grateful for these strangers. There was such an air of significance about Riley and Papà finally meeting that this dilution, the protective lubricatory presence of others in front of whom one had to be polite, was welcome. All was fuss: the coming to the table, comment on the warmth of the evening, passing of plates and the pouring of wine, the eating, the compliments to the food, a toast to Riley for finally having come so far to meet the in-laws. The jokes about language, the courtesies about journeys, the pleasantries about the dog. The stream gurgled invisible in its rocky hollow at the end of the dried-out lawn: crickets creaked, hands slapped at mosquitoes, Mama fetched the citronella candles and the medicinal smell rose. Nenna played her part, enjoying it, but watchful.

Over the artichokes, the artist said, 'So what about this war?'

'What war?' said the Russian. 'The Spanish one?'

'The one which is coming,' the artist said, glancing around, as if surprised anyone was thinking about anything else.

'Oh you English,' the Russian replied. 'You're always going on about the war.'

A small silence, while this sank in, and the table blossomed into a tiny tumult of glances: Nadine at Riley, Riley at Papà, Nenna at Tom. She was surprised by how strongly she wanted him to look – indeed to be – happy.

And then Vittorio, looking around first, quite aware that

he was about to be contentious, announced: 'Tom tried to run away to Spain, you know. Kitty said so.'

'Vittorio!' squawked Kitty, outraged at the breaking of a confidence, and Nenna too gave him a withering look in time to see him blow Kitty a semi-apologetic kiss from his fingertips.

'Well,' said Tom, quickly.

And then the adults tried not to look at Papà, except for Mann, who for an artist was very unobservant. 'Well done!' he declared, in the tone of one who is never in the company of people with different views to his. 'How far did you get? Why did you come back?'

Tom stared at his bit of bread for a while, then lifted his chin, as if he had made a decision, and said: 'No distance at all. I thought about it, and Riley talked me out of it.'

Mama suddenly got up and took some plates. Nenna could see her mother wanted her to join her, to break up the moment and change the subject, but she didn't.

'Really?' said Papà, and that just hung there.

Tom made a small noise.

'On which side were you planning to fight?' Papà said, after a moment. The Russian sat back. Riley sat up. Kitty glanced at Nenna, then pushed her chair back, admired the moon, and mentioned an inclination to take a stroll by its charming light.

'What a good idea,' said the heiress, but it was too late, because Tom, with a smile, dived in, and quickly (*as if before he could put it away again*, Nenna thought), he said: 'The Brigades, I'm afraid, Uncle.' And that did it. Everyone knew that Fascist troops were fighting for the Republicans.

The pause was heavy.

'What?' said Mann. 'What is it?'

'The Brigades are International,' Nenna said. 'Aren't they? Plenty of Italians are fighting for the Brigades . . .'

'*Comunisti*,' Papà said. His English dropped away. '*Anarchici. Questi Garibaldini e Matteottini . . .*' Mama reached out to touch his arm. '*Comunisti*,' he said again, and looked around the table, accusingly. '*Anarchici.*'

'They aren't the enemy any more, Uncle,' Tom said, so calmly. 'Things are changing.'

And then a sort of blanket of shadow settled over the table, over everyone and everything. Nenna found herself thinking of rabbits, running up and down a green tussocky hillside, dashing into burrows at the passing overhead of such a shadow. Tom – or his words – seemed to be that shadow. Nenna picked up his look when he raised his eyes. He looked helpless. *So what are you doing? What are you doing?*

Papà, big and handsome, his forearms on the table, his hands open as if to heaven, was staring at Tom, who looked skinny and young before him. Nenna closed her eyes for a moment: *the anger is coming* – then opened them. *No, there are guests. It will be safe. Marinella is there, Mama is there* – an automatic checking, for their safety – *but there are guests.*

The cloud gathered in Papà's eyes.

And passed.

'So you're a boy of heart!' he cried. 'You believe! And you would fight for what you believe in! Come here!' he cried, and was standing and enfolding Tom, and Nenna thought,

Thank God and she swallowed, and did not look at her mother, as Aldo congratulated Tom, and chided him gently, and clasped him again.

'But—'

Nenna recognised the ghost of relief passing along the table. She knew it well.

~

'What's the matter with Tom?' Nenna said to Kitty, as they carried the plates in and piled them up, sweeping oily detritus from the meal into the bin.

Kitty rolled her eyes, and said: 'I haven't the faintest idea. I'm really not the person to ask. He seems to think he's an adult, or something. He's certainly full of ideas. But really, I'm the last person he'd say anything to.'

Nenna left the others to tidy, and fetched the grappa and glasses for the men. She wanted to get back outside. She crossed the terrace carefully with the tray, breathing the night air, hearing the voices floating. The Roman guests were leaving, the moon careered blindly behind the cypresses, and cicadas sang with glorious abandon. She laid the tray down, and poured, and handed the glasses round.

Riley was sitting next to Tom now. Nenna slipped in at the shadowy end of the table as, with the tiny glass in his hand, Riley said: 'So, Aldo, you're a Fascist?'

'Of course,' said Papà.

'Why?' asked Riley.

Nenna smiled. *Why!*

For a moment Papà looked puzzled, then he laughed.

'What else should I be?' he said. 'Italy is Fascist. I am Italian. I am Fascist.'

'Doesn't it worry you?' Riley said.

She was interested. This was not something people asked.

'Why? Oh – no, I see. You think we should have voting, a choice, like you. Of course. We had a choice! We still have! I could choose to run about throwing bombs and striking and causing trouble – or I could choose to work hard for Italy. Easy choice for me. Twenty years ago in the Red Years, we could choose for Italy to fall apart in shame after the war, or we could choose to stand together under a strong leader.' He looked to Riley, eyebrows up, smile broad, for an understanding nod. But Riley's face was closed.

'I am a practical man,' Papà continued. 'I prefer to build. You know my dream? Nice houses for people to live in. Well built, red tiles, space for a vegetable garden, communal olive groves, hospital, pretty piazza, safe place to park bicycles, little schools, electricity for everybody, *dopolavoro*, water from a tap in their kitchens. This is what we are building in Agro Pontino.' Again he looked for a response, for the glow of natural agreement, and, failing to get it, continued again. 'Do anarchists let me build this? No. Do communists have the money to build this? No. We need organisation, unity and discipline – and we have it!'

Still Riley was silent, listening. Tom too. *But Tom knows all this,* she thought, *He knows Papà.*

'You should visit,' Papà said. 'See our reclamations, see Littoria and Sabaudia and Pontinia and Aprilia, our beautiful new towns. Four beautiful cities, since 1930. See what

306

Fascism is. What it does.' The smile was still wide, and his pride was palpable.

'And that's all?' Riley said, mildly, and Papà smiled mildly back, and said, 'That's what Fascism is for.'

'You don't feel it's changed at all?'

What are they getting at?

'I think one of the things that Riley might be referring to,' Tom said, suddenly and quickly, 'is the government's recent announcement that Jews are not Italian.

Nenna's head jerked.

What?

She leaned, gently, futher back into the shadows. *Papà? What is this?*

Papà had turned a mild gaze on Tom. 'A mistake!' he said.

'A mistake!' Tom exploded.

'Ah, you, you boy of heart!' Papà cried. 'Yes, a mistake! The Duce will put it right. Come here!' he cried, and for the second time he was standing and enfolding Tom, chiding him gently, and clasping him again.

Tom pulled back, like a man aware that his little darts are having no effect, a man looking for a bigger blade.

'Mussolini is in alliance with Hitler,' he said. 'Doesn't the Nazi policy on Jews worry you?' His words were carefully picked and claggy with freight.

Papà?

Aldo took a moment to clarify them – then looked up at him, clearly and frankly, and said in astonishment: 'No! Never! What. You think—? Oh no, my boy, the situation of the Italian Jew is completely different to the Jew in Germany.

We are not Polish, or Lithuanian, or anything – we are Italian! For two thousand years! We are not wandering Jews. We are not Zionists, dreaming of another country to which we have more loyalty! We are the most loyal citizens – more loyal than Gentiles, because we have always had to prove our loyalty, and they never had. Did you know,' he said, leaning in and twinkling, 'that half of Italians think there are no Jews in Italy? Because we fit in so well?'

'But you have seen the *Manifesto degli scienziati razzisti*,' said Tom.

The what?

'Oh Tommaso – Mussolini has always been a champion of Jews – Finzi! Ovazza! – because we work hard and we are good people.'

Tom glanced at Riley.

'We have Jewish naval officers!' Papà went on. 'Tell me – where do you ever see that? Jews in boats! That, my friend, is assimilation . . .'

Riley smiled.

'But it's been confirmed.' Tom said. 'They published the names of the scientists.'

'We are as safe as good modern houses,' Papà said, and Nenna smiled in the dark, at the broad generosity of the man who is right, smiling and loving, hospitable. Susanna came out and wondered if anybody would like more coffee, because she was going to bed.

'As safe as good modern houses,' Papà said again. 'Here – more grappa,' he said, and he poured, and he laughed, and the rightness he felt about himself overflowed with his bonhomie. Vittorio and Stefano came out to say goodnight.

For a moment, before his sons went in, Aldo looked like the finest of patriarchs, flawless. Nenna relaxed.

Then: 'Has Susanna seen it?' Tom demanded. 'Nenna? The boys?'

'Tommaso,' Papà said, gently. 'A man does not bother women and children with every little thing.'

Oh, thought Nenna. *Oh*.

Nobody wanted more grappa. Nenna slipped away, as the men rose and said goodnight to each other, and went their ways. She fretted, a little, in the course of the night, but when she woke in the morning she found that she wasn't worried about this manifesto, whatever it was. Papà said it was all right.

~

Vittorio, as it happened, had seen the paper. His friend Orazio, a muscly young *squadrista* of twenty-four who gave him wine and cigarettes, and showed him off to his friends, had shown it to him in Rome, during one of their long siestas at Orazio's father's empty flat. Vittorio, accustomed as he was to taking the words of older men at face value, wasn't bothered by the manifesto. Life was too enjoyable.

'It makes no difference,' Orazio said, tapping Vittorio affectionately – or perhaps dismissively? – on the nose. 'We need to be a bit more careful, that's all. But we can carry on,' he said, with a smile, and he carried on: kissing Vittorio's red mouth, and removing Vittorio's shirt and trousers, delighting in the good young Fascist masculinity that was revealed.

~

Tom couldn't sleep, that night. Telling the truth, actively, was – enlivening. He decided to walk down to the lake in the dark, alone in the soft air. Across the meadow, all the flowers were closed for the night.

Tom did not need lectures from Aldo in what Fascism was, and what it did. He knew. For every beautiful new town with a town hall built in the shape of an M there remained thousands of shoeless children hungry in slums; and those newsreels of the bloody Duce with his shirt off pretending to sow or harvest the reclaimed land were no more true than the notion of grateful Abyssinians longing for Roman ways – Abyssinians who in reality have been gassed and slaughtered and raped, their villages burned. *It doesn't work, is the problem. It isn't TRUE. It's a great big lie and they're all still staring like sunflowers.*

He thought about Bertolini's uncle, and the quiet, urgent, dispirited way in which Bertolini had told the story. He remembered the club swung by Aldo's friend, three years before.

The thing is, he had been certain Riley would say something important, something which would change everything here. Something which would mean he, Tom, would not have to be the one to say it. He had not got what he expected. He thought: *We wait, and we take things into account, and we hope something will change to let us off the hook, and the next thing you know you're up to your waist in it and you can't move . . .*

He took his shoes off on the black sand, and stepped in to the silent mirror-black water. Ripples flowed out: circle after circle moving out across the lake towards invisibility or disappearance, whichever came first. A tiny, silent surf broke on the shore behind him. Too late in the year for fireflies. In the trees an owl was calling, soft and strange: 'Quilp! Quilp!'

It has been a long time coming, he thought. *And of course it was bound to come in the end, but nobody wanted it to, and we have all done so well, for so long, pretending it doesn't exist – but now the depth charge has been dropped, and it will emerge in due course. Aldo has chosen not to rise, but Aldo is not the only person here.*

~

The next morning Tom walked the same route with Riley, down the field to the lake, early sun hot on their shoulders, chicory nipping their ankles. It was his first opportunity to ask Riley if he'd read the manifesto.

'The which?' Riley asked. He was absent-minded.

'What we were talking about last night,' Tom said. 'The Fascist declaration that Jews aren't Italian and there's to be no interracial breeding.'

'Fascist,' Riley said, and his tone, gentle but precise, stopped Tom in his tracks, and his words in his mouth.

For a moment he was silent, then, 'I should have told you before,' Tom said.

'Yes,' said Riley.

Tom bowed his head to the punishment.

After a while Riley said, 'All these years, and not one of you has mentioned it. Why didn't you tell me?'

Tom stopped. And started again. And stopped.

'I was publishing books on the evils of totalitarianism,

311

Tom,' he said. 'A biography of Mussolini and the roots of Italian Fascism. About what a danger it is to Europe.'

'Because,' Tom said. 'Because. Ah, because they always were, and I didn't quite realise, because I was so young. And Fascism really wasn't the same here as it is in England. And because it has always been presented to me, here, as something normal and good – it was just white socks and gymnastics and railways. Because I didn't want to cause trouble, because Nadine was – very fond of him, and Nenna was like a sister, for Kitty and for me, and Vittorio and Stefano were little brothers. Because it was entwined with everything else Italian, which we all love.'

Riley said, 'Reasons? Or excuses?'

'Reasons, I think,' Tom said. And pushed on: 'Why didn't you challenge him more, last night? You started but then – why didn't you talk about the violence? About dictatorship? Mussolini admitted murdering Matteotti years ago, and nobody ever did anything about it; they outrage the League of Nations daily, Abyssinia, they're allied with Herr Hitler, and the Blackshirts just beat people up who disagree with them. Why didn't you talk about the ludicrous empire-building? I don't understand why you let him off. He can patronise me, he still sees me as a boy, but he would have to take it from you—'

'What, now, am I meant to do something about it?'

'You're angry,' said Tom.

'Yes,' said Riley.

Tom bit his lip.

A lark was rising and falling over the corner of the meadow, pouring out its miraculous song, near where the chestnut horses still stood, ankle-deep at the edge of water as smooth as slate. Poplar leaves shivered, and the velvet folds of the hills beyond still held the deep shade of the night.

'It's too beautiful for all this, isn't it?' murmured Riley. 'Different types of Jews, and different types of Fascists. Divide, divide, divide. Is it all right to be anti-Semitic against some kinds of Jews? Are some kinds of Fascism all right?'

'No! But – I did think Fascism was good for Italy. For unity – for strength—'

'What's the point of strength if you're not free?' Riley said.

Tom stared.

'Of course,' he said. 'But I only properly realised a couple of years ago. It's why I didn't come back, these last years.'

Silence.

'I didn't want to upset the girls,' Tom said. 'Or you. I hoped it would go away. I would have told you if I'd known you were coming.'

'Well,' said Riley.

They kicked on in silence through the clover and grass, *mentuccia* and chamomile, livid green and wet from the irrigation channels after the early morning opening. Tom wanted to lie down and stare at them, as he had when he was young: at the tiny bright green clover leaves and spears of grass, and miniature flowers baffing about in the clean cold water rushing over them. He reached out and pulled a white lacey umbel from a patch of Queen Anne's Lace. *Drop of dark blood in the middle where the queen pricked her finger with a needle. And this pretty flower looks just like hemlock, and gives Kitty a rash.*

313

After a while Riley said, 'I'm sorry I didn't back you up. But all those reasons you gave are also my reasons.' He stumbled a little on the Rs, which required a slight forward movement of the jaw which would always be awkward for him.

Tom turned his face away from Riley's vulnerability. He expected so much from him. What he, Tom, had fretted over for three years, he was asking Riley to deal with over-night. On top of what Riley had been dealing with every day for the past twenty-one years, and dealing with so well that it became invisible to those who loved him best and should have helped him most.

If war is coming, Tom thought, *it will be mine. Not Riley's.*

'What's going to happen now?' he asked.

Riley said: 'To us here? Or . . . on the larger scale?'

'Both?' said Tom. Way behind them he could hear the voices of Kitty, Marinella and the boys, who were dragging Aldo's canoe.

'I don't know,' said Riley. 'There are so many ways in which things can go wrong. But we have to stick with what's right. As best we can.'

'But – can you stay here, knowing he's a Fascist?'

'I think we can be idealists without being prigs,' Riley said. 'He's a man, not a regime.'

'But . . .' said Tom.

'Did you want me to save you from it?' Riley said. 'I'd like to. But you all love him, don't you?'

Tom laughed. 'Yes.' Then, 'Should I have kept quiet?'

'No,' Riley said.

'Are you going to talk to Nadine about it?'

Riley walked on. 'Not yet,' he said. 'She's not political, you know—'

'There's no such thing as not political,' said Tom, hotly, and Riley smiled.

'Well I agree with you,' he said. 'But Nadine doesn't, and has a right not to. That's what differentiates us from the Fascists.'

'You know that's not good enough,' Tom said.

'Yes,' said Riley. Then, 'You know, all I can think of is losing my temper, and I don't think that will help. There's a lot going on here. He paused to swallow. You need to think about what you want to happen.'

They reached the little strip of black sand, bright against the green meadow edge, and dropped their towels.

'They'll need encouraging to come to London,' Riley said. 'Your job, I think.'

Tom shot a look at him, then ran out, with massive splashing, tiny fish scattering, and flung himself into the water, a long low dive heading for the gap in the bright green reeds.

When he surfaced, rolled over and glanced back, Riley was up the meadow helping with the canoe. It was Nenna standing on the sand, staring at him.

Tom shook the water from his head, and swam slowly back in.

~

'About yesterday,' she said, as he brought himself awkwardly upright in the shallow water.

She wanted him to apologise, that was all. *Apologise*, she thought, *and say it was all nonsense.*

'Which bit?' he said, shortly, not looking at her, bending down for his towel. She watched him, the pearly white skin over the long slender muscles of his arms and back, droplets of lakewater running as he moved. His body, for a moment, disarmed her.

She passed him his shirt, and waited while he put it on, and buttoned it up. His hair was standing on end. They started to walk up the field.

'Better?' he said, and there was something in his bright blue eyes which made her blink and clench her teeth for a second before she said, 'Are you anti-Fascist?'

'Yes,' he said, rather nonchalantly.

She couldn't believe it. *What madness! Is that how England is? You just say what you like with no thought for the consequences?*

Beyond him, Riley went by with the canoe held over his head, laughing with Kitty and the others. Nenna could hear their feet splashing in the watery meadow. 'Then we are not friends,' she said, simply, and with sadness.

He stopped. 'What?' he said, and she shook her head at his disbelief.

'Why are you shocked?' she said. 'You are against our whole lives. Don't speak of it again. I don't wish you harm, so I tell you – don't speak of it again for your own sake. And don't come here again.' She turned to walk on; he stopped her with a hand on her arm, and the feeling of it confused her.

'Nenna!' he said.

'You are anti-Fascist. We are Fascist. So you are anti us. We are not anti you. You have put yourself there.'

'Nenna, I am not anti-you! I could never be anti-you! I'm anti-Mussolini! And Mussolini is anti-Jew! Which means, and this really isn't very complicated, that HE is anti-you.'

'Shh!' she hissed: an urgent short hiss.

'Nenna!' he said. 'Why are you shushing me, in the middle of the beautiful countryside, far from anyone or anything? It's ridiculous.'

'You cannot talk like that to me,' she said. 'And you must not. People don't like it. You will get in trouble and you will get us in trouble.'

At this, Tom laughed. 'That's it!' he said. 'That's exactly it. The Blackshirts will come and beat me up? That's exactly why I am anti-Fascist, Nenna! ANTI-FASCIST! ANTI-FASCIST!' He shouted it out, in English and in Italian.

She was staring at him, her face tight. *He's lost his mind.*

'And you call yourself political,' she said. 'Is that your politics?'

'Yes!' he said. 'The right to shout what I think in a field. That's exactly it. Exactly.'

'Tommaso,' she said. 'We are not friends.'

'But—' he said, 'Or is there no room for but?'

'Tommaso, we live in reality.'

'And do you know about the reality?' he asked. 'Do you know what goes on? Which version of reality are you living in, Nenna?'

She flashed her eyes at him, and said: 'Do not bring harm on us.'

'It's not me,' he said. 'Really, it's not me. Did you see the manifesto of the racist scientists? Did you read what they're saying?'

'I don't know what you're talking about,' she said, but she knew what she had heard the night before. She wanted him to shut up.

'Well you should,' he said.

'I don't know what you're talking about,' she said again.

'Well, you should—' But she was striding off. Little clouds of grasshoppers sprang away under her steps. She didn't want to hurt them but she just needed not to hear.

'Nenna!' he was calling. 'What do your friends think? Have you talked to them?'

But you went to him for clarity.

'Nenna!'

No, I want him to shut up.

She didn't stop marching, up the field, up the white road past the house, past the cow shed and the farm, past the cantina and the peach orchard and the *orto*, until she was far up into the woods, in the dim shade and the dead leaves and the muffled quiet, heading uphill, trudging. When she stopped she lay down, helpless, and wept her confusion until she ached and threw up.

'It's like with the sandwiches and pullovers,' Kitty said to Tom, later. Nenna had gone somewhere with Aldo and the boys, and they were playing *scopa* on the terrace table. 'You have to call them *tramezzini* and – oh, I've forgotten it. Apparently Benny Goodman is Beniamino Buonuomo, too. Everything has to be Italian. Except for Jews. Apparently.

And you're not allowed to call people *lei* to be polite, because it's soppy girly to use a feminine form to a chap, and also too old-fashioned when everything has to be NEW.

'Nenna's not talking to me,' he said, picking up the best card – the *sette bello*, and – Kitty saw – not even noticing.

'I thought that might happen,' she said. 'She asked if I was anti-Fascist too.'

'What did you say?'

'I said I wasn't political, and she hugged me.'

'But you are anti-Fascist, aren't you?' he said, suddenly worried.

'Of course I am!' Kitty said with a smile. 'But I'm also anti-family arguments, and anti-arguing with the people you're staying with when it would only upset Nadine. I dare say it's hypocritical but let's be practical.'

'That's not enough,' he said.

'Well obviously not, but people are what they are, you know. You can't go changing them. *Eccoci qua*—' Here we are. *But here we aren't*— He wasn't even listening. Had he ever listened to her? She stared right at him as an experiment; he didn't notice, didn't raise his eyes. *Maddening boy,* she thought, and reminded herself: *don't be maddened by him. Don't want anything from him. Tom does not give you what you want.*

But he's my brother – he's my real family . . .

When she looked at Tom, she saw how her parents worked together: Julia's big eyes, exactly the same as in the photographs. Peter's elegance and languor, but young, and healthy. Something in her still wanted to cry when she looked at Tom. He looked like what everything going right between

319

Peter and Julia would have looked like. But he still never looked happy.

'Listen,' he said, dealing the cards. 'I'm not coming back to London with the rest of you. My life has to be here for a while. I've got to turn her round—'

'Italy?' Kitty asked, mildly acerbic. 'Or just Nenna?'

And then he looked at her. 'I wish I could save both,' he said, with humility and self-importance combined, which infuriated her.

'So can I have your motorbike?' she said, gaily. *Save Italy! Marvellous. God!*

'No,' he said.

~

She thought about it all later.

It wasn't that she didn't like Italy. Italy was glorious of course; *blah blah we know all about that, and Rome, good Lord.* She and Nadine had taken a day trip in on the train: the flower stalls everywhere and all those handsome men in white suits, and the lovely horse-drawn carriages, and the compliments, heavens, the compliments – Well, she knew she'd emerged, as it were, gone was the dumpy duckling, and here was some kind of swan, but to walk down the street and have these good-looking cheerful men just offering you the gift of their admiration, in that somehow innocent, old-fashioned manner, well it was charming. You knew they weren't going to do anything, or be unpleasant. Except sometimes the older men, in cafés. They had sat at a place in Piazza Navona which turned out to be full of horrid old roués in bow ties trying to pay for one's drinks. Johnny

Carmichael had very gallantly rescued them there, swooping down just as some particularly ghastly old prince had put his hand on Kitty's knee even though Nadine was there! And afterwards Nadine said he had his other hand on *her* knee!

But no, she was seeing, this summer, how things had changed for her in Italy. Tom had claimed it. He'd claimed the country when he had claimed Nenna as 'his girl' three years ago, and now Italy and Nenna like most things – Italy, and Nenna, were all his, and not interested in Kitty. And she couldn't make them so. She didn't want to. She was proud. Her confidence was still not up to actually claiming things, or people, for herself. Plus the Fascists were just unbearable now, everywhere you looked, throwing their weight around. No, Italy was absurd, and Tom was obsessed. She would look elsewhere.

She shivered a little though at the thought of returning to London. *What on earth does one do?*

I shall develop a passion, she thought. *I shall . . . focus my desires. And I'll have a love affair. It would be shameful not to have a love affair. I'll get a job in a place full of fascinating men; I'll do something fascinating there, I'll live in a flat with girlfriends, and . . .*

But she wasn't trained to do anything. No matter. *I've got all my certificates, I'll just – I'll—*

I'll get confident, she thought. *That's what I'll do. It's just a decision, isn't it? I'll flick that switch. I'm not stupid. I'm not ugly. I'll buy that book about how to win friends and influence people. Vera and Jennifer aren't round my neck any more – I'm going to go back and find something important and give myself to it.*

And at the back of her mind ran this thought: *and if there is war . . .*

War is passionate and important. War is fascinating. War is full of men. Peter and Julia had their war; Riley and Nadine had theirs. Aunt Rose found her career in war. War is big. She closed her eyes for a moment, and felt half ashamed, because it was as if she longed for the war, but she didn't. It was – *If war comes, I will find my place in it, and it will form me.*

~

Nenna was mending a dress later that afternoon at a table on the terrace, when she felt Tom touch her gently on the arm. 'Do you remember,' he said, 'that night we saw the spider eating the firefly?'

'Yes,' she said.

'How it kept on flashing, and in the dark we all thought it was so pretty, even though actually it was being eaten alive?'

'Yes,' she said.

'And if we hadn't chosen to cast a better light on it, and look closely, we would never have known?'

'Yes,' she said.

He put down in front of her the battered copy of the *Giornale d'Italia*.

'Page three,' he said. 'Read it now. Please.'

She glanced at it.

'Is that what you were talking about last night?' she asked.

He looked puzzled, so she snapped: 'I was there, Tom, when you men were talking after dinner. I heard you!

"Doesn't the Nazi policy on the Jews worry you?"' She said it in English, mimicking his accent.

'And doesn't it?' he said.

'No!' she cried, exasperated. 'That's the Nazi policy! Not the Fascist policy!'

He is so dim sometimes.

'You're not concerned for the Jews in Germany and Austria?'

'Well of course, but what am I meant to do about them?' she said. 'I thought we were talking about here.'

'Read it,' he said, and because her father had read it and dismissed it, she picked it up, made a face at him, and read it. It was the sort of thing people – politicians, men – said when they're not really saying anything. She read it calmly. And then, towards the end, she cried out.

Something, or someone is wrong. Or the paper, or the scientists, or – someone has made a mistake.

'So,' Tom said, after the necessary silence.

'Well,' Nenna said. She felt the tightness in her voice. 'But it's not true, is it?'

'No, it's not true. There is one race: the human race. It comes in many varieties.'

'Not that – I mean – I know it's not true – I mean about – us. We have the same name we had in Israel. Our two names – Elia for the prophet from the Torah and Fiore for our family's business – most people were in cloth, but we sold flowers. Famiglia Fiore. It's not true that nothing has remained of us . . . we are here! Look!' she cried. 'I'm here!' She was patting and poking at her forearm.

'Of course you are,' said Tom.

'I'm a *Giovane Fascista*. I was a *Piccola Italiana*, and a *Giovane Italiana*,' she said, too fast. 'I was in the parades every term at school, in my little cloak and shoes. Very boring it was too. I was in the gym displays. You saw me! Pa was in the army! His blood won the Trentino! Now they say we are not Italian?'

'Nenna,' said Tom.

She could feel that something peculiar was happening to her breath, as if it were running away from her, hurtling down a hill like feet about to trip—

'Did my mother not give up her wedding ring on the Day of Faith? Didn't she? There were fifty Jewish generals in the army during the war. The oldest and the youngest recipients of the Gold Medal – both Jews! Luigi Luzatti, Prime Minister of Italy, 1910 – Jewish! Ettore Ovazza, newspaper founder, a founding Fascist like Papà – Jewish! Ernesto Nathan, Mayor of Rome, 1907–1913 – Jewish! Seven Jews among the One Thousand who marched with Garibaldi! In 1922, two hundred and fifty Jews in the March on Rome!'

'Nenna,' Tom said.

'I don't understand. Why do they write that? That we are not Italian!'

'That's the kind of thing Fascists believe,' Tom said.

'That's not true!' she said. 'The Duce has never been against Jews. He has a Jewish mistress! La Sarfatti! She was an inspiration of Fascism—' She stopped herself.

What am I thinking!

She breathed, and felt the smile return to her face.

'It is a mistake of course,' she said. 'They don't mean us. They mean the foreign Jews. Of course not everyone who

324

wants can be Italian. Papà will make sure. He will be making sure right now.'

Calm descended on her. *Of course. Of course.*

'Nenna!' he cried. 'Does it say in the Manifesto that there are different types of Jew? Have you ever heard a Fascist say that? Nenna! Why would they care? Even if they knew? And Nenna – anyway – so what? It doesn't matter what the Duce has always said. He is aligned with Herr Hitler now, and he is saying what Herr Hitler wants to hear. The Duce has agreed to go along with National Socialism. Do you understand that?'

She glanced up at him, and picked up her sewing.

'Nenna – how could it possibly be all right just because it's about other types of Jew?'

Her mouth was so tight she could hardly speak. Her jaw ached as she pushed the words out.

'Papà will sort it out,' she said. She shook out the cloth of the dress; ivy leaves in two shades of green, printed on pale yellow cotton. 'And anyway, we would always choose being Italian over being Jewish.'

'Nenna.'

She peered at the seam at the waistband where the skirt had come away.

Tom threw his hands in the air, and walked off.

She felt as if she had won. She put the dress down and went inside and again she threw up.

~

Tom was going into Bracciano with Riley, to watch the newsreels – or rather, the LUCE propaganda reels.

'Come with us,' he said to Nenna, charmingly, in front of everyone. She didn't look at him, she just said no, very coolly, and went to her mother.

There was Herr Hitler on the silver screen, quickstepping along: the announcement said that the Fascist dagger dangling from his belt on little links of silver chain was a present from Mussolini. There was a clip again from his Italian visit in May, where he swore that the Alps would always be an insurmountable national border, and the band played 'Deutschland Über Alles' and 'Giovinezza' to a silent, serious crowd, and the floodlights shone on the sailors' round white caps so they looked like so many full moons. Tom pulled softly at his lip in the dark, and felt the breath rise and fall in his chest.

Afterwards, he stopped at the hotel and after some finagling with the night clerk, a moody youth with curious teeth and a flat cap sliding around on overpowering hair oil, was able to telephone London. Luckily it was Vernon, who liked Tom, who picked up the phone on the foreign desk. Vernon heard Tom out, and said he would see what he could do. Tom said he would file something in the meantime, and ring again the following afternoon.

Walking back, Tom said to Riley: 'Is it going to be like Germany? Will people have to leave?' and before Riley could answer he said: 'Because we must help them. Even Aldo.'

Riley looked at him, and said: 'Do you think there will be war?'

'Do you?' Tom answered, and he saw something pass over Riley's grey eyes, a sadness, a ghost, an emptiness, a terror.

'Riley?' Tom said.

Riley flicked his gaze, and looked at Tom, and said, after a moment of thought: 'Tom, forgive me, I'm going to be allegorical. You recall the Masaccio Virgin and Child in the National Gallery?'

Tom didn't. 'All right,' said Riley. 'Georges de la Tour. Caravaggio!'

These painters Tom could recall: the formidable chiaroscuro; deep recesses of shadow, gleaming points of clarity and light.

'They use a single source of light,' Riley said, 'to throw everything into such deep relief.'

'So?' said Tom.

'Fascists and Nazis have only one source of light.'

'Oh!' Tom cried in recognition. 'Sunflowers!'

'Exactly,' Riley said. 'Whereas normally we have all the strands of everything we've ever cared about casting different lights on human existence, and we operate by that complex light, with changing shadows, and things coming in and out of view, and subtlety, and nuance, and we work it out for ourselves, and it shifts as we go along . . . So when you accept a single light source and deny others – history, education, the experiences of other peoples, science – your light and dark become black and white. People do it in times of chaos. They think someone clear and strong will rescue them, and that they will not have to take responsibility for themselves.'

Tom had never heard so much from Riley. He breathed very gently, so as not to jar the moment.

'It seems safer – the wrong, over there, and the right, here,' Riley said. 'But it can't work. Because it's not true.'

Tom thought: *When you buy into something that takes*

over your conscience, your judgement, your vision, then you
lose subtlety. And human nature is inclined to subtlety. And
change. And chaos. So you lose your humanity.

'. . . so yes,' Riley was saying, 'I do think there will be a
war. And the irony of that is, that war itself throws everything
into black and white. We're us, they're the enemy. It's very
refreshing. For a while.'

Tom was surprised. 'Was that how it was for you?' he
dared to ask. 'Before?'

'On one level, yes. Once you had flung in your lot, it was
very simple.'

'Refreshing!'

'All this bloody to-ing and fro-ing, all this moral fiddle
faddle!' Riley burst out.

'But you can't want . . .' Tom said.

'I don't want any of what's currently on offer,' Riley said.
'I want everyone to settle down, so we can get on with
solving the problems we already have. Poverty and disease
and injustice and so on. To be honest, I want a treacherous
Nazi with a silver bullet for Herr Hitler.'

'Would that be enough?'

Riley laughed his restricted, harlequin laugh. 'Evidently
not,' he said. 'Evidently now we need a treacherous Italian
Fascist too.'

'I showed the latest – the racist manifesto – to Nenna,'
Tom said.

'And did she understand it?' Riley asked.

'It's clear enough.'

'Well, that does for Nadine and me,' said Riley. 'Dear God.
Just as well you're not really our son, eh?'

Tom did not know what to say to that. *Joking? About this?*

'Sorry,' said Riley. 'It helps, with a particular mix of the unbearable and the idiotic . . .'

He looked sorry. He looked, suddenly, terrible.

'What Aldo said last night,' Tom said, 'that it's a mistake – but it's been confirmed, with names – yet there's this silence. As a founding Fascist apparently he thinks he has some sway. Nenna of course says it's a mistake, too, and even if it's not, they don't mean Jews like them, like her family. They mean foreign Jews.'

'And does she think that makes it all right?'

'I bloody hope not!' Tom said. Then, 'No, I don't believe she does. I believe she's parroting her upbringing. And beginning to doubt. I'm working on her! As a result of which, she's not talking to me. And the irony is, there's so few Jews in Italy anyway.'

~

Back in the kitchen, getting water to clean his mouth, Riley felt flummoxed. *Founding Fascist?* He thought. *Not just going-along-with-it Fascists. They're real Fascists. Hundred per cent think-it's-all-marvellous Fascists.*

Nadine was at the stove with a coffee pot. He looked across at her, and before he could stop himself he said, 'I wish you'd told me earlier.'

Nadine looked bewildered.

'That this family is Fascist,' he said. 'All this.' He gestured into the room, the whole thing.

There was a pause before she said, 'I do too. I'm sorry. You see, but you don't see, and then it's too late.'

329

She doesn't realise, he thought. *She doesn't see . . .* He lit a cigarette and accepted a tiny chicory coffee. *If I were them I would take my entire family somewhere else. America or Australia or Britain. Right now.*

'Where's Aldo anyway?' Nadine was asking.

'In Rome,' said Riley, 'no doubt bending Mussolini's ear about the comparative merits of different kinds of Jews.'

'Six hundred and thirteen,' Nadine said.

'What?'

'Different types of Jew,' she said. 'The image of the pomegranate: six hundred and thirteen seeds yet we are all one fruit.'

He smiled. 'How do you know that?'

'I have no idea!' she said. 'It's one of those things I've always known. My mother must have told me. Oh! Yes – it's the number of mitzvah. The Commandments, in the Torah.'

'Was Jacqueline concerned with the Torah?'

'Not in the least. But I suppose she learned it when she was young.'

Nadine had that look of loss on her face that meant sorrow not for Jacqueline's death, but for not having had her properly in life.

'One fruit,' Riley said. 'It's nice.'

They were silent for a moment.

'But if they don't see the risks,' she said, 'or don't believe in them, what can anyone do?'

'Keep talking,' he said.

Chapter Fifteen

Bracciano, Summer 1938

There is a feeling that rises in a loyal person when the object of their loyalty becomes itself disloyal. There can be physical manifestations: a certain lack of safety in the joints of the body, a nervousness underfoot. Insecurity is part of it, where that which has been relied on is no longer a friend. Mentality has its own nausea; dizziness; weak ankles which will turn and let you fall; a glass which slips from your hand; an angry roar which erupts at a small provocation which did not deserve such a response. In some cases these feelings are immediate, acknowledged, and pure. In others they are followed wherever they go by a phalanx of disbelief, unwillingness, reluctance, self-interest and blindness. Thus it was with Aldo. So complete was Aldo's devotion that nothing the beloved could do would arrest it.

Dux Mea Lux. Right from the beginning. From the miseries of the war and the chaos that followed it to the gleaming streets of Littoria today; from the dangerous drunks and strikers and villains of 1919 to the tough, obedient, phalanxes of men sweating over their wheelbarrows, long files of them, shifting Italian soil to make Italian fields for Italian families – he saw it every day. Every day. Human happiness and hard work. Systematising the rivers, clearing the ditches, dragging away load after load after load of underbrush, load after load of mud. Dig and dump, dig and dump. As with the land, so with the men, and as with the men so with the country. Redeemed, by work and by community. The symbolism of it filled him with joy: as with the earth, so with the hearts and the minds.

One man made all this happen. One man knocked us into shape.

Walking up the dusty lakeside road from Bracciano with a brown paper bag of peaches, he smiled. He was thinking about a glass of beer and how one day, all ditches will work effectively, all roads will be metalled, everyone will have a little car, and there will be no more donkeys in Rome . . . Controlling nature. Driving out the mosquitoes. No more malaria. No more need for anyone to eat acorns and frogs, and die young. Though actually he liked frog. Fried with a little lemon, delicious.

How lovely it was, in the cool of the evening, as the flies and the wasps disappeared; the stream singing alongside the road, the sky so high, just beginning to fade into violet. Exercise was itself a patriotic activity – but it was not for that that he walked. In his hardworking days, walking was what gave him his moment of peace, during which he would count his blessings and consider, though he would always deny being in any way a religious man, his mitzvahs.

Recently, he had been listing every reason the Duce had to love him, Aldo, personally.

My war service. a) I was a volunteer; I did not wait about, I was happy and proud to spill my Italian Jewish blood for Italy in the mountains and let me tell you, boy, the mountains were as hard as the trenches were where Tommaso's kind-of papà lost his voice and his looks. We were fighting for the existence of our country. Il Duce understands that and he will never forget it. And, b) I was decorated. No, I'm not going to tell you what I did. The memory of my friends is good enough for me. They know, and that is enough. It was good enough for them, for my commanding officers. I didn't desert. I got my bronze medal.

I enrolled as a Fascist in 1919. 1919!

I was there for the March on Rome. Of course I didn't have to march very far – but I was there. They gave me the scarf.

My work – he greets me when I am in the group around him at work. He knows me. He said so. He said, 'Hey, I know you. You still here? Good man. Good work.'

And how often am I there in the crowd outside Palazzo Venezia, listening to his magnificent speeches? He sees me – I know he does. He knows me, and what I have done. I have been there for the inauguration of every one of the new cities: Littoria, Sabaudia, Aprilia, Pontinia.

My children. Four is not so many, but they are good and strong, and they serve as they should. Nenna in her cape and beret!

Four children, four towns. Lovely symmetry! *Perhaps we should have another, for Pomezia.* He had never mentioned it to Susanna, but in his heart he wished they had named the children after the towns. Of course the timing was wrong. *But Fernanda Littoria Elia Fiore. What a name! Marinella Pontinia . . . che bella.*

Laying the miles of white concrete into the hard-won channels of the new canals; the network of new roads, cambered and tarmacked and water-resistant, lined with new trees; the acres of land growing wheat and corn and beets; the vineyards, the olive groves. Trees and fields, ditches and towns, piazzas and football pitches, town halls and post offices, schools and hospitals, Green of Paris sprayed all over against the malaria, and quinine all round. The six beautiful great pumping engines as big as aeroplanes.

So much work. So much achieved. And next year, Pomezia! So much still to do.

He tried to think of anything that was wrong. His feet ached a little in his boots: the toes that were mangled by the frostbite of 1917–18. But he hardly noticed that any more. *What did boys know? The idea that you can build without a bit of destruction, some discipline and decision-making. Making* frittata *without breaking eggs. These children . . . The man though, the famous Riley . . . Well, it's just as well he is English, and going home soon. Not the kind you want for a cousin. Not here, not now.*

He was glad to be away from Rome. There had been a scene at Di Veroli's shop. A silence when he entered. A couple of the younger men giving him looks, and old Seta – not Seta next door, his brother – Daniele's father – who was clearly in a mood about something, said: 'Oh, look, here he comes. Hey, Aldo – tell me – you say you're not a Jew, and the Duce says you're not an Italian – so what are you going to be now? Have you thought about it? Got many choices?' Aldo had laughed, of course, and gone to embrace the old fool, but Seta said 'It's not funny—' like a toad falling, and the men around let a curtain of chill circle them, so that Aldo had had to leave making a 'well you're all crazy' gesture which actually, as he ducked back out into the sunshine, made him feel a little ill.

So he was glad out here with his family, away from all that. That pessimism, that expectation of oppression. His father had warned him about it: a Jewish thing, how we hold ourselves down with it . . . *Don't fall for it! Be the man to break free of it.* Yes, better to walk and swim and see these lovely trees, Susanna making her own ricotta with the farm women, the great copper over the open fire, the little baskets of white curds put out to cool. Better to bring home the eels in a bucket; take the boys out to shoot, play *sedid sediola* with Marinella, rocking her even faster on his knees, pretending to throw her out of the window.

Aldo swaggered in just in time for dinner, smiling. Nenna ran to him like a worried dog scenting salvation before he could even put the peaches down. He flung his strong arm over her shoulder.

'What's the matter?' he said, surprised by her sudden warmth. 'What is it, *bambina*?' Her face flooded with the fresh pinkness of relief.

'I saw the newspaper, Papà,' she cried.

'Were you worried?' Aldo said. 'There's no need! Oh, come here.' He put the bag down on the table, and wrapped his arms around her, all love, all fatherness, glad to have the opportunity with this big girl who so seldom now came to him blinking for comfort. 'Some fools are saying it came from Minculpop, that the Duce approved it. Well that can't be true, can it? I have written to him, and his reply will explain everything. He'll write back soon. I've been telephoning too. Everyone knows it's a nonsense, some little stupidity. Fascism is unity, *tesoro*, isn't it? Isn't it? Collective and equal? For the Slovenian and the Arab, the Jew and the Libyan, the Sicilian and the Venetian – all of us equal in the Empire?'

He was crooning to her now, and looking over her head to Susanna, sharing his reassurance.

'The Duce has always said so,' he murmured. 'He will knock this on the head. It's just a stupid insult, a mistake. It means nothing.' He smelt her clean hair, and his heart was full of her, his first-born lovely girl. For what had he suffered, if not to keep this girl safe?

'I said to him – do you want to know what I wrote?' She nodded. 'I wrote that of course I do not doubt him in any way, indeed that it's my very faith in him that causes me to believe that he himself would want to calm your foolish fears! Because the Duce is as another father to you – all wise, all loving. Like me! So, we know he will write back! But we know too that he is a very busy man.'

Susanna was clattering, cutting onions, casting them into the warm oil, their fragrance rising. The boys were arguing

336

about who would lay the table; Tom was collecting the plates, the bread, the salt. On the wireless, Louis Armstrong finished singing 'On the Sunny Side of the Street'. 'And that was the ever-popular Italian musician Luigi Fortebraccia,' said the announcer, blandly.

'What?' said Tom, in sudden, harsh disbelief.

'What?' said Susanna, to Tom.

'Did you hear that?' Tom said. '"Luigi Fortebraccia"? He's certainly not Italian. He's an American negro. It's Louis Armstrong. A black American negro.'

Nenna looked up from her father's shoulder and stared at Tom.

'It's a mistake, Masino,' Aldo said kindly. 'It's all just a mistake.'

For a moment Tom looked as if he was going to throw the pile of plates, or swear, or—

'Isn't it just,' Tom said, and walked out to the terrace, his back rod-straight.

Aldo looked from his wife to his daughter and shrugged and made a face: crazy boy!

~

It was Susanna who decided that the English had to stay longer at Bracciano. 'Please don't go,' she said to Nadine. 'I am happy to see you again.' There was something in her voice – what, a strain? The very slightest echo of strain? – that made Nadine stop for a moment.

'What is it, Susanna?' she said – but neither her minimal Italian nor Susanna's few words of English was enough. The very spareness of Susanna's communication though gave it

337

a force. Please don't go. It could be courtesy; it could be desperation. Nadine smiled and said, 'Shall I get Nenna to translate?' with a gesture towards outside, but Susanna shook her head. '*Non è niente*,' she said, which Nadine knew to mean 'It's nothing.' Though, literally, she thought, it translates as 'It's not nothing.' *Hm.*

She spoke to Riley about it later.

'Well, they're all over the place, the lot of them,' he said. 'Perhaps she sees things her blinkered husband doesn't.'

'Might you talk to her?' Nadine suggested, knowing as she did that—

Riley looked at her. Really?

She didn't know. Perhaps it was *niente.*

When Aldo saw them he started bellowing: 'So glad you are staying long; stay a long time! Whenever you like!'

'He's some kind of monster, isn't he?' Riley whispered to Nadine.

She gave him a look.

'Sorry,' he said.

~

The announcement a few days later, that Mussolini was absolutely behind the new racial manifesto made Tom's heart leap. *Now*, he thought. *This is the moment.*

But it had no effect whatsoever on Aldo's thoughts. He continued seamlessly: 'Well, he doesn't mean us, the Italian Jews. He means the foreign Jews. Certainly he doesn't mean those of us who were Fascists from the beginning, from the March on Rome. These journalists!' he cried, cheerfully. 'No sense of detail, no knowledge of history . . . And you seem to think,' he told Riley, 'that because something is said, something will happen! Ah, such touching faith. So literal, the English. Nothing is happening! This isn't Germany – all right, we can get the railways into shape but that doesn't mean people will follow rules. Let me tell you about the viper invasion. Years ago – you remember, Susanna? Nenna? – there were suddenly vipers everywhere, a plague, so the mayor promised five lire for every dead viper that was brought in – and half the neighbourhood set up viper farms overnight. Fellow at Trevignano built a new bar out of vipers. The *contadino* is *furbo* and so is everybody else. Why would they waste their time with this? The Italian Fascist has better things to do than start to hate his neighbour . . . He has too much pride. Tommaso, do you see anybody doing anything about any of these declarations? No. So please,' and he dropped his voice to a whisper, 'will you stop scaring Nenna? I need to go to work and not come back to scenes of hysteria. This Jew has an appointment with the government to finish off another city.'

Aldo didn't know what they did all day while he was working. Ate lots of food that he paid for, he hoped. In the evenings they all drank wine and played *scopa*, and at *Ferragosto* they all went to the *festa*. The fireworks were superb that year; Aldo bought nut brittle, sharp and sweet in the mouth, for everyone.

'This is a Christian celebration, isn't it?' Tom said, as the Holy Mother of God lurched through the streets on her gold platform, on the shoulders of her agricultural devotees.

'The assumption of the Virgin Mary to heaven,' Aldo said, and wondered why Tom seemed amused.

～

After Ferragosto, after the shooting stars of San Lorenzo started filling the night sky, they all returned to Rome, and it was time for the English to go back to London. Most of the farewells were fond, no declarations were made, and there had been no actual fights in the past week, so Aldo was happy. Only one thing was said which annoyed him.

The English were in their car, ready to leave, and Nadine leaned forward out of the window like a queen on a balcony, and said, with gentle formality, to Aldo and to Susanna: 'We wanted to say – all of us – that if you find you would like to come to London at all, for whatever reason, please come. *Se vuoi venire a Londra.*' She wanted Susanna to understand. 'We would love to be your hosts and help you.'

Well that's sweet of her, Aldo thought, and he said, cheerfully, 'Ah, but with this war everyone's so sure of, how will that ever be?'

'I mean,' Nadine said, 'If, because of the war . . . As Jews.'

'AAOOW!' he cried, a great big mock-furious noise. 'Not you too! I thought you were the sensible one, my sister! Of course we will visit you one day soon, and we will go to Brighton and complain about your horrible English sea and bad food. Now go on – time to leave before I cry. Tommaso, get in, *vai*!'

'Oh, I'm not going,' Tom said. 'I'm staying here for a while. Unfinished business.'

They all stared at him.

'You are so jammy,' said Kitty, peering out of the window behind Nadine. 'Bye!'

Aldo made a special sympathetic face for her, clicked his heels and gave her a Roman salute – at which a complete chill fell over the group hanging out of the windows. Kitty's hand twitched – but she did not make the salute back. Nadine gave a rather ghastly smile. Riley in the driver's seat barked a bitter laugh, and looked at Aldo, a true look, eye to eye, and pulled out.

'My friends,' Aldo said, smiling.

'*Arrivederci!*' called Nadine, her hand out of the window, waving, and he saw that her face was white as bone, suddenly.

'Aldo!' she yelled, leaning out, her hat in peril – 'Aldo! *Arrivederci!* I mean it!'

Chapter Sixteen

Rome, September–November 1938

The city feeling of Rome enveloped Tom quickly: fractious, noisy, exciting. It was still terribly hot. Laundry hung limp from the balconies and across the roads; even the fleshiest geranium leaves were going a little brown and brittle at the edges; donkeys leaned into slivers of shade at midday, pining for autumn. The women were unbearably beautiful, and the house too small for the grown children and the unspoken conflict inside it. It all made him nervous. The former ghetto was quieter, cautious. Dark-eyed girls smirked up at the young toughs on whose arm they hung; shopkeepers kept more indoors than he remembered. There did seem to be fewer people around.

The day before the family had gone back to London, sitting out on the low wall by the river, Tom had had a conversation with Riley. He said, 'The paper says they can use me here. I'm going to get my Italian really up to scratch before I go down to Palermo. It's ridiculous, really, that my tenses are so limited. I practically only operate in the present, like a Buddhist . . .'

Riley had said: 'Are you sure?' to which Tom could only say, 'Yes.' Riley did not like the plan, Tom was sure of that.

'It makes sense,' Tom said. 'The paper's really happy about it – their correspondent here is very political, so they want a bit of more social reporting. I'll do some vignettes of everyday life, that sort of thing. What the man in the street thinks. They say I can use a nom de plume.' (This was not the complete truth. The foreign desk had already liked, and printed, his piece on the dilemma of 'Armando, the Fascist Jew of Rome'.) 'They won't pay much and there's no guarantee about the job when I go home after Palermo,' he said. But this way, he felt, he could achieve . . . something.

'And your real reason for staying?'

'That,' Tom said. 'Plus I'm going to make them come to London.'

Riley looked across to the low glow of Trastevere.

'Are you in love with her?' he said.

'Good Lord, Riley!' said Tom. 'Course not. We hardly talk.'

'That's why I ask,' Riley said, drily.

'How could I be in love with a girl who's besotted with Mussolini?' Tom said, and tried to laugh.

Riley looked at him.

'You don't have to stay in love with the same girl all your life,' he said.

'I'm not in love with her!' Tom's face now was scarlet, he could feel it, and there was nothing he could say which wasn't protesting too much. 'She's my sister. And I'm responsible for her.'

'But she doesn't seem to be taking it in.'

'Well perhaps we're wrong!' Tom said. 'Perhaps this isn't leading anywhere. I have to try though. Don't I?'

Riley smiled.

'Yes,' he said. 'I suppose you do. And if it doesn't work, this is what you do: you give up, and come home. Set a time limit on it.'

~

So, he had to try. He registered with the *Prefettura*, found a tutor with a thorough knowledge of irregular subjunctives and the future perfect. He studied, he wrote, he made friends with some chaps at Reuters, he filed stories. He was staying at Johnny's again but he visited the cousins regularly; chummed up a bit with Stefano and Vittorio. Summer burnt out into autumn: something Tom had never seen in Italy. There was something real about being there out of holiday season. He tried to hold on to that, because almost everything else felt frail and artificial. Autumn, yes, felt more genuine: working, buying socks and a jacket like an actual man. He had not realised that he did not feel like an actual man. He lifted cigarettes to and from his mouth; felt the solidity of the china of his coffee cups. Inhaled, exhaled. He let Nenna ignore him, and he waited.

Late in September he was surprised when Susanna made him dip apples in honey before dinner.

'It's Rosh Hashanah,' she said. 'Didn't you heard the shofar today? Or see the people emptying their pockets into the river? Apples and honey, chicken *polpettine* with celery. Happy New Year! And I've ordered a mullet for Yom Kippur.'

'I thought you weren't Jewish like that,' he said.

'Some things you needn't change,' she said. 'Everybody likes chicken *polpettine*. And cakes. I've made *sfratti*.'

'They're shaped like sticks,' said Nenna, coldly. 'For bashing Jews with. It's traditional.' She had herself been to the cemetery with Susanna, and placed stones on Aldo's ancestors.

Several times he was overtaken by a profound inability to do anything at all. It was following one of these that he bought the jacket. Tweed was not available, so he got something in a curious substitute from Corsica. Rome's September had been as far as could be from the aching chill of his recent autumns in Cambridge, the east wind over the flat lands, but by October the evenings were offering the damp that settles into your bones, and the darkness creeping in earlier and earlier.

~

A few days after Rosh Hashanah, Nenna came over to Johnny's to wave a newspaper at Tom.

'So what about this?' she cried out. 'No war! Look! It says so right here. The Duce has negotiated a peace – just in time for Yom Kippur. You see? Peace with honour, your Chamberlain says.'

'Let's go out and celebrate,' Tom said, but she refused. She had only come to make her point.

~

Johnny, when he came back that evening, said to Tom, with a mixture of embarrassment and anger, 'You can't really stay here, old boy, if you're going to be visiting them all the time and having them visit you. It's not entirely safe.'

345

'How do you even know she was here?' Tom asked.

'Exactly,' said Carmichael.

'So are you asking me to move out?'

'I'm asking you, again, to make up your mind.'

'You know what side I'm on, Johnny.'

'Act like it, then.'

～

Peace with honour. The sigh of relief across Europe moved like the wind, and for a moment Tom too let himself breathe out. But then, in its wake, the follow-up presaged by the Racist Scientists' Manifesto began to make itself known. *As if the peace agreement had given it permission*, he thought. The Duce growing bold on this diet of approval. Tom did not believe in this peace. In its existence. *There is no peace. There is stalemate.*

He went to the island the day the next announcement was made, ready to catch her if she gave him a chance. She came home in tears, bewildered, suspended: new laws said Jews could no longer go to school. Nor could they be employed in any capacity in any Italian school, from nursery to university. 'Papà!' she cried again, and again Aldo went into the recital, the words stale by now, but as comforting as a nursery rhyme for her. This time there was a new verse: 'We are *Discriminati*! The Duce has said so, you see, I was right! As I was wounded in the war, and as a founding Fascist, of course this does not apply to us! And anyway, the women are setting up a Jewish school. You can teach there. Everything is all right my darling. Have faith.'

'But where am I to study?' she asked, and Aldo told her

346

to be patient, he would sort it out, there was some paper-work, of course she would be going back – and so she was patient. Some of her friends – Jewish friends – who had matriculated already were told they could stay on. Those who had not were not admitted. She waited. Not for long. In October came the government's Declaration on Race, which the entire family ignored. It didn't have anything to do with them. They were after all *discriminati*.

Tom stood alongside, and stared in disbelief as yet again she closed her eyes and let her father hug her.

Then she looked at him, and said, 'What? Your know-all eyes are full again – what is it now?'

'So it's all right to throw other Jewish children out of school?' he said. 'If their father wasn't wounded, or if they've only been here three hundred years, not two thousand? As long as it's all right for you?'

She went very pale. 'Of course not,' she said. 'But this is the world. This is the real world.'

'Your head has been poisoned,' he said, and she started to shake.

'I didn't make any of this,' she said.

'Exactly,' he said.

He found himself staring at adults, proper adults, men and women in their forties and older. *All these people have known war, and they're just carrying on about their business.* And at young people too: *all these people, their parents were in it, one way or another – do they talk about it? What have they been told?* In the English bookshop he found copies of

347

All Quiet on the Western Front, and *Goodbye to All That*, read them all. *Oh, Dad*, he thought, over and over, just that phrase. *Oh, Dad. You were younger than me now*. He realised he meant both Peter and Riley, and that he somehow meant Aldo as well.

He had developed the habit of reading the foreign papers at the agency: you couldn't get them anywhere else, and the local press was uniform in its Fascism and its bellicosity. Nothing looked good. Nothing.

On 11 November – Armistice Day! – Tom picked up the *Washington Post*, and read, 'The greatest wave of anti-Jewish violence since Adolf Hitler came to power in 1933 swept Nazi Germany today.' The diplomat who had been shot in Paris a few days before had died. Tom read of the riots across Germany and Austria which had followed – 'as a result'. The Hitler Youth, the Gestapo and the SS had been out smashing up synagogues, robbing and burning and destroying Jewish shops and factories and businesses, and murdering Jewish people, and taking them away. Thousands of them.

He picked up another paper: 'Mob law ruled in Berlin throughout the afternoon and evening and hordes of hooligans indulged in an orgy of destruction. I have seen several anti-Jewish outbreaks in Germany during the last five years, but never anything as nauseating as this. Racial hatred and hysteria seemed to have taken complete hold of otherwise decent people. I saw fashionably dressed women clapping their hands and screaming with glee, while respectable middle-class mothers held up their babies to see the "fun".'

A slow heat started to skulk about under his skin. A full

physical weakness crept up him, and the unanswerable questions – *what am I doing about this? How can I stop this? How can I find those people and bring them back to their families, how can I stop those women, comfort those babies, bury those dead, rebuild those buildings? How can I do anything?*

He knew perfectly well what he could do. He, like the boy Grynszpan who had shot the diplomat, could go over there with the silver bullet and put it through the head of this monster . . . or he could go out today and try – and no doubt fail – to shoot Mussolini.

I'm no better than Nenna, he thought. *There is going to be a war. Hitler's just pushing it because he thinks no one will stop him. Mussolini's pushing it because he's in love with Hitler. But – if Chamberlain didn't put his foot down for the Czechs in the Sudetenland, why would he for the Jews? For Germany's own Jews? Well then Chamberlain will have to go, because there is too much anger now.*

Is Aldo, across town with his fake coffee, reading this? Will this open his eyes? Will Susanna stand up, finally? Will Vittorio or Stefano? Will Nenna?

Will I?

There was a photograph of Grynszpan in a cheap suit and a pale raincoat, hair slicked down like an adult, looking terrified among French policemen. He had lived in the same *arrondissement* as Nadine's family. He was much younger than Tom. His story dripped out over the next days and weeks, in the newspapers and magazines. Tom read all that he could find. Herschel was an immigrant eastern boy, not a native Sephardi like Nadine's family – the wrong kind of

Jew, by Aldo's standards. He had been born in Hanover in '21, his father a Polish tailor with three children dead already out of six. Herschel was clever and lazy with a good memory and a hot temper. He was dark, sickly, religious, proud. On the Sunday, he'd had a big fight with his uncle Abraham, known as Albert, of Maison Albert on the rue des Petites Ecuries. Herschel's papers had expired. Papers were essential but no one would provide them. He wasn't German, though he had been born in Germany, and he wasn't allowed to be Polish though his parents were, and though living in Paris he couldn't be French because France wouldn't have him. Without papers he had to leave but nowhere – including where he'd come from – would let him in. Also, he needed money: he was forbidden to leave France with it, or to arrive anywhere else without it. But even if anyone had any to send him, it couldn't be brought in. At every turn, he could not do *x* without *y* being in place, but *y* was banned to 'his kind'.

Paris seemed much closer to Tom than Germany, or Poland, or Czechoslovakia. The French were neighbours; the Germans were the old enemy. You expected better of the French. *And it's right there, between Rome and London. Between here and home. Right here.*

Herschel had been staying in the *chambre de bonne* of the flat that Abraham had left because it wasn't safe for the family to stay there unless they threw the boy out – and they couldn't do that. *Why?* Tom asked himself, and looked at the picture again, and thought: *well, look at him, 100 pounds, if that, imagine him, vulnerable and furious, with his eyelashes and his ulcer and his won't-work-on-the-Sabbath and his four-days-to-leave-France. It would be a hard-hearted uncle who could bring himself to throw him out.* Then a postcard had come from a sister Bertha at Zbaszyn on the Polish border: Herschel's family in Hanover had been grabbed from their homes with nothing and dumped there – thousands of people dumped there, foisted on the Poles before the law could be changed – nothing to eat – in the woods. Bertha had apparently crossed out where she had written, *could they send money?* Well, she'd known they couldn't send money.

So Herschel had stormed off, and his friend Nathan went after him to calm him down, and they spent the day together till Nathan had to go home. Herschel went to a place called the *Tout Va Bien* – the All Is Well – for something to eat – Abraham and his brother went there looking for him, later, but the waiter said he'd left an hour before. He had gone to a little hotel in the Boulevard Strasbourg. The staff remembered him, so young. They noticed his lamp on, late into the night in the little room. On the Monday he drank black coffee and smoked and went and bought the gun. When he asked at the German Embassy, the clerk told him he was in the wrong place, to go to the Consulate. Herschel – he must have been so used to being in the wrong place, so used to perfectly good places becoming the wrong place by dint of his presence in them – declined the advice and insisted, so the clerk in the end sent him up to see Ernst vom Rath, he could deal with him. Herschel shot vom Rath, five times.

Symbolic, pointless, mad, magnificent, Tom thought. And the result! Five shots in Paris; thousands of people in

351

Germany and Austria. The day vom Rath died, two days after the shooting, was the twenty-fifth anniversary of the foundation of the Nazi Party. Many dinners and celebrations were being held. And so, when the news broke, it was simple for the Nazi leaders to all telephone each other and unleash this spontaneous patriotic response. Which, by that logic, 'the Jews' had brought on themselves.

Tom visited the island that evening, and left the paper there, on the table where any of them could see it. When it disappeared, he had hopes – but Susanna had used it to light the stove. *It is all marching on*, he thought. *Until it happens, whatever it is, there is no proof that it will, and every time something does happen, the goalposts are shifted about . . . Christ, this has been building up for a long time.*

~

Tom dreamed that night about Herschel Grynszpan's cousin, Bertha. He pictured her in an abandoned horse stall at Zbaszyn, sitting on concrete steps outside, to avoid the old damp straw within, the dirty smell of which seeped through her clothing – the only clothing she had, not nice after two weeks, but they had no opportunity to bring anything else, only some food which they had eaten and the cash which had been taken from them at the border . . . Waking, he wondered if she even heard what her cousin had set off.

~

Johnny Carmichael said, over a glass of red in a dim *bottega*, that about 11,000 people had been sent to a place called

Buchenwald, and 11,000 more arrived in the three days after Kristallnacht, and were put in a separate part, with barbed wire in between. He said 'My Country Right or Wrong' was written up over the gateway.

'They are systematically removing from daily life all active members and officers of any other party, and any other people they don't want in their new world order. They are classifying them: politicals get a red triangle; criminals a green one. The workshy – i.e. gypsies and people who refuse to be moved about for munitions work – get a black one. People who didn't want to move house! The International Bible Students get lilac. Sexual perverts get purple.'

'So what is it,' Tom said. 'The removal of undesirables from the ideal society: political persecution as social planning?'

'They'd call it state planning for the benefit of the community,' Johnny said. 'With forced labour, but they're not clear what it's for. Could be building and extending the camp. They thought it was for POW camps, or giant hospitals.'

'At least at the Agro Pontino it wasn't forced labour . . .' Tom said.

'No, but they were moving people around, and paying them hardly anything, and destroying everything so they could start their social experiment on a blank canvas. What about the people who lived there before? They'll tell you there weren't any. What about the locals who weren't offered any of the land? It all went to impeccable Fascists from the north.'

'But it was about housing war veterans.'

'Of a certain type,' said Johnny. 'But yes, the Nazis are

worse, and not only for being more efficient. This could be about labour policy: future slave-labour camps using populations from invaded territories. It's not new. The Spartans did it, with the Helots. Thus other races would be destroyed, morally, spiritually, economically and physically, and Germany would repopulate Europe and ultimately the world.'

'You're making this up,' Tom said, a little nervously.

'No I'm not,' Johnny said. 'Three-stage Nazi war. One, get Germany. Two, get Europe. Three, get the world. During each stage, train men up in grand-scale cruelty to be able to effect the next stage.'

Tom fell silent.

'Tom, do you really think I'm making it up? Because if you do, if you can just sit there and say that, you need to go elsewhere, Tom. You really do.'

Really?

'Nobody's happy about you being here. You're a risk to us and to be frank you're a risk to your cousins as well. I did say. Personally, I think you should just go back to London.'

'I'm not going back to London.'

'Wrong answer,' Johnny said. He glanced sideways. 'The right answer would have been along the lines of, "No, of course, I hate the Nazis and the Fascists." You're rather hogging the grey area, Tom.' Johnny gave a little snort, and gathered himself. 'Actually,' he said, 'it would be best if you go back to your Fascists. Or somewhere – anywhere. Just don't be here. End of the week.'

Oh.

❧

Damn damn damn damn damn.

Not that he blamed Johnny. Johnny was right. He could honestly say he hated Fascism, but he didn't hate all Fascists, did he? No, he didn't.

He moved into a tiny hotel room he couldn't afford, and thought about Chamberlain, with his piece of paper 'symbolic of the desire of our two countries never to go to war again'. He thought about Riley and Peter. He thought about Nenna and Aldo and Susanna and the boys, and of how Europe was becoming a swamp-like thing, untrustable. But full of real people, as real as him, all living their lives and suffering. Some more than others. It seemed to him that there was far too much, now, just too much happening, everything wrapped round everything else, intertangled like a ball of serpents. This did not look to him like something which could be disentangled. Once, long ago, Peter had explained to the children the concept of the Gordian knot. Tom thought about clean swords, and immense cannons, and the judgement of Solomon. Those things looked good to him.

I wonder what you do, he thought, *when what happens makes less sense than what doesn't happen. When reality takes the path of the surreal.*

He had a fair amount of time to brood. *But I'm going to need to be strong . . .* He took to exercising in the parks and gardens. Autumn was red-leaved with the lowering sun. His body wanted and needed something. *You should just go home. Johnny's right.* But he couldn't. He had forgotten Riley's advice: set a time limit on it.

❧

Just a few days after Kristallnacht came a new announcement. New laws: for the Defence of the Race. They forbade Jews from having most things a contemporary human being might want or expect, from wirelesses to the right to work, they restricted property ownership, forbade inter-marriage and the placing of newspaper announcements, expelled foreign Jews, revoked citizenship. They covered all aspects of what it was to be normal. They were familiar enough, from Germany.

And again Tom went straight round to the island, sniffing the possibility of a crack through which sanity might creep into their minds. *Perhaps this time – surely. Revoking citizenship?*

But no. At the dinner table, Aldo, charisma gleaming, still smiled and said: 'Don't worry, my chicks. It doesn't mean us! The Duce will never let us down.'

Tom wondered if Aldo was actually going insane.

The boys and Susanna turned to their plates. Tom could almost see the delicate smoky coils of their unspoken fears rising on the air, curling magnetically towards Aldo, and evaporating in the glow of his confidence. *That*, he thought, *is why strong leaders are so attractive. People like me are sitting and thinking and rationalising and fearing and taking into account and trying to work things out; someone like Aldo, or the Duce, is smiling broadly and saying 'But everything is fine! There is no problem!' Of course people like that. They can give up responsibility. But it's a lie. These leaders are like psychopaths – they don't see results. They have no long-term relationship with reality. One light source . . .*

'But you are no longer allowed to be in the telephone book,' Tom said. 'The telephone book!'

'Oh my dear boy,' Aldo said, joshing, sweetly. 'The telephone book! Of course we are – as if they would take the trouble to print new ones. It's all going to be fine.'

'Then why have the Orvietos left?' Susanna said suddenly. 'And the Setas? Why are people taking themselves off the register at the Union?'

'What union?' Tom asked. This was new.

'Of Italian Israelite Communities,' she said. 'People don't want to be Jewish.'

'Cowards!' Aldo said. 'Converting! No faith of any sort.'

Tom hoped Susanna would continue, but she just darted a look, and sort of slid back, and was silent again.

'Even the definition of what is a Jew has changed,' Tom said. 'To be honest, it's so complicated it must be hard for people to know whether they count or not.'

'Like the Roman aristocracy!' Aldo crowed, and laughed, and then threw him a look.

'You know people are leaving,' Tom said.

'Cowards and fools are leaving,' Aldo intoned, with impatient patience. 'And of course foreign Jews. There is nothing to fear. These are the over-reactions of those who have . . .'

Oh for crying out loud!

'Papà,' Nenna said. 'Even if it's not us, it's someone.' And that, perhaps, was the moment.

Aldo squinted at her, confused.

At this, Tom leaned gently against Nenna, sideways, and murmured, quietly: 'You can leave. Come to London.'

She turned in shock to stare at him, and her glance quickly

quartered the table like a bird of prey: her brothers, her sister, her father, her mother. 'No!' she said. 'Of course not!'

'Of course not what?' said Aldo.

'I am inviting you all to come to London,' Tom said. Quietly. Clearly. Even Aldo could not read this as an invitation to go on holiday.

But Aldo only gave a little smile of polite bewilderment. 'Why?' he asked.

Tom looked up at him. *Be bold and courteous. Be truthful.* 'Many people,' he said, 'think it would be wise. Under the circumstances.'

Aldo leaned forward, glared under his eyebrows – he even banged his fist on the table. 'And by that, they prove that they are not Italian!' he pronounced. 'Or worthy to be Italian. Of course we are not going to leave our country. This will all be—'

'Oh for Christ's sake Aldo!' Tom cried.

Susanna smiled nervously.

Tom stared at her. *How can they still pretend to be reassured? Are they all completely mad?*

'Your rights are being curtailed,' he said carefully. 'Even in Germany Jews are still allowed to go to school. Nothing here has improved in the past year. Perhaps travel will be next.'

'Why would we want to travel?' Aldo said benignly, holding his hands out, palms to the heavens. 'Masino, please. Don't insult us!'

Tom took hold of Nenna's wrist under the table and held it very tight in his fingers, pressing almost till it must have hurt her, till she turned her head.

I can't bear this, he thought. He smiled quietly, and pressed a button inside himself to start the thing.

'Aldo,' he said. 'Forgive me, but you are wrong.' An aerated feeling ran down his arms.

'My boy,' Aldo said, smiling.

'Stop that,' Tom said. 'You're deluded. They all trust you because you are a wonderful man in many ways, but you are very wrong and it is very important that you open your eyes.'

'Don't speak to me like this, Masino, at my table.'

Tom stared at Aldo, seeking for any sign of doubt in his eyes. There was none.

'You have deceived yourself, Aldo, and you are not admitting it even to yourself. Don't *you* speak to your family like this, lying to them.'

'Tommaso!' Aldo cried, and stood.

'Is every other Jew leaving Italy a fool?' he said, nervous, loud. 'And only you the clever one?' *Oh, no, I am shouting. Ah well – so let the shouting begin.* 'You *know* what is happening in Germany, Aldo. And tell me – tell your wife, and your children – has the Duce written back to you? Has he? In all these months? To say, Oh don't worry Aldo, everything's all right? No he hasn't. Nenna, has he? No. And if he did, why would you – *any* of you – believe him? He says anything he thinks will work for him! He's happy to sacrifice you and every Italian Jew to suck up to Hitler . . .'

He was becoming incoherent, but it didn't matter because Aldo was shouting back, and Susanna was crying, and the boys had stood up, a chair had been knocked over and it was all turning hopeless.

'I love you,' Tom was shouting. 'I love you all and I want you to be safe!'

Nenna was staring at him, her face paralysed with shock, suspended in time.

'You're bloody idiots the lot of you, stupid fools stuck in the headlights and Aldo, *you*—'

'You rat,' Aldo said. 'Our guest, our friend, our family. Like our son. You're a filthy slimy little rat.'

～

Ten days later, two policemen came to the little hotel; tall fellows in smart coats. News had reached their ear that an unregistered foreign Jew was living there.

'That'll be me,' said Tom, affably: six foot two, blond, cornflower-eyes, lilac smudges under them and a sleepless look. He smiled, and made his Italian accent more English. 'Do come in,' he said. 'Tea?'

Had Tom been living with the Jewish family Elia Fiore?

Yes he had, though not for a while.

Was he a relative? Nephew, they gathered?

Tom started laughing.

The taller man held Tom's papers between thumb and forefinger.

'Not by blood,' Tom said.

They thought about that.

He was damned if he was going to explain it to them. He smiled, and stood, while they murmured, glancing up at him from time to time.

They requested that he let them know, should he move.

'But of course,' said Tom. 'Thank you so much.' He was

due in Palermo anyway. He closed the door, and he was breathing shallow.

Someone has told them to find me, he thought, *because I am, on some level, a foreign Jew.*

It was a very nasty feeling.

I'm a free-born Englishman, he thought. *This is the twentieth century. And if I were a foreign Jew it would still be the twentieth century.*

He had in his English mouth a nebulous aftertaste, the ghost of a possible future, a parallel universe swerving perilously near. *They just want to know who I am, and where I am. They're not going to do anything bad to me . . .* And as he said to himself, of course not, that's nonsense, he heard the words in Aldo's voice, and he felt Aldo's excuse: they don't mean me. And he felt his own argument back: *so that makes it all right, does it?*

And Nenna had said that. Even if it's not us, it's someone. *Bertolini's uncle.*

Tom had done nothing to merit ill treatment by the Fascists.

Perhaps it's time I did.

The following day a letter arrived from the university, saying that as he was of the Hebraic race under the new laws the post provisionally offered to him was no longer available.

Even me! he thought. *Neither Jewish nor Italian, but I am on some list somewhere.*

And with that he realised that after all it was he who was going to have to leave.

But without them? Without her?

No.

~

He tracked down Bertolini.

'What can I do?' he asked. 'Is there anyone who can use me?' And Bertolini said, sympathetically but decisively, no. 'You're too tall, you're too blond, you're too English. You're too visible. Your family are founding Fascists.'

'But,' said Tom.

'You're known,' said Bertolini. 'And anyway, I don't know anyone. And don't go round acting like a fool. The wrong people will hear you and the right people will see your idiocy.'

I should go home, Tom thought. *My own country could use me.*

Or I should shoot him. Provoke a crisis and let the detritus fall where it will.

He thought, for a second: *Come on war, hurry up. Let's get on with it.*

~

He went to see Johnny at the Consulate.

'I'm sorry,' he said. 'Of course I'm with you. I'll stay away, but I need us to be friends. And I'm taking her with me. Is that fair? Tell me, how can an Italian citizen – well, a revoked citizen – come to Britain?'

Johnny, relieved, was full of information until he ascertained that the revoked Italian citizen in question was not herself inclined to go.

'All right,' he said. 'Can you give me a certificate or a formal letter saying I'm not Jewish? Because they've got it into their heads that I am.'

'Tom,' said Johnny. 'Calm down.'

~

Mid-December, on a dingy morning of a type he would never have imagined happening to Rome, Tom went back to the island and banged on the door.

Susanna answered.

'I've come to say goodbye,' he said. He said '*addio*' – 'to God' – not '*arrivederci*' – till we meet again. He stood in the hall, thin and pale. 'And I wanted to say, to say formally, for the third time: Please come with me. If you say you will come, I will stay, and I will arrange it. I'll do everything I can. The boys,' he said. 'Marinella. Aldo too.'

Susanna kissed him on both cheeks, and breathed out a little sigh through her nose. '*Buon viaggio*,' she said. 'Aldo will never agree!' as if it were a little joke, Aldo and his little ways . . . 'Next summer by the lake!' she said, in English, their old end-of-holiday greeting, and his eyes filled with tears.

Nenna came down behind her, a dark figure on the white marble stairs. She reached for her coat from the hook behind the door.

'I'll come with you to the station,' she said. He looked at her in wonder, picked up his suitcase, and said, a wild and stupid gesture, 'Bring your passport. We can get you a ticket at the station, and clothes in London.'

'Masino,' she said, cautioning, and shook her head.

But they walked out together, across the bridge and into the old Ghetto. It was both cold and warm; odd slithery weather. He could smell her coat: lanital.

'Nenna,' he said. 'Did you read about the attacks in Germany and Austria? Now that Mussolini is aping Hitler he is moving faster than Hitler did. He has legislated against you having a life at all. Your father . . .'

'. . . is a fine man,' she said, quite quietly.

'But he is wrong about this,' Tom said. 'In fact he is wrong about almost everything in the wider world. And you are old enough to look at the wider world, Nenna. It's not just about the fact that he loves you and you love him.'

She stopped for a moment, on the corner before Piazza Mattei. The stone tortoises and the fountain glowed and played for all the world as if it were a sunny day in summer long ago.

'I feel,' she said, 'that I have grown in a garden where I was planted, a beautiful garden, and that you want me to climb up and look over the garden wall.'

'Yes,' he said. 'Yes, I do. Because you are growing anyway and will see over soon enough, and even if you didn't, those walls are coming down. Or—' He was about to go off on another image, something biblical, expulsion from the Garden of Eden . . .

There was no need. She knew. It was in her face, her eyes. He looked at her, properly. Her cheeks were thinner, her eyes darker. Her mouth held a shape he had never seen before.

He was terribly, terribly relieved.

'Then come,' he said. 'Please.' His eyes caught hers, and

held them. It seemed years since they had actually looked at each other.

'I know he is fair, and kind, and good,' she said. 'I understand about everything, and yet. And yet.'

She was crying, of course. He thought: *she loves him the way I love Riley. Imagine if Riley fell to pieces before my eyes* . . . The thought made him feel weak.

'I am very afraid,' she said softly.

He stopped her, and folded her in his arms. How often must she have looked the truth in the face and turned from it, intelligent girl that she is. Tom had ignored the truth himself, and been able to avoid it just by staying away from them. *I've been a coward*, he thought. *I've let her down.*

He had always known that he would never be as strong as Riley; as brave as him, either on the battlefield or in the life that followed it. No one could be. He used to assume he would never get a chance to be – but now all that looked different. And right now, his arms full of a weeping girl, he felt strong.

'I have been dreaming about him,' she was saying. 'I see him wearing a golden shield, a woven armour, chain mail, glowing and shining, and then through it starts flakes of rust, a corroded spot, here or there, something eating at the fabric from inside. I want to touch it but I can't touch it in case there is worse beneath, like a rotten wall beneath rotten paper. If I touch it this armour will fall apart, and the body behind it will be rotten.'

'Oh dear,' he said.

'I always thought,' she went on, 'it is right to put yourself with the strong, to support the government. Certainly when you have a family! If he hadn't, how would he have worked, and earned a living? Only a – a fool would go against society.'

'It depends on the society,' he said, and she looked up at him, and said quietly: 'How is England?'

'We have elections,' he said. 'People laugh at Fascists in the street. There are all kinds of things wrong but you can say what you want about anything.'

'Masino,' she said. 'I can't talk about this to anybody.'

And that, said on the public street under the sky, iron wheels rattling over cobbles, a policeman's whistle, was to him like a horse's kick of reality. *She can't. She really can't.*

There was a silence, in which he willed her to continue. 'You can talk to me,' he said.

'You're leaving,' she said.

'So come with me.'

'I can't,' she said. 'Not now.'

'It will be more difficult later on,' he said.

She shook her head and gave a weak laugh. 'Oh, I can't leave my family. Never mind my father – my mother! And the boys – and Marinella!'

'If you come, perhaps they would be more likely to follow you,' he said, seeing even as he said it how the suggestion sank under the might of its own unlikeliness. Anyway, Nenna didn't even acknowledge it. 'Everything will be all right,' she cried. '*Attesismo!*'

'What's that?'

'Waiting,' she said. 'A Roman speciality. A Jewish one too.'

'You can't!' he cried.

'Oh, I must,' she said. 'Go on. You'll miss your train.'

'But—' he said, and

'Oh—'

And the law of not missing the train came bearing down on them; the obligatory continuation of normality, and they had to say goodbye, so they did, because *heaven forbid that anyone miss a train trying to turn the life of someone they love in a different direction*, he thought, as he turned away and walked along the platform – and then turned back, in one movement, a swerving realisation that for Christ's sake he had his own capacity to do what he wanted, what he thought was right. *We're all sleepwalking*, he thought, *wake up! WAKE UP!* – and he walked back, back down the platform, back on to the concourse, back out the tall stone entrance and across the road to where the tram he knew she would be taking would stop. She was standing there in the street, small and alone.

'Nenna,' he said, and put his hand on her arm.

'I thought you'd gone!'

'There's one thing,' he said.

She smiled at him, confused, and in itself there was something loverlike about that. *But I am not in love with her . . .*

'Marry me,' he said.

She turned her head sideways, mistrustful.

'You don't love me,' she said.

'I—' he said. 'It will help, later on. When I come back for you. It will give us a claim on you. And Marinella. When you change your mind.'

She shook her head.

'You're changing it already,' he said. 'Can't you see?'

She wouldn't acknowledge it.

'And I do love you,' he said.

367

'Not like a man and a woman,' she said.

Does she want me to? Is that what she's asking? Should I – Can I?

She's a fish on the line, I mustn't scare her away—

'We don't have to be like a man and a woman,' he said. 'But where can we find an official to give us a certificate to say we are brother and sister? And that I am sworn to you? Nenna,' and here he held up his finger, with the fine white scar on it. 'Look,' he said. She smiled and held up her own.

'Come what may,' he said, 'and that's all very well but it won't wash with any border police or Blackshirts.'

He gave her a moment. Then he said: 'All right?'

'I'll think about it,' she said. 'If you insist. Though I think it's mad. I think.'

~

From a café he rang Johnny, who was willing to try to ease the issuing of a copy of Tom's birth certificate and a *nulla osta* – a declaration that there was no legal impediment to Tom's marrying. 'But they won't marry you, old man,' he said. 'Not if she's Jewish.'

'That's why I'm asking you,' Tom said. 'It's only because she's Jewish that I need to marry her.' He knew that he had left it too late; that the web he wanted Nenna to escape had already quietly slipped into place around them.

'Welcome to modern Europe,' said Carmichael, and Tom thought *damn I'm a fool*, and again Herschel Grynszpan spun across his mind, younger than him, driven mad.

'But they think I'm Jewish,' he said. 'I'm on some list – the police came round. Give me a letter saying I am Jewish, and we'll marry on that.'

'Last time I saw you you wanted a letter saying you weren't Jewish,' Johnny said. 'Make up your mind!'

'Or, as I'm British, couldn't we marry under British law? Couldn't the ambassador marry us?'

'I've a feeling there's a limit to how many lies the Embassy can issue on your behalf,' Johnny said.

'So let's just work out which one would be most effective, and stick to that,' said Tom. 'Eh?' He leaned in to the receiver. 'Johnny,' he said. 'She's changing her mind. She doesn't fully understand what is happening. I am afraid for her safety in this country. It's my cousin.'

'I did work out that it's your cousin, old man. I'm not a complete nit. And you understand that if you take her to England and there is a war, sooner or later she'd probably be interned for being Italian?'

Tom shook his head. *Every way you look* . . .

'Could Father Harkness help? At All Saints?'

'It's a Christian church!' Johnny said. 'She'd have to convert. Which I suppose is rather exactly not the point. And it would still need to be under someone's law.'

'But if we can't have a religious marriage in either religion then we must have a civil marriage and a civil marriage by Italian law has to be by Italian law.'

'Yes.'

'So it would have to be by British law.'

'I'll see what we can do,' Johnny said.

Before he rang off, Tom asked, 'Is there much of this sort of thing?'

Johnny said, 'You're the first!'

Down by the yellow river, Tom leaned and waited for her.

'It's going to take a little longer than I thought,' he told her. 'Christmas is getting in the way. And there's the Banns . . .'

'Banns?'

'*Pubblicazioni di matrimonio*,' he said. Today's new phrase, and one he wished he'd never heard. Twenty-one days! He was terrified she would change her mind. He'd thought – *what, that he could just buy a few bottles of good prosecco for the officials, and five white roses from the Sicilian on the bridge?*

Yes, he'd thought something along those lines.

The day before Christmas Eve, Johnny said he could manage the *nulla osta* and a copy of Tom's birth certificate, 'some time in the New Year'. 'But we can't give you anything saying you're Jewish because A, you're not, and B, HMG doesn't see a chap's religion as their business any more, so there's nothing we issue which would have it on,' he said. 'You could apply for Italian citizenship and say you're a Jew, but I don't imagine that's the route you have in mind, is it?'

'No,' said Tom. 'And anyway they're revoking Jewish citizenships, not handing them out.'

'If you could find a ship's captain who's also a judge or

a registrar you could marry at sea. But I've asked around and there doesn't seem to be such a person in Rome just now.'

'No,' said Tom.

'So if you lied to the vicar you could have at least a religious marriage – Rev Harkness is a nice fellow, and I very much doubt he can tell a Roman Jew from a Roman Gentile on sight. Would Nenna pretend to be Christian? It still wouldn't be legal, but it would be something, and you could formalise it later at home. But we can't pull off British law in Italy, I'm afraid.'

It's such a simple thing, Tom was thinking. *I just want to get married.*

'But look, don't lose heart. I'm intrigued by this now – I'm sure there's a way. Of course if you could get her to come to England . . .'

Tom laughed, but not.

It couldn't be done, and even if it could it couldn't be done quickly, and even if it were done, it would mean nothing under Italian law.

~

Tom bought two bottles of good prosecco anyway, and five white roses from the Sicilian on the bridge. He took one of the former to Johnny in thanks for his efforts and got invited to Christmas lunch, and the latter to Nenna, who he met in a café behind Piazza Navona.

'We can only marry in England,' he said. 'We've looked and looked for a way. Can't be done.' He found that he felt ashamed of himself. He had wanted to be able to act on this marvellous noble whim, and for England to offer a wonderful swift manly solution to this rising chaos.

'So we can't be married,' she said, holding the roses and looking sad. For a moment it seemed absurd. Tom and Nenna! They had never wanted to marry anyway. Their decision had been purely circumstantial, and yet here they were, minding.

He glanced down at her. 'Sorry,' he said, and it seemed far from sufficient comment. 'Johnny's still looking into it,' he said, rather hurriedly, 'but – if you came, if you would just come to England—'

'Do you want us to be married?' she said.

'I want you to be safe,' he said.

'But you're not in love with me or anything?' she asked, looking at him, straight and serious.

'No! Lord no,' he said, automatically. And felt confused. Because—

Jesus, am I lying?

'*You're* not in love with *me*, are you?' he said. He was smiling. *We're talking about love!*

'No,' she said brightly. 'I love you but I'm not in love with you,' and at that they nodded, serious, believing profoundly in that great artificial distinction so important to the very young. They caught eyes, each trying to look more sensible than the other, then suddenly found that they were terribly embarrassed, and looked away.

'But I wanted to be sure,' she said, 'because—' and she smiled again, and then held something out to him. A piece of paper, folded.

He opened it out and read it. It told him that on

September 1, 1938, the marriage had taken place between Thomas Ellington Locke of London, British citizen, and Fernanda Fabia Elia Fiore of Rome, Italian citizen, at the Comune of Santa Ippolita in Puglia. It was stamped and signed and sealed and reeked of officialdom. And it was post-dated.

'Puglia!' he exclaimed.

'Far from any border we are likely to cross,' she said.

'Good Lord,' he said. 'But—'

She leaned in and whispered to him: 'When a girl is stopped from doing anything, she has to find something to do.'

He still didn't get it.

'You opened my eyes, Masino,' she said. 'And now they are open. Sometimes people need papers they don't have. And my handwriting is – flexible. And my friend Tullio has a little press.'

He was astounded.

'So, we're, um, married?' he said. The term gave him a little sexual thrill. *Sposati.*

She laughed. 'Are you pleased?' she said.

He found he was.

'Well,' he said. 'Bouquet,' gesturing the roses. 'Prosecco. Congratulations, darling.' *How had she done that? How had she turned so quickly, from her father's lamb to a forger? Look at her! She's so pleased!*

'Congratulations to you too,' she said, looking right at him, with her open eyes – and she leaned across the table to kiss him – and as she did, her hair, her cheek – it struck him like cold silver water all over his skin, shivery and brilliant – he wanted her to kiss him. He wanted to kiss her.

He moved his head. He took her kiss with his mouth – surprised her. And suddenly everything was very different.

As they came out of it, she said cautiously, 'But we're not in love.'

'No,' he said. 'Odd.'

They looked at each other.

'Odd,' he said again. 'Puzzling. Or perhaps just—'

He shook his head, as if shaking water out of his hair, and looked at her.

'I don't know,' she said. 'I—'

This is it, he thought. *This is something.*

'Come on,' he said, and as they left the café he took her face in his hands and kissed her, properly. Properly properly. Long enough for some wag to shout an incomprehensible bit of Romanaccio as he walked past them.

Nenna pulled away.

'Ah!' she said. And Tom said 'ah', in a very surprised way, and then turned sideways and took her arm in his. Fraternal. The street felt suddenly too small for them.

They walked together. After a moment they had to unlatch their arms.

'Well,' he said, 'If we're married now,' and he grinned, 'you have to obey me. Come to London.'

'Marinella,' she said.

'Bring her.'

'My parents,' she said, her eyes bright.

But it was different now. Why? Nothing had happened.

374

A forgery, and a surprising kiss. And, of course, her acknowledgement of the truth.

They both felt as if anything were possible. They were a team. Finally on the same side again.

He smiled at her so broadly, like an angel's wings.

'Who keeps the certificate?' he asked.

'Oh, you can have that one,' she said. 'I made two.'

He folded his up and tucked it into his inside pocket. 'You've broken several of Mussolini's laws with this,' he said, gently. 'Um . . .' he said, wanting to ask, but tentative. But wanting to be sure.

She looked up. 'You want to know? What's going on in my heart? Just ask, Englishman, just ask. I'll tell you – bitterness. Confusion. Fury. Loyalty. Confusion. But, to be clear: I have pulled my head out of the sand. Look, you can see it streaming from behind my ears. I have' – and she closed her eyes for a second, giving the words their due weight – 'torn the Duce from my heart. I hate him, what he has done to my family and my country. I fear him. I would come with you, Tommaso. I would! But now that I understand, I can't leave my family alone with him. Irony, yes? What you have revealed to me makes it impossible for me to come away as you want me to. You should have just seduced me, left out the politics.'

'I probably would have,' he said. 'If things had been different.' Then they laughed at some length, at the concept of 'if things had been different'.

~

Later, he took her to meet Johnny, who was sceptical but quietly encouraging.

'She's seen the light, Johnny,' Tom said.

'She was born and bred in Fascism,' he replied. 'Do you think that can change overnight? Even for your lovely blue eyes?'

'It really hasn't been overnight,' Tom murmured. 'It's been years, actually. But now I just want to get her to England, and we'll deal with the rest of them from there.' But he knew he hadn't been able to help them from there before. And it wasn't as if anything was getting easier.

He would persuade her. It would just take a little time. *Long haul.*

Walking Nenna back to the island through the empty dark stone streets, Tom trod quietly, feeling the echoes of other people's lives from behind the closed shutters. The occasional voice, calling; a little dog yapping, a shaft of light as someone adjusted a shutter or a curtain. Clouds were scudding around the moon, between the high walls, and a light chilly rain started. He put his arm around her and the cobbles beneath their feet began to gleam.

After a while, without breaking step, he murmured, 'So, Nenna, are you my girl?'

And for the rest of his life he regretted that he had not turned to look at her and seen the expression on her face. She stopped, she turned to him, and suddenly she was weeping and kicking him and bashing his chest like a girl in a silent movie, though she was far from silent, she was yelping and hiccupping, and he had to enclose her in his arms and hold her until with her ear against his heart and his hands holding her, she said, to the cloth of his coat, 'You idiot, you idiot.'

'Is that yes?' he said.

'Yes,' she said. 'I was always your girl. Stupid man.'

When they walked off, the angels' wings had spread to his feet.

❧

She didn't sleep that night. She left her shutters open and moonlight fell on her bed, and it filled her. *I give up*, she said to the moon. *How can I make this choice?*

The moon didn't care.

At around three in the morning, a thought skipped across Nenna's mind, like a water boatman across a calm dark pond. *It's not just Mussolini you hate. It's your father. Perhaps your mother too, for not protecting you. Your brothers, for not opening their eyes. Let them rot, all of them, before they kill you with their fear and stupidity.*

It is only Tom who has come back over and over, to help you.

Across the bedroom, Marinella mewed in her sleep.

I can take her with me.

❧

Alas there was no time. Someone, it seemed, had been noticing Tom's articles in the *Chronicle*. He, his foreignness, his anti-Fascist opinions, his nom de plume – fake identity, as they saw it – and his putative Judaism – had been identified and added up into a diagnosis of undesirability. The policemen – God knows which of the myriad forces they

377

were from – returned and invited him, as an alien, a Jew –
ha! The irony – and a spreader of lies about the Duce, to—

Bertolini's uncle

—leave the country. On the next train.

His first thought was of his own idiocy. *I should have expected this.*

The tall one was strolling round his little room, glancing at things, picking them up and putting them down again in a mildly insulting way. Tom was so surprised by the sudden immediacy and reality of these men being in his room, saying and doing these things, and so simultaneously relieved that they weren't punching him or bundling him down the stairs, that he wasn't even able to make up his mind whether or not he should be demanding to take his wife with him. *If I do, will that simply bring her and the family to their attention? What if she still says no? What if they find the friend's press – what if she is in danger already? And that is why they've come for me?* The what-ifs tumbled around him; he could not get his hands on any of them long enough to see it properly, and part of him was still thinking *this is all nonsense, things like this don't happen, not to English gentlemen who have done nothing wrong . . .*

And thus, he thought, *it moves. More real every day.*

They allowed him to step into the café to ring Johnny, and tell him briefly what was happening.

'Try to let her know,' he said. 'Tell her I'll be back.'

Then they put him on the train north, sat down with him, changed with him at Milan.

~

Their fellow travellers avoided his escorts, looking away and taking distant seats. At the border, these same people queued with them: families and couples, small suitcases, overcoats, misty breath hanging on the air. It was cold; the mountains in the distance snow-topped. He was following the general movement when the short one tugged his elbow, steered him round a corner of the station building and swiftly, effectively, knocked him to the floor.

Tom was still wondering how he got there when he felt the first blows, heavy swipes to his ribcage, a thud on the back of his head, a powerful kick in the small of his back and one to his belly. *Pain, nausea, inability* – and the two men stood back.

'We have plenty more for next time,' the tall one said. The short one was slipping something back into his overcoat pocket, and the word came to Tom: *manganello.*

'Show the bruises to your mother,' the short one said. 'Now come along!' – and he sighed impatiently as Tom took his time trying to stand up, trying not to vomit.

'That way!' the short one said, and the tall one handed him his hat, with a smirk, and Tom rejoined the queue almost as if nothing had happened.

'Plenty more, any time you like,' the tall one cried, and Tom realised this was absolutely nothing, to them. Absolutely nothing. A way of amusing themselves during a boring job. He raised his head, and bit his lip. *I have a lot to learn. Self-discipline. Patience. How and when to apply physical courage.*

He thanked the thug for his hat, and put it on at a gangster angle, tipping it just so. He didn't brush himself down. He turned and put out his hand to each of them, his eyes as blue and clear as they could be. 'Thank you for accompanying me,' he said. 'I'll be all right on my own now. Goodbye – till we meet again. *Arrivederci*' – and he went up into the crowd around the desk, where someone was saying, 'All owners of Austrian passports who cannot show an entry visa to Switzerland are to be turned back,' and, 'These passports were issued after 15 August 1938 . . .' as if that explained everything, why these families were standing here and could go no further. One guard was calling for advice. 'Should I telephone the Police Department?' Tom heard his boss murmur, 'One can assume that the holder is a Jew, if the passport is valid for only one year.'

He didn't look back, and his companions did not come after him. He thought he heard a chuckle, but he was trying to breathe through what felt unavoidably like a broken rib or two.

As he came to the front of the queue, the mother of the group in front of him was examining the document which had been returned to her. 'Turned back,' it said, and a stamp saying 'COMO', crossed out.

Tom had no visa, but his passport was old and British, he was tall and blond, and no doubt his companions had some arrangement for the chucking out of foreigners. Cleared and checked, he wanted to return to find the woman, and ask her where they would go, what they would do now. But he had been handed over, his suitcase thrown after him, and was being steered through to customs *dogana douane zoll*. Pyjama bottoms, he felt, would be the best thing to try to strap himself up with. He smiled politely. What else could a chap do, at this stage?

~

It was, to Aldo, a simple matter. If somebody is damaging the unit, well, it's like in war. Or as with Matteotti. You don't keep and protect someone who is betraying the brigade. You get rid of them. *Just as well that the Orivietos and the Setas have gone. A curse on the other fainthearts who insult me. May they all go. Good riddance.*

Tommaso, I am not an idiot. There is a limit to how much trouble you can cause in my household before I throw you out. You think I don't know what you are doing when you go on about Kristallnacht, about war, about passports, about Herr Hitler? You think I haven't noticed? How you undermine my authority, how you insult the Duce, and try to break our loyalty, which is our strength?

And Tommaso. Do you think I don't know my daughter? Do you think I don't see how she ebbs and flows around you? How this summer she hated you, and now she comes home with you, her eyes alight, laughing like the full moon? You think I am blind?

White roses, Tommaso? Please.

He conceded it would have been more honourable to throw Tom out of the country himself; to beat him up a little or frogmarch him to the border personally. But he remembered the scene on the riverbank and the look on Nenna's face that night. It was clear he would have to get someone else to do it. He could not have Nenna looking at him like that. That would be self-defeating.

All your talk of trouble to come, Tommaso – this is one trouble which will not come. If there is war, it must be very clear which side we are on. You go on about Jews being in danger! Our loyalty and our Duce are our strength and our safety, they are, they are. And my girl will not be in love with a boy who is on the other side. You won't dismantle us, Tommaso, and there will be no Romeo and Juliet here.

Part Six

1938–9

Chapter Seventeen

London, Autumn 1938

As soon as she got back to London from the summer in
Italy, Nadine sat on her bed and rang up Rose and Peter to
invite them to Sunday lunch. Her purest happiness was
having everyone round one table. She knew by instinct who
should be there, and flickered momentarily over Tom's
absence. The recent oddnesses in Rome just made having
the family together all the more necessary. She looked at all
that and it made her tired. Or perhaps it was just being
forty. Perhaps it was having to acknowledge that this was
her life, this was all there would be—

It wasn't that she minded, enormously, not having her
own child. It had sort of made sense, particularly as there
was Kitty and Tom. There had been so much to be set in
the right direction that introducing something new had for
a long time seemed irrelevant. But there had always been
the possibility – at least, they had thought there was the
possibility. The doctors had said there were things they
could do . . . but she and Riley had not wanted to do things.
They had not even wanted to talk to doctors. Perhaps,

looking back, that was a pity. And forty – well, this seemed the moment to recognise that the little tiny dead baby, that half-formed thing, the baby that wouldn't – couldn't – didn't stick – well, that was her only baby. Her belly clenched at the memory of it. *As it always has; as it always will.*

Anyway.

Never mind! she thought, and the words brightly sprang into her head. She hoped she wasn't being bright about it. But even so. *Que sera sera, and so forth.*

At least Kitty had gone to stay with a friend this weekend. Nadine didn't mean it badly, but Kitty was moodier than a girl of nineteen should be, and with all the goodwill in the world, it was tiresome.

Peter, when she spoke to him, said, 'Put Riley on the line, would you?'

Nadine still hesitated. Though of course it was up to Riley. It was only Peter.

When she handed the receiver over to Riley, she couldn't make out what Peter was saying – not that she was trying to – but she heard the liveliness, and the sudden warmth and enthusiasm of Riley's 'Yes! Of course!' in the middle of Peter's stream.

'What was that?' Nadine asked, when Riley hung up, grinning.

'He said, "Look here, Mabel and I are engaged, I blame you, and I couldn't be happier. Would it be mad of me to ask Nadine if I can bring Mabel on Sunday."'

'Engaged?' said Nadine. 'Mabel?'

'Yes,' said Riley.

'But who is she?'

'She's a singer,' Riley said.

'Have you met her?'

'Yes.'

'Why does he blame you?'

'I've been in favour of it. She's a wonderful woman.'

Nadine didn't understand.

'So you've known all about it?'

'Yes.'

'But you didn't tell me,' she said, a little bewildered.

'I was respecting his privacy,' Riley said gently.

'But the children!' she said.

'His business?'

'Really?' she said. 'Really?'

'Have I done wrong?' Riley said.

'Riley – darling – Peter is to marry a singer! What kind of singer? "She's a wonderful woman"?' Nadine sat down again. 'Sweetheart,' she said. 'You should have told me. Who is she?'

Riley explained Mabel. 'She's American, a jazz singer.'

Nadine may have raised her eyebrows—

'At the better sort of club,' said Riley drily, 'a respectable person, a proper musician, don't worry.'

'I'm not being bourgeois!' Nadine said. 'But Peter is a catch, you know. Any – disreputable woman – would want him. It must have crossed your mind.'

'He's in love,' Riley said. 'Mabel is good news. They will need our friendship. So, family blessing, all right?'

'Of course,' she said, and as he left the room another thought grabbed her. *Kitty will be back on Sunday, and does she know? Perhaps Peter has told her – or not – should I check? Should I tell her?* Nadine remembered sitting Tom on the kitchen table to tell him Julia was dead; not knowing if that was her job or not, and making the decision that it was. *Of course – because that's the point of a woman in a family, isn't it? To fill in all the gaps, and occupy all those positions. Even in a sweet marriage like ours.*

She started trying to find the telephone number of the place where Kitty had gone for the weekend. 'It's in Wolvercote,' she was saying to the operator. 'It should be under Thomson. No, I don't know the initials. Wolvercote, Oxford.' No luck. *Well, it's Peter's business to tell her,* she thought. But she was in doubt.

What Nadine didn't know was that Riley had forgotten to tell her that Peter had said, 'And I might bring someone else.' Or indeed that Mabel was black, or any other bit of information which might have helped to prepare the family for these sudden new members.

It was still warm enough for lunch in the garden, and given the failings in communication beforehand, the lunch started well. Rose and Nadine had had several confabs in the intervening days. No, Peter had said nothing to Rose. 'What!' Rose had said. 'I had no idea! Fiancée! Jazz singer!' And she had whispered what Nadine had thought: 'She's not some terrible nightclub floozie is she?' – which made Nadine feel a bit better about having thought it herself.

She was able to reply, 'I gather not. She's made records! She's almost famous, apparently! And Riley knows her! And likes her!'

When Rose arrived she and Nadine stretched their eyes at each other in the hall, checking and confirming that their views aligned – *my gosh, what will she be like? We'd better keep an eye on Kitty and Tom* – and despite their maturity, they giggled. It was a very pure happiness they felt for Peter, and a faith, which each saw in the other, that now, he would have chosen well. And of course if Riley liked her then she was bound to be—

Of course when Mabel came in and was negro, and had with her a young negro girl, their eyes caught and stretched a little further. There was a moment when everything hung, surreal – and in that moment Nadine realised that the grace with which Mabel waited, head slightly to one side, for her hosts to catch up was the same grace with which Riley waited for people to take stock of his scars; a grace which said: *I know, I am not normal to you. You do not know what to do with a person who looks like me. Please, take your time.*

And so Nadine thought, *This woman deals all the time with how she is seen, and the assumptions made. Just as Riley does* – and the moment passed with Nadine rushing to Mabel, grasping her hands in hers with a true affectionate warmth, and blurting: 'So it's you, you are the reason he has been so happy after all—' And then she felt something of a fool – but a good fool, and not embarrassed. *Blather on*, she thought. *Why not. Unless – does it embarrass her? She doesn't seem embarrassed.* It seemed a pity that embarrassment was even a possibility.

After that, courtesy and natural good character upheld the occasion, and nobody said or did anything thoughtless they were sorry about afterwards. If Rose was surprised to find that Peter's beloved was a negro woman, she hardly showed it. If they were curious about the shy stately daughter not much younger than Kitty, that was only natural. After the blackness, a daughter was just another surprise. Peter, God bless him, seemed hardly to notice that it was an unusual situation, and Nadine shared looks with Rose: *he's so unworldly!* Mabel, accustomed to being made a show of, behaved with perfect low-key courtesy, offering amusing asides, frank answers, and an appropriate domestic version of the charm which held audiences entranced. Nadine and Rose were duly entranced. Iris, dignified and girlish, said very little. Her eyes, Nadine noticed, were glued on Peter. And of course everybody was so engaged with all of this that none of the hosts noticed that the daughter did not address her mother once, nor even sit beside her; nor that the glances the mother cast towards the daughter were anything other than a mother's natural concern for her daughter being in a new place among new people.

Kitty arrived just before the roast beef, swanning in in a rather sporty outfit, back early from her trip because she was longing to see her dad.

She sort of jumped on him and wrapped his head in her arms as he sat, then looked up around the table, grinning proprietorially. 'Hello,' she said cheerfully. 'I'm Kitty. Who are all of you?' She was, actually, agog. A beautiful glamorous negro woman at Sunday lunch, with a young girl! She wondered if perhaps she was writing some kind of sociological book for Riley. *A Guide to British Society and Culture for the Newly Arrived African* perhaps. Though she was rather well-dressed for an intellectual.

Peter stood up, and Kitty fell back rather, as she wasn't expecting it.

'Dearest,' he said. 'This is Mabel Zachary, and this is Iris.' Kitty stuck her hand out gamely across the table, and said, 'How do you do, how do you do.' Mabel and Iris had to semi-stand, and there was a little physical awkwardness. Mabel said 'How do you do' back, with mild amusement, but Iris said 'Very well thank you,' so Kitty knew she wasn't entirely educated. And the woman was American!

Rose, very suddenly, with a very quick glance at Peter, tapped her fork on her glass and stood up.

'Ladies and gentlemen,' she said. 'This is a very special family occasion, and Peter has something very special to tell us all.'

Peter looked up. 'Do I?' he said.

'Yes,' said Rose. 'You do.'

Kitty said: 'Hang on a mo, let me pull up a chair. This sounds good!' She leaned forward, elbows on the table and chin in her hands.

'Of course,' Peter said, and blinked a little, and then stood up again, properly. 'My dear family,' he said. 'Kitty, Rose, Riley, Nadine, and good old Tom in absentia. I have to tell you some astonishingly good news. Um. This lovely woman, Mabel' – here he looked at her, so so did Kitty, and caught the expression of exquisite embarrassment and shy pride on her face – 'has, rather to my amazement, agreed to marry me—'

Kitty shrieked. She didn't mean to but she did. She put her hand over her mouth immediately and whispered, 'Sorry.'

'—and before you get carried away,' Peter continued, thinking quickly now, because Rose's glare, Nadine's silently imploring face and Kitty's shriek had galvanised him into realising that he had almost everybody he loved in front of him, and hardly any of them knew anything, and it was rather extraordinary – he should have thought this out – 'I would also like to introduce you—'

He stopped suddenly. *This is huge.*

No turning back.

'—to someone who I have only known myself for a month or two – in fact, let me tell you – I've known Mabel for nearly twenty years,' he said, and for a moment he seemed to be losing his composure – he was in fact thinking that losing his composure might be best – but then he fell silent again, and looked at them all, staring up at him. Mabel, alone, was looking at the table, with that humorous little smile on her face that she wore while waiting for people to get round to things she'd understood forever. She glanced up, and she winked at him.

He took courage.

'This is Iris,' he said, helplessly. 'She's my daughter.'

He gave them no pause after this, no comma or semicolon within whose reach they could make a decision or fall into a position, semi-informed – he pushed straight on through: 'I didn't know she existed. Mabel had her reasons for not telling me. Kitty, my darling, she's your sister – Iris – this is Kitty. Rose, Nadine, Riley – this is Iris. Iris, this is my family.' But he was not listened to now, because with the introduction Iris had glanced up at Kitty, and under the electricity of the gaze between Kitty and Iris everything was silenced. Kitty's chin was up, her head back, and she stared down the table, blue eyes shining.

'And did you know about me?' Kitty said. 'Iris?'

'I was told two weeks ago,' Iris replied.

Kitty's eyebrows went up. 'Two weeks,' she said. Her breathing was heavy. She looked around the group. 'Gosh. Well, no reason I suppose why I should be told at the same time as you.'

'Kitty,' said Nadine.

'Well, a funny way to go about things. Has anybody else got any announcements? Any more children to be produced out of the blue? I suppose by now I should be used to unexpected additions and unlikely arrangements.'

'Kitty,' said Nadine.

'Take their side, Nadine, why not,' said Kitty. 'We all know you're not interested in me and haven't been for years.'

'Now hold on,' said Peter, and Rose said 'Darling' and Kitty made a face which said clearly, *You see what I mean?*

Iris sat with her head down.

'It's not because you're negro,' Kitty said to her. 'Don't think it's that. It's because nobody told me. I find it faintly humiliating to have things foisted on me in front of everyone. I dare say some of you can understand that.'

Her face was twitching a little; she could feel it. 'Well,' she said, with a brittle smile.

'Nobody knew, darling,' Nadine said. 'I didn't know. I – Iris,' she said, with a warm and loving smile, just the word of welcome that the girl needed in this excruciating moment.

Riley, watching, saw how yet again Nadine's desire to give everybody what they wanted and needed tore her in half, because the needs and wants were conflicting, and Kitty would see kindness to Iris as cruelty to her.

'I didn't know,' said Rose mildly.

'Nor did I,' said Riley, and so Kitty flinched and said, 'Oh well then, I'm ridiculous, clearly. Never mind, Ridiculous Kitty, with her ridiculous feelings . . .' Even though she knew she was making herself all the more ridiculous.

Riley was the one to stand up and go round to Mabel, to bring her to her feet and embrace her, and then offer the same to Iris. 'Don't mind my face,' he murmured to her. Nadine and Rose reached their hands across to her, and as each did so, the other held her hand out to Kitty.

They all sat down. Nadine shunted up so that Kitty could sit next to Peter. They subsumed her, her shock and her disconcertion and her bad behaviour. Rose patted her knee. Riley winked at her. She thought, *I know they mean well but I am not to be allowed to feel what I feel. This isn't being loved. This is making do.*

She froze herself into position and didn't let her shoulder touch her father's, so that he would understand how hurt she was, and everything she was feeling.

~

Everything she was feeling?

Kitty, in her bedroom, was bitter. She lit a cigarette and turned to the mirror to do her hair. There was a postcard

394

stuck in the side of the frame; she'd bought it years ago at Porta Portese, the flea market: a sepia picture of a tragic lady clutching a flower and leaning against a window, with *Tutta la mia vita fu amore e dolore* in curled writing printed across the bottom. All of my life has been love and pain. She used to think love and pain would be rather glamorous – *when will it start? Love, adventure, tribulation?* – and longed above all for experience.

When she was little she used to make lists of what she loved. Shepherd's pie. Mummy, even though she's dead. Daddy, even though I haven't seen him for three weeks. Tom, even though he's horrid to me. Nenna, even though she's so far away. Chocolate. Max the dog, though he did die too. Nadine and Riley, even though they don't really care about me, they just wish they'd had their own real child. Daddy, even though he's marrying someone new and turns out to have had another daughter ALL ALONG.

This other daughter . . .

Iris . . .

With her mother.

How kind of you, Papà, not only to have another daughter all along but to have one who has a mother. A kind, beautiful, sensitive, tender mother all of her own.

Iris. Her name is Iris. With her Mabel.

Kitty hummed, and looked at her nails. She was still burning, and the burn was getting deeper. It wasn't the shock of being told like that in front of everyone. It was the utter, profound betrayal. This girl was eighteen. Kitty had wanted to ask her birthday, but held fire.

Well, I have had as ladylike an education as anybody but

I'm not a fool. She didn't know if everybody else was just too stupid to notice. Or if they genuinely didn't care. This girl had been made while Mummy was still alive. Father had been with that woman not only while Mummy was alive, but the year she died. Tom said Mummy was bad but perhaps Daddy had made her bad. Perhaps she wasn't bad at all. *Because it's pretty bad to go making a baby with someone else when you have a wife and children of your own already, isn't it?*

And if he was well enough to be making babies with someone who wasn't Mummy then that whole thing, that vast shadow over everything, when we were little – Daddy always in his study, Daddy in the cottage, Daddy doesn't come out, Daddy doesn't join in, leave Daddy alone, Daddy smells funny, Daddy shouting, Daddy's damaged by the war, not all wounds show – well he was all right enough in 1919, wasn't he? To make that glamorous woman sleep with him?

And she's not that old. She must have been very young then.

And for all that time, this girl has existed – and even if Daddy didn't know, that woman did.

She was combing over what she knew to be true and what might be true. *They must have been seeing each other. How could he have not known Iris existed? You can't want to marry someone without even knowing they have a child. It's absurd. He might have known them both, all along, all those years. My entire life.*

It all led nowhere, except to one very simple, very difficult truth: *he might be lying.*

She glanced at herself and made a mean face. It looked good, with the lipstick.

What do I love now?

None of the above, none on the list, because They Don't Love Me. Here then, though not in the expected form, is love and pain.

She sucked in her cheeks, taking a drag on her cigarette. '*Ci*garette,' she drawled, with the American intonation. '*Ver*mouth.'

I could, she thought. *I might.* She was thinking about running away to New York. Hollywood, perhaps, to be an actress. Though even thinking about being an actress was simply admitting she didn't have a clue who she was or what to do. Trying on personas, trying on the persona of someone who tries on personas for a living . . . She tried to look at herself: *you've finished school, you've passed a few exams, cheered at leaving the place where you never got very far beyond feeling inferior, and you've learned to type. Much of your attention is taken up by not eating. Your plans, such as they are, don't involve being plump.*

She was bored with being resentful. *What am I then? What am I?*

Hungry, she thought.

Who knows what is going to happen? None of us. Look at Riley's face and Mummy's death and the many ways in which Daddy has changed. No one knows. Anything could happen. Like this war. People seem to think that because one's young and female one is totally ignorant and dim, and doesn't notice the slightest thing.

She felt, really, like a table with too many wobbly legs. Nothing to trust. She had read somewhere that trust was a decision, and had been thinking about that. She didn't think it was right. *Trust is an instinct*, she thought. *You can trust someone you don't much like; you can mistrust people you adore. I think I made myself trust Daddy – against all advice, really. I trust Tom. I think.* She really really wanted to talk to Tom. Everybody else was falling over themselves to be good about this bloody wedding – because they didn't want anyone to think they minded about the woman being negro, she thought, but she knew she was being mean. They probably liked her. *Daddy's over the moon, embarrassingly so, and no doubt she's a perfectly nice woman. I wouldn't know.*

Kitty hadn't spoken to Iris or to Mabel since the lunch. Hadn't approached either of them, hadn't had any approach from them. She felt like the first wife in a tale of the *Arabian Nights*: her situation was respected; she had the power and the status – but the new wife had the attention from the king. Though in fact Kitty had no idea if Iris had attention from Peter. She didn't know how they lived. She didn't want to. She didn't want to be involved. Or, more precisely, she wanted them to come and get her.

And where *was* Tom? No letters, no response to letters.

Tom, darling,

Where are you and please will you write back? I know you've heard the news, I mean family news, not imminent war news – though you know as war is imminent it might be an idea for you to come home? Nadine told me she's written to you and I can't imagine that even in his clouds of amour Daddy would neglect to tell his only son – well, as far as we know his only son – that he's marrying a coloured jazz singer and has had a child with her all along.

Or perhaps he would. After all, he's never told us before. Perhaps he has a Japanese child somewhere, and one from Borneo. Or Alaska. We could make cigarette cards of them in national costume. Please come home. I'm fed up with the lot of them here. I dare say it's all very nice for you just being in Italy and not having to face any of all this – but you are leaving me to deal with it on my own and I need someone to say horrid things to, as none of this lot are being less than saintly about it. ARE YOU COMING TO THE WEDDING? PLEASE COME. I terribly don't want to go but I suppose I shall have to because bemused though I am by all this I don't want to be the one to make a big fuss about it. Well I do, of course, but – oh look it would be much easier, my dear and only bro, if I had you to go with. Sending this now to catch the post. RING UP if you possibly can. COME BACK.

Yr sis Kitty.

~

She did go to the wedding, without Tom. Westminster Registry Office, and practically nobody there beyond family. Nadine had been saying it should be church; he was a widower and she a spinster, why not, but Kitty liked that it was small like this. What did Nadine want, after all? Men from Peter's office that he practically never went to, Granny in full fury, and rows of jazz musicians looking embarrassed? Dear God. Granny wasn't there, in fact, so that was probably as well.

Everyone seemed terribly happy. Not so much for the wedding, but with a sort of fluttering of possibility, with relief about the Prime Minister's announcement. Peace with honour – no war! Everybody was talking about it: can we have faith in it? Will it be real? Is it strong enough to last? But overall, for today, be happy. It was as if they were instructing themselves. It bewildered Kitty, really. *When something is so vast, what is the point of having an opinion? Let alone desires . . . The politicians will do what they do.*

Mabel thank goodness hadn't put on a wedding dress, just looked rather slinky in cream satin and some lilies, her hair short, oiled and curled under a tiny hat. Iris dressed like an invisible person, Kitty noticed. She smiled at Iris as best she could and moved on swiftly, loosening her arms from Rose and Nadine, still both intent, God bless them, on making things nice. *Sorry my dears I don't feel nice.* But she was aware none of this was Iris's fault. This contradiction was giving her a headache. Iris had an intelligent face. *I wonder what it's like to be negro*, Kitty thought. The only negro people she knew about were tribes people in magazines, grass skirts, or slaves in America in the old days. But Iris spoke and dressed like anyone else. *I hate her.*

And Peter? Peter looked so happy, across the room, that Kitty couldn't rest her eyes on him for fear of burning. She didn't speak to him, just sat towards the back, almost fainting from the smell of lilies, thinking about the days when she was the only person who was Peter's friend, when she would go down to the damp cottage in the woods with bunches of buttercups for him, and put his slippers out in front of the fire. She didn't know if he even remembered that.

Afterwards, as everyone came out, a man with a camera zipped up, took some pictures, and then grabbed Kitty.

'You're the daughter, aintcha?' She thought he must be the official photographer, and said yes. 'Miss Kitty Locke?' he said. 'So how d'you feel about your dad marrying a fuzzy-wuzzy?'

'Who are you?' she said, and he said he was Smithers, or something, from the *Mail*, and it made as little sense to her as his manners.

''Pparently she entrapped him? Any comment?' he said. 'Who's that other nig nog – that girl?'

And something in Kitty moved quickly and suddenly into a sort of checkmate. To be put in this position was an insupportable extra insult to her as a result of her father's behaviour. The way this man was talking and the story he was after was an even more insupportable insult to Mabel and to Iris. *Ergo*, she was required to be on Mabel and Iris's side. Not to be would be the most insupportable insult of all.

'Go away,' she said to him. 'You're disgraceful.'

The man went. 'All right!' he smirked, as he went, as if she were a lunatic. He lit a fag, and glanced back at her.

Horrid, horrid man. A toxic anger rose in her. *How dare he?*

How dare they bloody all! Why does nobody look after me? She was shaking.

Parents are meant to look after you. That's what they're for. Julia never could. Peter never did.

Peter and Mabel were standing now at the top of the steps, looking glamorous, cosmopolitan, radiant. That magic web was all around them, glowing, binding them together, excluding all others. A smile, hope, relief, conviction.

Look at him there, she thought, and she looked and knew for a fact that she was not the most important person in the world to anybody, and never had been. She turned away to light a cigarette – *why yes, I shall smoke on the street!* – and so didn't notice Iris approaching the happy couple, kissing her father and clasping his hands, ignoring her mother; the tightening of Peter's face, the collapse of Mabel's as Iris moved on. She was too busy wishing Tom were there. He would loom up and say 'Everything all right, old girl?' and scare the journalist off. He would make a face or a joke that would make everything all right. Tom being absent, it was easy for her to imagine that he would do what she chose to imagine him doing. All the right things, for her. *Tom is actually devoted to me. He just can't let his devotion show in public because it would be undignified, and that's why he has to tease me or ignore me or torment me. Deep down*, she thought, *we have a very special relationship, based on our shared loss. We are loyal only to each other when the chips are down.*

She grimaced, the twist of eyes and mouth that comes with total concentrated self-absorption, an expression which makes anyone who chances to see it wonder what on earth is wrong with your face, and are you perhaps insane.

Really? Tom and I have a special relationship?

He didn't come back for this, did he?

You're still taking buttercups to people who don't much care, Kitty . . .

She had already decided to give the reception a miss. If someone had taken her by the elbow and said 'Come along with us, Kitty!' she would have gone, of course, flush with

402

the joy of being wanted – but without that, no. So when, as she slunk rather embarrassedly away, awash with double-negatives about what *she* really wanted, her elbow was taken firmly by a gloved hand, she looked up in expectation of relief. What she saw was her grandmother, Mrs Orris.

'Granny,' she exclaimed. 'I didn't see you – I didn't know you were here!'

'I wasn't here, my dear,' she replied. 'I wouldn't have dreamt of being here. But I wanted to catch you, because I knew how upset you would be.'

'Oh!' was all Kitty could manage, because her grandmother had never before shown any signs of perception or sympathy, or indeed interest.

'I wondered how you are,' Mrs Orris said, her eyes keen.

'Well I am rather upset,' Kitty said. 'Actually.' She was thinking of the horrid journalist as much as the wedding itself, the situation.

'Of course you are,' said Mrs Orris. 'Let's go and have a cup of tea.'

Mrs Orris – Granny – leaned forward, attentive and generous. There was cake, and there were questions. She wanted to know how Tom was; took his non-presence as disapproval of the match, and invited Kitty to come and live with her.

'In Berkshire!' said Kitty, rather horrified.

But no, Mrs Orris had taken a small house in Kensington some years ago. She spent about half her time there. There was room for Kitty and indeed for Tom.

'All this,' she said, 'is the fault of the War. If the War had never happened, Julia would not have been in the condition she was in, so worn down by suffering that she lost her strength. She would never have died. Peter would not have been so difficult, Tom could have stayed at home. Everything would have been perfectly normal.'

She dabbed her eye with her tiny lawn handkerchief, and Kitty thought: *you are my flesh and blood. You are my mother's mother . . .*

Mrs Orris had noticed the scene at the top of the steps. 'Did you see?' she said. 'The girl didn't even greet her own mother. Must have been brought up in a barn. Or a Jazz Club! Unless the mother is an utter monster, as she may well be.'

Kitty smiled.

Neither of them observed that between the two of them they had failed to greet their son-in-law and their father.

'You might like to Come Out,' Mrs Orris said. 'As a debutante. I think we could manage that. I don't suppose it is the sort of thing that Mrs Purefoy would have the chance to think of. It's so important at times like this that one should do what one can.'

But Kitty didn't need these Jane Austen blandishments – she was already persuaded. Her father would hate it.

A few weeks after the wedding, Kitty surprised Nadine and Riley at tea.

'I have a job,' she said blandly. 'I shall be typing, at the Foreign Office. So I thought that as I have a wage and so forth, I'd better be moving out.'

'Are you going to live with – Peter and Mabel?' asked Nadine. She looked utterly surprised.

'No!' said Kitty. 'Of course not. Why would I?'

'Because he's your father and she's your stepmother,' said Nadine. 'Why not?'

'I'll be living in London, Nadine,' Kitty said.

'You're not old enough! You can't set out and—'

Kitty said, 'I too am setting up a new family home. I too am informing everybody after the fact. You can tell Dad. If I am to put up with his wife and child then he can put up with me living with Granny.'

She thanked them for everything they had done for her, avoided any emotive language, smiled and kissed them and promised to see them soon. And went. There was absolutely no point sitting about, continuing this unsatisfactory childhood. The chips were going to come down, pretty soon now. She could feel it, even if Chamberlain – and everybody else – couldn't. This peace, this reprieve – she was unconvinced. It was time to launch out, have all the fun she could, and make sure she was an adult in time for whatever was heading their way. *War will form me.*

But wherever she went, whatever she was doing, one thing was on her mind: the daughter, with a mother of her own.

Chapter Eighteen

Como, January 1939

When the moment came, Tom didn't get back on the train. He couldn't. After he passed through the bureaucracy he headed up a quiet street to find a quiet place, his torso rigid with pain, his shoulders hunched in his jacket. He glanced back across at Italy. The trolley bus wires stopped dead, he noticed, at the border. *Now what?* he thought. *Now what?* He was in something of a daze by the time he reached a small hotel, and sat in its bleak little parlour. He had no Swiss francs, but seeing his blank look the girl accepted his lire, and brought him coffee. Real coffee! The shock of pleasure at the taste booted him awake, and he smiled, and the girl noticed, and they exchanged pleasantries. It was nice. He felt the absence of the tensions he'd been entangled in, and asked her name. Elise. Thank you Elise. Can you help me?

She could.

She brought bandages, told him to save his pyjamas. She bound him tight, and he could tell she had done it before. 'Fascist villains,' she said, and he was pleased to hear those words said aloud by a stranger. He took a room, and lay down, and thought.

Home? He didn't want to go home.

He certainly wasn't going to stay here.

Back into Italy then, back to Nenna.

Back into Italy?

Bertolini's uncle.

They wouldn't do that to an Englishman.

Oh, you know that, do you?

Illegal, dangerous. And for what purpose?

To get Nenna. Nenna who you have kissed. Nenna who has erupted inside your heart. Nenna who it always was, who you love and who loves you, with whom you are in love, who is in love with you.

Downstairs someone had a radio on, and the songs came drifting up the staircase with the smell of furniture polish: a woman singing about how she took a trip on a train, and thought about you. Peter would know who the band was, and the singer. It was a sweet lilting voice, and one of those perky tunes with sad sad words, and a blue note just waiting there, to do you in . . . *I peeped out the crack and looked at the track, the one leading back to you, and what did I do, I thought about you . . .*

Nenna Nenna Nenna.

When he didn't stop and divert the flood, he burned up at the thought of her.

He'd kissed girls before. He'd had what one might term a liaison with a frolicsome Cambridge barmaid, which he

407

felt a bit bad about. Someone's voracious sister had attempted to mangle him at a dance in a way which rendered him a combination of ecstatic and hideously embarrassed. He hadn't been interested in love, and the power of sex had alarmed him. He hadn't wanted to do the wrong thing. Especially with Nenna. Well, now, of course, he very much wanted to do the wrong thing, and only with Nenna.

Now he was away from her, he could let himself think about it. But then equally he couldn't, because it was—

Oh God.

He didn't understand. *This is all so—*

It was simplest to concentrate on saving her.

But I have no more to bring to the situation. I need more evidence, or ammunition, or whatever it is that I need . . .

It occurred to him that he might be able to – *ah! Now here's an idea, possibly even a practical one: a British passport, in her name, on the strength of the marriage certificate! Would that work?*

Well.

He wrote to her. What else could he do? He was exhausted and fuzzy with the painkillers Elise had brought him.

My darling,

God knows what you are thinking. Well, I am all right. I've been chucked out, and am now up an Alp, staring back, staring forward. To be precise, I am lost. But my love – are you my love? You are, aren't you? Good. My love, I'm going to go home and sort everything out. Don't be scared.

408

Everything will be all right. My heart is very full tonight. There is no doubt in it.

Masino

He slept badly that night in the little hotel, body aching and mind whirling with the same old stuff. What will it take for her to accept the level of danger they are in? The boots on the stairs and the banging on the door? Images of Herschel Greenszpan, pale in his pale raincoat, and Gavrilo Princip when he'd just shot Archduke Ferdinand. Bloody great bags under their eyes, looking ten years older than they were. *My age, or younger.* Thoughts of Riley at eighteen and twenty-two. And in the end: thoughts of her, images of her, memories of her, fear for her, desire for her.

Each time he moved he rolled into pain. Twice he woke in a panic and had to count his money before drifting back into restless sleep, to dream of her.

～

Early in the dawn he looked out the little window, flinging it open to the bright air, and saw the railway line, how it laid out this way, and that, sneaking between the snowy mountains. It was cold, up here. He put his suitcase flat, and opened it to look for a jersey. Inside, on top of his stuffed-in shirts and dog-eared books, tied with string, lay a pile of letters. They were addressed to him. Each had been opened, and, presumably, read.

He had not put them there. He had not tied them with string. He had never seen them before.

Tom stared at the little bundle. *How kind of the Duce*, he thought bitterly, *to return my mail*.

He took the letters out. He knew the writing on the top one: his father.

For a few minutes Tom sat and stared. He read it again.

Anvedi oh! he murmured. *And we think nothing happens when we go away . . .*

Married!

And a child!

His first recognisable feeling, and he was proud of that, was pleasure. A small but definite, warm little spark of delight. Here was a totally unexpected good thing. Peter, doing something normal, and good, which suggested the likelihood of his being happy. Imagine! Peter, happy! But also Peter doing something really very unusual. A child out of wedlock? And a jazz singer?

But what kind of jazz singer would marry Peter?

Tom pictured a floozie, perky and coy and *boop-boop-a-doop*. He pictured a sultry Lana Turner type in satin with a retinue of gangsters. He pictured a breathy suburban dimwit who would put her hand on Peter's arm and say, 'Now, dear.' He pictured Ethel Merman. She would have to be quite old – Peter after all must be fifty by now. Well. Good. A father with a new wife is probably a happy father with someone to look after him.

And a daughter!

A letter from Nadine put him right on some of his wonderings. She was American, a wonderful singer – they'd all been to hear her – even Grandpa had come out to the nightclub, and loved it, and had told her how much

Rachmaninoff loved Art Tatum, and invited her to the Albert Hall – and that she was negro—

That did stop Tom. Negro!

He was just thinking that he would never have thought Peter modern enough for that when he remembered: the family he had seen on the corner of Lexington Street. He closed his eyes and tried to let the image float back – the three figures, their ease, the girl looking back at him.

Sister.

And he thought – *aah*. And then: *Good old Dad!*

He found he wanted to know how old she was, this Mabel, and what she looked like close up. Now he pictured others from his father's record collection: Billie Holiday, Mildred Bailey, Josephine Baker.

October! *They'd be married by now then.*

I have a negro stepmother. It was so surprising, without having the individual woman to look at and form an opinion of, that he found himself feeling slightly dizzy. *Is she going to set up at Locke Hill? An American would be strange enough, for the types down there. Even Londoners count as exotic in Sidcup. What will the servants think? What will Granny think!* And that thought made him laugh out loud.

If Nenna and I were to actually marry, we could tell the amusing story at the wedding, of how we 'married' to escape the Fascists, and how it was at just the same time as my father married.

Hang on. I have a negro sister.

Bloody hell.

Perhaps Mussolini had heard about that, and that was why he'd been expelled. *God, now I'm black by association,*

411

as well as Jewish. Though I'm neither. Dear me, we're a pickle for the Racial Laws, aren't we?

She is after all as white as she is black. Biologically. Hmm.

His ribs really hurt. There had not been a single incidence of pain in Tom's life that had not been accompanied by the thought of Riley. *Buck up, fool,* he thought.

That was the only letter from Peter. A thick handful were from Kitty, confused, and cross. He read them briefly, but did not empathise. He leaned back, and closed his eyes, and found that he felt so bloody far away from them that it was difficult to picture their faces without distortion. And these new people. New sister. *Take that, Benito! Take that, Adolf! The finest English blood, the Lockes of Locke Hill, with the blood of a negro American, i.e. former slave blood – i.e. perfectly likely to be African royal blood. And think of the gene pool! This being where eugenicists always get it wrong. Blood should be mixed. It's the etiolated old aristo inbreds who end up with jaws so huge they can't eat, and haemophilia and so forth. A bit of brand new blood from another continent can only be a strengthener.*

How things can move and change and come round in this world, sometimes even for the better. He wanted to meet this new branch to his family, and hear their story.

Peter. You old dog.

My third mother!

~

He bought a stamp and thanked Elise courteously when he left. Perhaps he was flattering himself but she seemed a little sorry that he was leaving so soon, so he took the pension's card and said he'd come back, if ever in the neighbourhood. 'Who knows!' he said, and she raised her eyebrows in a parody of the impossibility of foretelling anything in these uncertain days.

He walked gently back down to the station, suitcase in hand. The pain was nothing when he muttered *buck up, buck up* to himself. In the square, he posted the letter to Nenna, his breath hanging in the cold. *She is there all alone, beginning to realise the danger, nobody to help her. After all this time of trying to persuade her, only now when I have been booted out is she starting to see.*

It made him jumpy.

Riley would know. London would know. London would be on his side.

~

On the train he read the French newspapers, which were rather enlightening after several months of the Italian ones. Every rattling circuit of the wheels' chorus on the tracks sang him closer to home, to reality, to impossibility, to whatever it was that was imminent but still had not arrived.

It's going to happen. There will be war.

He was full of desires. Edgy, irritable desires. Now what? Now what? Every day that passes it would get more difficult.

I will go back. As soon as I can, however I can. So go back. Go back now. Jump off the train.

No, I'll go back with a British passport for her, and visas for the family. Riley can offer Aldo a job. Susanna can be – oh I don't know. Something.

Or am I scared to go back? Scared she'll never say yes?

413

Scared the squadristi *will beat me up – that I'll get a* manganello *in the mush?*

Because I'm going to have to deal with fear, before all this is over. Aren't I?

By my age, Riley had finished his war.

~

He wrote to her again on the train, a long letter, his handwriting jiggly, and posted it the moment he arrived in London. It ended:

The thing is I love you, and this situation is insupportable. Violence and the law (!) may have chucked me out for now, but God only knows what will happen – if anyone does – and so all things are, in theory, possible. When I think of your courage, and your position, my beautiful girl, I think above all of the strength there is in you. All that you devoted to your father for all these years – all the passion and power you put into being wrong, will now help you as you turn around. Believe it. Don't be scared. I do believe that your father will see sense, and if he can't, that you will recognise it, and make the decision about your own life. You are not only their daughter. You are your own extraordinary self. These circumstances which entangle you are not all you are. And if that's not enough – Nenna, my old friend, my new love – I need you as much they do. I will not be able to go into this war with you over there. You belong here. Not by birth, but by your heart, which is just, and no longer fooled by what it was brought up in. Do you remember you spoke about the garden you were planted in? Time to

414

leave the poisoned garden. I could start to run wild here with the imagery – tendrils round your ankles, creepers tying you down, those who are too deep in the rampant undergrowth for you to pull them free – darling – I know. Of all people, I know. Tell me you will do it. Machete at the ready if need be. Nenna – my friend B's uncle was turned in by his own relatives. It is no longer possible in these times to put family first and that is not your fault, nor the fault of any other decent human being. But you must do something about it. Sides are lining up. You cannot be – you are not! – on the side of the violent, the unjust, the Jew-haters, the liars.

Darling. Come.

∿

And there, in London, sat his old life. It was, if he chose it, pretty much as it had been before – *if I forget about Italy, I could just go back to work and carry on following my imme-diate nose.*

But my immediate nose wants to lead me back.

I can't believe I have left her there—

He went back to his job on the paper.

After work one dingy dark evening, rain diagonal in the streetlights' glow on the huddled overcoats scurrying to get out of it, Peter took Tom to meet Mabel. The Serpentine was a haven of warmth and escape, and the gold-digger idea flew out the window at the first sight of the relaxed, professional way Mabel clicked her fingers to her pianist. Tom clocked the strong arms, the green sequins, the lazy smile, and leant over to whisper, 'Gosh, Dad!' Peter, it seemed to him, was excited, and apprehensive – waiting for approval? *For my approval?* Tom thought. *Well that's new.* He withheld it for a while. She looked to him interesting and independent; she sang, it turned out, beautifully, in that way that sculpts you inside and changes something there.

As the second song closed he leaned over to Peter and murmured over the nightclub buzz and clatter: 'She's bloody marvellous.'

Peter was smiling like a boy. 'She is, isn't she?'

And then she sang, oddly enough, 'I Thought About You'. So Tom thought about Nenna. In the lull after she finished, Tom leaned over again.

'Dad,' he said. 'I'm marrying out, too.'

Peter raised his eyebrows.

'Nenna,' Tom said. 'I'm going to do it. Papers, passports, petitions to the Home Office.'

'Well I'll help in any way I can,' Peter said, and each had the same little furrow in their brow during the next few songs, as their private complexities shifted and lifted and disappeared like morning dew.

Later, over sole at Sheekey's, Tom told Mabel how he had seen them on the corner of Lexington Street.

'I saw you too,' Mabel said. 'On the corner. For a second I thought you were Peter. But Peter was standing right by me.'

~

He had gathered that Iris and her mother were on some kind of complicated terms, but his own approach was simple. He rang, Iris said come to tea, he went.

416

She was tall and nervous, and offered him cake immediately she opened the door of the flat in Eaton Square.

'Do you live here alone?' he enquired, looking around, and she blushed, just a little, so he said, 'Sorry, not my business,' and took his coat off and went through to sit down. Gas fire, books, piano. Long white curtains drawn already. Midwinter.

'Well!' she said.

'Oh God,' he said. 'Was Kitty horrid to you?' – whereupon Iris laughed – a single bark.

'She's such a—' Tom said. 'At least she can be. Prickly sensitive little thing, Kits. Don't worry. Soft as a sausage inside, just self-obsessed – and it's contagious! Look, we're talking about her, when we should be saying, Good Lord, I have another sister! Or, you know, you can say, I have a brother, and we should just be being sort of being amazed at each other.'

'I am amazed,' Iris said.

'Me too,' he said. 'Do I look all right to you? I do hope so. Must be a bit of a shock.'

'You look all right,' she said, warily.

'You look all right to me too,' he said.

There was a silence.

'Is that it then?' she said. 'We agree we look all right?'

'Well, we could have cake.'

She started laughing then. Her rather steady face cracked up into movement and he liked her.

'You are so like my – your father,' she said. 'Our father.'

'I'm bloody not,' Tom said – and stopped. She's family. *She's new but she's old. This is very very strange.*

'Am I?' he said.

'Oh, yes,' and her smile flickered, and she swallowed, and said, 'Tea. Let's just . . . have some tea.'

It seemed to him she might be the sort of girl he might make friends with. If he'd just happened to meet her somewhere, he would have wanted to talk to her. *Well thank Christ for that. Ha!*

~

Nadine and Rose were all over him, and Mrs Orris was leaving messages. Kitty was trying to get hold of him but it was all complicated. In the end they met at the American Bar at the Savoy.

'What's all this about you living at Granny's?' he said. 'Everybody's rather upset with you.'

'Serve them right,' Kitty said. She had a very smart little hat on.

'Why?'

She shot him an awfully forlorn look. 'Because of everything! Daddy just – oh for God's sake, Tom, you stay away for months and then just swan back—'

'Am I missing something?' he asked. 'Dad got married, he's happy, so what?'

Kitty blinked at him. 'He lied,' she said. 'To us, to our mother, to everybody – he's been with that woman for years—'

'Not interested,' said Tom. 'Sorry, but really. Here and now, darling. He's been miserable almost his entire life, so let's just let him be happy for a bit, shall we? You can amuse yourself dragging it out, but to be honest I don't

418

think anyone's noticed it's a protest vote against the new Mrs L.'

She frowned.

'Oh for God's sake, Kit, don't tell me you've turned into some kind of racialist?'

'It's not that!' she cried, indignantly.

'Well you'd better move back home then, before anyone starts thinking it is. Is it about money? You think he's going to leave everything to them? He can't – I'm still the eldest son.'

'Thank you Tom, I am neither a racialist nor some gold-digger inside my own family.'

'Well what is it then?'

'I thought you might like to come and live there too,' she said quietly.

'What, with the Mastodon?' he barked. 'No bloody thank you. Perfectly happy with Riley and Nadine for the moment. Hardly ever there anyway.'

Kitty raised her eyebrows and took out a cigarette. She waited for Tom to light it, and kept her nostrils a little flared.

'And what did you make of Iris?' she asked.

'Nice girl,' he said. 'Thought we should all go dancing. What do you say? Break the ice?'

Kitty blew smoke down her nose, a measured move, a dragon breath. He knew exactly what she was thinking: *Typical! Nobody gives a damn about poor me.* The old 'Poor Little Kitty' performance.

'How about Friday night?' he said. 'Iris and I are going anyway,' he lied, making it up as he went along, knowing

419

she wouldn't be able to resist. 'I might bring along some of the chaps. Johnny's in town. Go and hear Mabel sing, then go on somewhere. Make a little party of it. Come on Kits, you know you want to . . .'

He smiled at her, and she melted a little, and he was glad to see that she still melted at it, and still pretended not to.

~

Iris was delighted at the suggestion of going dancing, but very much wanted to hear another singer; would they mind awfully?

Well, Tom had promised the chaps they'd be seeing his new stepmother – it was rather the point.

'Of course,' said Iris, and Tom could hear her adjusting her expectations. He rang Peter later.

'Do Iris and her mother not get on?' he asked, bluntly.

'Slightly minds that Mabel and I knew each other all the way through, and Mabel didn't tell her about me,' Peter said. 'You know how girls don't like to feel left out.'

'Well then they're all in a flap,' Tom said. 'Kitty's livid about Iris. I'm trying to take them out, in a brotherly manner—'

'D'you want me to come?' Peter asked.

'Good Lord no,' said Tom.

~

The chaps were Johnny Carmichael and Vernon from the paper, spruced, joshing, and torn between flirting and talking European politics. Kitty, of course unable to resist, arrived in dusty pink chiffon, glowing; Iris was lean and elegant in a white dress of her mother's, let down and taken in, with her hair oiled and a flower behind her ear. Kitty immediately felt fat. Iris breathed very carefully on this, her first proper social outing with people sort of her own age. The chaps blinked, and opted absolutely for flirtation.

The Serpentine Club was busy: glittery, smoky, scent and laughtery; bias-cut satin and scurrying waiters. They had a table with a velvet banquette, near the front; the table Iris usually used to go to, with Peter. Mabel knew they were coming; a small fuss was made.

They drank cocktails and smoked (not Iris though) and Carmichael entertained them with improper tales from the Embassy in Rome, at which Kitty shrieked with laughter. Vernon couldn't take his eyes off Iris, and asked her so many questions that he might as well have been interviewing her. By 'What was your favourite subject at school?' Tom stopped squashing his irritation, and asked her to dance. They glided out: the music was light and instrumental; waiting for Mabel to come out and electrify the scene.

Holding Iris, out on the hardwood floor, Tom had to remind himself that she was his sister. He found himself looking at her and sensing her flesh under his fingers: flesh of my flesh. So different! He glanced at her hands, her fingertips on his.

'Are you searching for similarities?' she asked him, leaning away a little to match his gaze.

'Tall,' he said. 'Slender.' And then he was stuck. Not fair, not bony, no blue eyes, no thin mouth, no floppy blondish hair, no dark circles under the eyes.

'Intelligent,' she said. 'Musical. Little bit repressed and

moody. Keen on Greek and Latin.' She gave him a slight curl of smile, and it was – it was! – the identical of Peter's charming smile – Tom's own charming smile.

He gave her the same smile back, and saw that she recognised it. For a moment there, circling in each other's arms to the faintly depressing strains of 'Melancholy Baby', hardly dancing at all, they just looked at each other, smiling.

'I wish we'd known you before,' he said simply, and her eyes filled with tears. He squeezed her hand, in a buck-up, brotherly sort of way, and she blinked, so then she had to go to the powder room, and he squeezed her hand again as she went, and worked his way back to the table.

'Lovely girl, our new sis,' he said, and Kitty smiled politely.

'I gather she's not talking to her mother!' she said. 'Imagine, all those years without a father and the moment she gets one, she stops talking to her mother! Didn't even talk to her at the wedding. Ridiculous girl.'

Johnny was kicking her under the table and Tom said 'Kitty!' warningly, but Iris was there, behind her by the banquette, and heard enough.

'Came back for my bag,' she said, expressionless, and Vernon located it and passed it across to her. She turned away, back rod-straight, and Tom was preparing a most withering condemnation but then Iris turned back, and looked down at the back of Kitty's head. 'I gather you're not talking to your father,' Iris said, calmly, not unkindly. 'Had him your entire life, and the moment he finds some happiness you turn your back on him and make sure he's still got something to be miserable about. Didn't even talk to him at his own wedding. Taking him for granted, I suppose.'

Kitty didn't turn round. Her eyes were fixed on the table: the tiny vase of carnations, the candle, the cocktail glasses gleaming in the low light, the ashtray with Carmichael's cigarette burning down. The moment hung in the air.

'Well,' Kitty said, and started to bustle on the velvet seat, looking for her bag. 'You stay and listen to your mother sing, why don't you, how lovely. I think I'll—'

'Oh for God's sake Kitty, don't—' Tom started, but Johnny broke in, taking Kitty's arm and saying, 'Come on darling, it's our foxtrot!' which of course was ridiculous, because it wasn't a foxtrot, and she wasn't his darling, but he pulled her out from behind the table and on to the floor, and in a moment had her fully enclosed in his arms, safe in the familiar pattern of nondescript English dance steps, her head hidden on his chest, her tears unheard and unseen.

'You're a lovely girl, Kitty, a lovely girl,' he murmured. 'Something of a little fool, sometimes . . . but a lovely girl.'

Kitty looked up. Her mouth was tight. 'Thank you Johnny,' she said. 'But I don't care to be patronised.' She extricated herself, went back to the table, and picked up her bag. Her heels felt perilous beneath her. She snapped good-night to Vernon, and to Iris, sitting down now, she said: 'I'm right, though, aren't I? Still, at least you've *got* a mother.' She shot a look of pure venom at Tom, and turned to fight through the crowd.

She almost missed Iris's valedictory shot. 'Oh sure, honey, we're both *right*' – as if rightness was the least of it.

Tom rolled his eyes apologetically at the chaps. Vernon said, 'Shouldn't you . . . ?' but Johnny was already going after her. On the little stage the musicians had stood down their instruments, but they picked them up again now as the pianist leaned in, and said, 'And now, ladies and gentlemen – hell, do I even need to say more? The woman we're all here for – our endlessly, blessedly, helplessly recklessly, heavenly velvety ebony speciality – Miss Mabel Zachary!'

She slipped on, sweeping the room with a lazy smile and those dark eyes that hardly anybody knew were looking for Iris.

Before the song started up, before Mabel even saw where they were, Tom leaned over.

'I don't know what it's all about,' he said to Iris quietly, firmly, 'but for what it's worth I'm glad to have you both, and I wish you'd make it up with her.'

'Kitty's made it clear—' Iris began.

'Not Kitty,' Tom said. He nodded his head towards the stage. 'I'd love to be able to call Mabel my mum and you my sis,' he said. 'Two new dreamboats in the family . . . Dad happy . . . Everything in the garden lovely.' For a moment, that phrase, *Everything in the garden lovely*, made him blink—

He pulled himself together, and looked at Iris, a little sideways. 'Don't you think?'

The players had started up, a slinky rhythm.

Iris met Tom's gaze, and rolled her eyes, and Mabel started to sing: *When they begin . . . the Beguine . . . it brings back the sound of music so tender*

Iris choked back a little laugh.

'What's funny?' he said.

It brings back a night of tropical splendour

424

'That was my lullaby,' Iris whispered. Tom, glancing up at Mabel, caught a little recognition in her eye as she watched them, as she saw Iris smile and speak.

It brings back a memory evergreen . . . Mabel's voice, as she sang, tendrilled among the velvet seats like cigarette smoke, entwining and embracing every person in the room, their pasts and their futures, and none more than Iris and Tom.

~

Johnny caught up with Kitty as she stepped outside.

'Sorry,' she said, and she shivered, ascertaining the level of London night chill: considerable. She could already feel the cold of the pavement through the slight soles of her evening shoes. 'Strange days!' she said, gaily. 'Heightened emotions!' She made an amused ironic face, like a madcap girl in a comedy romance. Myrna Loy, she thought. *Though Myrna Loy never made stupid outbursts like that.*

'Bus?' he said. 'Or nightcap?'

She turned up the collar of her coat.

'Both,' she said, and glanced over at him. 'Nightcap first.'

He gestured, and she clicked down the road, then stopped and turned back to him, and rested her forehead for a moment on the front of his coat, leaning in at an angle like an exhausted person. It smelt of cold wool and another life.

'She is right,' she said, and her face wrinkled up again, invisible.

'How very annoying of her,' he said. 'But well recognised. Come on. You can tell me all about it over something strengthening. Soup and chocolate, or strong liquor?'

She looked at him. *If I think, nice eyes, does that mean I don't think he's attractive?*

'Strong liquor!' she said, ruefully. 'But just the one. What time is it? Is it awfully late? Because I think I'd better go and see my father. I mean, probably not now. But first thing tomorrow.' Her eyes filled with tears and she thought for a moment that she couldn't look pretty at all, but it didn't matter because she was being true and honest with someone, with a man, an attractive man, and that was rather wonderful. And she was going to forgive Peter. And, perhaps Iris. Whose fault it wasn't. And that was rather wonderful.

'Good girl!' Johnny said. 'Oh! Sorry – is that patronising?'

'Yes,' she said, and she smiled.

Chapter Nineteen

Rome and London, January–September 1939

Jan 1939, Rome

My Dear Masino,

I only need to change two letters to make that my dear marito, Masino mio marito . . . I am still laughing, Tom my Husband.

But I am not laughing, because I have received your letters. How can I tell you the strength your words give me? Your words, your admiration, your encouragement, your faith, your love – you love me! – each inspires more of the same in me. I wish to know everything but fear to ask. So is it permanent, this departure? I will go to the embassy to see JC, if he is still there; I am talking – trying to talk – to Papà, to wear him down. I am drips of water against a stone, and it will take a thousand years. He is the Fontana di Papà, I am the Acqua Figlia, tourists will come to see us in years to come. Masino, I recall the poison garden, I understand your machete, but but but. It is my own heart wrapped round with tendrils, my own blood in those tangles. I am not laughing. I remember you standing in a field and shouting your views to the sky. Now I am not sure anything can be written on paper. Will there be war? You make it sound inevitable. Nobody here wants it – well only the stupid young men who think it's glorious. I see little Stellina out with them, hanging on their arms like a pretty handbag, making eyes . . . my first kiss, my second and my third. You know what I am talking about. Masino mio, anything that you know, that I do not know, please write and tell me. I feel only knowledge is real, I can only hold on to truth. And it is hard to find, specially since I realised I am no judge of it and never have been. Yes I have been wrong, my entire life. Yes! Tom – you think I am strong but there is a weakness inside me as a result. I stop in the street, or before I speak, and I think 'Are you sure?' I am not used to this. I don't know how to estimate things now. And now is a terrible time to start – here where everything is either confused or wrong or lying. You will be my *Bocca della Verità* – I will put my hand in your mouth, and you will bite my follies and my errors.

I still cannot say that I will do it – you know what IT I mean – alone. I am the only one earning now; what would they eat?'

She could not tell him the details of this. Who knew who read what letters? She had got false papers from Tullio in a non-Jewish name, and she walked an hour each day to work to clean a *palazzo* on the far side of the city, polishing marble floors in tall dim rooms, the mop swabbing to and fro, dustmotes in shafts of sunlight through the shutters, stone steps and dark oil paintings, where nobody knew her. She gave the money to her mother. She kept her real papers in her other pocket, for when she came back to her neighbourhood, in case she was stopped, and she was convinced that something as stupid as taking the wrong papers out would be how she would ultimately release herself from this intolerable situation. She had her story prepared: *Oh, yes, I just found these in the street. I'm taking them to the police station.* She mapped routes, and thought about which police station was where, so that she could be pretending to be on her way to a particular one if challenged. *But why aren't you going to the one just behind you, signorina? Oh, I didn't know there was one down there – thank you! – I'll go there instead.* The 'thank you' was a good touch. *After all, I am a Fascist too. Grateful to these blackshirted boys who look after me so well.* She wore her party badge at all times. Someone had said all Jews were no longer allowed to be party members. She didn't even know. *And how long before I have to wear a yellow badge alongside it?* Now she had opened her eyes, she was learning fast.

Some of her friends had left. Some were carrying on as usual. The better off were for once worse off – their fathers' jobs were more official and therefore more officially ended. The poorer people in Piazza just carried on making the best of things, as they always had.

These were not things to write down. Her letters to Tom developed a curious language of their own, a mélange of English, French, Romanaccio, Italian, code from their childhood. No names; *il pischello* (a Roman word for boy) for the Duce; and she signed herself, from your little sister.

She continued:

Mama has sold the good sheets. I wish, in a way, I were a proper Jew; I would look to God for relief. I swear when I see our friends and neighbours coming out of synagogue they look lighter than when they went in – but alas no one is coming from the mountains for us. Or if they are, they are not people we wish to see.

Anything that you can do for all of us, tell me, and I will obey.

Dalla tua Sorellina

Tom read this in the office, back in his original role. The paper hadn't been that impressed by his Italian adventures. You had to have a certain status, it seemed, before getting into trouble would be admired. Even Vaughan had smirked a little when Tom was put back in his box – hanging round the magistrate's court, cracking his knuckles and listening out to hear who on the foreign desk was retiring/moving on/about to be sacked. Out of hours, he started an advanced French course held in a primary school; he sat on a ridiculously low stool at a tiny school desk, his bony knees sticking up, one of them constantly jiggling with the nervous energy which was becoming his constant companion.

Being back in London made not being in Italy feel utterly impossible. From the safety of here, the urge to be there, to fight back against what was going on there, grew stronger day by day. The anger grew stronger. The fear grew stronger.

He could smell the badness coming. He was beginning to feel . . . up for it.

~

February 1939

Carissima,

I like that you might be laughing – a splendid response to all this. But I have only one thing to say: COME. COME. COME. You see I say it three times. I will say it as many times as it takes. COME. At the very least, say you will come. I am putting things in place. Please send me IMMEDIATELY two little portrait photographs, signed on the back by a lawyer as your true likeness, and a copy of your birth certificate. When I have you in place HERE I can start to work for the others. Everybody might be able to come. I enclose letters from Riley's company offering employment. Aldo will be a translator and Susanna I'm afraid must be our cook. So that, and the marriage, may make it all right re the visas. I have to say 'may' because so many people have come already, and it's all a bit of a bunfight. But I am doing my best.

Yes, the paper has decided not to send me back to Rome, what with my expulsion, my lack of experience of the political side, my youth, etc. But that is not so bad, as it is by concentrating here on the paperwork that I am most likely to be able to bring things to a happy close. It takes time. Time! I am not sleeping particularly well. *Forza, sorella mia, forza e pazienza.*

Darling. Come. Now that everything is polarising. You

have to be here, under the same light source with me. COME COME COME SAY YOU WILL COME.

February '39

Masino mio,

If by repeating that word you could remove the fact of my family, then by all means repeat, there would be a point to it. (Though it wouldn't be necessary – I would already be there.) But can repetition change facts? No. So. How about this? If I can ever come, I will come. About the photos. The Jewish lawyers have already left, and the rest like everybody else are dancing on their toes on a hot roof where we are concerned. I am sure I will find some old drunk though who will do it. Or some other way out. Will you not need photographs of the others? I can make the boys and Marinella do it, but I don't know about Mama and Papà . . . or perhaps you are still hoping I will forget about them.

There is not much to say. I am tired. Yesterday I sang with our friend from Piazza for the first time in a long time. My voice creaked like an old door. I must sing as I do my work, like a Rossini housemaid.

I should have so much more to say to you. This is hardly worth the cost of a stamp. I am so full, Masino, of so many things, and yet I am already exhausted – but you don't need to hear about that. I have given up reading. There are now so many reasons, spiritual, biological, political, all contradictory, as to why I am a lesser being that I cannot make sense of it. I see my old schoolfriends joining in; people we have known all our lives. There is a theory of envy – it is all because we are more intelligent than others. But I am not intelligent enough to understand. Or it is because we are rich, an international web of bankers taking over the world – yet I don't have money to sweeten a lawyer to sign a photograph. Or because we are a communist plot, an international web of socialists taking over the world. Don't you see how I have taken over the world? I was reading a student journal: it listed all the places from which we are to be chased (cafés, schools, gardens, swimming pools, streets, hills) and it used the term 'civil death', for us. Civil death?

Papà sees it all now as a test of his Fascist faith. As God tried Job, so *il pischello* is trying my papà. The backbone of Fascism is obedience to authority: so Papà continues to obey. He keenly and devotedly excludes himself, according to *il pischello*'s laws. He agrees he must no longer use the library, if that is what *il pischello* wants. He no longer works, because *il pischello* does not want him to work. He will stride nobly into his own civil death, for his beloved *pischello*. His pride is magnificent. He will never change his mind. He may as well kill himself. It is after all what *il pischello* wants. He said to me – you can imagine how he spoke. He said, how do you define faith? Faith is what rises above the challenge of rational doubt. He rises so far above rational doubt that he flies. He is the Icarus of rational doubt. So he is irrational to the point that he will sacrifice us all. He might as well spank his own bottom. He will thank the hangman, offer him help to tie the noose around his own neck, congratulate him on ridding the world of one more horrible Jew. My papà.

433

I am so sorry. You know what about. And so angry.

We get no sympathy. Sympathy is unItalian. It is weak, old-fashioned, unpatriotic and punishable by law. And still on occasion Papà produces the old cliché: if the *pischello* knew about this he would of course do something . . . our *pischello* is a kind *pischello*, he is only tough for our own good, his minions betray him, it is they who are corrupt/violent/incompetent, not him – if he had the means, the information, the whatever, he would be the first to rectify the situation, to solve all our problems, to answer every petition . . . There were old *contadini* women kneeling as he passed, in Torino. Even if I were not banned now from the cinema, and even if I could afford to go, I would not. The newsreels make me sick.

Your *pischello Inglese* was here. You probably know. He brought an umbrella; *il pischello Italiano* thinks umbrellas unmanly, and believes therefore that the English will never enter a war. He has forgotten that they were in the last war, and didn't do so badly.

Blessings to you
Tua sorella.

~

Nenna wrote this letter at the kitchen table. She could hear her father next door, talking quietly to himself, rustling papers. Before she went upstairs, she looked in on him. As she thought: he was standing, leaning over the desk, absorbed in the smooth white field of a set of plans. His sleeves were rolled up and his forearms were strong in the low lamplight, fists resting on the leather desktop. Every now and again he issued a low admiring chuckle, or leant in to smile at a detail.

He looked up, his smile creasing as he called to her, '*Buona notte, amore!*'

'*Buona notte, Papà,*' she murmured.

~

Tom and Kitty were back in the American Bar at the Savoy. She wouldn't meet anywhere else now.

'How can you afford it?' Tom said. 'On your typist's pay.'

'It's an investment,' she said. 'I need to meet a nice class of chap, and move in interesting circles. Anyway, what's going on? You look positively green.'

'What, Carmichael not nice or classy enough for you?' he said.

'Johnny's perfectly charming,' she said, 'as you well know. Don't change the subject.'

Tom grinned. Kitty made an amusing Woman of Mystery – she almost had it right, but there was something innocent about her which shone through the cigarettes and the flippant comments.

'Perfectly charming!' he said. 'That's good, I suppose. I'll tell him you said so.'

'You will not. Now why are you green? And could you please stop twitching your leg, it's a horrid habit.'

'Am I green?' he said – and she gave him a very straight and familiar look, the one she used to give him when he was being that bit too naughty, too likely to land them in trouble; a look containing both pride and a touch of *please,*

Tom – the look of a girl who knows him very well and is concerned for him.

He smiled.

'I'm in love,' he said. 'I actually am.'

She squeaked and jumped and waved her arm to order champagne. 'Who with? Do I know her? Tom, that's marvellous.'

'It's Nenna,' he said. 'I'm properly in love with Nenna.'

Kitty sat down.

'But—' she said.

'Exactly,' said Tom.

～

For three hours Tom and Kitty sat and drank and talked, and when he got home Tom wrote this:

Nenna,

There's something I need to say, and in all the talk of bureaucracy and papers and family I'm not sure that I have made it perfectly clear. Something has happened to me and I don't think it will ever unhappen, whatever the future brings. I have fallen in love with you. I am in love with you. I am in love with everything about you, with your heart and soul. Take this fact and keep it close and do with it what you will. I am yours. I always will be.

Tom

～

Nenna wept when she read it.

Here he is – here he is.

436

That night in her boat-like bed she wrote his name, Masino, on the soft skin inside her forearm, with the point of her compass. The scratches were delicate and white like the frond of a feather. She pushed a little harder: beads of ruby blood along the pearly scratch. It all looked so clean and beautiful. It hurt. She pushed a little harder, and smiled.

That night she dreamed for the first time in years of the island pulling itself free and sailing away.

~

She read his letter again the next morning, and at every possible opportunity. The glory with which it inundated her made her suddenly bold to her father at table.

'I saw Gelsomina today,' she said. 'They're leaving too, did you hear? To America. New York!'

His reaction was immediate, pre-sprung.

'When you speak to me like this,' Aldo cried, flinging his fist to the table and his eyes to heaven, 'you are like the proselytising Christians, trying to force me into a conversion I don't want. I will not convert! Do you understand, my love, how offensive you are in asking me to? The Duce is my leader, torment me as you will.'

All around the table the members of the family curled up beneath it, silent, dark heads tucked down, snails hiding from salt. *But I have a shell*, Nenna thought, *and this can't go on*. She didn't particularly want to challenge him in front of his sons, his wife, but round the table was the only time she could say anything to him. He was out of the house, all the time, as if he were going to work – *but what work?*

Has he, miraculously, of all the Jewish professionals in Italy, not lost his job? They did not know. He did not say. Susanna would not ask. But the law, now, forbids him to work.

'Do you think I don't know history?' he was saying, pumping himself up, the familiar rhythmic inflation of his self-assurance, his conviction of his superior knowledge, his justified resentments. 'You talk to me of liberty,' he said, 'and imprisonment – were you born with the filth of the ghetto under your fingernails? What do you know of Venice and Trieste, of Napoleon? What do you know of Pius the Seventh, of the Inquisition? Does the terror of the generations flow more strongly in your blood than in mine?'

No. But I see that you are terrified, that you have inherited that terror and can't admit it.

'Do I know nothing of the gratitude due to the princes of the House of Este? Of the duplicity of the Spanish who expelled us from Spain but allowed us at Milan, under Spanish rule – until they expelled us again—'

It was the kind of blind proclamatory shouting to which it's both pointless and impossible to respond out loud.

Yes, you know so much, Papà – so why can't you know this too? This one thing which it is necessary to know?

'Ask your mother about the Jews of Mantua!'

Now – see – he slaps his napkin – faded and shiny from long use and too much washing – out in the air, snapping like laundry in the wind, and settles it down on his chest, tucked in at the collar. As he always does. Now – hands down on the table.

'Yes, I am all for Rome,' he said, elbows out, face stern. 'But I know what has happened elsewhere too. And above all I know that Rome has produced our saviour, yes, a

438

saviour who through no fault of his own, through practicality, has had to take issue with those foreign Jews, with no national loyalty to Italy – he understands that our land cannot afford them though with the generosity of his generous heart he would, he would, if he could – but a land is only so big, it would be foolish, immoral even, to let everyone who wants our beautiful land to come here—'

He does not see his entire family cowed before him. He doesn't know that his sons mock him behind his back. That Marinella flinches when he raises his voice. We who love him hate him. Papà.

'No,' he was saying, 'Benito Mussolini is our man, our leader. He loves us, he will protect us. Look around! He has done us no harm! Has he? Look, there are our plates, here is our roof, here is our food on our table.'

Aldo spread his arm wide. None of them looked up. Marinella seemed absorbed in her piece of bread, murmuring to it, a little song of her own.

'If we reject him,' he said, more gently, 'will we not anger him? Then, will he not punish us, show us his fury, throw us out, as any father would whose children turn against him?'

A big heat expanded inside Nenna's head.

'Is that what a father does?' she asked.

Susanna closed her eyes. The brothers, eyes wary, chins pointed, glanced to and fro between father and sister.

'When a child insults, a father punishes,' Aldo said, grandly.

'What if a father misunderstands?' Nenna replied, and looked up at him, straight.

439

'Oh, Nenna,' he said, with his beautiful smile. 'A father knows best.'

'What if a father is wrong?' she persisted.

'What father is wrong?' he said, disbelieving, indulging, fond of his clever daughter – and she almost smiled, because his wilful blindness was so adaptable that she could almost believe he didn't know what they were talking about. 'The Duce is not wrong!' he said. 'What father—?'

'You will not see it,' she said, 'because you fear to—'

Beside her, Susanna sighed deeply, deeply, as Aldo rose and expanded into his glory.

'Fear!' he cried. 'To a hero of Caporetto, you say fear?'

'We lost, at Caporetto,' Nenna said. 'Humiliatingly, because of bad leadership and misplaced loyalty. I say this to a Jew who will not see his enemy for what he is.' And then, dropping it into the silence of his shock, she said, scarcely believing she was doing it: 'And to a father who will not see that his daughter is right.'

Silence. Then:

'What is this?' he said.

'It is a loving daughter telling the truth,' she said.

'How sharper than a serpent's tooth it is,' he said, 'to have a thankless child. It is not truth. It is disrespect.'

'It's truth as I see it, as it has been demonstrated to me. And Papà, have you not noticed that everybody else agrees with me?'

'You think I'm frightened, and wrong.'

'Yes,' she said.

'You don't respect me,' he said. 'So go. Go on! Go!'

'But you are right to be frightened,' she was continuing.

440

'Only a fool would not be frightened. I just wish you would act on it.'

They were talking over each other; neither quite hearing what the other said. How wide and deep can a chasm suddenly be . . .

'Go!' he cried.

Susanna stifled a gulp. 'Papà,' Vittorio said. Susanna nudged him, glanced – *leave the table.*

'No,' said Aldo. 'This is their sister. Let them stay.'

'You don't want me to go,' Nenna said, raising her head, looking him in the eye, *big beautiful brown eyes of my father.* That was true, she knew it. Her voice was shaking; throat very small for it to fight through. *But you have to say it.*

'Sharper than a serpent's tooth,' he mused. His face was closed.

'And Stefano?' she said. 'Vittorio? Mother? Marinella? Are they to go too?' They all looked up.

Perhaps I will vomit.

NO.

Vomit up words. Go on – let it go. All of it.

'Or are they all to stay here, terrified of your blindness, "protected" by the man who forbids them to own a radio, forbids them work, education – who loves Hitler who murders Jews, throws them – us! – out of his country with nowhere to go, keeps their property, robs them and humiliates them. What have those Jews done wrong, even in the eyes of Hitler, other than be Jewish? Does Hitler know or care where a Jew's grandparents lived? This bossy new friend of Mussolini, does he know or care that Jews have been in Rome since before Jesus Christ? Are those children he throws out an international communist conspiracy? Or are they children with nowhere to lay their heads, now? That will be us, Papà. That will be Marinella and Mama. Papà, I don't care. I can go. I am strong, full-grown but young – I can go. The boys are boys, they're growing up – they can go. We can sleep in barns and lie and steal food. But Mama. And Marinella. Marinella, Papà. How can they steal food and sleep in the street?'

He was trying to talk over her, to talk her down, and in the end she stopped. The boys were staring unnerved.

'And you!' she cried. 'You'll be old! You!'

'Child,' he said. 'Be calm. Be calm. Listen. Do you recall the life of Edgardo Mortara? No, listen. A Jewish boy of Bologna was illegally baptised—'

'What are you talking about! There will be war, Papà! Italy will be on the side of the Jew-killer, because of your Mussolini!'

'Shut up. I am telling you something of great importance – illegally baptised by a Christian maidservant, a thief, who claimed he was mortally ill – and he was taken from his loving parents, adopted by the very Pope, because a Catholic cannot be brought up by Jews, and he was now, by that act done on him without his or anybody's consent, by an illiterate girl, a Catholic . . . this was not even seventy years ago—'

The family fell silent before the barrage, fell into the torpor of those accustomed to a parent who goes on and on and on . . .

'Papà—' she murmured.

'—that boy is still alive – a Catholic priest in an abbey in Belgium, despised universally and internationally for his constant efforts to convert Jews to Catholicism. But listen: the Pope – Pio IX – offered the boy back to his parents, if they would only convert – they would not. They would not. Stupidity! Listen, my stubborn child. The only way to deal with this world is to reject all religion, all superstition, and to put one's faith in strength and clear modern principle. Which is what I do. Do not fall victim to the webs of religion, my dear girl. Modern principle – such as Fascism offers. This is the way. Il Duce himself said that priests were black spots on humanity, he himself said that they were at fault in blaming the Jews for the death of Jesus, he himself said the sacrifice of blood of Italian Jews in the last war was vast and great and generous – I have it here—'

'It was the Romans who required Jesus to die,' Nenna said. 'He suffered under Pontius Pilate. Pilate was a Roman.'

'Do not involve yourself with any machinations based on religion. Do not concern yourself!'

And what do I say to that? We, so proud of our Jewishness, despite our scorn for religion, are now to declare ourselves nothing to do with Jewishness? Again, as if those who hate us would care!

She said: 'Only a crank, Papà, deals with the world as if the world is as he wishes it to be. I do not believe in water, therefore I am not drowning. I do not believe in your right to behead me, therefore I ignore your guillotine. I swore loyalty to you twenty years ago, therefore I do not see that you are betraying me now.'

He sat stony.

'Papà, please! No decent human soul, Jew or otherwise, could look at the acts of Nazism and think them right.

443

Gentiles across the world denounce it – but we are Jews! We are not only witnesses, we are victims! There is no doubt. Papà, you love your Mussolini as if he were a god. You gaze blindly when you gaze on him.'

'Blindly?'

'Blindly.'

'Blindly' he said.

'It is reality, Papà. We can leave, if you will come. Or do you want us to curl up, loyal and loving by your side like a spaniel in a folk story, and suffer the fate your folly brings down, because we love you?'

He heaved, and he subsided, and he heaved again.

He's a volcano. Is he about to erupt? Or is he spent?

'Because we love you,' he said, finally, and with some difficulty, 'we will not throw you out of the house, so long as you *shut up*,' he barked, 'with your disrespectful "truth". We are a loyal Fascist household. Your chatter is not to bring danger to us. If you wish to leave, to break your mother's heart, and mine, to destroy your future and to submit to who knows what danger, and bring it also on to your family, well, you are nineteen years old and you know everything, so I am sure you will be safe and happy. Go on! If that is what you want.'

Nenna glanced round the table. The boys, agog. Susanna, holding her hands together and looking, if one had not known that this was a secular household, as if she were praying. And at the end, in her little chair, clutching her damp bread, Marinella. Three years old, fat cheeks, big eyes staring at Nenna. *I am old enough to be her mother*, Nenna thought. *Marinella Marinella Marinella.*

'So you admit there is danger?' she said, raising her head

444

high this time, staring him out. 'In a safe and civilised place, you know, people can say what they think. There is no reason for people to live in this arbitrary fear.'

'Arbitrary!' he said. 'Listen to the words she uses . . . You sound like your English Tommaso . . .'

'You educated me,' she said. 'So that I could bring glory to Italy. So I will. So I will.'

Susanna was shaking her head.

'Such trust and love I had for those people,' Aldo was saying. 'For that boy. He educated you.'

'It doesn't take any education at all to see what is happening, Papà. It just takes opening your eyes.'

'Listen to her!' Aldo said. Bemused, almost. 'He put this into your head. That English boy.' He stared at her for a moment then said, 'And what else did he put into you? What else did he open, eh?'

His meaning was perfectly clear.

Nenna turned her face away. And then swung back at him and hissed: 'I did not hear that filth from your mouth, Father. I did not hear it.'

Her father was leaning back a little, glaring at her, red-faced, a little sneer on his mouth, a little 'huh' escaping his lips. 'Well,' he said. 'Look at her. Now we know.'

Susanna was crying. Stefano was crying. Vittorio was biting his lip. Marinella gave a low soft wail.

'Now look what you've done,' Aldo said.

~

She didn't leave. More and more families did, anyone with money, or a cousin in London, or a son in America. *We have cousins in London. We have a little bit of money. We can sell things. We can still go . . .*

The people who stayed carried on: selling their vegetables, sewing their clothing, going to the synagogue, sitting on their doorsteps. Would they leave if they could? Were things quieter? Or was that her imagination? The neighbourhood was covered by a light, immovable, indomitable veil: *Attesismo*. Waiting.

Or was it quiet because nobody was talking to her? *Because I am the Fascist girl?*

It was as if she had never felt shame before.

But I am loved. Tommaso wants me, in London.

But my mother! My little darling, Marinella – my stupid brothers who I love so much.

After the fight with Aldo, Nenna had no more letters from Tom. She accused her father of withholding them, in a mighty rumpus, tempers matching, Marinella cowering, and a slap to her face. She accused her mother, whose quiet denials she had to believe. She lost many nights' sleep at the thought that they might have been intercepted by OVRA, the Duce's secret police, so mysterious that nobody knew what their acronym meant. She thought OVRA would now come in the night and take away the whole family. She tried to remember what she had written. Her stupid attempt at code would be transparent to half of Rome – anyone who could read, knew any Romanaccio, knew any English. She expected, nightly, the crack of *squadristi* at the door. But then no, surely. OVRA had better things to do. But then they

446

had picked up that guy who had wondered – wondered! – why the *pischello*'s son-in-law Ciano had so much time to play golf.

'Tom doesn't care about you,' said Aldo. 'Sweetheart, men can be like that. Forget about him. You're young. You've got your daddy!' And he held his arms out to her, and she went into them, her head on his chest, and she said, 'I'm sorry, Papà, I'm so sorry,' and he stroked her head.

As the Duce kept saying, this was no time for sentiment. It was time to toughen up.

~

Stefano, fifteen years old, would glue himself to his seat during the fights. A man does not run. A man stands his ground. A man is not scared of women. A man respects his father. He seethed with incomprehension, but one thing he knew. Tom was the root of the unhappiness and fear in the house. The letters with the English stamps were the poison. A man must take responsibility and protect his family. So Stefano stole the letters.

Then, fearing his own foolhardiness, he didn't know what to do with them. For a while he kept them in his school-books, but Susanna was teaching the boys herself now and it wasn't safe. As Nenna became sad, looking for the post each day with an ever-shrinking spark of hopefulness, misery grew in him, and haunted him. He wished he had never started it, he wished he could put them back, he thought about throwing them into the river; about posting them again. They sat there like a snake in a box. But even he knew that the English were weak, dissolute people who scorned Italy. He had to protect his sister, whether she wanted him to or not.

He didn't talk to Vittorio about it. Vittorio had grown silent at home, and was out much of the time. Stefano didn't like out. The *squadristi*, marching about with their *passo romano*, made him nervous. Vittorio chatted to them! Such confidence – anyway, Vittorio was away. He had talked their parents into letting him go fishing in Catania. So much for school at home!

Inspiration struck Stefano: a way out of his impasse that seemed both honourable and convenient. He posted the backlog of the letters, and each new one that came, through the Bocca della Verità. Let the great round cheese-faced moon-faced stone mouth of truth eat them.

❧

Receiving no letters, it became impossible for Nenna to write. The words of Tom's last letter burned in her mind: I am in love with you. I am in love with everything about you, with your heart and soul. Take this fact and keep it close and do with it what you will. I am yours. I always will be.

She did not know what to do. She went back to the Embassy, but Johnny Carmichael was not there any more and what could she say to anyone else? *My English boyfriend has stopped writing to me, you must tell the King of England and make him sort it out—?* She came away thinking that had Johnny been there she might have begged him on her knees.

Sometimes it was just about safety. And then it was about the kissing: desire stuck her through, and she was a speared animal, immobile, open-mouthed, desperate. *He has left me. He has met someone else. He has given up on me because I resisted him at every point. He didn't mean it; he only said it because he is fond of me and thought it would make me go to England . . . He doesn't love me.*

He has been found and hurt by Fascists in England – they have killed people in France before, why not in England?

He is sick.

He has had an accident.

And: *Who would love me anyway, a stupid Fascist Jewish girl? Everybody will hate me. The Jews, because I was Fascist. The Fascists, because I am a Jew. Tom because I am stupid and I have let him down. I have made myself nothing. A nothing.*

Was. Past tense. A shift I would have done well to make earlier. I have only myself to blame.

～

Each day was hot and difficult, more difficult each day. Less money, fewer ways to make a little, less to eat. Susanna getting thinner visibly, as she gave every possible bit of food to the boys and Marinella. Nenna was wise to that; she refused the larger piece of bread, the slightly fuller bowl of soup.

Papà – oh, he said nothing. His shirt collars grew shiny, he called her stubborn, he changed not a whit of what he believed. *Clinging*, she thought. *He's clinging to a sinking branch. And I'm just as bad, clinging to him.* Night after night he sat with the windows open, going over the plans for Pomezia. Night after night, she sat on the other side of the house, thinking about Tom. She hated him. But whenever a man looked at her in the street or at someone's house, blue eyes appeared before her, blue eyes and white roses and his voice in her ear. *Are you my girl, Nenna?*

I was always your girl.

And then the brutal suddenness with which he had been whisked away just as—

Just as—

Just as—

—and then she would cry, and cry, because she could feel the touch of his mouth, his hard slender chest against her breasts, that moment when they were both so surprised that this – this instantaneous heat and hunger – was something – that their years of mocking affection could be set on fire just like that – that she wanted him to come back and finish it – or start it – to do what a man does to a woman . . .

Ever since her father had mentioned it—

She hated her father more than she hated Tom.

She adored him, she was crazy for him, she would do anything for him.

—and then his letters, promising that the help would come, could still come, the talk of visas, of employment for Aldo, of it being possible, of love

even then

and then the letters stopping, and the nothing.

It's up to me then, she thought. *I must start to make up for this.*

450

She went round to Tullio's, and waited with his mother until he came. They walked together. 'I'm at your service,' she said. 'If my handwriting or my innocent looks or anything else are of use, you and your friends can make use of them.'

Tullio looked at her with some sadness. 'The daughter of Aldo Fiore?' he said. 'I don't think so. The boys weren't even happy about my doing the certificates for you.'

'I've changed,' she said. 'My eyes are open.'

'I dare say,' he said. 'I believe you.' And he shrugged, and moved away, leaving her there on the street.

It took Tom a while to notice that there were no letters coming from her. He read her old ones – the ones he liked, the recent ones – and he wrote to her, scraps of news when there was no time, longer romantic letters at the ends of his long and busy days.

When he realised it had been ten days since he had received a new one from her, he was not too worried. It would be the post. He wrote to Bertolini, asking him to pop round if he didn't mind, and see if she was OK. It was when that letter had no response, and then came back another three weeks later with 'not known at this address' on it, that he wrote to Susanna, and heard nothing back, and started searching his mind for other reliable people in Rome, someone he knew well, to whom it would be safe to write, someone he could trust, who was still there, who would not be put in danger by his writing to them.

He rang Johnny. 'Give me the name of somebody kind

at the Embassy in Rome. I have to know she's all right.'

Johnny said: 'Leave it with me.'

~

Another letter had come to the island. Official, from Sicily. Aldo opened it before supper; the pasta was boiling; Stefano was reading, Nenna was laying the table.

'We write to inform you that Vittorio Elia Fiore of Rome was arrested . . . along with other men . . . a dance . . . a sexual aberration that offends morality and that is disastrous to public health and the improvement of the race . . . an evil which needs to be attacked and burned at its core.'

Vittorio Elia Fiore of Rome had been tried, and found guilty, and he was now in internal exile with the other convicts on the island of San Domino in the Tremiti.

Aldo read it out loud, disbelieving.

Susanna fell to the floor, knees buckling, a puddle of woman, weeping and howling, hitting her face with her hands, pulling her hair.

'A faggot?' Aldo said, standing up. 'My boy is a faggot? Impossible.'

Nenna grabbed the letter from him and sat, reading it through.

'Is it true?' Aldo cried. 'Susanna, you're his mother – is this true?'

She howled, shaking her head.

'The little bastard,' he said. 'Catania! Fishing! With that little bastard Orazio – and him a *squadrista*! Serve them right, the perverts – the Duce—'

And Susanna leapt from her swirl of misery on the floor,

and sprang to where her husband was. She flung her head back and stared at him, and she slapped him. She clawed his face. She spat at him.

'You,' she said. 'You are the bastard, and you are the fool. YOU are the bastard.'

Aldo put amazed hands up to his face.

'Nenna,' Susanna said, 'go to England. Take Marinella. Find the Jewish people there, find a synagogue. Your Tom might help you but find the Jewish people. Jews have to help each other. You hear that Aldo? You remember? Jews have to *help each other*! It's the law. I will go to San Domino, and your bastard father can rot in hell.'

Nenna turned to look at him. Tears were rolling down his face, much slower, really, than this all merited.

Susanna said: 'Don't you understand, Nenna? He's lost it, everything. Gave it all up.'

'So did you,' Aldo said, very quietly.

'At least I gave everything up for a man I knew,' Susanna said. 'For you. Women are meant to give up everything for a man. A man is not.'

Nenna stood silent.

'He gave up being Jewish, for Benito Mussolini. He gave up God. For a man. For a Golden Calf.'

For that evening, Nenna thought that the bursting of Susanna's banks signified relief, clarification, change – possibility of improvement even. She sat upstairs with Stefano; they played *scopa* and pretended they did not have antennae out for the voices below, the shouting, the weeping.

Stefano said, very quietly: 'What has Vittorio done? What is a faggot?'

Nenna looked at him. 'You can ask him when he comes back,' she said.

'Will he come back?'

There was a feeling at the back of her neck as if she was being gripped. 'It's not like murder,' she said, but she couldn't think of anything better than that.

In the end silence fell below.

'Come on then,' she said to Stefano, and they cautiously stepped down the stairs.

Papà will have listened to Mama, she was thinking. *Things will be different now.*

But Aldo was sitting alone.

'Where is Mama?' Stefano said.

'Gone out,' Aldo said, smiling.

'Gone where?' said Nenna.

'Oh, she'll be back soon,' said Aldo, the smile in place.

Never in Nenna's lifetime had Susanna gone out of the house in the evening on her own. Looking at Aldo's face, Nenna recognised that this was collapse.

'Where?' she shouted.

'Oh, just, just – she'll be back.'

'It's night-time, Papà. What do you mean?'

'She'll be back,' he said. It sounded almost airy.

She's left us. She's left Papà.

'Has she gone to find him? What did she say? What did she say!'

Aldo sat there, beaming. Nenna felt her strings cut, then. Her mother gone, her brother imprisoned, her beloved silent

454

and so far away, two children to be cared for, and her father—

'Come,' she said to Stefano, and together they ran out into the night. To the tram stop, to the station, running, asking, panting. No sign. It was two before they got in, and Stefano was almost in tears.

Nenna looked in at Marinella, fast asleep, angelic. She looked in at her father, lying fully dressed on the bed like a dead man, his breath soft. His hair looked a little thinner. She touched his hand. He didn't stir.

~

In the next days, waiting (though she pretended she wasn't) for her mother to return, she raised her eyes and looked around at the wider world. Larger items than her mother were making their moves. On August 23 Russia and Germany signed their non-aggression pact. On August 26 Belgium mobilised. On August 27 Hitler demanded Danzig and the Polish Corridor. On August 28 the Netherlands mobilised. Chess pieces were on the march; ingredients for the explosion lined up.

She went to Aldo, who was sitting in his suit at the kitchen table, his curls limp in the heat, his jacket on, his briefcase on the floor at his side. He was reading a book, and weeping. Marinella was at his feet, picking through a little bowl of dried beans. When she saw Nenna, she jumped up and hugged her.

Nenna picked Marinella up, and with the child heavy on her hip, told him the news. He glanced at them for a second, and said 'Hm', with a little shrug, still holding the book.

That sight: the book, the jacket, the tears, the immediate return to the page he was staring at, made her realise that her father was actually being driven insane.

'Where is Mama?' Marinella asked.

'Gone to see Vittorio,' Nenna said. 'Don't worry, you have me.' She smiled at her. 'Here. Fold these clothes.' While Marinella folded, Nenna wrote.

28 August, 1939

Dear Masino,

I haven't heard from you for so long. Have you given up on me? I wouldn't blame you. But as things just get worse and worse I have to ask you again: please help us.

Tommaso, I don't know how to write this. These words. Vittorio is in internal exile. In other words, in prison. It is an island. He was with some men. This is a special prison for men like this, to remove them from 'decent people'. His friend is a Fascist, but what they were doing was not apparently Fascist. He is there too! So at least the law is equal about that. I have no words – none beyond these, not good enough. Mama hit Papà. War is inside and out. She has gone to Termoli, the nearest she can get to San Domino, where Vittorio is. I don't know what she thinks she can do there. Stefano says nothing – nothing. He wants to join the army but even if they want fifteen-year-olds (I don't think they do) they do not want Jews. You may wonder about Papà. My love, he is losing his mind. He looks at maps and plans all day, and he smiles at everything, and at the same time he cries. There is no Jewish doctor to look at him. Anyway the Jews are not

456

talking to us. So I am cooking and holding the house together, a bit. Marinella is

She paused a while, to think what she could say about Marinella. In the end she crossed it out.

My love, did you get the photographs? They weren't very good. I went to the Embassy: I spoke of Carmichael and the man said he knew him and gave me 50 lire, so if he asks for it back from Carmichael or you then you will know that I need your help. But when I went back he was no longer there.

I know you had ideas; I don't know what has happened about them. But things are not going to get better. Soon we will lose on both sides: Italians, enemies of England; Jews, enemies of the Nazis. So then what, for us? I cannot imagine. I can only hope that the war will keep them so busy they will have no time for tormenting us. Again I ask the ridiculous question – are my letters not reaching you? I don't understand why I do not hear from you. Please. I am sorry for all the times I didn't listen to you. Is it that?

Please help us now.

My love, are you my love? I am yours.

Nenna

The letter was tear-stained, and she didn't like what she said, nor how she had said it, but there was no more paper.

'Stefano, look after your sister,' she said, as she left the house to post it.

He looked at her, at the envelope.

'What did Vittorio do?' he asked.

'I don't know,' she said. 'It doesn't matter. Everything a Jew does is wrong now anyway.'

'Who are you writing to?'

'Tommaso,' she said. 'I'm going to England.'

'What about me?' Stefano said.

'You can come too,' she said, and pinched his cheek. She didn't have to reach up; he was not tall.

'No,' he said. 'I don't deserve it.'

'Ah, sweetheart,' she said. 'It's not your fault. It's all bigger than us. Good that you can learn to see clearly now.'

'No,' he said, and set his downy chin firm. 'It's not that. I stole your letters. Lots of them. From England. I put them in the Bocca della Verità. I wish I hadn't but I didn't know how to say—'

She slapped him, so hard, and he reeled.

She closed her eyes and put her hands to her own face, biting her lip to stop unforgivable words coming.

When she opened her eyes he had gone, footsteps across the piazza, nothing.

Marinella was looking up at her.

'Stefano!' Nenna yelled, and ran out, Marinella at her heels. 'Stefano!' – the word echoing across the cobbles, between the buildings, yellow and grey over the river. Nothing.

'Which way did he go?' she cried, too loud, to Marinella. The little one pointed a shaky arm, and her face crumpled. Nenna picked her up, hushed her, lurched up to the road – looked to the bridge, and to the other. Nothing.

'He'll come back,' she said to Marinella. 'Come on!'

She posted the letter. Then anger hit her again as they stormed down the Lungotevere and across to Santa Maria in Cosmedin to where the old stone face stared anciently, blandly out. Its size and dimness stopped her only for a moment – *I didn't kill Jesus* – and she stared it in the eye before smoothing her hair and going to find a priest.

No, he knew nothing about any letters. The signorina could call back. What name was it? *Poverina.* From her *fidanzato*?

She could see he pitied her, thought her a dupe, and had observed her Jewish name.

'I will come back,' she said. 'Thank you. It is important.'

'They're real letters,' said Marinella. 'Tom is real.' She smiled up at the priest and he blessed her, automatically.

~

Standing outside the ugly church, fretting, Marinella at her side, Nenna hit the side of her head with the ball of her palm, and directed herself to the post office. She counted her coins. Her telegram read: WILL COME WITH MARINELLA EVERYONE ELSE MAD OR GONE STEFANO STOLE LETTERS SEND FOR US WHATEVER YOU SAY I LOVE YOU

Later, when Marinella was asleep and Stefano wasn't back, and Aldo was chuckling over a map and the house was quiet, Nenna went out again. In the ivy-leafed cotton dress she had had since she was fifteen, and despite her mother's admonitions that she must not sit down on stone, it wore the seats of her clothes so badly, she sat on her favourite

459

fallen column in the Forum, polished smooth by generations of backsides, and she asked the ghosts of Rome and the god of Israel what was to be done, and she wept.

Chapter Twenty

London, Summer–Autumn 1939

Twice a month Nadine went to tea with Rose in her rooms behind her GP surgery. There they would talk. Not about Tom and Kitty, nor Peter, nor Riley. After an initial ten-minute exchange on everyone's being all right, these subjects were banned. They would talk about politics, art, literature, music and about developments in medicine, and in social and health policy. Of course these topics did sometimes overlap with talk about Peter and Riley; Tom and Kitty. The two women had become far more interested in race relations, for example, since the arrival of Mabel and Iris, and of course the Woman Question was always coming back to Kitty, who had left her grandmother's and moved in with some girls, and what on earth she was up to? And foreign affairs led to Nenna and the Roman family, and when the imminence or otherwise of war barged its way in, as it increasingly did, that of course led to Tom, and sometimes even to Riley. But today Rose had been reading an article about whether a girl should own her own tea set, or did it give an undesirable impression of independence?

'Did you see it?' said Rose, pouring from her own teapot into her own teacups. 'Quite droll. It made me think of Kitty in her flat.'

'I don't like it,' said Nadine. 'Too self-aware. I'm glad she's working though. It's better for a girl to be thinking about things outside herself.'

'Like we were at her age?' said Rose, with a look, and suddenly they were on the subject, the unavoidable subject that was lurking round every corner, at the end of every innocent comment.

'Ha!' said Nadine, with a touch of bitterness. 'God forbid.' She stopped for a moment. 'But when you look at the world . . .'

'It won't be how it was for us,' Rose said. 'Even if it comes to it. There won't be trenches.'

An image came to Nadine: looking up, from underground, after that god-awful terrifying night at Étaples, and seeing almond blossom against the pale Flanders sky.

'Won't there?' she asked. She considered, for a moment: Kitty, smart little Kitty, in the chaos of the mud and the terror of a bombed-out slit trench . . . It gave her a swirl of sickness inside. *Why are we so powerless, over and over?* 'Do you promise?' she said, with a bit of a smile.

'Aeroplanes,' said Rose. 'It will be very different.'

'Will,' said Nadine.

'If,' said Rose.

After the requisite little silence Nadine jumped up and gave a little kind of 'aaagghh' sound of frustration. Then, 'Oh, Rose,' she said. Then, 'Do you think—' but Rose cut her off.

'I'm just fighting my own little war down here,' she said. 'Against measles and flu and polio and rickets and syphilis and drink and black eyes. I don't know. There's nothing for us to do about it, and if there is, I dare say they'll let us know.'

'Will they want us again?' Nadine was forty-two now; a strong and capable woman. Rose was fifty; in the prime of her knowledge and capacities.

'No!' said Rose. 'You have children and a husband, and I'm still treating the wounded from the last war.'

'The last war,' said Nadine. 'It used to just be called the War.'

Rose laughed at that, a little bitter laugh. 'Nadine,' she said. 'Remember your technique. Don't worry about anything unless you're able to do something about it, in which case do something about it, and stop worrying. How's Tom?'

'Flying,' she said, and looked up. 'Flying! As if he can't wait! He's signed up with the RAF in some way through the UAS, you know, making himself available . . . I won't – can't – listen when he talks about it. He looks more like Peter every day, only with Julia's cheekbones and her great eyes . . . He might as well be carrying a gigantic banner saying "sacrifice me". Aeroplanes, Rose! Aeroplanes and bombs and weapons up in the air! And human bodies!'

Rose observed her, kindly, and Nadine shook her head briefly to shake off the images.

'Anyway, how are you?' Nadine asked.

Rose turned bright red, and started to speak, but stopped herself.

'Rose?' Nadine asked.

Rose started laughing, and then said: 'Oh Lord,' and then, 'Nadine, I'm to be married, don't laugh.'

Nadine laughed and laughed. Rose laughed too. He was a cardiologist. She had known him for a while. A childless widower. He did not want her to give up work. His name was George Mackesson. He played the violin and liked Thackeray. She liked him very much. They would live in Bloomsbury, to be near his hospital. She would join a practice nearby, perhaps in Camden. She was very happy.

'You're very happy?'

'I'm very happy.'

Nadine too was very happy. Something like that, at a moment like this. Priceless.

~

Mabel and Iris were doing their best at Locke Hill.

Mabel had been finding it hard even before Iris agreed to come down; now, seeing her daughter also subjected to the . . . limitations . . . that she herself had hoped to see off, it was worse.

At first she had gritted her teeth and accepted that she had to give it a go. *Nature*, she thought. *The lovely piano. The beautiful garden. Lots of room. Um, walks.* And above all, Peter's sense of home.

Iris had come for Christmas, though she maintained her chill, which made Mabel miserable and compounded the chill she felt all around from neighbours. When the vicar called, his confusion was so total that he stayed only five minutes and couldn't exchange a word with Mabel beyond a greeting. At least the Purefoys visited, with Kitty, occasionally, and Sir Robert, and Rose. Mabel had feared feeling like an exhibit; personally responsible for the success or failure of race relations in Britain for decades to come; *if this family fails*, she thought, *I will have proved that negroes have no value, and whites have no heart. Or vice versa.* But it was all right. They all got to know each other better, and that actually was all that was needed.

Mabel and Nadine went Christmas shopping together. As they came out of a glove shop (soft green leather, for Iris, and pale blue for Kitty), Nadine said: 'Is it always like that?' to which Mabel responded: 'That depends how you think it was . . .'

'Self-conscious, and slightly panicky,' Nadine said. 'Them not you. With an undertone of disrespect.'

'. . . because, you see, I don't know what it's like when I'm not there,' Mabel said.

Nadine, who had never in her life been the only white woman in a room of negroes, thought about that.

'You know what's tiring,' Mabel said suddenly. 'Being the beginners' course for everybody. Always being talked to about your skin colour. Or being looked at, knowing they're thinking about your skin colour, and specifically not talking about it. Or not being looked at, because your skin colour is too confusing for them even to see you.'

Nadine wanted to say sorry, but it didn't seem right. 'Let's have a cup of tea,' she said, and steered Mabel towards her preferred tearoom. Yes, the waitress gave them a doubtful look; yes, Mabel – and Nadine too – stared her down.

'The other day,' Nadine said, 'I was at dinner, and someone

465

said to me, no Jew is safe in Europe – and then she stopped, as she realised what she had said, and apologised to me. I couldn't think why for a moment. I thought, Oh, does she know I have Jewish relatives, in Italy? – and then I realised she meant me. You know, I didn't used to be "a Jew". Nobody was in the least bit interested. But now apparently I was a Jew all along. I'm starting to think, all right, I'll go to a synagogue and see what it's all about – but that's absurd for me, really – I'm not going to start to be religious now. But the anti-Semitism – would I even have noticed, if I didn't have my Italian cousins? I mean, Mabel, imagine if I read in *The Times* one morning that I wasn't English, that my marriage was invalid, that my parents' marriage was invalid, that I and my children are impure, that I can't have a Christian servant, or work . . .'

Mabel looked at her.

'No Jew *is* safe in Europe,' she said.

'But apparently nor are inverts or gypsies, or – would you be safe in Europe?'

Mabel looked at her coolly. 'Under the Italians,' she said, 'You and I would not be allowed on the same bus. And Peter would have five years in jail for being with me.'

Nadine was flummoxed by this. 'Are you sure?' she said.

'Well, maybe that's only in Ethiopia,' Mabel said. 'Maybe they have one set of laws at home and one in the countries they have invaded. Like they have one for the ruling class and one for everybody else.'

'How do you know about this?' Nadine asked.

'London is a place that people come to,' Mabel said. 'And when they're here, they talk to each other.'

Nadine said, 'Are you safe in London?' She was feeling an abyss opening up around her: *so much that I don't know, that I have not seen.*

'Safe is something you can feel sometimes,' Mabel said. 'Not something you ever are.'

Nadine looked at her, and one of her waves of tearfulness surged up inside her.

'This sort of thing could be against anybody, couldn't it?' she said. 'There's no logic. How long before it's old people, or one-legged people? So it has to be fought, and then if there is war . . . and then we're back to that, fearing, for everybody, all the time . . . and the only comfort for that is the idea that nobody is actually safe anywhere anyway, in wartime or in peace, because we can all fall sick, be knocked down by a motor car, and that's so dispiriting and you know it only upsets other people if you indulge it, so you have to cheer up and be brave and put the damned kettle on . . .'

'Yes,' said Mabel, mildly.

Nadine looked up at her and grinned.

'Sorry,' she said.

Mabel raised her hand, in a tiny movement which conveyed everything of understanding, affection, forgiveness, and humour. It reminded Nadine of Rose.

They each took a sip: the sip of the moment passing, the sip of relief. The sip of punctuation.

'If there is war,' Nadine said, then stopped herself and asked: 'Where were you, in the last one?'

'I was a child,' Mabel said. 'In London, and touring the country with my mama.'

They talked about that for a while, and about Nadine's

467

war, and each began to see what an exceptional woman the other was, and they ordered more tea.

'So do you feel Jewish?' Mabel asked.

'No. I hardly even knew I was. I wonder if my mother did that on purpose.'

Mabel smiled low. 'Not a choice I have for Iris.'

'But would you?' Nadine asked. 'If you could?'

'No,' Mabel said. 'That would be a lie. There's no problem in being what we are. The problem is in how we are treated. And, you know, the world may improve.'

'I've never had that,' Nadine said. 'Because it's invisible, I suppose. Nobody ever knew I was Jewish. I slightly feel I'm letting the side down . . .'

'Depends which side you're on,' Mabel said. 'And what you think the sides are. And whose geometry you accept.'

'Moral and social geometry?'

'I'm on the side of the kind,' said Mabel.

'And the honest,' said Nadine.

'And the hardworking.'

'And the peace lovers—'

'Yeah, we're getting kind of biblical here,' said Mabel.

'I *am* on the side of the peace lovers,' said Nadine, and Mabel cried out 'Nadine – why do people fall for it? For those Big Boys' Gangs?'

'A need to belong, I think. It's easier to feel you belong if you can point to someone else and say "They don't belong."'

'In the States,' Mabel said, 'the poor whites need the poor blacks – someone to feel better than.'

'Hm,' said Nadine. 'I honestly don't think I need to feel better than anyone else.'

'That is a lucky position to be in,' Mabel said. 'It's because you're all right.'

'I am,' said Nadine. 'I am.' And then the tearfulness roared up again, and she started crying, and the next thing was she was telling Mabel about Aldo and Nenna and the others, about Tom's campaign and how they had tried to help, about how since Kristallnacht politics had become suddenly very personal.

'Sweetheart,' Mabel said, and the word made Nadine cry the more, because despite Mabel being younger than her it was motherly. 'I know. And people say they're not interested in politics, as if that means politics won't be interested in them.'

'They're Fascist and Jews,' Nadine said. 'They'll be everybody's enemy . . . we've invited them, I'm proud of what you said – London being a place people can come to. Riley's said he can give Aldo work; they can stay with us—'

'Not unless you turn the house into an internment camp—' Mabel said.

'You see! You see? Mussolini declares that they're not Italian because they're Jewish, but the British government won't go along with that, they'll say they're Italian therefore Fascist – and they are Fascist.'

And that surprised Mabel. Nadine attempted to explain.

'It's all the same nonsense, in the end,' she said. 'Surreal nonsense. By Fascist law, I'm not allowed to exist. Mabel, if there is war, would you go back to America?'

'No!' Mabel said. 'You know what US laws forbid me to do? Be married to my husband, number one.'

Nadine fiddled with her teaspoon and asked: 'Do you

ever feel you should be over there, campaigning, and so forth?'

Mabel yelped.

'What, are you going to go campaigning for the Jews in Nazi-land?'

Nadine said: 'Perhaps I—'

'Stop that right there,' Mabel said. 'When the fight comes, we join in. It ain't so likely a couple of middle-aged ladies can start the fight. We carry on fighting our little fights, spreadin' the word. Anyway, I don't feel American any more. And my blood is from everywhere, insofar as I know. In America, I'd be the most uppity kind of negro – one who not only left, but succeeded. I ain't going back till I play Carnegie Hall. And I ain't never gonna play Carnegie Hall.'

'Your voice has gone more American,' Nadine said.

'Does that when I get relaxed,' Mabel said. 'Or excited.'

~

They all went to church on Christmas morning, crunching up the frosty path. They all sang out, side by side, and Nadine smiled to see Peter, Mabel, Kitty and Iris's eyes all fill with tears at the same glorious crunching chord in the penultimate line of the chorus of 'Hark, the Herald Angels Sing'.

Afterwards Kitty put a handful of Christmas roses on Julia's grave, mossy now, and settled, and Mabel held Peter's hand tight.

~

Iris came back to her mother in the New Year, sheepish, lonely and forgiving, after the night at the Serpentine with

Tom. The massive relief when she did so seemed energy enough to carry them into this new life, down here. They still had the flat in Belgravia. Lexington Street had gone, taking that life with it. They were no longer three generations of black women making music and going to church. They were the exotic (how they grew to hate that word) musical wife and daughter of an English gentleman, and eyebrows rose when they came into the room.

Iris had hoped to start lessons at the Royal College immediately, to go up on the train, stay at the flat, but that proved not possible. Mabel thought – *if I had been open, earlier, could she have been studying all these years, at this higher level?* But that made her think about Thornton, and the past, the great and full past . . . she couldn't regret anything. After a false start or two they had found a piano teacher in Sidcup, an older woman, strong on technique. Sir Robert introduced her, and Mabel could not help realising that it was this connection which made the woman accept Iris. Mabel wondered if he knew it. She found that she could not ask him. So Iris worked, and worked: listened, learnt, played. Sir Robert took her to concerts, and sent her tickets. Once or twice Mabel and Peter found them heads down together over a score: Debussy, Rachmaninoff, the sweetness of shared obsession and concentration.

Mrs Bax, Julia's old bridge partner, and two of her friends, came to call. They quite simply stared at Mabel and Iris as if they were creatures in the zoo, and asked if they could pat Iris's hair. 'They might as well be taking notes,' Iris hissed, in the hall, as she and her mother both left the room pretending to be looking for Mrs Joyce. Mabel laughed.

Mrs Joyce caught them giggling together, for a moment, but then Iris said she wasn't going back in there to be peered at and reported on to the ladies of the neighbourhood, 'half of whom probably wanted to marry Peter themselves'. At this, Mrs Joyce looked at her with new respect, so later Iris wandered into the kitchen and explained to her about how dull it is for negro people to have their negro-ness gone on about all the time.

'Quite apart from the fact,' she said, 'that I'm as white as I am negro anyway. And I am a daughter of this house. Peter's daughter.'

(Mrs Joyce said to Mr Joyce later that she was grateful for the conversation. She had been a little concerned, about how to behave, as it's not what a person is used to, children from long ago suddenly popping up fully grown and being presented as if they'd always been there, and – you know – illegitimate – but then not illegitimate after all – but of course the girl – Miss Iris – was right. The parents were married now and Mr Peter had put everything right, even if the new Mrs Peter wasn't, um, English.)

∾

In the spring and summer the English countryside, it turned out, *was* beautiful, and the garden *was* lovely, and Nadine came down with Riley, and Kitty came a few times. But when Iris cycled back from her class in tears, because the teacher had said she could no longer teach her because other pupils' parents had complained, on the same day that the girl in the haberdashers had again ignored Mabel, simply ignored her, said not a word, as she served customer after customer before her, and nobody – nobody – said, 'Oh, I think this lady was before me' – Mabel bit her patient lip, threw some cushions at Peter's cello, still reclining there in the corner of the beautiful sitting room, and cried out that enough was enough.

'Please, please can we go back to town,' she said to Peter. 'I'm not getting this English negro country lady thing right. Or it's not getting me right. Please. Please.'

And he said, 'Of course, my love, of course.'

Later, he said: 'At this rate they'll be needing the place as a military hospital before the year's out anyway,' but he had recognised their needs, and that was what mattered.

Chapter Twenty-One

Norfolk, September 1939

Riley watched the weeks slip away during that odd summer. He was reading the papers all the time, and taking everything in: Czechoslovakia in the spring, the end of the fighting in Spain, Mussolini and Hitler signing their 'Pact of Steel'. Initially it had been going to be called a 'Pact of Blood'. *Dear God what is wrong with these people?*

His mind of course turned to Aldo. Was blood and steel what Aldo had in mind? *Of course not. Aldo, Nadine's flesh and blood.* Now flesh and blood was a pact Riley understood. Flesh and blood, or blood and steel . . . *Hardly a difficult choice, you'd have thought.*

He noticed that babies were being given little gas masks of their own. Evacuation plans were drawn up. The country was hovering on a starting line, waiting for a starting gun which didn't go. It was terribly hard for everyone to concentrate, as their fears and desires and opinions flickered about the place, bouncing off each other, ricocheting. War or not war. The Up-And-At-'Em school; the Never-Agains. The young people who knew nothing, the practically minded, and those who were still like Peter used to be. He assumed there were others who were still like Peter used to be – in their sheds, their pubs, their back parlours, their street corners, saying nothing, paralysed, still, twenty years later. Not everyone had been able to heal up in Peter's symbolic ten years. *And here we are, another ten years on.* He did not want to see a baby in a gas mask.

He found that he was fiddling with his splint more, unscrewing it, screwing it up. It was uncomfortable. *Nerves,* he thought. Nadine came in one day when he had taken it out, and found him just staring at the gap, in the mirror. She took the splint from his hand, and put it down, and kissed him.

It really did make him nervous, and then the fact that it made him nervous made him nervous again, in a slightly different key.

~

Nadine had arranged the family holiday. It was to be two weeks of calm and rest in a hotel on the Norfolk coast from the end of August. There would be walking, and bathing or sailing if they wanted. Kitty had agreed to come for a few days – they hadn't seen much of her for months. He and Nadine were glad that she was coming. He wanted very much to keep tabs on everybody, everything. He had held his wife closer, since Kristallnacht.

A couple of days before they were to go, the Nazis and the Soviets signed their non-aggression pact. *Well, that's it,* Riley thought. *Hitler's got nothing to be scared of now. He'll just carry on, barging around . . .*

He spent his time in the hotel library, reading and asking himself questions which the newspapers didn't answer. *What will happen? What will happen to Tom? What will happen to Kitty?* He thought about how quick they had all expected it to be, last time, and how quickly those who had expected it to be quick had died. The term 'last time' took on a life of its own in his mind. *Last time,* he thought, *it was the war to end all wars.* He thought he'd better concentrate on the particular. What does a publisher do during wartime? *There'll be rationing, of paper almost certainly – there'll be messages to be put across, propaganda – I can do that.*

When Nadine told him to go and get some air, he did. Sometimes he sat in a deckchair on the breezy beach wrestling with his newspaper. *It's all set in place like buoys at sea, a runway, a flare path. This is the route; that's all. Nothing to be done.*

~

Kitty arrived a day later than the others, screeching into the hotel's drive in a tiny car with the roof down. Johnny Carmichael was driving it. She looked utterly enchanted with herself as she burst on to the verandah where they were having tea: pink-cheeked, windblown despite her scarf, convinced of her own adulthood.

'Darlings,' she said. 'I do hope you don't mind, I've brought Johnny. Tom knows him and he's quite adorable. He's booked his room and everything, and will be perfectly happy to take people out in his simply fantastic car.'

Riley had to stop himself laughing at her – dear Kitty. He shook hands with Carmichael and wondered how he felt about this. A gentleman caller! *Well, he looks like a gentleman, for what that's worth.* When Tom came in from striding the dunes, he was delighted to see Carmichael, and that sent the visitor up in Riley's estimation.

The delight didn't last long. Kitty had brought the post from Bayswater Road. 'Here's one from Nenna, I think!' she said.

As Tom took the envelope from her his hand shook.

'You haven't heard from them for a long time,' Nadine said. Tom was just staring at it.

'Let me,' she said, and he let her take it from him gently. She opened it, and handed him the flimsy sheet of paper.

Riley could see the tearstains. *Oh*, he thought, and Carmichael said, 'Old man—'

Tom looked up at them, looked round. 'I'll read it to you,' he said, and someone said 'Oh Tom are you sure—' and he shushed them, and said, 'We're all rather in this together now, aren't we?' so then everyone was quiet and he read.

Dear Masino,

I haven't heard from you for so long. Have you given up on me? I wouldn't blame you. But as things just get worse and worse I have to ask you again: please help us. Tommaso, I don't know how to write this. These words. Vittorio is in internal exile. In other words, in prison. It is an island. He was

Here Tom broke off, and scanned the next few sentences. He paused a moment and blinked before taking up again:

477

I have no words – none beyond these, not good enough. Mama hit Papà. War is inside and out. She has gone to Termoli, the nearest she can get to San Domino, where Vittorio is. I don't know what she thinks she can do there. Stefano says nothing – nothing. He wants to join the army but even if they want fifteen-years-olds (I don't think they do) they do not want Jews. You may wonder about Papà. He is losing his mind. He looks at maps and plans all day, and he smiles at everything, and at the same time he cries. There is no Jewish doctor to look at him. Anyway the Jews are not talking to us. So I am cooking and holding the house together, a bit.

Did you get the photographs? They weren't very good. I went to the Embassy: I spoke of Carmichael and the man said he knew him and gave me 50 lire, so if he asks for it back from Carmichael or you then you will know that I need your help. But when I went back he was no longer there.

I know you had ideas; I don't know what has happened about them. But things are not going to get better. Soon we will lose on both sides: Italians, enemies of England; Jews, enemies of the Nazis. So then what, for us? I cannot imagine. I can only hope that the war will keep them so busy they will have no time for tormenting us. Again I ask the ridiculous question – are my letters not reaching you? I don't understand why I do not hear from you. Please. I am sorry for all the times I didn't listen to you. Is it that?

Please help us now.

Nenna

'Is it too late?' Riley said.

'It was always too late,' Carmichael said. 'Sorry, Tom. For Fiore, certainly. We can have a go for the children. Do they have passports?'

'She does. I don't think Marinella and Stefano do.'

'Their father would have to apply for them.'

'Oh Christ!' Tom burst out, and turned away.

Nenna, Nenna, Nenna. Tom's legs felt a little lame. He'd been trying to put through a call to Rome: no luck. Just long empty noises hanging in space and distance. It didn't sound as if the phone was even ringing. He pictured it, black and squat on the credenza in the hall. Aldo might answer, or Stefano. *She is in such pain and trouble—*

Tomorrow morning he would telephone to the Embassy in Rome; he would go back to London – he'd take Carmichael – and they could draw up an actual plan. Now she was willing – at last, thank GOD, she was willing – now they could get papers and money to her.

They were all waiting for lunch in the hotel restaurant, around a table with a slightly grubby cloth on it. It was a nervy group: Tom had been on the phone again all morning sending telegrams, and was jumping with frustration, about to head back to town; Nadine had insisted that he eat before he set off, which he didn't want to do, and Kitty was trying to hide her disappointment that Carmichael was going with him. Lunch was to be chicken with white sauce, and

479

treacle tart; Riley was thinking that he could probably manage the chicken when the manager came in, coughed importantly, and made an announcement.

'Ladies and gentlemen,' he said. 'Excuse us for the interruption but we thought you would like to be informed that we have just heard on the wireless that Herr Hitler has invaded Poland.'

Riley's heart seemed to lie down within him, to spread and melt, to disappear almost.

Breaths were taken. Silences and murmurings ebbed and flooded around the room. 'What?' said someone, fractiously. 'What?'

'Is that it, then?' asked Nadine.

Tom unfolded himself, raising his long pale self like some kind of wraith.

'Tom,' said Riley, and paused. Nadine put her hand out.

Tom touched it, gently, as he walked past on his way to the telephone cubicle. Carmichael rose and went with him. There was a glow in Tom's eye. 'Fighter or bomber?' he said to Kitty, as he passed.

'Fighter,' said Kitty. 'Knowing you.'

'I'm not so sure,' said Tom. 'Could go either way.'

'And me?' Carmichael said.

'Intelligence, of course.'

Kitty was as white and as bold as her brother. *Paper children*, Riley thought, *and mine, though I never deserved them. And now I shall lose them.* He watched Tom go. *They don't know. How could they know? And everybody who used to know has forgotten. Everyone has forgotten.*

Nadine stood up. For a moment she stared in the direction

480

Tom had gone; she looked to Riley. It was a desperate gaze she gave him, her mouth hanging a little open, her eyes imploring but at the same time knowing that they must not implore. She was shaking her head.

'It might not be,' she said. 'They might—'

'But all this has been going on for so long now,' Riley said.

'Like in America,' she said. 'Where people dance day and night for weeks, hoping to win ten dollars, and fall over from exhaustion . . .'

'Nadine,' said Riley, helplessly. 'Not much we can do about it.'

'Are we just back to where we were?' she said. 'Is that it? We're back there again?'

'The Prime Minister will have something to say,' Riley said. 'This isn't necessarily it.' He didn't believe himself.

Tom came back half an hour later. 'Twenty minutes queueing and then I can't even get a bloody operator,' he said. 'It's no way to run a war. I should probably sign up as a telephone engineer – that's what they need. What are you going to do, Kitty?'

'*I am* in the Foreign Office, Tom,' said Kitty. 'I'll see what they've got for me. What did girls do in your war, Riley? Nurses and typing I suppose. Perhaps they'll let us drive and ride motorbikes this time round.'

This time round.

'Oh, girls rode motorbikes,' Nadine said.

Of course, Riley thought, *of course Kitty will be brave and fine because Nadine, not her own poor mother, has been her model. And Tom will be brave and fine because the example* of Peter's turnaround is stronger than his weakness. *They will volunteer, and go, wherever they have to go this time, and do their bit, whatever their bit turns out to be, and they will try to be as good as us, and maybe get their face or their mind blown apart too, and spend their lives trying to be as good as we have been at living with that. Better than us.*

Children, he thought. *Children. They know nothing. They've been nowhere. Oh God.*

'Might join the army myself,' Kitty was saying now, grinning boldly; more boldly than she could possibly feel. *Surely. Surely they understand?* 'If I could have a motorbike. Do the right thing!'

But girls were killed too, motorbike or no motorbike. Slit trenches full of nurses, Gothas raining down on them; Spanish flu, infections and syphilis and the sinking of the Marquette . . .

Riley looked up and saw Nadine, watching them across the room. *How do they look to her, these children? Like her life's work, about to be smashed to pieces? Are we really so stupid? Are we?*

Riley dredged around inside himself for the courage he used to have. *It must be there somewhere. Where is it? Has it melted away, because it's not needed for me now, but for them?* His heart beat fast and light: pitter pat, pitter pat.

Tom and Kitty remained, alert, strong, on the nice little armchairs around the low table. *Not our war. Your war,* Riley thought. *Look at you, so beautiful. Your war, that we couldn't prevent. Babies . . .*

Kitty said: 'And what are we going to do about Nenna?'

'Everything we can,' Tom said, pushing himself up again

from the chair, and it was as much as Riley could do not
to weep.

~

The day turned into a tangle of frustrations and indecision.
Johnny's car wouldn't start, the phone lines were overloaded,
Tom trying to telephone, Kitty deciding she wanted to get
back too, there were no cabs to get to Norwich for the train,
everyone wanting and failing to go here or there, and
changing their minds, until in the afternoon Nadine made
them all sit down and have tea, and said: 'Enough. No point
everyone running around now. Tom, you can get hold of
them tomorrow. It still might not be . . . Go and get some
fresh air,' she said, as if he were twelve. 'Go and stride about.
I might come out. Kitty? Riley?'

'Are we allowed?' Kitty asked.

'We're not at war yet,' Tom said. 'And they won't invade
here. They have to invade at Thanet, or somewhere.'

'Well someone thinks they might,' said Kitty. 'There's rolls
of barbed wire already out there on the beach.'

'I rather think that's for fencing, sweetheart,' Nadine said.

'They'll come by air,' said Tom. 'Thousands of para-
troopers.' At which Riley got to his feet, feeling the weight
of tiredness, anger, and sadness on him as he went towards
the stairs. He trailed his hand along Nadine's shoulder as
he left, as if saying, 'I don't need you to follow me.'

The others stared east, as if the Nazi planes and troop
carriers might already be massing just beyond the horizon.

~

In the end, Tom and Riley went out. By the time they got on to the marshes it was a beautiful evening: the sky so very high and deepening blue, the sun behind them in the west gleaming low and gold on the samphire-studded mudflats; the gilded pools rippling silently as the tide slipped in to fill them. There was the odd bird.

Tom was a little ahead of Riley, towards the base of the last bank of dunes before the open sea, and Riley could see his bare shining head, *not in any damn uniform, with any damn hat, thank Christ*, his boots clagging with wet sand as he trudged on. Somewhere over to the left – not far – shots were being fired – *a poacher?* A harrier suddenly rose, clacking its alarm, and along the beach in the distance someone whistled for their dog. Riley heard the dog barking just as the low, loud tide siren started to moan, and drown it out.

It all became terribly clear to him as the siren started, and the dark figure on the slope before him went to scramble up. Fillets of sand were crumbling beneath his feet, and a smell of cordite drifted on the air. Tom climbed on up, long legs, arms reaching, not even a tin hat on, and Riley saw, suddenly and as live as day, this son crucified on the parapet, in No Man's Land, and all the other dear boys running towards him; he saw barbed wire and limbs, and the rain of bullets beyond, and he saw the sky falling in, again.

Riley thought, *I could shoot him now. It would save so much time and trouble.*

He shook his head clear. *None of that.* He gave it a minute. A poacher's gun. A tide siren.

He almost laughed. *Leadswinging by proxy, now, is it?*

That is the past. That is the past. What's coming now is—

∼

On the way back they stopped in at the pub; and it was such a silly thing that set it off. Such a silly thing. A man in an unfortunate jacket, standing at the bar with some other men, red-faced, been there since opening time by the look of them, excited about the news about the imminence of war, war war war, everyone was saying, eyebrows up and under-informed bravado at the ready, *a kind of premature ejaculation*, Riley thought – well, this one said, 'But we should be with Herr Hitler. He can't keep his flies buttoned when it comes to someone else's country, but he's some good ideas. He's right about the Jews!'

So Riley turned to him, mildly, and said, quite clearly and identifiably sadly, 'My wife is Jewish.'

The man looked at him, with a sort of sneer, which swiftly curdled up with the bewilderment of the 'What's wrong with your face?' look, and so then he gave a sort of snort and, in a gesture of default self-defence, he waved his hand by his temple in the 'he's-bonkers' twirl. So one of his mates said, 'Steady, George,' but Tom was on his feet towards him, and George, twitching, burly, old enough to know better even in a public bar, said, 'Oh I stand by that, I do!' and then, seeing the height, youth and expression of Tom, lashed out, flailing and useless, but he managed to catch Riley a wild hard crack on the right of his jaw.

The crack of bone, the thud of flesh, the cry of pain. Blood and teeth. And the splint, askew, falling weird and alien and semi-attached out of Riley's poor mouth. He felt it. Mashed up.

'What the fock's that,' the man said.

Riley had bitten his tongue. Oh, that taste of his own blood in his mouth!

A couple of blokes were holding Tom away. He dropped his head and came up calm. He turned to the men around him and said, with a nod to George, 'Well, you'll remember whose side he's on. Attacking a decorated veteran of Ypres and Passchendaele, for having a Jewish wife.'

Riley tried to speak, tried to smile at his own attempt to speak, swallowed some blood and thought briefly about the curious effect your own blood has on your faeces when you swallow enough of it. He thought, *I really wasn't asking for it. Nadine can't be angry with me, it's not like in Wigan*, and then he had to think about Ainsworth, and then he sighed, the vastest sigh.

Actually it hurt a lot.

~

Tom walked Riley back, holding him steady with a clean pub dishcloth against his face. The landlady had wanted to call the doctor, but Tom said no, his mother was a nurse, they'd go back to the hotel. Of course Riley remembered his long walk outside Zonnebeck.

Kitty ran to embrace Riley, and reeled back. He stood there, confused. He had reverted: *wounded Riley, who does nothing. Someone else take charge.* His grey eyes were emptying with the pain. He did not say anything, or give the small sideways smile.

$$\sim$$

Nadine's head swam slightly at the sight of him, the napkins under his jaw, the look on his face. But her thought was, *Thank God. Thank God we are in a peaceful place, we have a car, there is petrol, we are not so far from London, we are twenty years on, there are not thousands of him, we have Mr Gillies in his clean and tidy office, there is none of the crisis, none of the filth, none of the*... She did not care to remember the things there were none of. She sent Kitty for the hotel first-aid kit; allowed a doctor to be called solely to provide some morphine, and carefully cleaned Riley up. He seemed to want to unscrew the splint on the other side, but she couldn't hold the damaged side up in the right way for long enough, and even putting his finger in his mouth made him gasp and catch. She couldn't really see what was happening in there. She thought the bones might be shattered on both sides. The blow had come from the left, Tom said; the splint could have jarred the bone on the right as well and ... well. There was a fair amount of blood.

$$\sim$$

Tom telephoned everyone he could think of, to get Gillies' home number. The lines were still impossible, and for a moment he had the illogical thought that he should be able to get a line, because the imminence of war should only be affecting telephone calls connected with imminent war. In the end they just drove off into the dark, Tom at the wheel,

Kitty map-reading with a torch, Nadine holding Riley upright in the back. They got home after midnight and Tom half-carried Riley inside.

~

'There was some kind of bust up,' Nadine said. 'I wasn't there.' She had never been to see Gillies with Riley before. It was early, before his clinic was meant to open. She hadn't slept.

Riley pulled his bandage aside, and spat blood into an enamel kidney basin. He gestured for a pen and paper, and Gillies handed it to him, observing both of them.

Mortified. My fault entirely. Took exception to an anti-Semite.

Nadine slipped forward and took the paper from him with a gentle touch, and handed it to Gillies, who read it.

Riley leaned back, suddenly, and looked from one to the other. His face was white as bone.

'Let's take a look,' said Gillies, and Nadine again stood away, and let them do what they had to do. Riley's head fell back. Gillies washed his hands, unwrapped him, peered, dilated, murmured.

'The splint is a goner,' he said. 'Which is good. I've been trying to get him to get rid of it for years.'

'What do you mean?' Nadine said.

'So I can give him a graft,' Gillies said. 'Bit of rib, or tibia. Much stronger, more longlasting. This jaw is like the Treaty of Versailles – it was never going to hold, and it's a miracle it's lasted as long as it did.'

She didn't understand.

'We can finish his treatment,' Gillies explained. 'Do what we should have done in 1919.'

'What?' she said.

'He wouldn't let me,' Gillies said, and her face told him, and he said, 'I'm sorry. You didn't know.'

'I didn't,' she said. 'I thought that was it.' She glanced at Riley. She hoped her face didn't look accusing, but she feared it probably did. He looked so helpless there, in the chair, throat naked, mouth adrift. *I know he's in the best of hands.* 'The best of surgeons and sisters' – the phrase came to her, where was it from – ah – the field postcard. 'I was admitted with a slight/severe wound in my . . . fill in as appropriate . . . I am now comfortable with the best of surgeons and sisters to do all that is necessary for me.'

She thought, looking at him, *I will protect you and love you in every way it takes. Now, then, always, forever.*

'Well,' Gillies said. 'We'll admit you now, Riley, and I'll try to fit you in tomorrow. It doesn't look too complex. Don't worry!' he said, and his smile was a bright flag of confidence. 'We're much better at it than we used to be.'

Riley made a noise Nadine hadn't heard for years: the noise of bitter laughter through a wound.

~

The Prime Minister spoke on the radio. He told the country that the British Ambassador in Berlin had handed the German government a final note stating that, unless he heard from them by eleven o'clock that they were prepared at once to withdraw their troops from Poland, a state of war would exist between them. The Prime Minister said he had to tell them now that no such undertaking had been received, and that consequently this country is at war with Germany. He said it was a bitter blow. He said, Up to the very last it would have been quite possible to have arranged a peaceful and honourable settlement between Germany and Poland, but Hitler would not have it. He said, His action shows convincingly that there is no chance of expecting that this man will ever give up his practice of using force to gain his will. He can only be stopped by force. He said, The situation in which no word given by Germany's ruler could be trusted, and no people or country could feel itself safe, has become intolerable. He said he was resolved to finish it. He said, Play your part. He said, Calmness, and courage. He said, May God bless you all and I am certain that right will prevail.

Riley was in Gillies' office. Everyone knew an announcement was to be made, and Gillies, who shouldn't really have been there on a Sunday, had invited him in to listen. As the words proceeded, Riley could feel something else in his face which was familiar from long ago: a lowering feeling, a cutting off, an accepted and unmentioned resentment. *And so it goes. The freedom has all been a mirage; now all is boss and instruction and fear once again. Will they want me? Perhaps in ten years' time when they've used up everyone else. No – I will have nothing to do with that side of it. I must stay while others go – boys—*

'Well,' Gillies was saying.

Riley grunted.

'What do you think?'

He wrote:

490

Nothing to say, is there?

Gillies was silent, and then said: 'I think it was kind of fate to give us those happy years, before turning the lights off again and drawing down the curtain. Though there were those for whom the curtain never lifted.'

Riley wrote:

We always knew we'd have to fight them again.

Gillies was staring. Then he shook himself, and read the note, harrumphed, and said: 'All the more reason to get you done and out of the way, eh?'

Riley's cheeks tightened a little, and he covered his face with his hands. *I have no choice*, he thought. *Gillies will cut bone off my leg and dismantle my face again to get it in, and finish off the job.* He kind of, almost, laughed. *Yes, best get it done now, before the crowds.*

Later, he gazed out of the window. The high redbrick and white stucco buildings of the West End sat as they had sat for generations, scarlet geraniums in their window boxes, front doors and black railings shining. *Those will be carted off for ordnance, sooner or later . . .* A sense of terrible importance lay on the tense and muted streets. He felt rising from the people passing below a need to do, and no knowledge yet of what to do. Outside the pub on the corner men muttered, in low voices. Women clicked by anxiously, their shoulders nervous in their jackets, their shopping bags twitching as they rushed home.

They're all ready to roar off from the starting line, Riley thought – *but when they look over their shoulders, they're running against nobody. Things should be happening, but nothing is happening yet. They're all going to get prepared, with their new socks and gas masks and evacuation plans. All right, boys and girls, this term, we'll be fighting the Hun . . . They've invaded everybody else and now they're going to invade us.*

But never mind. As Gillies had said, 'We're much better at it than we used to be.'

～

Peter and Mabel were at Locke Hill. It was Mrs Joyce, listening to the radio as she was ironing, who came hurtling from the laundry room, and called them. They all stood around the ironing board. At the end the women looked at Peter with the same expression, one he found helpless and irresistible. He said: 'Well we knew it was coming, didn't we?' and Mabel said, 'Did we?' because she didn't, really.

'In a way,' said Peter.

Iris was staring at a small pile of tennis balls, wondering whether this would affect her going to the Royal College. She remembered the moment for the rest of her life.

～

Rose had stopped in after church for a cup of tea with the vicar. He was a younger man, and he looked up at her with a glint of query in her eye, and she thought, *I am a veteran.*

'I don't know,' she said to him, before he could ask. 'I suppose it will all be very different. It's not as if everyone just heads back to the Western front, or the Med, or Egypt. I have no idea what it means.'

Later, in her sitting room with Mr Mackesson and a glass of sherry, he said: 'Bombs, is what it means. We will

492

all be needed here as much as anywhere else.' Rose had blinked, a lot, and he had held his arms out to her, so she had gone to him and leant against him, her head on his tweed shoulder and his arm around her, and to be honest her thought was not of war, but of love: *Why didn't I allow this before? Why did I protect myself from it, deny it to myself? Could I have had this, with someone else, twenty-five years ago?*

And then: *No. Because it is him. This is him, for me. And how much easier it is going to be to face all this with him here.*

~

Kitty was in her flat, woken by Johnny on the telephone. When he told her, she felt, in order, vindicated, sick, and excited, and called to her flatmates to share the news. Cynthia rushed to the window to look out, wanting to see if the world had visibly changed. Ada told her to come away, she was in her dressing gown and people would see, before lighting a cigarette, and trying to look bored. Cynthia burst into tears.

~

Nenna, when the news reached Rome, cried and cried, she couldn't stop crying. She could hear Aldo's voice saying: 'Sweetheart, Italy is not in the war. It is Germany with whom England wants to fight.' And she shouted at him though he wasn't there. 'Blood and Steel, Papà – what you want and here it comes. We will all be killed.'

You cannot desert your father . . . she whispered . . . then she closed her eyes, spat three times, and made her mind up. The men could do what they wanted – Papà, Vittorio, even Stefano, who had not come back, and whose friends said he had gone to Naples. *Naples! Why?* It was beyond her. *This was men's work and men's fault – to hell with them all.* Blood and steel would separate her from them, whether they loved her or cared about her or remembered her at all or not. They must look after themselves.

And Tom? A trail of memories flared up in her heart, right back to the beginning: Tom and her as children together by the river; when she asked him in the church if she had killed Jesus, and he wrote down the words to look them up. Him shouting in a field, his hair shining in the sun. His face when she produced the marriage certificate – his voice cracking as he shouted down her father – the intensity with which he had tried to help her, for so long, despite all her resistance. His kisses. And now he had to be the enemy and she had to be with the Italians fighting alongside the Nazis – *Such nonsense! Such hideous nonsense!*

The world became very small to her, suddenly. Shrinking what you cared about to manageable proportions seemed the only possible response. *My mother, and my little sister. Feed them, comfort them, keep them safe. Marinella and Mama. That's what matters.* So that meant Marinella, as Mama had not come back from her dockside vigil for Vittorio. *So. Head down, hard work, Marinella. That might be achievable.*

And England. She didn't know. She waited to hear. He must have had her letter by now, her telegram.

The following day a telegram came: GO EVERY DAY TO

EMBASSY MENTION CARMICHAEL TAKE PASSPORTS
LOVE ALWAYS TOM

Marinella had no passport. Aldo would have to sign for
her to get one. *Pah.* Tullio would have to make her one. She
would do whatever it took.

And she would go. Every day.

~

Aldo was in Pomezia. Just watching. He just wanted to see.
It was looking beautiful. He'd come down a few times now.
One evening, he had seen the Duce on his Moto Guzzi: he'd
heard the rumble, the cracking echo of the big V-twin
echoing across the plain, unmistakable. He'd chased after
him – like a fool. He just wanted to ask him face to face,
to make absolutely sure; to see if the Duce could give him
any idea about when he'd be able to reverse it all, when
he'd want him back – he was going to tell him how he was
using his time constructively, studying, keeping up with
things – he was pretty sure what the plan was: stick with
Germany, then when they had won the war together,
everything could go back to normal.

People were sitting out on the bridges and the low walls
and along the embankments for the evening *passeggiata.*
They stared at him.

He'd helped to build five of these cities, and the canals
that permitted them and gave them strong foundations,
and the roads that linked them. The flag of the new city
was to be red and blue, for the earth and the sea. This
afternoon he saw three people he knew: a tractor driver,
who waved and yelled a greeting. A foreman, who looked

embarrassed, and frowned. And on the other side of a gleaming white canal channel full of murky water, he saw an old man he hadn't seen for years, thin, poorly dressed. Aldo squinted, trying to recall him, his name or face or function. It came to him: it was Olivieri, one of the brothers who used to sell him frogs, right at the beginning. Aldo cried out to him, cheerfully; Olivieri squinted back at him, raised his hand in a knowing and weary salute, and walked on. There was no bridge nearby, or Aldo would have gone to talk to him.

Nadine was at home, alone, packing a small bag of things to take to Riley. She listened carefully to the Prime Minister's voice, and took three long silent breaths as it came to a close. Tension rose off her shoulders. *So. Now. What's to do?*

She would speak to Mrs Kenton. She would remind her that no foreign soldier has invaded England for nine hundred years. And to her father, and she would telephone Rose. Then – carry on. She would take Riley's things down to him: the operation was tomorrow morning, and he would stay in for a couple of weeks. After that she would nurse him at home. The supplies had been ordered. They were giving him a naso-gastric tube with a little pump, through which he could have broth and beef tea and eggs and cream, bypassing his mouth completely.

She wondered how soon rationing would be introduced. *Is this going to be a long haul? It feels like the start of long haul.* They would give her instructions: recipes, amounts for a balanced diet. He would manage the pump himself.

It would give him something to do during healing, which would take a while.

Lots to be done. Lots to be done.

We fight all our individual battles alongside this big one. How big will this be?

Another long silent breath.

It will be hard. It will be hard. But we know what to do. So do it.

~

Tom was on a train south with a package of papers and cash. He had four return tickets in his pocket and a tune stuck in his head: '*Lucciola lucciola vien da me ti darò il pan del re . . .*' His heart rattled like the train itself for the thousand miles he travelled. He blocked it all from his mind for the duration, and slept like an exhausted child after a long sickness. He woke, he ate, the trucks coupled and uncoupled, he stepped off one train and on to another. Day into night into day. And then St Peter's appeared in his window, and fled again, and he stood, and stretched, and checked the times for the return train that afternoon.

He went directly to the island, and told the cab to wait. The door was open to the piazza, late summer sun drifting in. She was in the kitchen, looking at some chickpeas. Marinella was at the table. Aldo was singing softly in the next room.

Tom went to Marinella first, and said: 'Go and get a bag, put your favourite book and toy in it. And some clothes.'

Nenna turned.

'You too,' he said. 'Now.'

497

They went. Nenna moved as if in a trance, wading through something. He didn't open his arms to her; he didn't kiss her. He could hear her speaking softly to Marinella.

'Passports!' he shouted up the stairs. 'Anything valuable. If you're not going to bring it, hide it.'

All right.

He went in to where Aldo was, and saw him sitting, staring, crooning.

'Are you coming?' Tom said.

'Tommaso!' cried Aldo, with a kind of joy in his voice and Tom said: 'If I try to push you into the cab, will you come?'

'Come where?' Aldo said. His voice was a soft echo of the joviality of former times. It made Tom flinch, and feel sick.

'Or will you hit me again?' Tom said.

'Tommaso!' Aldo said, and his smile was idiotic, his eyes dull.

'Here's your tickets,' he said. 'Visa, letter with a job offer. Get your passport, and go and get in the cab.'

Aldo sat there.

Nenna and Marinella appeared behind Tom.

'Papà?' she said, so gently, and at that Aldo scowled, and stood, and said: 'I'm going to the bar.'

'Papà!' she cried, and Tom felt that if he heard her cry out one more time to her father for the common sense he no longer had – and actually hadn't had for years—

'Nenna,' he said.

'You won't get any other answer from him.'

Her eyes flared.

'Coming, Marinella?' he said. He held out his hand and she took it. She turned, looked up at Nenna.

Marinella and her little suitcase.

He picked up Nenna's case, and said 'Got everything?'

Outside the driver helped him put the bags in the boot. Marinella clambered in the back. Nenna stepped forward. He didn't offer her his hand. *It's your decision*, he thought, but he didn't say anything. He didn't dare.

She climbed in.

Triumph? Not yet.

He looked around. 'Aldo?' he called, but Aldo was not there.

'Keys,' he said to Nenna, and he went and closed the door, and locked it. Leaning against it, he scribbled a note, and went to tuck it under the Setas' door.

'They've gone,' she said. He glanced over at her, and moved across to the next house along.

Nenna was frozen immobile when he got into the car beside her.

'Budge up,' he said, and she budged.

'To the British Embassy,' Tom said to the driver, and he ducked his head, as if to avoid anything Nenna might say or do, as if hiding from her potential to change what was happening.

'Where are we going?' Marinella said.

This is where I pretend it's all a huge adventure, he thought.

'As far as we can,' he said, and smiled.

$\approx$

He held his breath on the train until it started up, shuffling and shuddering, and left the station.

Somewhere north of Civitavecchia, Nenna started crying,

and he put his arm around her, and couldn't tell her shaking from the train's. Marinella leapt up from her seat and stood by them, patting her, saying, 'Nenna, Nenna, what is it?' in that insistent, plaintive way, until he said to her, 'Marinella, sweetheart, it's all right. It's difficult, but it's all right.' Somewhere north of Bologna he felt Nenna go to sleep, and he held her head close to him. Marinella curled up as best she could on the other side, trying to lean on Nenna, each of them trying to negotiate the hard seats and the stupid armrests.

He remained nervous and wakeful. The border loomed ahead in his mind: the mountains, the queues, the officials, the trolley-bus lines which stopped where Switzerland began. Muscly thighs and unpleasant magazines. A stamp saying COMO, crossed out. Beyond all that, a memory of clear cold water, wild strawberries in an impossibly steep green meadow, an eagle circling overhead. But somewhere north of Milan he too slipped into sleep, and the train rattled on, carrying them towards the mountains, into the night.

Acknowledgements

And thanks go to

Charlotte Horton, for eternal Italian support in every way for such a long time.

Derek Johns, for twenty years of top agenting.

Natasha Fairweather, for inheriting me so seamlessly.

Alexander Stille: without his exceptionally interesting book *Benevolence and Betrayal*, these characters would not have taken this path or, indeed, existed.

Milton Gendel, Anna Gendel and Monica Incisa della Rochetta, for Rome then and now, the Island, Piazza Mattei, the house, the story of the little room.

Armando and Lina Olivieri, Renzo and Roberto, and Angelo.

Elisa Sesti, for some things she said, and the loan of her hair.

Don Alessandro and Donna Amelia Odescalchi, and Don Francesco Massimo-Lancelotti, for Vigna Grande.

Sergio Bertelli, for Trevignano.

Ilaria Tarasconi, for native Italian grammar and culture.

My lovely publishers old and new – Katie Espiner, Suzie

Dooré, Cassie Browne, Louisa Joyner, Charlotte Cray, Ann Bissell and all at Borough Press.

Andy Ryan and Look Right Look Left Theatre Company, Mimi Poskett, Oliver Payne, Katie Lyons and Magdelene Mills, whose ideas for how CityRead 2014 should present *My Dear I Wanted to Tell You* led directly to a scene in this book . . . Meta or what.

Isabel Adomakoh Young, first reader.

Robert Lockhart, who still managed to contribute so much, despite being dead. So typical.

Mum and Dad, ditto.

Michel Faber, for being good at these things.

ς